THUNDER IN YELLOWSTONE

THUNDER IN YELLOWSTONE

A CONTEMPORARY LITERARY NOVEL

E. B. LEE

Thunder in Yellowstone A Contemporary Literary Novel

Copyright © 2023 by Evelyn B. Lee First Edition

Publisher's Cataloging-in-Publication

(Provided by Cassidy Cataloguing Services, Inc.)

Names: Lee, E. B., 1957- author.

Title: Thunder in Yellowstone : a contemporary literary novel / E. B. Lee.

Description: First edition. | Pinehurst, NC : Little Brown Dog Press, [2023]

Identifiers: ISBN: 978-1-7364560-5-7 (paperback) | 978-1-7364560-7-1 (hardcover) | 978-1-7364560-6-4 (eBook) | 978-1-7364560-8-8 (Audio) | LCCN: 2023919773

Subjects: LCSH: Women journalists--Montana--Fiction. | Montana--Fiction. | Yellowstone National Park--Fiction. | American bison--Yellowstone National Park--Fiction. | Brucella abortus-- Yellowstone National Park--Fiction. | Ranchers--Montana--Fiction. | Small cities--Montana-- Fiction. | Rangelands--Montana--Fiction. | Wildlife conservation-- Montana--Fiction. | Justice --Fiction. | BISAC: FICTION / Literary. | FICTION / Women. | FICTION / Nature & the Environment. | FICTION / Small Town & Rural.

Classification: LCC: PS3612.E22358 T48 2023 | DDC: 813/.6--dc23

Library of Congress Control Number: 2023919773

Editing: Stephen Parolini www.noveldoctor.com; Proofreading: Elyse Lyon; Cover design by Lynn Andreozzi; Cover photograph istock © Boogich

Publishing Services: Little Brown Dog Press, Pinehurst, NC, USA

www.littlebrowndogpress.com

For George Barata, my brother
Near or far, you are always by my side

CONTENTS

PROLOGUE

MORRIS, Montana, does not exist, but the heart of its story, as presented in the following pages, does. Located in the Greater Yellowstone region, it is a place where cattle, ranchers, and bison make their homes. It is a place of peace and conflict. It is a place where justice must be defined for a small town and a nation.

1

MONTANA

I STEERED my car into Irv and Izzy Wilson's gravel drive, swung my right hand in the air in celebration, and whooped out a holler that was likely heard back in the City of Brotherly Love, where I had begun my travels twenty-two hundred miles away and thirty-two driving hours earlier. Not for nothing, I included several one-night stays at cheap hotels equipped with screaming children running hallways, and played unnerving games of cat and mouse with double tandems barreling past on downhills, falling behind on climbs, and speeding by once again to batter me with hurricane-force drafts.

While the drive was long, days were short. The February sun folded early into the western horizon, enjoying extra winks of winter sleep. Not a streetlight edged the roads out here, and the Montana sky was pitch black, though beautifully wrapped in a sequined starry cover. It couldn't have been more unlike Philadelphia. Welcome to my new home—Morris, Montana.

Had I sprung for more expensive lodging, I would have slept better, but I was frugal. Since college, I had survived on a reporter's salary and carefully guarded life insurance money, sadly compliments of my deceased parents. I anticipated increased pay at my new position and hoped to craft freelance work for additional income, but on principle, I refused to overpay for sleeping space and shower.

Seconds after I heard the stones crackling under my car's tires, the front door to the house swung wide open, and Irv and Izzy emerged with welcoming waves. From behind my windshield, I returned the gestures. Izzy's flapping arms morphed into a series of air hugs while Irv jostled past her and down the steps to begin his job as traffic controller, waving me toward the preferred parking location.

I felt like I was coming home from college for winter break. Mom and Dad used to wait by the window, then rush outside to wave me in with vigor equal to Irv and Izzy's, even though I had studied barely an hour away. I loved them to the moon. I loved Philadelphia as well. But I had decided to leave the nest, knowing I could always return.

That was part of the story. The rest was I had lost the man I expected to marry. Officer Jake Marshall, of the Philadelphia police force, and his K-9 officer, Olive, were ripped from my life while on duty. Jake in an instant, and Olive within weeks, despite a valiant fight. At least I said goodbye to Olive, who lay in my arms with trusting, loyal brown eyes looking back at mine. But when I did, I let go of my last lifeline to Jake. A precinct of support carried me through the first half year. After that, I was back to where I was before Olive, Jake, and I had happily intertwined our lives: independent, alone, and married to work. As I explored jobs and lifestyle options, I gravitated to another small community, though markedly different from the blue brotherhood, and became willing to chance a big move, finally ready to face adventure. I was becoming myself again.

The *Philadelphia Daily* would get on fine without me. Nine years of ferreting out crime stories for them was plenty. So, while I was half running, I was also taking a needed risk to move up the professional ladder, set a few more boundaries on my time, and try a new line of writing to become the best editor and feature story writer the new *Western TriState* magazine could ever have.

I put my car in park with a familiar upward lift to the gear shifter, turned off the ignition, and removed my foot from the brake. Then I slid my right hand to the dashboard and gave a grateful pat. "Thanks, Justice," I said, addressing my little four-door coupe.

Justice had come into my world more than a decade ago, after my first car, Liberty—the one I had shared through high school and my first three years of college with Eva, my identical twin—had finally moaned to a halt. Yes, we were Philly people through and through. Middle class, with hope and dreams. Scrappy. Determined. Wed to liberty and justice. In theory.

Irv interrupted my thoughts with a tap on my side window. I unlatched the locks and pushed open my door.

"Where's all your stuff?" he asked.

"That's half of it," I said, nodding toward the back seat. "The other half's in the trunk."

"This is it? I've never seen anyone move and pack so light. Especially not … well, you know, women. Shoes usually fill a bag. I hope you don't mind my saying so."

"Clearly, all those people don't have a fully furnished apartment compliments of the magnificent Irv and Izzy." This brought a warm laugh, followed by a bear hug. And then a mama-bear hug from Izzy.

"I'll take these up for you," he said.

"Be my guest." The suitcases were jam packed and heavy. I recalled Eva's and my determined struggle to zip them closed and haul them to the car. Then I considered how much we had sorted, tossed, donated, or recycled. How could I have accumulated so much?

With Irv on his way with suitcase number one, I called to him. "I hope I don't have to tip. I haven't started my job yet."

"It's on me," he said with a backhanded wave. Then he and half my luggage disappeared through the door.

"So, Amber, how were your travels?" Izzy asked.

"Fabulous, but arriving here is even better."

Izzy accompanied me to the second-floor garage apartment. It was bigger than I remembered from my visit, but its wood interior walls, mimicking those of a log cabin, were exactly as I recalled—cozy. With a beautiful view across the valley to distant mountains, I couldn't wait to see my first big-sky sunset.

Izzy took me through the particulars of the apartment. Then we toured the main house, where Irv offered additional instructions.

"If you're wanting to go outside when warm weather comes, keep yourself inside the fence line near the house. Most everything else stays outside of it," said Irv.

They had waited to greet me and hand over the key before speeding away to Florida. They didn't intend to come back for the summer and weren't running cattle any longer. I didn't know why they still had this place. I doubted my rent would cover maintenance costs, but I knew nothing of real estate around here. It appeared they had quite a few acres. Maybe that meant something.

Irv, eager to hit the road for the Sunshine State, claimed he was more than ready to leave the work behind and catch up on reading, to which Izzy exclaimed, "That's why you were helping Sam Nelson with his fence all week?" It was half question and half statement. All Irv said was "You know as well as any, Iz, he needs all the help he can get."

"You know how to reach us with questions," said Izzy. "Your boss can also tell you all about things here and anyone to call for unexpected repairs. The best place for food in town is Abby's Diner, and don't worry about a couple of chickens that occasionally show up. They either make their way home, or they disappear. I'll skip the details."

With that, she gave me another hug and said, "I hate to chat and run, but we need to make the best of the remaining light."

Irv, married to his task as first driver, had the passenger door swung meaningfully wide open, beckoning Izzy.

I gave a lasting wave and chuckled as I sent them eastward. *Who is the parent now*, I thought, *manning the home and sending the college kids to new adventures?*

In less than an hour, my bags were unpacked, and I felt free as a lark for having two single suitcases of belongings in my life, and nothing more. The next moment, an unwanted partner named Anxiety settled beside this sense of freedom.

"Oh, come on, Amber. You have this!" I actually said it out loud. I wasn't the first one around here to forge a new path and build a new future. It was time to buckle down the nerves.

With my freshly brewed coffee, I sat with my empty journal and began writing, while intermittently enjoying views of the magnificent rolling fields, awaiting sunset. It had been years since I had kept a real journal. As a seasoned crime reporter, I had become quite adept at keeping my anonymous leads anonymous and many notes cryptic. Today, I could begin blooming again.

A long night's sleep would have been most welcome, but there was something unsettling about the lack of traffic noises, the absence of airplane sounds, and not hearing trains wailing their deep-throated night calls into broken intervals of air currents. It was quiet, and I took a long time to drift asleep, eventually comforted, I suppose, by the noise of my active thoughts. Sometime between midnight and dawn, I heard sirens in the distance and several loud trucks racing along nearby roads. I knew the sounds particular to specific first responder vehicles: their engine noises when they accelerated and idled, their sirens and warning yelps. These were unlike any I knew. I vaguely wondered if weather had moved through and caused a wreck, but I didn't bother to check. Instead, as soon as I roused from sleep, I pulled up the covers and slid back into a new series of dreams.

It took little over ten minutes to drive to the center of Morris, home to my new office and a couple of banks, Abby's Diner, a bike rental, a food store, a feed store, and a post office, among other establishments. It was a respectable town, capable of serving tourists and locals alike. The roads were clear. The sidewalks were not. In a town of less than eight hundred, I had hardly expected to see dozens of people standing around. Not just standing, exactly, but gathered in small groups with pained expressions flooding their faces. Some even held a hand to their mouth or close to their chest. Temperatures were near zero. I parked in the first space I found, walked to Community Bank, and kept my ears wide open.

In the equivalent of a city block, the hornet's nest buzzed a front-page story to end all stories: one man dead, another in the hospital, all the result of a lone bison. The kicker was mention of possible suicide. Death by bison?

I inhaled deeply as I marched past the last group and entered Community Bank.

"I'd like to open a bank account," I said to one Mr. Frank Bishop, sitting at a desk with his name on an unremarkable nameplate.

Mr. Bishop, Account Executive, looked me over, gave an odd smile, and said, "You single?"

I stared. "Yes, a single account."

"Didn't answer my question." He gave me another look.

Less than four minutes later, I looked across another desk at Mr. Shane Walters of First West Bank. Mr. Walters cared about money details. Nothing else. Except for the events of last night.

"You hear the commotion?" he asked, with a slight lift of his eyes as he completed the paperwork.

"What happened?"

"A bison got into Sam Nelson's ranch and killed him. Sam, that is. Someone said he put himself in harm's way on purpose. Some tourist also got trampled. I think he was staying at Sam's loft. Weekly rental sort of thing. He's off at the hospital now."

My mouth was open the duration of the report and a good five seconds after. It seemed too remote to believe. Not to mention, Sam Nelson, the man Irv and Izzy had spoken of, was the only person I'd heard of in this town other than my boss.

At a very late lunch in Abby's Diner, I got just the dessert I needed with my end-of-lunch coffee and cupcake: a supportive conversation with Abby—*the* Abby—of Abby's Diner. We started talking when she learned I was new in town. For some reason, the Frank Bishop thing slipped out.

"If I ever see that Mr. Frank Bishop again, it will be too soon."

"Well, you know you will," she said, "Can't hide much around here."

"I didn't do a single thing wrong, but I feel guilty. Why?"

"Don't you worry about Mr. Frank," she said, her tone committed. "He's been doing that for years. Maybe decades. He doesn't mean a thing by it, and besides ... he's married ... and everyone knows it, including him." I must have shown my disbelief because Abby assured me again it was only harmless talk.

Sure, I thought, *other than it was harassment, gave Community Bank a bad name, was way beyond acceptable or legal behavior, and made a person feel crappy.* I kept this to myself but felt an odd sense of relief knowing Abby heard similar remarks. I found it peculiar in a state that was the first to allow women's votes and to accept women in governmental positions, both in my column of positives when I considered my move.

If experience told me anything, having a good diner friend would open many doors to people, their stories, or latest news. Abby, of course, had already heard the full spectrum of reports on the night's bison break-in.

"Gored him. The tourist, that is. Midsection," she said. "Close or mighty close to a main artery. Some are saying the horn went right in the front and out the side, so the poor guy had to somehow slide the whole horn out of his body to get free. That don't usually happen, and I'm not sure if it could."

"Sounds gruesome."

"He's in mighty rough shape. ICU. They're hoping he'll pull through to say what happened."

"When might they know?"

"Has to wake up first, but even if he could, they're likely keeping him semiconscious a while. And drugged. The nurses over there promised to keep me informed. Well, as much as they're allowed to, that is. Mostly so I can keep other folks informed, rather than letting the rumor mill run amok."

"Why would a buffalo, or bison, gore someone? In the middle of the night?" I finally asked.

"Now, that's the question of the day. And likely for the next five days or more. Why was a single bison even near Sam's ranchlands? It's not where they usually are this time of year. And it shouldn't have been charging unless it got chased or scared. If that was the case, we've probably got wolves coming mighty close to Sam's cattle ranch; also peculiar. No calves around there this time of year. That's what the wolves usually chase."

City rats slid down my wildlife least-wanted list.

"Someone was talking about insurance money," I said.

Abby raised her eyes to mine. Instead of leaning over my table to continue the conversation, she sat on the other side of the salt and pepper and pile of napkins, leaned far forward, and lowered her voice. "Sam hasn't been happy lately. His cows haven't been doing so good. Some people heard he intended to get out of the ranching business, so they went assuming things, and you know what that does."

"He wanted out?"

Abby nodded. "He talked about opening a dude ranch for artists, but hadn't shared much about it."

"It's an interesting idea," I said.

"It's unusual around here to turn away from cattle, being a family business and all for most of them. Heck, look at Irv and Izzy."

It was a smaller town than I thought.

"They're in no rush to sell none of their land, and they aren't even here no more practically," she said.

"I wondered about their thoughts on their future, but didn't ask. I figured I'd either hear or not." I realized around here, knowing one's landlords well enough to know their business, and maybe even their relatives, was likely not uncommon.

"When it's in your blood, it's in your blood, and it's in Irv and Izzy's arteries and veins, through and through. They just got too old and tired for it and couldn't ever have kids. But it wasn't exactly in Sam's blood. He came into it through his wife. Poor thing. Shelly. A sweet, sweet girl. Sweetest you'll ever meet, and tough as a hawk when she has to be. Like most of them. She's heartbroken, but I know she'll get through it. Some are saying she feared it was coming. That's why others are saying it might have been planned."

"How do you plan a bison break? Aren't they a bit big to push around?"

Abby laughed. "Big and opinionated. Just like the people around here. A lot of them will be thanking Sam to the stars if he planned a fake break-in. Though none of them would want him dead over it. No, ma'am. They just want the bison off the cattle lands."

"I don't follow. Why?"

"They carry a cow disease. So, if a bison causes a stir, it proves it don't belong. But that, my new friend, is for another day. I need to check on other customers. But, hey, here's a word of advice: don't be like a tourist and get yourself gored by a bison. If you see one coming, run. I mean it. Buy the postcard instead!"

I vowed to remember Abby's words and went looking for my new boss, Fletcher Marks. As chance would have it, I missed him by a few minutes. He was on his way to the hospital to follow the facts. *Tomorrow*, I thought, as I proceeded to tackle my final errand—groceries.

Back in the apartment, I lined up subscriptions to the dailies and regionals coming out of Cheyenne, Billings, Jackson, Helena, and Bozeman to stay abreast of area news and familiarize myself with regional reporters. Besides scanning the obligatory obituaries, or death notices as they were called—the inches of typeface that helped pay a paper's rent as well as spread the word of people's passings—I was drawn to a new palette of regional high school sports, college sports, and local rodeo reports. I followed this with a quick internet search, which revealed the closest professional football teams—the Denver Broncos and Seattle Seahawks—were each over seven hundred miles away. I was destined to remain a die-hard Philadelphia Eagles fan. Not a surprise. Then, I searched for the cow disease Abby had mentioned. Its name was *Brucella abortus*. At its worst, it caused cows to give birth to weak calves, or to lose them before they were born. It was a rancher's nightmare.

2

────────────

THE GAZETTE

I CAUGHT Fletcher in his office, coffee mug at the ready and eyes set to his computer screen. He welcomed me as he had during my interviews—with a warm, supportive smile. His shirt was off-white cotton. His pants dark denim. And his shoes were boots. What most caught my attention, beyond the sparkle in his eyes, was his bolo tie: two strands of shoestring black leather hanging from neck to waist. They were kept in place by a simple silver slide near his collar, and had silver endpieces near his waist. A cowboy hat, with a beautiful brim, had been slung over a hook on the wall, right next to a puffy winter coat and a camouflage hunting jacket.

Fletcher put together a most impressive daily—the *Yellowstone Gazette*. As well as carrying international and national news, he reported regional stories in a semiconservative tone and often had the investigative lead on other publications. The *Gazette* and its writers had won numerous awards. Fletcher, too, had a stellar reputation and was a big reason I was here and looked forward to a life ruled less by the lusty mix of emergency response and adrenaline.

"Amber Phillips, good travels?" he asked.

"Absolutely. It's good to be here."

Fletcher envisioned our new magazine as an eye-catching tabletop publication that would up the ante for the region. It would highlight the best of this tristate community and cater to tourists, future residents, future businesses, and locals alike. Fletcher believed an outside eye would do it best. He also demanded the new baby tell things like they were, not like a dull tourist publication. This one had to have the good, the bad, and the ugly. In short, it had to be real. Glossy on the cover but not in the words. "People gravitate to truth and imperfections. They understand them," he had said, "as universal elements of life."

Before my hire, I asked, Why a magazine launch? Other publishers were scaling back. Was it tied to personal interests, perhaps in real estate, or something else? Fletcher's answer was forthright. He had no more real estate than anyone else, but he believed in the region and wanted to both help it grow and retain its intrinsic natural and human values. Meaning, he emphasized, he wanted all its complexities to be illuminated so they would be appreciated, celebrated, and fostered in the coming decades.

"We might look like a bunch of small towns to everyone else, but when you put us all together," he had said, "we are a strong region. Often cohesive, but also having to work through a host of differing opinions. One thing for certain is we'll always share this land, and we'll always support our communities. It's what makes us."

When we jumped into the nitty-gritty of issues and topics, it felt as though we had already spoken and compared notes for hours. At meeting's end, we had our six headliners for the bimonthly's first year. The Yellowstone River would be our leading lady for issue number one. On yellow-lined paper, Fletcher jotted down a few words; then he reached forward to surrender his handwritten note.

"A couple of contacts to get you started," he said. I glanced at the list, with its left-handed slant.

"Perfect."

"I suppose you heard the news?" he said.

"The goring, or mystery goring?"

Fletcher nodded. "I might borrow you for a week of regular coverage. That is, if you haven't forgotten your journalistic beat skills on the ride out here."

"What's up?"

"I'm keeping our guy—Joe Morris—on hospital alert. Trying to keep up with the local authorities and anyone else coming close to the tourist, to get a lead on what the hell actually happened. It's not adding up. Sam always had a gun nearby, and no bison should have been anywhere near."

I must have nodded.

"I'm sure you've seen plenty like this," he said. "Unusual circumstances surrounding someone's succumbing to the Will of the Lord."

I had covered my share of mysterious deaths, but no one had ever described it like this. I managed a feeble response. "People come up with something new every day, even though I thought we had done it all."

Fletcher nodded. "It's never going to end. The good news is Joe's half brother, Burt Holcomb, works with the sheriff's office. That gives us a reliable source if anything comes out of ICU."

"I'm ready to help, but I don't want to mess up my first issue."

"Have faith, Phillips. You'll do fine. I'm good at picking winners."

He held forward a bowl of individually wrapped mints and said, "Here … sustenance. A person needs it out here. And schedule in Monday mornings."

"For what?"

"That's when I fill it with new candies. It's my way of

making sure people check in with me, so I don't have to go hunting them down."

We looked at each other with mutual respect, as though cementing our future working relationship. Then, Fletcher said, "Saddle up, settle in, and call me with anything you need. Ideas, new stapler, shoulder to lean on, or joke of the day. I'm here."

<hr>

The morning after meeting Fletcher and his candy stash, I climbed the four wooden steps to the *Gazette* building and stood a moment to admire the impressive porch, spanning the entire length of the building, some fifteen feet deep. I wondered how long ago it had been constructed. Fletcher nodded as I looked over at his trio of front-facing windows. From his vantage point, he could see everyone who came and went.

The *Gazette* was a good thirty-person operation. Bustling. Noisy. Lively. But familial. At least, this was my first impression. My space was on the second floor. Through my windows, I could keep tabs on the village's outdoor dining space. No one was eating out today, given winter's biting temperatures, but the tables and benches remained in place, framed by a pair of massive trees, which I suspected dated back to the town's incorporation. Abby's Diner sat on the left of the opening, and a real estate office, western store, and barber set up on the right.

My first step of settling in was finding a spot for my recently purchased desk plant. It had been an impulse buy but was planted in a perfect swirl of pottery, in my favorite colors—deep lapis blue and seafoam green. I had read it as western and warm, despite its cool palette, and with dark green foliage above, it had practically grabbed my hand. Surely, it would help having something so soothing watching me type. I carefully placed it on the corner of my desk and grinned. It was perfect.

"Knock, knock." A woman's voice, accompanied by a soft sound of a hand striking my door, startled me.

"Who's there?" I asked.

"I brought you a cinnamon bun."

It was Diane Mitchell, Fletcher's assistant and office manager. We had met when I interviewed.

"Smells wonderful."

"Tastes even better," she said. "Or so I've been told."

"Nice to see you again."

"Does it have a name?" Diane was petting the leaves of my new plant.

"Um … not yet."

"Let me know when it does. I call my philodendron Theodora, Teddy for short. Odd thing we do, name our plants, but just about everyone I know does it."

I devoured Diane's cinnamon bun in a matter of minutes and rushed out to visit Bill Smith, National Park Service historian and one of Fletcher's leads. Bill's afternoon of no appointments was my call to action. This magazine editor was wasting no time!

Two county sheriff cars, parked on the side of the road, caught my attention. Another two law vehicles, four miles further along, nearly caused me to stop. Could they be investigating Sam Nelson's bison? Fletcher would surely know.

Bill Smith was younger than he sounded on the phone—perhaps my age—but a bigger surprise was he wore street clothes. My last involvement with the Park Service was covering a ghastly murder/suicide outside the Edgar Allan Poe National Historic Site in Philadelphia. Each NPS contact, to a tee, had worn iconic gray-and-moss-green government-issue.

"Welcome to Montana," said Bill. "And welcome to your first local history lesson." He had a map and notebook of photos waiting.

"Your Yellowstone River," he said, "winds from south to

north through the entire park. Here, at Younts Peak and Thorofare Mountain, just south of the park's boundary, drops of glacial water begin to coalesce and put everything into motion." Bill pointed to the location on his map. I had never considered a river's beginning.

"Slowly growing, the river flows north for about seventy miles, until it spills into Yellowstone Lake and meanders calmly for roughly another twenty miles as lake water. Upon exiting the lake, the Yellowstone shows its multiple personalities. Here, for example," he said, pointing to another location on the map, "it races over rapids, and then further north, morphs into its calm robe again, as it flattens in the floodplains of the Hayden Valley.

"Years ago," said Bill, "the valley itself was a lake. Now, it is a broad lowland of river, floodplain, and grass, highly sought by wildlife. So, when we consider history, we can't look at short-term, human history alone. We must also consider glacial history and the big, universe-type history. It is what shapes a lot of things out here. And, by the way, in some cases, your Yellowstone River is the one responsible. Like right here"—he pointed again to the map—"at the Grand Canyon of the Yellowstone. It's where the river is its most dramatic. Water cascades over no fewer than three falls, and"—he held up a finger to accentuate his next words—"those falls were created by the water itself over time, eroding the surrounding rock. This," he exclaimed, "is history. Make sure to visit this spot. No place else you'll see sixty thousand gallons passing per second. Well, in peak season."

Bill shared many stunning photos, making sure I understood where each was taken. Then he said, "What's next?"

I didn't hesitate. "The name."

"Excellent," Bill said, sounding triumphant. "And muddy waters, too, Ms. Phillips." He enthusiastically pulled forward his chair.

"Lesson number two," he started. "You can't look at a name without looking at people."

Bill opened a separate notebook and displayed his first graphic.

"These twenty-seven Tribal nations have ancestral links to Yellowstone. In fact, Indigenous people might have lived in the park over ten thousand years ago. Only one Tribe we know of lived here year round, but many visited in summer months to hunt and gain access to obsidian, valuable for arrowheads. Historically, Tribes had different names for the Yellowstone region, and most centered around the geysers and hot springs. But a 1790s map shows the river labeled as the Crow River or Rock River. And a later map, dated 1797, shows it as 'R. des Roches Jaunes,' which translates from French to English as Yellow Stone River." Bill showed me copies of the maps in his notebook. Then he turned the page. I continued to scribble notes, having decided to work from informal discussion rather than a recorded interview.

"In the Grand Canyon of the Yellowstone, we do find vivid yellow and pink rocks, rhyolite lava. But along the lower reaches of the river, in eastern Montana, we find something else—bluffs of yellow sandstone, where the Minnetaree lived. As the story goes, French trappers coming to this region translated the Minnetaree name for the river as Roche Jaune, which translated to English as Yellow Rock."

"Eastern Montana?"

Bill smiled. "Several hundred miles as the crow flies, and the Minnetaree weren't known to travel to Yellowstone's Grand Canyon—the yellow rock region inside the park. Fascinating, right?"

Bill turned another page. "In this 1806 journal entry, William Clark mentions 'Rochejhone' when referring to the big bend of the river here in Livingston. Meriwether Lewis and William Clark recorded it as Yellowstone, likely based on this translation from the Minnetaree, but we have no direct assurance of this. So, all we really know is we now call it the Yellowstone River, and when we created the park, it was given the name Yellowstone National Park."

"Lewis and Clark?" I said. I was in lands surveyed by Lewis and Clark. My elementary school history lessons had become personal.

Bill next pulled out an atlas to show the reach of the river beyond park lands. It followed a serpentine path across the double-fold pages. Brooks and tributaries infused their waters with the Yellowstone's. Bill steered me toward Kendra Sloane in Billings.

"She's the expert for this. And tell her I sent you."

Fletcher called me into reporting mode through a succinct message I picked up on my way back from Bill's. He delivered the assignment in a vague but curt manner, giving me a location and a time at which I should arrive at the start of next week. Then he said, "Just report if any fights break out, and get a few quotes if they do." A nifty assignment, I thought, as I considered it would be Valentine's Day.

3

———

AMBUSH

CLOSE TO DAWN, I followed Fletcher's directions and wound my way into Montana north of the park. My expectations bobbed between odd assignment at best and atrocious shit show at worst. For the second time, I found sheriff vehicles marking my route. I arrived to see a group of people and a few dozen pickup trucks on one side of a graveled-over opening, and another half dozen men and women standing on the far side of the gravel near a mix of trucks, SUVs, and passenger cars. The truck group held guns. The others had cameras and notepads. What had Fletcher sent me to?

Before I knew it, the gun group began to move. Individuals took different positions and gave more space between themselves. Some set long guns onto tripods. The notebook group moved, too, turning in the same direction and lifting cameras. I looked back and forth between the gunners and the cameras. They remained still. Then, from a different direction altogether, I saw a beautiful sight: a group of bison gathering atop a ridge. They varied in size but were all bigger than I expected. Today was my lucky day. I had never seen bison in the wild. Now I was given a gift of twenty! But then, I recalled Abby's words and wondered, *How close could they come for us to remain safe?*

As they trudged forward at a deliberate pace, white puffs of body-warmed air streamed from their nostrils, then vanished. Several bison wore lumps of snow, matted into their fur.

Nothing less than pure peace consumed me as I watched the magnificent animals. Then, without warning, a loud blast rocked the calm. I jumped, and it vibrated through my midsection. Two of the gunners began making a racket and giving one another a high five, followed by a hefty whack on a shoulder. Others hooted. I looked across the gravel to the group focusing cameras. An acrid scent wafted past. I knew the scent of gunpowder. A single bison lay still on the ground. The others remained standing, milling about, as though nothing had happened. I watched them circle the fallen bison, as though to assess. Another blast shattered the calm air. A second bison fell. The cameras snapped photos, and gunners and cameras alike shouted. In an instant, I felt Olive lying in my arms again, ever courageous and unsuspecting that a human could inflict the pain of a gunshot. I pictured Jake being struck down, as well, likely trying to save Olive. The Philadelphia mass murders of two summers ago, and the brutal kidnappings of last fall, resurfaced, as though summoned by an evil sorceress. I felt ill. Another shot cracked. I didn't look. Instead, I walked a wide and wavering loop to the camera group.

A man with a megaphone was dressed head to toe in orange, with a yellow hi-vis reflective strap encircling him at chest level. With a clipboard wedged under his arm, he spoke into a hand-held voice recorder.

"Hey," I shouted to him. "What's going on here?"

He turned. "What does it look like? They're killing bison." Another shot sounded, and he continued his recording. I saw a dog-eared decal with the words "Bison Guardians" on his clipboard.

I looked back at the gunners and set my sight on a man I hadn't noticed when I arrived. He stood casually in front of his maroon-red truck, legs spread apart, arms folded across his chest. He held no gun, but plenty of words rang from his mouth. "Thataway, right shot. Make way for another. Keep your eyes on your mark. Bring your number when you've hit." He seemed to be directing traffic.

I watched in horror for a good quarter hour. It was an ambush. A shit show ambush. I looked back at the bison, now numbering more down than standing. A woman with the photographers took ahold of my elbow as another shot whistled. "It's the last hunt of the season," she shouted.

"Hunt?" I reached in my bag and handed her a tissue. Both of her eyes were tearing. "How can we hunt them? And this is no hunt. This is a ... a ... shooting gallery!"

"The Park Service has a cull number in mind."

"But they're part of the park," I said.

"They are until"—she contorted her face—"well"—and then gave a briefing. "These have gone out of the park. They're searching for better grazing spots, where snow is less deep this time of year. It's instinct."

This much I understood.

"But as soon as they set hoof out of the park, they're open season for those with a permit. Every year this happens."

"Every year? Why aren't they protected?"

"Montana ranchers don't want them on grazing land."

"Because of *Brucella*?"

She nodded. "And the parks people don't want too many bison for what land's in the park."

"So, we don't have enough land?" I shouted back. "What do you call this?" I swung my arm across the horizon to point out endless acreage. Another gun sounded. The woman flinched.

"Besides," I said, "I read there has not been a single direct transmission of *Brucella* from bison to cattle."

"You're right," said the woman, "there hasn't. But it doesn't stop the threat or the antagonism. We've been fighting this for over forty years. Today is the last day of the hunt."

I watched another buffalo fall. A youngster, encouraged by his father, had pulled the trigger of a long gun. Only the animal wasn't dead. It tried to stand. The back end stayed crumpled on the ground. It tried again. Without success. I lost count after ten attempts to stand with hind legs that couldn't move.

"Oh, my God. Shoot it!" I yelled. Misery needed an ending. Stunned by my words, I apologized to the camera people. The kid fired another few shots. Finally, a bullet streaked through the bison's hide and flesh and sent her fully to the ground. A resounding thud signaled the end of the animal's futile flailing. But I thanked God it ended. The worst part was seeing the smiles on the faces of the gunners and hearing the father shout "You did it!" I closed my eyes, but the vision remained clear.

When no more bison stood, I introduced myself to the man in orange. He was clearly the one in charge of a pitifully small and ineffective pro-bison lobby.

"I didn't want that bison shot," I said, "but it had to be done."

"You did the right thing," he said.

"I'm Amber Phillips. Fletcher Marks from the *Gazette* sent me."

"A friend of Fletcher is a friend of mine. Mel Headman. Nice to meet."

"Different circumstances would have been better. That was atrocious."

"Indeed, but we don't get to choose. Does Fletcher want anything in particular? Numbers?"

"Only asked for newsworthy fights. Looks like I don't have a story, except if this isn't a story, I don't know what is."

"Oh, this is a story, all right. A story that's gone on for way too many decades. I can fill you in, but we'll need a lot of time.

And right now, I have to head off. But some day … some hell-freezes-over day, we have got to make a sensible plan. 'Cause this sure as hell isn't it."

With that, Mel walked to his SUV. I shut my eyes once again to temper the shock of the kill and reflect on how beautiful these animals had been when they were snorting in the cold air, and how nobly they had walked toward their unsuspecting deaths. I wanted to hug and comfort them, even as their warm red blood seeped from their stilled bodies. And I wanted to shoot the whole lot of gunners, even though I had never raised a gun. I thought again of Jake and Olive. I was thankful Fletcher wouldn't need a story. From the sounds of it, I couldn't write anything that hadn't already been written many times over.

The next day, I sped from the park region to meet Bill's friend Kendra Sloane for another Yellowstone River meeting for the magazine. The more background information I could gather, the better I could assign a cohesive set of features, and one-on-one conversations always revealed interesting details. Besides, in-person introductions promised to settle me faster into my new home.

I shimmied past a row of cardboard boxes piled four high the entire length of a narrow hallway and followed another row of boxes barricading all but the corner of a laminate-top desk. If Kendra's voice hadn't answered my inquiring greeting, I would have turned to look for her elsewhere.

I waited for her to emerge from the man-made cave and followed her to a room with a fluorescent light flickering with an annoying twitch. Kendra flipped the light switch to the off position and then back on. The lights sent a clear beam overhead. Barely inside the room, Kendra looked me square in the face and said, "I heard there was an accident down your way."

"Accident?"

"A wildlife encounter."

She meant the bison. Sam's bison.

"It happened before I settled in here. The details are still sketchy."

My explanation sufficed. Kendra marched around the conference table—a twenty-seater—stopped near the corner of the room, and said, "Here is your river." She lifted her hand to a satellite image covering the length of the wall. I recognized the shape of the United States.

"Your Yellowstone starts in the Absaroka mountains." She reached to a spot and said, "Here. Wyoming and Yellowstone Lake. It flows northward and down the mountains into Montana." Her hand snaked loosely up the wall. "Several major rivers claim headwaters in the Rockies. A number venture over to the Pacific Ocean. Then, we have the rebel."

"Mellow Yellow?"

"Precisely. Except she's not so mellow everywhere she goes." I followed Kendra's hand as it continued a long wiggle to Montana's far northeastern corner and then crossed into North Dakota. I wondered if the river would spill into the Arctic. It was odd enough that it ran north. In my mind, downhill flow equated with southerly flow.

"So far," said Kendra, "we've gone about seven hundred miles, and this is where it becomes even more interesting, because here it joins the Missouri River. Once it hits the Missouri, the clear mountain rainwater and snowmelt that started their grand journey near Yellowstone National Park mix with a third of the water that falls on the state of Montana. Together, it all winds eastward, mile after mile, some lazy and some not, before flowing seamlessly into another big name—the Mississippi. Here."

I stopped looking at her hand and stared straight into her eyes. "The Mississippi?"

"Exactly. North of Saint Louis."

"I had no idea."

"You're not alone. From Saint Louis, it says 'fare thee well' to its easterly course, for it now travels south through Memphis, Baton Rouge, New Orleans, and … drumroll … into the Gulf of Mexico. This, in a nutshell, is your Yellowstone River."

I found myself clapping, both for the pact formed between the Yellowstone and other mighty waterways and for Kendra's wonderful telling of its travels across a good third of this country. "How long does it take?" I asked.

"Depends," she said. "It varies every year, based on amount of water and snowfall, temperature, and what we do to the land around it." I took copious notes as she shared.

By the time I left Kendra, I had learned more of the waters of the Yellowstone than I could have imagined. Many of its tributaries originating within and near the park had ancient ties to humans, even in this sparsely populated landscape, and would receive coverage in the first issue. Beyond the park, the river's impact only grew as it flowed its course. As Kendra has said, rivers were our connectors.

Through the front windows of the *Gazette* building, I saw Joe and another young regional reporter named Mitch sitting with Fletcher. When Fletcher had first mentioned Mitch, I had thought it was his nickname for Diane Mitchell, but I quickly learned Mitch was someone altogether different.

Barely two treads up the stairwell, I heard Fletcher's familiar voice. "Phillips, join us."

I took a seat.

"Joe was giving an update. The tourist is in an induced coma, but they are bringing him out of it. Getting help breathing. More details, Joe?" said Fletcher.

"Best case is he'll be breathing again on his own in a few days. They'll take out the tube and see how he does and if he can do it on his own. He's already had several surgeries. They expect several more. Legs, spine, punctured lung, broken ribs, other internals, and infections are all on the radar."

"So, with the tube, I'm sure he's sedated," I said.

"Yes. So, no communication yet, but hopefully soon."

"And no criminal charges that you know of?" asked Fletcher.

Joe shook his head.

Criminal charges for a bison? I thought.

"Keep us posted," said Fletcher. "That's it for you two. Phillips, sorry to send you to a bloodbath. Mel said it was gory as ever."

All I could manage was a two-word summary: "No fights."

Fletcher reached forward with his candy bowl. "Peace offering. They're new."

"When you asked Joe about criminal charges, you couldn't have meant the bison."

"Right. I guess I was thinking out loud. It still doesn't make sense."

"What do you mean?" I asked.

"In midwinter, roadways are an easy path for bison travel. Mel—the same Mel you met—checked the road for about five miles in both directions of Sam's and didn't see or hear a thing. The first neighbor to the north—John Forest—keeps feed for his cattle, so his ranch would be a likely bison magnet, but John hadn't seen any sign of a bison. The next ranch up, there is no feed, and there were no signs of a bull. At the third ranch beyond Sam's—Wayne Heller's place—Mel and Wayne saw hoofprints and snow trails, but nothing headed toward Sam's. What they saw looked like elk prints, anyway. Mel's inspections south of Sam's showed nothing. And no one he spoke with saw the lone bison before or after the accident. It's as though someone trailered it in, dropped it off, and picked it up after.

With all the emergency vehicles, well-wishers, and curiosity seekers pulling off the road at Sam's on the morning of, it's impossible to tell if a specific bison-carting trailer made a quick stop, not that this is very likely. Mel and I both believe something criminal is at the root of this."

My body bristled. "But why?" I asked.

"Exactly," said Fletcher. "Why?"

Following a quick stop into my office, I walked to Abby's, searching for any additional news circulating through Morris.

"What's up there, Amber?" asked Abby.

"I saw the bison hunt."

She quickly gathered two coffees. "You want yours dark again, this time of day?"

I would have helped Abby sweep and mop the floor if she had asked. She was exactly the kind of friend I needed and had hoped to find when I moved here.

"With all the homicides I've covered, none compared with the hunt," I said.

"It gets a lot of people riled. And I know it looks grotesque."

"It was more than that." I shared my story of Jake and Olive and said, "Just like Olive, the bison were innocent pawns on our human game board."

"Oh, jeez, Amber. Sam's passing must have hit mighty hard, as well."

"I'm through the worst of it. In fact, I want to reach out to Shelly and help her through it, since I went through the same."

"Well, sorry you had to see the hunt, on top of Sam's accident, given what you've gone through."

"Does the hunt have to happen? Is it etched in stone?"

"I bet you met Mel. He's the one to ask."

"I will. On a better note, I'm all set with most of my first assignments, I'm about to meet with Simone Sanders, my art director, to discuss photos, and I had another good meeting today. Workwise, I am all over it!"

"And I," said Abby, "am so all over it, I am taking tomorrow off."

We high-fived, avoiding any coffee accidents, and filled the booth with laughter for a good hour longer. Abby was a godsend.

Driving home, I recalled Kendra's words and considered rain from the mountain sky of Yellowstone spilling into a tropical ocean where sea turtles swam and we harvested shrimp by the boatload. The next time rain fell, I would reflect on how far the droplets had yet to travel. Though I knew it would only be a pittance in comparison to how far they would have already come.

At the start of the next week, I sat with Simone Sanders to discuss photography for my first *Western TriState*. She had already met with Jack Gordon on layout and gone over intended page number and ads. Simone's remarkable eye and expertise directed my thoughts to areas I would never have considered. She was a real pro. Her image library was huge and her knowledge of photography and freelancers even greater. I hadn't considered that the Yellowstone River should appear in all its seasons, as I had seen it only edged by winter, but Simone knew it could be no other way. As she shared glimpses of bright summer warmth, arresting fall foliage, landscape, waterscape, river meadowlands, and more, I became privy to much of the river's character I had yet to see. I would gladly leave the individual selections to Simone. She appreciated my trust.

While we worked, a nagging question poked at me every few minutes. It finally spilled out. "Simone," I started, "out of curiosity, or maybe a bit of envy, how is it you wear fashion boots and not cowboy boots like everyone else? And how can your pants flare loosely and your shawl look elegant, when everyone else here works in … well, let's just say 'rugged wear'?"

Simone's entire body lit up as she laughed with elegance equal to her outfit. "It's my one self-indulgence. Well, one of two. You've already seen my coffee indulgence." Indeed, I had. And she had seen mine as we had powered through our design session with mugs in hand.

"Seriously," I prodded.

"When I was younger, I worked in New York and Paris. High life. High stress. I am much better off here."

"Wow."

"Yes, wow. One of the most important things I learned about myself is my mind works best with flair. When I slip into sweatpants, I only think of curling up, with a book or TV, because my brain refuses to create. When I wear 'rugged wear,' as you call it, I am only half-ready for the world and my best work."

"Maybe I should try it," I said. "But what do you do when you're shooting outside?"

Simone smirked before answering most matter-of-factly, "Gucci." I reveled in her impish laugh but wasn't certain she was kidding. I would ask again another time, and also learn why she'd left her former life to live and work out here, where a skyscraper wasn't to be had for miles and we were at population near-zero. Although hadn't I done something similar?

"Now," said Simone, "here's what I think we should do with people. Maybe add in a few, but not scare everyone off with peak season crowds. I know Fletcher told you to show it like it is, but believe me, as open and calm as it is in winter, it is the exact opposite in the summer high season. It would scare the world." Simone pulled a few shots up on the screen.

"Holy crap!" I said. It was like opening assembly at summer camp, with people packed together like canned sardines. "How do this many jam onto a riverbank? I mean, I looked at plenty of photographs and read tourism statistics and regional demographic details up the kazoo before I accepted the job, but this is ... well, this is frightening. Did you use a wide-angle lens, or were you messing with settings?"

"This is the height of it. Start preparing now for a rude awakening," she said, "when RV season rolls around. It starts like a soft rain, but before you know it, and before you can get a road out of here, it pours down like a monsoon. A monsoon of RVs."

I pictured them dropping from the sky!

"And when someone sights a bear, elk, or bison and its calf," she continued, "there rapidly develops a swarm of photographers. Imagine," she said, "wildlife paparazzi."

"Here's to you," said Abby.

"And you," I replied.

We clinked our bottles together, and I took my first swig of Montana craft beer from the local watering hole, the Eagle Feather. We were celebrating my one-week anniversary in Morris.

"You're not from here, are you?" I said.

"No. Made my way out here from Missouri a decade or so ago and expect I'll be staying, although I don't always know why. I don't ski. Don't hunt. Don't fish. Don't do any of the stuff these folks do, but, somehow, it's home. The diner's been good to me. I guess that's another way of saying the people have been good to me."

"Why'd you come in the first place?"

"What do you think?"

"Not a man ..."

"Affirmative. But being here, and being with me, wasn't right for him."

"I'm sorry."

"Don't be. It was years ago, and it was best for both of us." Abby shifted in her seat. "So, have you gotten over the hunt?"

"Not a chance. When I was reporting, I could recall visual details like no tomorrow, and it often helped. I'm sure to see the hunt, hear it, and … in a way, feel it … for a long while."

"You should ask Mel if you can help. Maybe change something."

"Um … being a newcomer and all, I'll just try to blend in."

"Well, you keep stopping in my diner. I'll make you an old-timer in no time."

As soon as she finished speaking, I saw someone I had hoped to never see again. He made a beeline to the Eagle Feather bar. I grabbed Abby's arm. "Who's that? The guy at the bar. That's the one."

"That," said Abby, after making a subtle turn of her head, "is Brody Ross. He's single and available …" Abby quieted. "I'm sorry, Amber. That was insensitive of me. Why do you ask?"

"He's the pseudo hunt director."

"He's also a rancher. Has the most to lose from bison crossing his way. And … he's a mighty good marksman." Abby drew out her last words.

"What do you mean?"

"Let's just say, if you want to kill a dung beetle on a piece of dung three miles away, Brody could likely do it."

"Great."

"The man I was telling you about earlier—the one who moved on—he and Brody used to work together, but Brody got to be a difficult boss. I wasn't totally surprised. Brody had been through a lot. He lost his family at a young age and always seemed better on his own. Say, grab your drink and follow me. They don't call me the social director for nothing."

I followed Abby to a big round corner table where six chairs were filled, leaving two empties for us. As soon as we closed in on the group, greetings went up all around. The men stood. The women remained seated. Abby made the introductions. Within seconds, conversation ventured into the local goring, as though it was being discussed before Abby and I arrived.

"If I were him, I would have let the bison be. No need to get one of those things agitated." Others agreed with the man who had spoken.

"It would have left on its own."

"Shouldn't have been over there to start with."

"That's what I don't understand."

"No one does," said another.

As opinions flew, Brody slid into the group. The men acknowledged him with quiet nods. A couple moved their chairs so Brody could pull in a seat. The conversation continued.

"I heard Sam was in pretty deep with his debts. That maybe he was losing bets somewhere."

"You don't know that for sure."

"Hardly anyone ever knows anything for sure, but you can be pretty sure."

"The only bet he lost was trying to shortchange his land." Brody had everyone's attention. "His finances were fine."

"How do you know?"

"I talked with him. He just wanted to get out of ranching, that's all."

"Why would he want out?"

"Why wouldn't he?" said Brody. "Long hours. Birthing worries. Health crises, changing land leases, unstable prices. You name it. If it weren't for Shelly, he never would have gotten into it in the first place. He told me himself."

"Sam took pride in his stock," said another. "He didn't always make the best decisions, but he tried hard."

"I'm just saying, he told me he was making a change, and I don't blame him. If I didn't have to deal with these issues every day, along with scrutiny from reporters and those animal rights interests, I'd do something else too. We're animal rights people.

And we're land managers. Why should I spend my life answering questions from all of these other interests, anyway?"

He was staring straight across the table. At me.

"Well, that's a different issue. Maybe you'd feel different if you had family here."

Eyes darted to the man who had spoken. Quickly, he said, "I don't mean to hurt your feelings or nothing. That's not what I meant by that. I just know you might feel differently with more family support."

"No hurt feelings," said Brody. "But it wouldn't matter if my family was here or not." Brody continued looking at me when he talked. "I'm tired of fighting the conservationists for land we have a right to use, and for trying to make a living. It's tough enough without this."

Abby took the reins. "Let's all get talking about something more pleasant than people leaving and people getting killed. Who's still reliving the Grammy Awards?"

Everyone took the bait. Everyone except me. I let the newly animated conversation run past while I finished my first Montana beer. Then I made my excuses and left.

By the time I checked my phone messages from the front seat of my car, I saw none other than Brody Ross leaving the Eagle Feather. The sight of him put me on edge. He had practically stared me under the table. I pushed back against the seat and remained as still as I could until I saw the taillights of his truck disappear down the road to the valley. I took note that one taillight was dark.

4
———

FISH

I WRESTLED with morbid thoughts of bison bodies nearly my entire drive to Billings. Of course, people hunted, especially out here. I had to accept it. And I did, along with bison and cattle being part of the human food pyramid. But each victim was an individual that had learned to trust the safety of the park. They were supposed to be protected and their families left intact. Park visitors expected this, as well.

Finally, with concerted effort, I refocused my thoughts on the Yellowstone River, which had appeared along my route. It was not as wide or deep as I expected. In some spots, gravel bars snaked midway between the banks, the water ran so low. Was it the park that had caused the river's great allure, and not the river itself? Most of my encounters with rivers had come when I was stuck in traffic on a bridge and had no place else to look, or when a crime story had taken me to a watery location. It was surprising how many people dumped bodies in water, unaware remains often surfaced.

Michael Bertram, a Fisheries biologist, was more than happy to talk about a couple of Yellowstone's fish issues, as he called them. I understood why as soon as I stepped into his office, where I was surrounded by more fish than I had seen in my life. Several taxidermized, including one resting on the table between us, and others depicted in framed artwork gave immediate introduction to speckles and stripes, bright fish specimens and dull.

Michael dove right in. "Lake trout. Issue number one." He pointed out its framed depictions on the wall, both in photographs and illustrations. "You find these guys all over in parts of the park," he said. "Swimming around in abundance. But the thing is, they don't belong. They didn't start out here, and they shouldn't be here now. But people have a way of messing things up."

"Don't I know it."

"These, on the other hand, belong here." Michael touched the fish on the table, which didn't look much different from the known criminal on the wall, until I forced myself to look more closely. It was petite, and its spots were black, not white. A reddish tinge highlighted the part I would call a chin. "These are our native Yellowstone cutthroat trout," he said. "See how they have an orange mark on them? And these"—Michael pointed out several others in a photo lineup on the table—"are more members of the troublemaker group: brook trout, brown trout, rainbow trout. Either edging the cutthroats out of their own Yellowstone Lake, among other places, or hybridizing with them."

As a total newbie to fish issues, I had to ask, "Why is this a problem?"

"The biggest problem is a single lake trout"—he pointed his finger to the offender—"can eat forty or so cutthroats in a year. One lake trout in and forty cutthroats out. And you say, 'Who cares?'"

"Well …"

"The problem has to do with bears, eagles, and osprey because they love a trout dinner. Interestingly, the nonnatives live deeper in the water. It's like they know the best way to avoid becoming someone's meal. Keeping this other wildlife—the bears and such—in good shape means keeping the cutthroat population in good shape. So, the invading trout have to go. Cutthroat in, and the others in the frying pan."

"Is it possible? To eliminate them?" I asked.

"Well, we've figured something out. Anyone fishing in Yellowstone has to release native fish back into the lakes and rivers, but they are welcome to take unlimited or specified numbers of nonnative trout. People love the idea of free or all you can take. So, we're making progress."

Simone Sanders sprang to mind. She had described differences between Yellowstone summers and winters in both qualitative and quantitative terms.

"I heard fifty thousand people a year fish in Yellowstone. Is this right?" I asked Michael.

"Something like that. As long as they're removing the fish that don't belong, I'd be good with double that."

I softly laughed and said, "It sounds like you're onto something. I hope it works."

As I rose to leave, I said, "Here, let me get that for you." I carefully lifted the cutthroat trout with both hands and walked it back to its faded paint outline on the wall.

"Dang, Amber, how tall are you?"

Without interrupting the fish's placement activity, I said, "Six-one in soccer cleats. Six-five in stilettos."

"Goalie?" he asked.

"Backup. Starting striker."

"Well, let me tell you, I am so tired of hauling out a step stool to reach that darn fish ..."

"Patience, Michael," I said. "Platform shoes are sure to make a comeback. You'll be fine."

Three miles into my drive back, I found myself singing what I jokingly named fish scales. Starting in C major, I went up and down the scales, singing, "Fish fish fish fish fish fish fish fish fish. Bum bum …" Then in D: "Fish fish fish fish fish fish fish fish fish. Bum bum." I followed it with E … Honestly, if I didn't laugh, I might have cried … Fish scales. I jerked my head in the air and laughed, pleased I had had another excellent interview. Taking charge felt good, and my move was, once again, making sense, for all the good reasons I had anticipated.

Singing fish scales prompted memories of my college a cappella group. Maybe Morris had a similar group. Joining it would be a sure way to fit in faster. And a sure way to learn a slew of western songs.

I steered Justice into the parking lot and noticed a man in a sheriff's uniform slipping out the side door of Fletcher's office. The door no one ever used. He made his way to the marked sheriff's car, parked a few spaces from the building's end. I suspected this was Joe's half brother, Burt Holcomb. Then I noticed someone else checking the side-door exit: conservationist Mel. Mel ducked down in his front car seat a moment after the sheriff closed Fletcher's secret door behind him. When the sheriff wheeled away, I pulled into the vacated space and turned my eyes toward Mel again, just in time to see him returning to an upright position behind the steering wheel. I saw Fletcher through his office window. He, no doubt, had seen it all too. What was Mel hiding? And why? By the time I was inside the *Gazette* building, Joe and Mitch were marching in tandem toward Fletcher's office.

"Phillips," I heard him call. "Might as well come in too."

Aha, I thought, *the benefit of his front-side office.*

The three of us pulled chairs into a semicircle around Fletcher's desk. He started right in. "Word from ICU is the tourist is doing relatively well."

"Thank God," said Mitch.

"Yes," said Joe.

"But," said Fletcher, "Burt said he's far from out of the

woods. Heavily sedated. Major trauma to his midsection. Broken tailbone from being tossed and landing on it. His head took less of a beating than first thought, so he might be less jumbled than we'd expect. He's still in an induced coma and obviously not talking."

"It can take a while," I said. "I've seen it before. Hopefully … what's his name … will get through it without trouble. What is his name, by the way?"

"Tourist," said Fletcher. "No name being given yet."

Joe, Mitch, and I looked at one another.

"What?" To my embarrassment, I nearly shrieked. Calming, I added, "Surely Shelly knows."

"Edward Steele," said Fletcher, "but he goes by Ted. He has ties to a national wildlife association. We have been asked to keep it quiet. And we will."

Tourist it was. Joe and Mitch stood to leave.

Fletcher shot me a question: "How was your fish trip?"

Joe and Mitch whipped back around. "Relax, guys," said Fletcher. "She just ran up to see Michael at Fisheries. She wasn't ice fishing." Joe and Mitch departed.

"My meeting with Michael went well, but what's with Mel and Sheriff Burt? Do they have some history? Or is Mel some sort of suspect?"

"Mel?" said Fletcher. "Why do you ask?"

"Oh, come on. You and I both know Mel took to his seat like a truck-flattened pancake when Burt left your office."

Fletcher smiled. "Just messing with you," he said. "Mel's okay. He and I are a team when it comes to odd things around here. I'm the info snoop, and Mel's the in-the-field snoop. If I go showing up, a lot of people follow. If he shows up, they figure he's always looking around. So, they dismiss it quickly. We work well together. And have for years.

"Anyway," said Fletcher, "Mel's been poking around all week, like I told you, but he expanded his search. Bison can jump six feet, and Sam's fences top out at four, so he started looking around on Sam's land. Mel tries to stay out of the way of the authorities, but somehow, Mel overstepped some bounds, so Sheriff Burt wanted to let me know. Of course, don't you know, Mel and I were just about to have a quick chat when Burt pulled in. So, Mel ducked back into his SUV, and Burt asked me to remind Mel to give Shelly's ranch a bit more space. Mel likely didn't want to have the conversation."

"Sounds like you ought to put a leash around him."

"Not a bad idea," said Fletcher. "But before I go shopping for one, tell me where we're at with your first issue."

"Michael was another big help. I'm good with three possible stories related to the river and have the last assignments ready for you to review. Simone and I are clear on photo coordination. I'll be doing a bit more of the initial research the rest of the week. Advertising looks strong, thanks to your pushing ahead with it so far in advance."

Fletcher smiled. "Exactly why I hired you."

I left to compile fish notes and found myself quietly humming another few rounds of fish scales.

When I stopped into Fletcher's office for another candy du jour for my ride home, he reached forward with bowl in hand and finished a phone call.

"Any word on … Tourist?" I asked.

"Not in the last hour, if that's what you mean, but I can share a bit about Sam. His funeral is Saturday."

"Should I go?"

"I don't see why not. In a small town, your absence can be more noticeable than your presence."

"Except," I started again, "in the gunners-and-cameras groups I was telling you about, I'm definitely a prowildlife camera type. I feel I'll have a target on my back for all the hunters and ranchers who are certain to be there."

"You might have to hold your tongue," he said. "And I know how you feel."

"How could you?"

"Trust me," Fletcher said, "I've seen everything. The good and the bad." His tone got my attention. "I've hounded everybody at one point or another and have received plenty of backlash, along with support. Don't you let all these notions get to you."

"Sure thing, but here's a notion that *is* getting to me. Do you think Sam had anything to do with his own death, like people are suggesting?"

Fletcher shot me a look. "Trying to get himself killed? It's a bunch of crap."

"Oh, thank God."

"Between you and me and the walls around us, Mel thinks it was a setup."

"Setup?" I said.

"A way to make the bison look bad to gain leverage in the policy-and-planning arena. A way to show the world that bison need to go. Mel and I believe a bad-minded rancher would choose Sam's place to herd a bison into because Sam was looking to get out of cattle anyway, with his artsy dude ranch, so no cattle could have been infected—not that a bison bull would be a problem—and no real industry harm would have resulted from it."

Fletcher slipped across the room to shut his office door.

"Mel's equally curious about his 'cameras,' as you call them —the wildlife guardians. He's wondering if one of them might have gone rogue and gone overboard, trying to prompt a rancher into illegally shooting a trespassing bison. Either way, losing a human life certainly was not part of any plan."

"What do you think?"

"I think the answer will surface. Sam's done cockamamie things over the years, but he knew better than to invite a bull bison over for dinner. And he wouldn't waste a penny trailering one in either. Just keep your wits about you, your ears open, and your instincts intact," added Fletcher. "And paying respects to Sam and offering words to Shelly will go a long way. No need to dress up. Work attire will do fine."

"Thanks, Fletcher. I've been wanting to offer Shelly support. And, by the way, thanks for making it red licorice, not black."

He smiled and said, "Instincts come in handy."

Abby and I ended our day at the Eagle Feather, having both had rough weeks: she with a slight wrist sprain from awkwardly catching a broom falling from the wall, and me with a strange introduction to my new home, where the pace of life was not as slow as I had anticipated and very little felt normal. We both needed to talk. My need was undoubtedly rooted in having lived life with a twin sister, with whom I shared all. Abby claimed she enjoyed having a new listening ear—someone who might be a tad less opinionated than others she knew, or at least offer different opinions, like a proverbial breath of fresh air.

Within minutes, our conversation centered on Brody Ross. I had run into him a couple of times and whimsically suggested he might be following me.

Abby said, "Might be," and my chest tensed.

"I mean, he might have an interest in getting to know you," she said.

"What for?"

"Just 'cause. I heard him talking to another guy a couple of days ago, asking what anyone knew about you."

"I'm not interested. Not in Brody. Not in anyone."

"Well, don't go saying that …"

"Abby, no. Change of subject, please. How's your wrist?"

"Bad. But good news, I saved the customer from getting hit

by a broom. And my coffee's still the best in town."

Less than a second later, Brody walked through the doorway, scanned the room, and began winding his way through tables.

"Don't you dare leave me," I said, lowering my head.

Abby looked over her shoulder just as Brody said, "Mind if I join you?"

Abby started the conversation in her typically direct way. "How are your cattle doing with all the commotion? Your ladies doing okay?"

"They're fine. No harm from a little noise. Besides, they're far enough away."

"I didn't know if you were allowing them over the property yet."

"Not for a while. Footing's not quite good enough, and bison are still too close. For now, they're homebound in the near pastures, so I'm still doling out plenty of winter feed for a bit longer until the grasses start producing enough."

"They move?" I asked.

"What cow doesn't?" asked Brody.

"Well, I know they have legs, but I meant you move them to different areas?"

"Of course we do, or we won't have any grass left." I glanced at Abby after Brody's curt reply. She rolled her eyes.

Brody, impatient with cattle talk, surprised me by asking about my job.

"It's a new magazine Fletcher wants to put out. Print and digital."

"Why?"

"Lots of places have regional magazines. Some by county. Some by state. Some even by town or city. Back East, that is. He thinks it will be good for the region."

"It sounds like he's trying to spin some sort of image to bring in outsiders. I don't mean you. I mean outsiders to move out ranchers. Change what's done around here."

"Why would he do that?" asked Abby, suddenly animated.

"Don't get me wrong, I know he's important to this town, but I don't totally trust him."

"Now what exactly do you mean by that?" asked Abby.

I was curious for an answer but knew it wouldn't matter. I had already balanced the source of the statement against my knowledge of Fletcher. On the other hand, it made me face an unwanted fact: I knew little of Fletcher or anyone else.

"I challenge anyone to a game of darts." A voice boomed across the room, breaking my train of thought. "Two out of three wins it. Money on the table. Ten bucks. Put it down, folks," said the unknown voice.

Brody nearly knocked me down to make his claim to the challenge, pausing only to say, "I'm not one to turn down easy money. Apologies."

"I don't know who this guy is, but he won't know what hit him," said Abby.

True to Abby's word, Brody was a marksman, even at darts. He was methodical and unemotional and soon had ten bucks in hand. As he started giving tips after, I quietly slipped outside.

When I tilted my head back to view a beautiful full moon, the crackling sounds I heard in my neck reminded me of how much Brody put me on edge. Or maybe it was Abby's mention of his interest in me.

Once inside my apartment, I dialed my phone and waited, desperately hoping to bridge the gap between time zones in Montana and my sister's familiar voice in Pennsylvania.

"Eva!" I shrieked.

"Amber!"

"If I had to leave one more message or text, I would have gone nuts," I said.

"That makes two of us."

"I miss you. And I miss Philly," I said. "Everything is so different here."

"Just what you wanted, right?"

I told Eva about the goring and thought she had hung up when the phone went silent. Finally, she said, "That's not the kind of different I expected."

"There's more," I said. I detailed the bison massacre, and Eva gasped.

"Worst of all," I added, "it reminded me of the way I lost Jake and Olive."

"Oh, no! Amber, are you okay? I'm here for you."

Eva was always the most positive one in the family, and I found myself gratefully clinging to her support. Then she said, "This whole time you've been out there, I've been thinking of our family dude-ranch trip."

"Saddle burn!" I shouted. I heard Eva shouting the same in unison. Then she said, "Jinx."

Neither one of us could remember why Mom and Dad had booked a family trip to an upstate New York dude ranch, where the big attraction was milking a cow.

"The one chance we had to do something other than soccer, and we ended up there," I said.

"Instead of a week at the shore," said Eva.

"All I remember," I said, "is following Mom and Dad and that dude named Rocco around a bunch of fields and through trees that seemingly wanted to poke out every eye in the saddle, on a variety of severely aging horses, while battling horseflies and sunburn."

"And my newborn allergy to hay," added Eva. "Or maybe it was to horses. OMG. How did we survive?"

On cue, Eva and I blurted in duet, "Saddle burn!" It was the beauty of being an identical twin.

"Do you remember Dad," I asked, "with his running commentary on horse poop, as though he had never seen it?"

"Of course. But I also remember him swinging his hat in the air like he was at a Phillies game and a runner was rounding the bases. And Mom was trying out the bandanna cowgirl look," said Eva.

"While alternately focused on the 'gorgeous expansive land-scape' and her aching inner thighs from the saddle." In unison, once again, Eva and I barked, "Saddle burn!" My stomach ached from laughter. Eva and I must have gleefully shouted "saddle burn" a thousand times by now. It had long ago eclipsed the aching inner thighs and tight calves from which it was born.

"Don't forget the clothes swaps," I said, "to confuse every-one. And the switch we made in the tack room two stalls away from Rocco sweet-talking with his horse."

Eva and I both tried to say "Saddle burn!" but our uncon-trolled laughter left us gasping for air instead.

"You should know," I finally said, "that our little upstate New York dude ranch was nothing like the real thing out here. That was definitely the kiddie zoo compared to these Montana ranches."

"Well, then … congratulations on graduating," said Eva.

In a moment, reality hit again. "Of all the things I miss most here, it's you, Eva, and your family. I knew this wouldn't be easy, but I didn't think this part would be so tough."

"It's tough on us too," she said. "First time you haven't been in easy driving distance, or closer. Ever. Melody and Finn took it hard at first, but you know kids … a couple of hot chocolates and a trip to the outdoor skate rink, and all was well again. But it's good, right?"

"Yes," I admitted. "And we don't have to rely on pony express to keep in touch, even though it has been difficult reaching you."

"We'll get better at it," she said.

"Oh, Eva, what would I do without you? Everyone should have an identical twin." I hung up the phone, grateful I was finally old enough to know, year after year, she was the best birthday gift ever.

5

THE SERVICE

I DROVE to Sam's service, curious to meet townspeople and learn more of Morris as well as pay my respects. Brody's maroon-red truck sat prominently in the first row of vehicles, as did Fletcher's with its press card on the front dash.

The Cowboy Church was a place where many lives had been committed to the Lord and where special services accommodated the long hours of ranchers and their families. After a quick survey, I surmised every resident over the age of ten was present.

I sat alone, in a pew toward the back, until joined by an older gentleman with a rounded face, kind brown eyes, and short white hair, balding on top. He introduced himself as he reached forward his hand to shake. "I'm Pops. You must be new here, because I know everyone else."

I shook his hand, cold from the weather but warm from his heart, and said, "I'm Amber Phillips, new gal in town. I work for Fletcher Marks."

"Ah, Fletcher. I've known him for years. Decades, actually. If he hired you, you must be mighty special. Nice to meet you, Amber Phillips."

Sam Nelson had made quite a mark as a valued townsperson of Morris. Many kind words were spoken and touching stories recalled. Shelly met the day with grace. She kept her tears inside and shared a smile of everlasting love as Sam was given to the Lord. She knew, likely better than anyone, that her Sam was in a good place. And I knew exactly how she felt, facing her future without him. I had to speak with her.

The service was interlaced with song: glorious hymns and other compositions. Several times, Pops and I shared a hymnal, each holding one side. Our voices harmonized, as though sharing a single voice: he with a deep, full baritone rising powerfully from his chest, and I with my natural contralto. We enjoyed heralding Sam in this manner, with our private duet.

After, we gathered at Avalon Ranch, a welcoming western venue. I introduced myself to several people I hadn't met and saw Mel talking with Fletcher for quite some time. Then, he made his way over to me. After what Fletcher had revealed about a possible setup, I had plenty of questions for Mel but knew I couldn't ask. Not here. We kept our conversation strictly social. He was curious about Philadelphia, having spent most of his life in Montana. He had traveled as far as Washington, DC, several times but never had reason to go beyond. He was, however, an avid football fan and had a distinct distaste for my Eagles. As usual, it was a good bonding point.

"It's nice to meet under better circumstances than before, and I am glad you are here with Fletcher. We're sure to meet again," said Mel. He raised his glass, and I clinked mine against it. Then, Mel moved away to mingle and snoop, as he described it. As there was no longer a Mrs. in his life, he claimed the news and gossip were more difficult to come by. I doubted he missed much.

No sooner had Mel stepped away than Brody stood by my side.

"A shame about Sam," he said.

"It sounded brutal."

"I wanted to talk about the hunt."

"Oh, no. Let's not," I said.

He continued anyway. "You need to hear about the bison around here. It's our ranches on the line."

I was trapped.

"First off, East Coast, what do you know about cattle?"

I looked him straight in the eyes. "East Coast? Did you really call me that?" Brody smirked. "My name is Amber. And how did you know where I was from?"

"Word gets around. And no need to get defensive. I was only wondering what you knew about the ranching business."

"Nothing. But clearly, you already know this."

"Well, just a minute now. Let's start at the beginning and go through it."

I looked around his shoulders, preparing to half listen.

"Around this park, and all across Montana, Wyoming, and lots of the West and Southwest, too, you've got ranchers supplying beef and dairy to all you East Coast people, midwesterners, southerners, and foreigners. Without us, you'd be stuck. Besides, our cattle grazing these lands brings money in to the governments and takes away the headache of governments having to manage the lands themselves."

"This doesn't explain the hunts."

"Bison come in with a bacterium. You can't see it, of course, but a lot of them have it. Might be in up to sixty percent of the Yellowstone bison by now. If they give it to our cattle, we're as good as out of business. It causes the cows to abort and lose the calves they're carrying, and then we have to send the herd to slaughter. You have to trace the cattle to their herds of origin and check on them too. In a two-year timespan, a state can't have more than a couple of *Brucella* infections—that's what it's called: *Brucella* and brucellosis—or the entire state loses its brucellosis-free status. Then, you can't transport a single animal from the entire state across state lines without vaccinating, which is expensive. Trust me, it's a mess. So, bison and cattle can't mix. Big costs all around."

"Yes, I read about *Brucella.*"

"Right. So, bison moving down the valley lands has to be stopped."

Brody was suddenly looking like one of the bad-minded ranchers Fletcher had described. I wondered if he was here as a cover and had merely feigned concern for Sam.

"I heard this is a long-standing battle," I said. "Or maybe I should call it a management concern. I also heard there hasn't yet been one direct transmission from bison to cattle. Oh, and it was cattle that infected the bison in the first place, decades ago."

"Well, you call it what you want. Just don't be feeling sorry for a wandering bison. Ranchers have to make a living. We have to protect our cows. And we can't go hunting on park property. It's illegal."

With my inner voice shouting "Thank God!" Brody kept talking. "The thing is, there's only so much grass."

I stopped him right there to very slowly and deliberately speak my piece, while looking him straight in the eyes: "I see no shortage of grass."

"You'd be surprised," he said. "Bison eat a lot, and any extra weight they can put on their bodies they need to survive the winters. In fact, bison only sleep about one hour a day, and they eat about half of their waking time."

As Brody and I talked, I saw Fletcher look over. It happened twice for certain, and maybe a third time. It was unnerving, partly because he was my boss and partly because I wondered why he was so interested.

Thankfully, Fletcher turned his back to me when he moved into conversation with three older women.

Brody, too, seemed done with his bison lesson. I wanted to

grill the daylights out of him and shame him for his involvement in the hunt, but instead I said, "You have a big ranch?"

"Big enough to keep me plenty busy. I'm happy to show it to you. We could do it in a couple of hours if we took horses or the ATV."

"What exactly do ranchers do? If cows eat grass all day, it's not like you have to watch, keep them company, or hand-feed them."

"Actually, at times we do just that. Hand-feed them. Come another week or so, when most of the calving is happening, you'll think the entire town's shut down thanks to hand-feeding. And making sure the birthing goes well."

"I've heard only a little about this. And I've never seen it."

"You come around for that tour, and I'll tell you all about it. Might even let you try your hand at something."

A ranch tour sounded enticing. The journalist in me had surfaced. The part of me that asked infinite questions and needed answers. "Okay, I'll take you up on it. Maybe when the snow's gone."

"No need to wait," said Brody. "Next week would be good. No weather coming in that I know of."

With our conversation at a logical end but neither of us certain of a way out of each other's company, Diane proved a godsend, asking if she might borrow me for girl talk. I couldn't have smiled a more heartfelt greeting.

"I've known Shelly forever," said Diane. "And Sam and I went to school together as kids. He was such a kind man, and perfect for Shell. Say, did you notice they put plants on the tables instead of flowers?"

I followed Diane through people and chairs until she said "Let's sit here" and pulled out two chairs at once.

"When did you become interested in plants?" I asked.

"As a child, I was always trying to grow things. I wasn't

always successful. When I went to the university, I studied botany, mostly in the lab."

"Why aren't you in a lab now?"

"I married Gene. He's around here somewhere. I put my energy into cooking up a storm and helping him best I could. Then I saw this interesting job advertised, and I took it. I've been with Fletcher and the *Gazette* ever since. Over ten years. Good people. Makes me think. Gets me out of the house. Gene likes that I'm here too. He always says 'If you're happy, I'm happy,' and he means it."

"Has much changed over the years? Is Morris any bigger or different?"

"Things always change, Amber, but they also stay the same. The same families are around, mostly. Occasionally, new people come in, like you. But a lot of the thinking stays the same. Oh, sure, we might get a few more homes here and there, or a new street sweeper, but it's the land that keeps everyone busy and keeps everyone grounded. It dictates our lives. That's never changing."

It was mighty philosophical from my usually bubbly friend. What else was behind her exterior?

"Look over there—that's Gene. The handsome one smiling at me!" Diane's face lit up. Mine did, too, seeing Diane's joy. We both waved, and Gene nodded.

"Shelly's holding up well," said Diane. "I speak with her almost every day. Never a doubt that she's going to get through this. I told you once, she's the toughest one I know. But enough of me. How are you settling in here?"

"I'm settling. Abby is helping. And so are you. Thank you. I tend to be impatient, so settling will take longer than I want. Something tells me it will be worth it."

"Attagirl."

About fifteen minutes after the dessert plates were empty, I noticed a large but stealth exodus of guests. I joined the stream and found myself walking practically arm in arm with Banker Frank.

"Sorry if I scared you the other day. You know, asking if you were single," he said. "I ask all my customers about their family. It's how I was raised."

Abby, I thought. In a small town, I should have expected conversations would be private among closest confidants but otherwise easily open for public consumption. Frank's words sent guilt through me, head to toe. Where was that line between community creeper and concerned, honest, friendly questioning? It had become so fine as to be invisible. Maybe, in Morris, it wasn't so difficult to be nice. Or to care for strangers and not watch them run from you. I thanked Frank for bringing it up. Stepping into Justice, I felt less like an odd, newly discovered specimen for having spent a few funeral hours with a town of former strangers. I looked forward to growing here. Banker Frank had taught me a valuable lesson about community. But what was the meaning of Fletcher's glances? I doubted he cared how some easterner held her beverage glass.

6

TOURIST

I LOOKED at Fletcher and said, "I saw you watching me at Sam's service. Why?"

"I figured you'd notice."

"And?"

"I was curious to see how badly you might skewer Brody for his participation in the hunt. I didn't know if I might have to step in and save him. Or, at least, stop a brawl."

"I was on the verge. He even dared to call me East Coast."

Fletcher laughed.

"What will Shelly do? With no cattle, I imagine the ranch is going to become an overgrown, weedy mess, and she won't have income."

Fletcher leaned back in his chair. So far back, I feared he would topple, but he looked perfectly comfortable, a clue he had done it before and knew the limit. "Grasslands," he said, "know how to take care of themselves. One thing Shelly's got going for her is climate."

"Climate?"

"Summer can be mighty dry here. Hell, we're considered semiarid. Grasses have it all figured out. When rain is scant, the tops die back, but the roots reach one, two, sometimes three feet into Mother Earth's warm soil. Some weeds also run mighty deep roots. The lesson is it all works out. Shelly won't have to go mowing or brush hogging, or whatever you did back east." He spoke as a compassionate schoolmaster. "Her land will be fine. And beautiful. Sam and Shelly always had a mighty spectacular stretch of this earth. I was always happy for them being the ones holding the deed to it. Their whole family has taken pride in protecting it. And, as for finances, she'll be fine. She's had family behind her since before she was born."

"I'd like to meet her again, when she and I can talk. She had a presence about her at Sam's service, didn't she?"

Fletcher nodded and smiled. "You're getting it, Phillips. Now, you're getting it."

I playfully walked my fingers across his desk to his candy bowl, let my fingers hop in for a moment, and smiled when I brought the wrapped chocolate to my chest. "See you later tomorrow. I'm heading out for more fish news."

"I'd take another chocolate, if I were you. Tough subject."

As I began unwrapping the candy, Fletcher said, "I have news." His ringing phone interrupted. Joe, down the hall, needed Fletcher in his office ASAP to join a call for an emergency police report. Fletcher sprang from his chair. "Phillips," he said, "I'll be back. Stay."

How many times had I jumped at a first chance for a scoop with my old daily? I smiled.

As I faced Fletcher's desk and the window-framed scenery beyond, something on his bookshelf caught a stream of sunlight. The golden glow came off a statue, some eighteen inches tall, with the same image I saw on many Wyoming license plates: the cowboy on a bucking horse. The statue looked like solid bronze, although it might simply have been coated. It had an inscription on its base. The rest of Fletcher's shelves held a pair of circular rings, permanently interlocked; a dark wooden box; several news awards on plaques lined one next to another; and a sand-and lavender-colored ceramic vase holding a spray of dried twigs with dried leaves. What surprised me was the absence of family photos.

As Fletcher stepped back in, I turned from the sun's reflected fingers to see a serious expression combing his face.

"Our Tourist is doing well. He's talking, albeit under the influence of meds."

Fletcher paced as he spoke. Then, he edged himself onto the corner of his desk, using it as a seat, with one leg on the ground and the other dangling loosely over the side. He huffed, with eyes trained to the floor. As though convinced of a decision, he nodded slightly, looked directly into my eyes, and said, "I'll let you in on the latest. It *was* a setup. Not the goring. Not the ATV mishap. But the bison being there in the first place."

I inhaled deeply to absorb his words.

"Mel found out late yesterday afternoon, after Sam's service. We told Sheriff Burt, and we've been on pins and needles ever since, hoping to talk with Tourist." Fletcher continued. "Mel went walking the Nelson property as a tribute to Sam. You know, as his way of saying goodbye. They were mighty close, Sam and Mel. While he was out there, Mel spotted several breaks in the fence line. They couldn't have been done by any bison—far too neat, wire snips neat—and there were too many of them. A couple of gate hinges were broken as well.

"As far as Mel and I are concerned, any rancher would have the skills and equipment to get it done fast and steal away even faster."

"But why?"

"This is the loaded question. Was someone making a point about unpaid debts? Unlikely. Sam and Shelly's finances should have been fine. Was someone looking to frame the bison? Making a public statement that bison were getting too close for a rancher's comfort? Did someone have some other beef with Sam and Shelly?"

"Did he have any enemies?"

"Doesn't everyone?" Fletcher slid off his desk and into his chair. After leaning forward in silent thought and tapping his fingers on his desk a few moments, he said, "But Sam was too nice for anyone to have had it out for him. And I told you I don't buy the life insurance stories. The only person who'd frame a bison is someone who wanted them out of here for good. A conniving cattleman. Or woman. I don't put Sam in this category. He had a new dream, after all, and he was moving on to fulfill it." Fletcher studied his cowboy necktie and fiddled with its silver endpieces. "Keep this under your hat," he finally said.

The moment I stepped through Fletcher's doorway, a troublesome thought blazed through my head. I spun around to face him.

"How much do we know about Tourist?" I asked quietly, moving back toward Fletcher. "Not everyone who looks like a victim is a victim."

Fletcher nodded once, slowly. "Good point. And it's his word against the dark night sky." Fletcher's words hung in the air as we independently considered the implications. I turned again to leave. Fletcher's next words grabbed me, as though he had taken ahold of my neck.

"Phillips," he said, rising quickly from his seat, "come with me. I can't stand this secondhand news."

I hopped into Fletcher's truck and had barely shut the door when we lurched out of the parking space for a fast ride to the hospital. Sheriff Burt was waiting for us in the lobby. Fletcher cleared our passage with the staff as we traveled, but it would not have surprised me if he already had carte blanche access.

Tourist was dressed in a hospital gown and a multitude of bandages and tubes. He looked good for five surgeries, which wasn't saying much.

"We're not here for a story," Fletcher said softly. "Just anything you can remember about what happened. I won't print a word, but Sam's a forever friend. Shelly too."

Sheriff Burt said, "I know you've already shared a few things. I also know your mind might be fuzzy. We understand."

Tourist acknowledged his compromised situation with closed eyes and the slightest of smiles, as though to say, "You're telling me my mind is fuzzy. Fuzzy like a fur ball." He started talking.

"I don't remember everything. It happened fast," Tourist said in staggered breaths. "I saw Sam's ATV coming across the field. The headlights, at least. It sounded like he was gunning it. Heading right to left. Then circling to the right again. Swerving, really. All around. Then I heard Sam shouting 'Get. Get,' and I heard a gun go off. At least, I assume it was a gun. I wondered who was out there with him. I wanted to make sure he was okay. I watched. For a while. And walked toward him. Suddenly, he was coming right at me. I thought he was going to kill me. It was like he had gone crazy. He kept yelling something. Again, I think it was 'Get! Get!' I thought maybe he'd lost control of the thing." Tourist became silent. I flicked my gaze to Burt and Fletcher. Both remained focused on Tourist.

"And then," he started, "Sam called my name. I remember him shouting. I barely heard it over the engine noise. I thought he said 'Ted, run!'" Tourist's voice quieted as he closed his eyes and leaned forward to brace his forehead against his outstretched fingertips. "Well," he started slowly, "for this brief second, I thought I saw this dusky shadow. I mean, I barely saw it. I wasn't sure it was real. Sam's headlights shone straight into my eyes. Blinded me. Then, the lights turned away. It sounded like the ATV hit something. There was a crashing sound. Next thing, I felt like I was hit by a cement truck. Lifted in the air and I don't know what. Except ... I vaguely recall Sam grunting and yelling like ... like he was coming toward me. Like he was trying to help. And then I saw Sam. For four or five seconds. That's all.

He was closer. Staggering. Yelling. I heard another couple of gunshots. They sounded different from the first. And a woman was screaming. Lights were coming on. It was like a movie. Happened so fast, but also like slow motion. Every second lasted forever. I saw Sam fall. The animal went straight to him. Oh, God. He's dead, isn't he? Sam is dead."

Tourist unfolded his arm and set it by his side. He lifted his head with eyes opening wide, as though emerging from a trance. "I don't remember anything else. Except being here in a hospital. Going in and out of surgery, they say. I guess they did all sorts of procedures."

Fletcher placed his hand on Tourist's shoulder. "You're lucky to be alive."

Tourist smiled. "Sounds like a miracle."

"Tell me," said Fletcher, "what put you out after dark in the first place?"

Tourist stared off to the corner of the room. "The stars," he said, and smiled ever so slightly. "The sky here is captivating. For artists, it's a gold mine of inspiration." He looked at Fletcher. "And that's what they're doing, you know, setting up for artists." Tourist steered his eyes straight to Fletcher's and then froze his gaze. "Oh, my God. Sam is gone."

Sheriff Burt softly cleared his throat. "Now, don't you go worrying about things."

Fletcher's eyes caught mine. It was a signal to leave.

Three rooms down the hall, I said, "This tells us nothing about why it happened."

"Nothing at all. But it says Sam was not only a great man but a hero: he saved Ted's life."

7

SUSPICION

"Hello, Mr. Steele."

Minutes after Fletcher dropped me off at the *Gazette*, I had sped home to begin tapping keys on my computer. While Fletcher considered it important to refer to him only as Tourist to protect his privacy, I had taken note of the full name on his hospital wristband: Edward C. Steele. These days, everyone had at least a minimal public trail created by the insidious world of search engines. In fact, I had already searched, only to find an overwhelming number of Edward Steeles. Hopefully, having an initial would narrow the field. Even if I couldn't share the details, I could explore them. "So, Edward C.," I said, "are you from Nebraska ... or California ... or, crap ... about five blocks from my sister's home and my former office in Philadelphia? Holy Mother ..."

I pulled myself fully upright, rested my hands on my laptop, and considered he might be some sort of half neighbor. Then, I scrolled through more of the reported Steeles. Too old. Deceased. Too famous. I refined my search to include "artist." Then I did another refinement to investigate consultants. Sure enough, Tourist was most likely the Pennsylvania Steele. What's more, this Edward C. Steele had ties to a national wildlife association, exactly as Fletcher had said. After further searching, I stared at a blurb from my old daily. It had reported "the wildlife confrontation" with "a local city man." His condition was called life threatening. What seemed equally life threatening was the second paragraph, which put the accident in context, as it reported the need to finalize plans to balance bison lives with the safety and curiosity of tourists, and placate ranchers—a.k.a., I thought, the cattle industry. I read this to mean reduce herd size.

I pulled back from my computer. Could Steele's account at the hospital have been a lie? Could Steele have set up Sam Nelson? Was he secretly a bison proponent, affiliated, or not, with the Bison Guardians and their cameras, hoping Sam would shoot the bison without a permit? As Fletcher had growled, it was his word against the dark night sky's.

Fletcher must have seen the story by now, since every morning he had an edge on local, state, national, and world news before setting foot at the *Gazette*. I would ask after my visit to Clarke's Specialty Leathers. Our second issue was slated for regional art, and even with the Yellowstone River issue barely underway, I was assessing topics, including Clarke's, for the next issue, not to mention satisfying my personal curiosity.

The distinctive scent of tanned leather infiltrated my nostrils so swiftly it made them tingle. I would wear the woody scent for hours. Everyone would know I had visited Clarke's. I considered for a moment the oil I used to break in my one and only softball mitt, the year Eva and I tried a summer softball camp. Its scent was one and the same as Clarke's interior.

The store was deeper than it was wide, and stocked full with vests and boots, jackets and chaps, gloves and hats, and an assortment of belts, buckles, and ties, the likes of which I had never seen.

I gravitated to a wall lined with belts. Two rows were

braided; the others were not. Many were smooth, but a few showed the natural patterns of various skins and hides. Colors ranged from light brown to deep brown and black, in a continuum of shades. On another few racks hung more colorful offerings—everything from olive green to white, light pink, deep rose, and various shades of blue. I ran my hands against several of the hanging leather straps as I passed and listened to buckles jingling and the gentle sound of leather shuffling, one belt against another, after I let go. I continued to the vests. They were sleek and shiny. But what shone far more brightly were the belt buckles, precisely what had pushed me to Clarke's in the first place. The biggest were five inches tall by six inches wide. Silver. Bronze. Maybe some were gold, though I assumed plated. Those encased in a counter display, locks fastened, were likely the real deal. Most were engraved, like shimmering works of art. Yesterday, Brody had worn a bronze buckle, and I couldn't miss it. Perhaps that was the point. This was another reason I had come—to ask when the buckle had become the belt.

I departed Clarke's with a single item, a slender chocolate-brown strap with a turquoise-and-silver clasp, and felt another step closer to settling in. The leather artistry I had discovered did, in fact, merit an article. Mike, the owner and head leather artist, was more than happy to help and promised to supply leads to several who crafted the buckles.

"Fletcher," I said, making the call on my drive. "The *Daily* in Philly picked up Tourist's story. A week ago. I had nothing to do with it, trust me."

"So I learned. I looked it up again last night, after you put the bug in my ear. You know, about victims not always being victims. A lot of the eastern papers allotted space to it. Not too surprising. It's the sort of news that easily snags a reader. They might even have gotten wind of it from our first reporting, though someone else clearly ferreted out Ted's hometown. Don't worry, Phillips, I trust you."

Midafternoon, I heard Fletcher on the phone when I came downstairs, set on snatching a candy and checking in. His words stopped me short of his door.

"Amber? She's fine," he said. "No, I am certain. I took her to the hospital on purpose. Oh, baloney. I saw no sign of their ever having met." After a bit of silence, Fletcher added, "I will tell you if I change my mind about her." He hung up the phone in what sounded like an abrupt manner.

Had Fletcher taken me to the hospital as a test? I felt a piercing sting. It was followed by an even harder-hitting wave of disappointment, as I considered my bond with Fletcher broken. I quietly retreated to the stairs, prepared to hide in my office.

"Phillips? That you?"

I paused, with one foot on a tread, the other suspended midair and capable of stepping up or down. I considered not answering. Instead, I turned, ready to fire.

"You were talking about me," I said. "I overheard."

"And?" he said.

"You don't trust me."

"To the contrary," he said. "I trust you completely. Exactly what did you hear?"

I gave the report. Fletcher nodded thoughtfully. "The rest of the world wants facts. We—you and I—are mercilessly relying on our instincts to find just that—facts—or the proof everyone else needs. I could tell everyone in this town I trust you, which I do and have, by the way, and it would not carry the weight of an honest-to-goodness indisputable fact. So, for all those casting doubt your way, I can now, on unrelenting ground, tell them all to go to hell in terms they will understand. Of course, you and Tourist had never met."

"Who was that? I asked.

"Burt."

"The sheriff?"

Fletcher nodded. "He's doing his job. And I did mine."

"What do you mean?"

"You're from Philadelphia. Tourist Ted is from Philadelphia. You arrived here at nearly the same time," said Fletcher.

"I never considered my integrity would be scrutinized. Especially not by someone I believed trusted me."

"I have never told anyone I don't trust you, Phillips. Never. Don't worry about Burt either."

Following several moments of silent consideration, I lifted Fletcher's candy dish and reached forward to offer him one of his own candies. After a noticeable pause to inspect the goods, he theatrically selected one, and then gently took ahold of the dish, so that he might do me the same honor.

Late afternoon, Eva phoned as I snaked my way out of town for the short ride home. It was planning time for summer vacation, and she hoped to convince me to join Karl, the kids, and her at the Jersey shore. We had created many pleasant midsummer memories of people, beach time, and funnel cake near the ocean waves. It was a wonderfully odd marriage of offerings.

"You already know I can't, not with starting a new job," I protested.

"It's the first time in years you won't meet us for a day or two."

"Trust me, I know. I'm feeling left out already." Sand, ocean, boardwalk, and family sprang to mind, as though I were looking at a scrapbook.

"Saddle burn," said Eva.

"Yes, saddle burn." As if to ease my pain, I changed subjects and updated her on Sheriff Burt's call to Fletcher.

"So, maybe you'll be fired by summer and can join us after all," Eva said.

"Fletcher also told me he overheard a couple of locals reassessing my presence here since the injured tourist is from Philly, a couple blocks from home. Fletcher set them straight."

After I gave details of the hospital visit, the fence, and its implications, Eva calmly asked, "Did you look at the fence?"

"What do you mean?"

"You know exactly what I mean."

Immediately after our call, I put Justice into a three-point turn in a long stretch of open road and prepared to detour past Sam's ranchland. If Eva and I knew anything from playing soccer, it was how to inspect and hop a fence. We had done it a million times. All kinds of fencing—wood, metal, split rail, chain link, and more—chasing errant soccer balls or sneaking onto locked fields.

I parked some fifty yards north of Sam and Shelly's home and headed straight for the Nelson fence line around what appeared to be an enclosure. Sam and Shelly's ranch used flat rails, three total, with the highest about four feet tall, as Fletcher had said. The entire stretch was weathered, and several boards boasted rot holes straight through. Many posts revealed a tangled mess of silver screws as evidence of recent repair work meant to secure the tops to their rotting bottoms. Irv had been right about Sam saving money on proper repairs. Also evident— plenty of boots had walked the line before me.

I strode quickly and made equally quick mental notes. Dirt piled up barely an inch around the base of many posts caught my attention. Gouges cut in the earth, also around many posts, and scattered sawdust added to my suspicion. I grasped a single post and gave a gentle push. It wiggled like a loose tooth. Why were they sawn nearly through but left standing? I had never seen this repair technique. Something was amiss. What else would I find?

I reached a section where imprints of boots fanned out in all directions, and the ground was more disturbed than if a bison had wallowed in it. An opening indicated two sections had been removed. Had the bison broken through here? Or was it emergency access? No one had mentioned any such thing. A single post between the sections had been busted off near ground level. I studied the stub left in the ground and then glanced at the bottom of the post, which lay to the side and should have been attached. It had been cut. By a saw. Like all the rest. I snapped a photo and took note of another loose piece of fence post lying on the ground ten yards away. Mud covered part but not all of it, and something about it seemed off. I focused my camera again.

I crossed the matted ground beyond the fence to a spot some forty yards away, where police tape and flimsy metal stakes formed an eerie, isolated rectangle. I had seen plenty like it. Surely, it was where either Sam or Tourist had taken a beating. Nothing looked particularly significant. Not until I saw a very large man coming from Shelly's back door.

"Hey!" he shouted, barely out the door. "What are you doing? Get out of here!" He headed straight toward me. And he carried a gun.

"I'm looking—"

"Hell no, you're trespassing. Get!"

He stopped, raised his long gun, and pointed it straight at me. If there was one thing I didn't need, it was to die a trespasser in rural Montana. Especially not after my recent conversation with Fletcher about trust. I yelled an apology, waved my arms above my head, and began trotting toward my car. Would he really shoot me? He hadn't given me the chance to introduce myself.

Loping along the fence line, I saw a second car parked near Sam's house. I recognized it as Mel Headman's beat-up SUV, with a kaleidoscope of bright decals on the driver's front door. Inside, I noticed Mel taking photos through his open driver's side window. Was he taking them of me? Or the confrontation?

Was he going to use them against me? To prove I was involved with the tourist and this whole bloody mess? To my surprise, Mel stepped from his car and called to the man, and last I saw, from a quick glance over my shoulder, they were shaking hands and shaking heads.

My heart continued to race, but I slowed my steps. As I neared the road, I took stock of the facts. Posts had been sawn, but not completely, so they remained upright; several posts had shoddy repairs; a section of rails was broken through, perhaps intentionally for emergency vehicle passage; Sam and Tourist's collision site was marked with tape; and a single splintered post was left outside the collision tape and fencing, and something about it was suspect, at least to my eye.

With barely a glance in my rearview mirror, I raced Justice straight to the *Gazette,* hoping Fletcher hadn't left yet.

"Sheriff called," said Fletcher. He gave me a grave look. "The one you saw—with the gun—is Hal Tanner, one of the staunchest cattlemen in this part of the state. If you want to choose the wrong one to mess with, he's the one."

"What the heck? Why was he there? And I didn't see Burt anywhere."

"Hal is Shelly's cousin. He's trying to keep newspeople away since your old daily and others got ahold of the story. In case you hadn't noticed, you fall into this unwanted-reporter category, even if you are a local. Hal's trying to keep it quiet and civil for her."

"By chasing people with a gun?"

"Success rate runs higher than words."

I said nothing.

"Anyway," he continued, "Sheriff Burt stays there when he can, to shoo people away before they have to meet Hal ... so we don't have another unwanted headline in this town. But Burt can't stay all day. Mel was stopping in to let Hal know he had some recruits to help repair Shelly's fencing."

"I had to see the fence," I confessed.

"And?"

"I've seen plenty of fences and know how they accidentally break and how they not-so-accidentally break."

"We already know someone was up to no good. And you mean to tell me you went walking all over tarnation to find those fence breaks?"

"What do you mean all over? They were right at the house."

Fletcher gave a quizzical look. "Near the Nelsons' house?"

"Off to the side."

"What?

I paused. "They were nearly all weak links. Each one that wasn't recently repaired looked to be recently sawed at the base and covered up. They were standing by a thread, and sawdust was plastered into the mud. They had to be recent."

"What are you talking about?" he asked.

I lowered my head and cocked it slightly to stare Fletcher down. "The entire fence near the house was messed with. I know for a fact."

"Near the house?" Fletcher brought his hand to his chin. "You mean the horse corral off to the side? Mel was following the fences away in the fields. Where a bison could have passed unnoticed. You're telling me the corral is broken?"

"Much of it."

"First I heard of this. It sounds more like outright malice," he concluded. "Planned vandalism. With no thought of bison. Except for those outer sections Mel found."

"Which leads us back to the question of enemies," I said. "Who would want to hurt Sam?"

"Or his ranch?" said Fletcher.

Fletcher pulled up photos onto his computer screen. "These are what Mel shot for me right after the accident," he said. "Jordan Jones, a local photographer, took official photos for the sheriff, but I didn't want them."

We inspected in silence. As Fletcher lifted his hands in defeat, I caught sight of an incongruous detail. "Wait," I said, lurching my face closer to the screen. "That's not right. What's that?"

Instead of closing out the exhibit, Fletcher zoomed in for added detail.

"Technically or nontechnically?" he asked. "They're grasses. Likely fescues or bluestems. But what the ..."

"They weren't out there today."

"I bet not. Shouldn't be in these photos either. At least, not green like this. I didn't look at these before. Just chose the one with the house."

"Forget about green or not. It's bare ground. No grass." I recalled the gouge marks surrounding the posts.

As Fletcher and I inspected the photos, I saw more discrepancies between what was on his computer screen and what was in my memory.

"These aren't at Sam's," I finally said quietly.

"No?"

"This broken rail section, perhaps, but the others are wrong. There's no dirt pushed around the posts either."

"Or someone was out there tampering the last couple of days," he said.

"Or nights," we said, nearly in unison.

"Which would rule out Tourist," he added.

Then I dug into a lingering box of suspicions. "Any reason for Mel to photoshop these? To make things look different?"

"You've lost me."

"You said you know Mel well?"

"Known him a long time, at least."

"So, how do Mel and Hal come off as friends when they are likely on opposite ends of the bison situation?" I asked.

"They don't have to agree on everything to be friends," said Fletcher. "Bonds can be cemented simply from knowing someone a long time. It's hatred that grows like a snake strike, particularly when ideas don't mesh."

"So, why was Mel taking photos today? From his car? It felt like he was clicking pics of me, not the fence. Between the news story showing up on the East Coast, Sheriff Burt questioning my integrity, and Mel putting me in his lens, I feel I am being framed."

"Oh, Phillips, don't be crazy."

"Seriously, I've seen all kinds of things, and these earlier photos don't match what I saw just now. Fletcher, this is going to turn ugly."

"Phillips," he said again, "Mel's not like that."

Within a moment, he was leaving a phone message for Mel.

"I'll let you know what I learn," he said. "In the meantime, get some rest but don't get arrested. I told Burt I had sent you out there, to deflect a bit of the heat back at me, but landowners take trespassing seriously around here. Mind your step."

As soon as I set foot inside my apartment, I phoned Eva.

"I saw the fence. I also saw the wrong end of a gun." Eva remained silent as I shared details.

"You need to stick to your magazine," she finally said. "Leave the bison to Fletcher and the sheriff."

"I wish I could. That's part of the problem."

"Do it, sis. Don't wish it!"

"I'll try. In the meantime, I want you to know I'm going to Brody's ranch tomorrow, in case I disappear."

"Amber! Don't say that."

"Sorry, I just wanted you to know. If I'm living in Morris, I have to see ranching firsthand. I'll phone or text as soon as I leave him."

8

RANCH

BRODY'S RANCH spread over four thousand acres, much of it his property, but a thousand or so added acres courtesy of the federal government's grazing-lands program. How did a rancher come into this much acreage? Back in Philly, ten to twenty acres was an estate, and woodlots and other working farms topped out at five hundred to fifteen hundred. Brody pointed across the landscape from his porch: flat grasslands covered roughly six hundred acres around his home and barns, lowlands with a small creek bed spread from there to the eastern boundary, but he claimed no direct access to the Yellowstone River. This meshed with another five hundred or so acres that rose to a plateau in the northwest. To the southern side, he had his best two thousand acres. It wove into lands he paid the government to graze, federal land that was part of the national forest.

"A forest allows grazing?" I asked.

"Why not?"

I contemplated his surefire answer.

"That tree line, beyond the small hills and close to the mountain base, is about where the property ends." My sight line followed Brody's verbal description and his outstretched arm a long distance to the horizon. "It's a couple of miles away. And I aim to show it to you. We'll ride." Brody stepped forward. I didn't budge.

"I don't ride," I said.

Brody urged me along with a tug to my elbow.

"Helmet for you," he said. "And helmet for me. Gloves? Check and check. I'll hop on, and you'll get on behind me. I'll keep the pace so slow a turtle could pass us. And if you need me to stop, tap my arm or my shoulder or give a gentle helmet-to-helmet, but nothing like you see on those football games I hear you watch."

"Did you name her?" I asked. "This machine of yours?"

Brody's lips turned upward. He answered just before he started the engine. "Gunsmoke."

"What?" I shouted, though I was certain I had heard him.

"No explanation," he shouted back with a turn of his head.

I continued to stare at the side of his face as he carefully directed Gunsmoke through the open snow.

I was glad to have given Eva details of my visit as we traveled away from any other humans, across acres of desolate land, but Brody's sensitivity to my presence behind him and his sheer willingness to offer a tour in the first place put me at ease. We slowed to a stop atop a small hill. He cut off the engine to talk.

"Here's where I set the cattle out late April. Most snow's usually gone by then. It's the benefit of the lowland. Usually, it's plenty clear for a new grazing year, which saves me money and time. I'm one of the few who does late-season calving. I feed my pregnant cows through winter and let the grasses here do the rest in the final month before the new ones arrive."

Although not grasping all the timing details, I saw, without a doubt, it was beautiful land. Flat for the most part, edged by gently rolling open hills. I found it odd to not find a river bisecting the flats. Only open land, sprawling in all directions.

Being in the valley, I concluded Brody had a fine space for his cattle, but knew bison likely found it equally inviting.

"You asked about work," he said. "Here's your first calving lesson. Most cows give birth just fine, but you have to be around in case of a problem. Some of them are breech, facing the wrong way. Some need help getting born. So, you have to manually get the job done. And this time of year, cows give birth at night. It's a fact." He paused and nodded. "Once little one and mother meet, you need to know Mama's going to care for it. They have to bond. She has to feed it. Sometimes one or the other doesn't happen. We become surrogates of sorts: bottle-feeding, keeping the newborns warm. Sometimes you have to pen them together, hoping they take to each other, while continuing to make sure everyone's getting nourishment. If they give birth and the temperatures are too low, you have to towel them dry and warm them up. Otherwise, they'll die of cold. This is why the town looks like it's closed in some of February and March, and why the ranchers are dragging, despite being highly caffeinated. I do things differently. My work's done by nature, but it costs me a bit more hay in the winter, keeping them a good weight with little ones inside. Others also feed through winter, but it's slightly different."

I considered the weeks to come.

"Now, the supersmart rancher is the one who's going to move their cattle to fall birthing," said Brody.

I looked inquisitively.

"Don't ask me why, but fall births happen during daytime."

"And you ..."

"I am a smart rancher, but not yet supersmart. I'm slowly shifting breeding times, but I am not there yet." He smiled, clearly proud of his plans. Then, he restarted Gunsmoke, and we covered another lengthy stretch of open grassland before coming to another stopping point.

"Now, here are a few more things you have to know. What

looks like a lot of land isn't as much as you think when it comes to grazing. One of the things about Sam's land is he didn't move his cattle as much as he should have. He let some of it get overgrazed. This can ruin a place for years. All good ranchers are good land managers. You let your cattle graze one area and then you move them to another. This lets the grass in the first area regrow, like mowing. If the weather's dry, you have to maybe move them around faster. If you overgraze, you'll get weeds and bare ground. If you don't graze enough, the grass plants might not grow as much. They'll be getting shaded over by all the old stuff that settles down on top of it. Grazing helps grass, and grass helps grazing. Around here, each cow/calf pair—that's a mama and her calf—needs roughly three acres of land a year, and you want to have some lands rested so you know you have good, nutritional forage for them all. When you're planning spaces, you have to consider what the wild animals are eating too. Small animals, medium animals. I'm not talking bison. These wild ones might consume a quarter of your annual forage, so you have to plan for it. And you have to have water in all these different places, because cattle like to settle around water. This is why every rancher is a land steward. I doubt anyone outside of ranching realizes this."

"It sounds like ranching would be a good topic for a future magazine issue."

"I bet it would," said Brody. "I'd be happy to tell you more about it any time. Except during calving."

As we motored around an edge of trees, I saw what looked like a long, thin pole sticking through the trees atop another ridgeline. I tapped Brody's shoulder. He brought Gunsmoke to a stop.

"What's that?" I asked.

"Church."

"I don't see a building."

"Oh, it's there. Your friend Fletcher can tell you all about it. He's on the council."

I knew Fletcher was a man of strong faith. I hadn't gotten around to receiving details.

"It's the newest church on the Montana side of things. And he's mighty tied to it. Surprised he hasn't told you about it already."

Brody's tone of voice told me there was a tangled backstory hiding among his bluestem. For now, I would drop it. It didn't mean I would forget it.

"This is where I see trouble brewing," he said at the next stop. He directed my gaze with a nod of his head and a point of his uplifted chin. I saw them. Bison. A cozy herd, heavily coated and slowly making their way single file. I couldn't draw my eyes away. They were the pillars of this western land.

Brody broke the peaceful silence. "Like I told you at the funeral, these are a threat to every cow on my ranch and every ranch within a couple of hundred miles of here. Trouble across the state, next state over, and every state around."

Brody shared, once again, about a microscopic bacterium that went undetected by our eyes but packed a killer punch.

"Dead cattle aren't worth a dime," he concluded.

"But we both know a bison has never directly infected a cow," I said to him, as I had said at Sam's service.

"Maybe. Maybe not. Yellowstone bison are still carriers. So, they better keep distant."

The dark look in his eyes, and his slightly clenched jaw, told me just how personal it was. It was Brody versus Bison. And Brody wasn't about to lose. It gave pause to otherwise enjoyable parts of the afternoon. From what I could tell, he was oblivious to my silent anger. While I better understood the problem, I questioned why we couldn't find a different solution, to make the conflict disappear.

"It's one of the reasons I keep my cattle from calving earlier in the year. I can let them out to the other rangeland after the bison have moved on. It's also why I come out here nearly every day this time of year. Checking for any that have come too far. Bison, that is. That water over there—you can see the edge of it," he said, raising his arm toward the church, "draws everything. It's a blessing and a curse being near it. It bubbles up warm, but not like a hot spring. Not like a regular spring either. Bison like it. But that makes it a real danger zone for my cows."

His words explained the many snowmobile tracks I'd seen as we made our way over here. He confirmed it when he said, "Those bumps, or moguls, we went over back there are from chasing a couple of bison. It's not as fun as it sounds."

Gunsmoke snorted as Brody started her up again, and we began the final leg back to his home. As we crested atop another hill, he slowed again but didn't bother shutting Gunsmoke down.

"There they are," he shouted. "At the hay lot."

Down the rolling hillside, I saw a large group of cows, looking like any other cows I had ever seen. Brody appeared to say something.

I tapped his arm for him to quiet Gunsmoke. When I told him I had missed every word, he repeated his thoughts.

"One hundred and eighty head of your best Montana stock, keeping warm for the winter and nourishing the calves inside them. You're looking at money. Rancher's gold. Or so they say."

"You sound cynical," I said. "And I heard you say something about moving the other night at the Eagle Feather."

"Oh, I'm plenty fine. Figure I'm here for a reason."

"Aren't we all?"

It didn't take Brody long to heat coffee on his stove. If I had to guess why he invited me in, I'd say it was as much for a look at his rustic decor—horns, antlers, and several furry heads with slightly open mouths and partially exposed tongues—as it was for a warming beverage. Of course, a bison head hugged the trophy wall above the rest. I didn't say a word. Just drank my coffee and swallowed the conversation before it started.

I phoned Eva as I was leaving Brody's ranchland. Then I thought about Brody and his ranch the entire ride home, as though I'd never left. He had shown me how massive this land was down at working level and how long a day's work it demanded every single day to do what every rancher did. No wonder Brody had called me East Coast. Few people knew what others were doing for them when they raised their beef. I had not given credit where credit was due; another western lesson for me, and certainly a future magazine topic!

9

INTRUDER

VERY FEW PHILLY residents had likely ever heard of brucellosis. And back in Philly they would likely be calling a bison a buffalo another five hundred years from now. But in Morris, and throughout the region, everyone knew the dreaded enemy. My follow-up search of brucellosis revealed we had vaccines for cattle—young-age vaccines and older-age vaccines— but our attempts to vaccinate bison and rid them of the bacterium hadn't worked. And while eradication programs in cattle, started in the 1930s, had left the industry clean across the country, Yellowstone bison were still known carriers, lone holdouts. Except, it turned out, they weren't alone. Brody hadn't mentioned elk.

With a visit to the diner after lunch, I shared with Abby my findings and details of Brody's accommodating ranch tour.

"I told you Brody was developing a soft spot for you," she said. "I doubt he's given anyone else a ranch tour, save grassland management people and the like."

"Does anyone talk about elk?" I asked Abby.

"Elk?" She wiped a damp rag across the countertop and

straightened her back to consider my question. "Sure, for hunting. It's a big catch, an elk is."

"Abby, elk have *Brucella* too. And no one seems to be chasing elk off their lands. In fact, Wyoming's leaving food for them in winter feedlots. I'm missing something."

"This sounds like another Mel question. Or ask Fletcher."

I doubted Giana Guthrie had many visitors. A lost tourist, perhaps, or a bear here and there. Each road narrower than the last took me several turns off any semblance of pavement to finally park outside her single-story double-wide trailer, a structure desperately in need of paint. I felt a stirring of nervous energy being so far from the main road. At least Giana had a big-ass truck parked alongside her trailer. She needn't worry about getting in and out of her hideaway.

As soon as Giana and I started talking, the river plot twisted into another man-versus-nature tango. Competing motives and our relentless battle for control were at the forefront.

"Do we build levees and irrigation lines or let the river flow freely?" she asked. "Do we make reservoirs held in by dams or allow unfettered journey? Develop and cover land or live by hands-off conservation? Put down riprap and build up embankments or leave natural embankments and floodplain? Leave our mark with oil spills or leave a legacy of untainted water?"

As Giana threw me into conflict upon conflict resulting from humans manipulating land, water, lives, and surroundings, the New York striped bass came to mind. It was a fish that had prevented reconstruction of a waterside highway after the highway's partial collapse. Snail darters, I also knew, continued to hold the ace of spades in eastern Tennessee. Sometimes, wildlife won.

"Out here," said Giana, "it's the pallid sturgeon that's dividing everyone and dividing the river's future."

"I've heard of sturgeon but thought they were ancient and only existed in museums."

"You got half right. And almost the other half too."

I awaited an explanation.

"The sturgeon we're talking about, the pallid sturgeon, is a pale, light-pinkish-colored fish. Its scales look more like plates. It's a rather ugly fish, sad to say, and yes, it's also ancient. Since it's down to a few dozen wild individuals in the lower Yellowstone River, our sturgeon's limited population trumps its external physique. Sturgeon are fighting for their life in court. Decision after appeal after decision. Their only home might soon be a museum."

"It sounds ugly," I said. "I mean the situation."

"It's this fish, and some odd sense of pride, or maybe it's nostalgia, that has kept the Yellowstone River dam-free all these years. No other major river in the lower forty-eight remains undammed. But my guess is it won't last much longer."

"What are the chances?" I asked.

"Mighty small, I'm afraid. This sturgeon used to swim freely from Montana to New Orleans. Think of it! Could you do that? Come spawning time, they swim upstream. Then they move along again with the river. Their ancestors were swimming over seventy million years ago. *Tyrannosaurus rex* was walking Montana while these guys were swimming in the water. Of course, this area was more like a hot and humid southeastern swamp, similar to what Louisiana looks like today. When glaciation came along, these fish somehow adapted, persisted, and survived. Made it through all the great uplifting of the Rocky Mountains, starting about seventy million years ago, and all the subsequent changes to the drainage basin east of the Continental Divide. Made it through ice ages from 2.5 million and 11,500 years ago. Imagine it. This fish did all of this. A fish, for heaven's sake! People, as we know ourselves, have only been walking this planet eleven thousand years. Not seventy million. In my mind, that makes these ugly ancient fish amazing and worth saving."

All I could say was "Wow."

"On top of this, it's one of the largest freshwater fish in North America. Some grow to six feet end to end and seventy-five pounds! Any one of them might live fifty years. So, what gives us the right to send them to extinction? To not share better our natural resources?"

Greed, I thought, and said out loud, "Or simply being human. We do it well."

"These days, there's increased talk and action aimed at putting up a dam."

"Why?"

"To get the water where and when we want it."

"If we dam the river, will they die?"

"Engineers will tout the benefits of fish ladders. Then, they'll build a dam and put in a fish ladder. 'That'll give a way up,' they'll say. 'That'll do it.' But I can tell you, it's not that simple."

"They use them back east. I thought they worked."

"Oh, sure. A ladder might help the remaining fish get back upstream to the other side of a dam, but dams and levees do more than hold and move water. Dams and levees change flow, temperature, water level, rapids, cover, and oxygen in the water. Without getting too technical, I'll just say this as an example: fish eggs fall to the bottom in man-made reservoirs, and down there, there's not enough oxygen, and it's much colder, so the eggs die. Adult sturgeon have lived in murky water for millions of years. A dam and levees change this too."

"So, they'll go extinct."

"The odds lean that way," said Giana, her voice trailing off.

Driving home, I considered the dam and wondered who the

Mel Headman of the fish world was. Pallid sturgeon needed a champion.

———

"Knock, knock."

Diane's familiar greeting was like sunshine every time she rapped on my open door and sang her way into my office. Today, she came bearing chocolate chip cookies. Someone had already warmed a few in the microwave. The *Gazette* smelled like a bakery.

"What's new with you?" I asked.

Diane sat. "I'm sure you know our patient is being moved to a rehab center next week."

"Yes."

"Well, I'm heading to Shelly's after work to do some things around her house. She's hoping she can bring Ted ..." Diane quieted.

"Don't worry. I know his name."

"Phew. I figured. Anyway, she wants to spring him out of the rehab center and bring him to the house every so often for a change of scenery and to boost his morale. I'm planning to give Shelly some company and help her set things up to make it easier for him to maneuver around the house. I'm bringing cookies too. The truth is, I know she doesn't need help, but I want to stop in. Did you know she's my cousin?"

"I did not."

"Her father and my mother. Siblings."

"I heard Hal Tanner was also a cousin."

"Oh, Hal. Yes. Aunt Charlotte's son. Charlotte's the sister of Shelly's father, Jim. I guess that makes Hal a sort of cousin-in-law to me, but not a blood relative."

"Small world."

"Sometime, when I go to Shelly's, you'll join me. I know you two would hit it off. Today's probably not the best day."

"I would like that. Given Shelly and I have a somewhat shared experience, I have felt guilty not visiting for support. But I also know time alone is valuable to healing."

"Shelly needs friends more than ever," said Diane. "Not gossips. We have a number of those. But friends. Especially as time goes on and she works to get her ranch back up and running. It's always when the hoopla quiets, and you find your-self sitting alone too much, that you need your friends more and more. I'll bring you over when she's ready."

"Please. And tell her I am thinking of her."

Diane winked, folded a pair of cookies into a napkin, and set them on my desk.

"By the way, have you named your plant yet?"

"Not yet."

"Jeez. It's not like I'm on pins and needles waiting to mono-gram anything, but we might have to give you a deadline."

10

CONSERVATIONIST

I PULLED into a strip mall parking lot on my way to Cody, and almost immediately, Mel's call came through.

"I'm glad you got out of Hal's crosshairs the other week," he said.

"All thanks to you for distracting him."

"Happy to be of service. Fletcher shared your findings of post tampering at Sam's horse corral."

"And?"

"Your investigating has set me on another path. Thank you. Emergency responders did break a section of corral fence, by the way, to move Sam and the tourist as fast as possible."

"Were you taking pictures of me?" I asked.

"I wanted Hal to think I was catching a trespasser on film to butter him up, but I wasn't snapping any."

"What about your photos from the accident?"

"Fletcher's an excellent newsperson, but an even better person. He knew the story itself would get plenty of attention without putting the accident's grisly stuff all over page one. He was shielding Shelly. The photo he printed of the corner of the house and a single fence section was definitely from Shelly's and was just enough to show the location. The other fence photo I gave him was a stock photo, in case he decided to stay clear of her ranch altogether."

"He has good instincts," I said.

We set a date to compare fence notes and discuss bison. Then, he asked where I was traveling. When I told him Cody, he advised I would get a good lesson in bison eradication. He also asked that I give his regards to Eleanor at the museum. His cousin.

Nothing could have prepared me for Cody. Immediately inside the first building, I came face to face with a pile of bony white buffalo skulls mounded to the height of five and a half men and spread out some thirty feet across the earthen ground. They had been stilled by a camera's lens and its inner workings in the year 1870-something. Was it art or a record? It appeared posed, to allow the bulky stationary camera of its day enough time to capture the ghostly scene. A single man had climbed atop the pile. I could only imagine the crackling of his boot-steps. A couple at ground level stared at the camera. The photographer's name wasn't known. Nor was the exact fate of the skulls. But Mel's cousin Eleanor said they likely became fertilizer or charcoal. The original photo had been taken at a carbon works plant in Michigan.

"At least they weren't wasted," I said cynically. Then, I asked, "How did they die?"

Eleanor clucked her tongue. "Gunshot, arrow, run off a cliff, perhaps. Some might have been followed by horse or targeted from the comfort of a train. It was different back then."

"Was it?" I asked. "A month ago, I saw them culling at Yellowstone. I'm sure your cousin gives reports."

"Yes and no," she said. "I tend to stick to the history even though it isn't admirable. I'm a firm believer historical record has value for shaping our future."

The figures she shared were agonizing: from 1800, some

thirty million bison were slaughtered in less than a century. Only three hundred and twenty-five individual animals, including twenty-four in Yellowstone, remained. In 1873 alone, our government stopped more than one and a half million bison from ever thundering across open lands again.

"For what?" I asked.

"Oh, all sorts of tangible goods—food, leather belts for steam-driven machines in Europe, carpets, sport trophies, refined sugar, bone china, and bows, to name a few. When the railroads came through, quite a number were downed as a preventative measure because the trains couldn't stop fast enough to avoid collisions with the animals crossing the rails. And, not least, the killings, as you likely know, were intended to destroy different Indigenous peoples' ways of life—the nations intimately tied to the way of the bison. As I said, this is why I am here. So we understand it and don't repeat it. Ever."

No wonder Mel told me this trip would give a brutal introduction to the saga. I felt shame for being even remotely connected to these massacres.

"How'd your cousin Mel come up on the other side of this bison conflict?"

"Dear Mel," she started. "He was always a kindhearted soul. But more than that, he was our family peacekeeper. Fair as fair could be. Always wanting to equal things out and avoid conflicts."

"Some way to avoid conflicts ... taking on the ranchers," I said.

"Well, we were never ranchers, but we grew up with many. Mel doesn't see it as him versus the ranchers, though. He simply sees it as a problem that needs a solution. One that's amenable to everyone, once and for all. He's certain it can happen and the killing can end. Of course, I've heard him say this for decades, but he firmly believes it. 'If the politics and egos would step aside and allow it,' he has said time after time, 'a solution is waiting.' For decades now, he's been looking at a broader picture, well beyond setting cull numbers. Other people are just too petty or small-minded or stubborn to see it. Mel says it would take but a little bit to open up some lands and make it work for everyone, people and bison alike. It shouldn't be so difficult to open up land and close down land."

"Not out here," I said. "It's plentiful enough."

"Not to mention, people haven't owned the land for nearly as long as bison traveled it before. Not even a fraction as long. I hope we get there soon—to that balancing point," she said, "because Lord knows I worry about him. If a person wants to get rid of someone out here, there're a lot of ways to do it, and there're a lot of places to make them disappear."

I gave a pat to Justice's dashboard as I drove back home and thanked him for keeping me safe. In a few weeks, I would drive him to the dealership, where I would pick up keys for my new truck. Goodbye was never easy, and this felt as though I was abandoning my best friend.

I detoured around the valley and caught a glimpse of the northern herd. Several swung their massive heads side to side to push snow from atop winter-worn prairie plants for any nourishment the tufts might offer. I scanned the horizon beyond the busy herd, wondering how far the land stretched before these lowlands fanned out of the park. And I prayed the shaggy brown beasts, puffing like sturdy steam locomotives, stayed inside the invisible lines. I wished I could have seen them as they used to be, nearly covering the continent. Why, exactly, were we so stingy with this land? How had an imported cow come to receive preferential treatment? And how hard would it be to change it back? I hoped Mel had an answer. Right before I turned to leave, I spotted elk. Within the cover and shadows of several trees, they were well concealed.

11

———

TARNISH

Yᴇʟʟᴏᴡꜱᴛᴏɴᴇ ᴡᴀᴛᴇʀ, I had learned, was some of the country's, and perhaps the world's, most pristine. It had avoided man's filthy touch. But Ginger Sharp, a state hydrologist, was about to share the ugly scars of mining operations. Several waterways had suffered horribly, including Soda Butte Creek, a small tributary to the Lamar River, itself a tributary to my Yellowstone. I was gauging the value of including a related story in our first issue. Fletcher believed it would be a good eye-opener.

"I hope you can handle bad news," she said. "The Soda Butte story is a rough one."

"I used to cover crimes," I responded.

"Very well. This is Soda Butte Creek."

I stared at photos of a shocking-orange streambed. "How bad does it smell?"

"Not bad. But metals have leached into the creek for more than eighty years, and those are bad. They've killed off plenty of plants and aquatic critters. The orange you see is iron. Copper and zinc are in the mix."

"What happened?"

"The short of it is a couple of trappers discovered gold in 1869, and within the year, surface and underground mining had begun. Prospectors were taking precious metals—gold, silver, and more—before Yellowstone National Park was even established. It was 1933 when people discovered the big ore deposit. This led to five years of underground tunnels, followed by opencut surface mining until 1953. That year, they abandoned the mine and all that went with it."

"Abandonment sounds good."

"Mining's biggest blemish is usually the leftover material it creates. Thousands of cubic yards of tailings, which, in this case, were placed smack in the Soda Butte Creek bed. It was originally a settling pond setup, like a lagoon, but its walls were frequently breached, and heavy metals flowed straight into waters heading toward the park. Postabandonment, leaching continued for years. So did the washout of sediments into the creek and floodplain."

"So, the creek's filled with tailings?"

"Exactly," she said. "A few decades ago, they diverted the creek around the tailings pond, but overflows and breaches continued. What's more, mining also made the water extremely acidic. While water, oxygen, and certain bacteria naturally break down pyrite, a rock common here, wide-scale soil and rock disturbance—precisely the fingerprint of mining—speeds the process and intensifies the results. Acidity goes way up.

"About five years ago, we received cleanup funds, but you and I both know federal agencies move slowly. Someday, we'll remove the contaminated soils, remove the tailings, and treat the stream water and contaminated groundwater."

"How exactly?"

"By running it through treatment plants, adding calcium to neutralize the acidity, and other chemicals to capture the metals. It will be a giant of a project."

"But definitely worth it."

"For Yellowstone? You bet."

"I'd like to have one of our freelancers, George Gomez, give you a call and Simone Sanders reach out for photo suggestions. This is exactly the story we need for the first issue."

As I rolled back to town on this early March morning, I realized how quiet it had been of late, and I recalled Brody's words about calving season. A few people I had never seen were in the food store. They must have had the earliest calves. Others had gone undercover—likely fully entrenched in the labor and tasks of the season. Wayne Heller was getting coffee from Abby, instead of Lucy Heller and Wayne together. I guessed they were playing a husband-and-wife tag team. The Eagle Feather, too, had been like a ghost town. In another few weeks, if Brody's word was true, Morris would settle down to a more consistent pace of grazing and growing, unless a late snow put itself on the calendar.

"How's it going, Phillips?"

"F-Man! F-Man! He's the one!" I marched into Fletcher's office waving invisible pom-poms and vocally blasting the fight song.

Fletcher stared. Finally, he said, "Frightening."

"Oh, no fun."

Leaning back, he said, "Okay, okay, I'm giving you five minutes of gloating time to share your latest good meeting. Then I have to finish this up."

"All I really wanted to do was say hi. But, since you asked, I have four of the Yellowstone River articles assigned and am about to send you a contract for another. We have drafts in for two of the first assignments. Simone is as organized as a filing cabinet. I feel great about the visuals."

"All good," said Fletcher. "I saw you were considering assigning the mine tailings story to Gomez. Did you get my email about Warren's interview with Ginger? The one in the *Gazette* when the request for cleanup funding was first made?"

"I already passed it along. The background information will be helpful."

"Excellent. And make sure to check with Donald on current ad space requirements."

"Will do!"

Our first issue was humming along. So was I. And I might have heard Fletcher mutter "Sisk boom ba" as I took on the first two stairs to the second floor in a single step.

"Karl?" I said. "What a nice surprise."

Eva's charismatic but steady Karl was the best possible mate my sister could have found. Seeing his name light up on my phone and hearing his voice, I couldn't wait to tell him news about the magazine.

Karl's tentative tone sounded a prelude to trouble.

"What's wrong?"

Karl was clinical about it. Eva's cancer had returned.

While my shoulders dropped, my body rose into an odd version of full alert. Call it panic, adrenaline rush, and shock in one quick injection. Just like years ago, when Eva battled and overcame the ugly, insidious grasp of Enemy Cancer. I shook as Karl shared details.

"A doctor found it on a scan after she mentioned pain and fatigue and they checked her blood," he said.

My heart sank deep into my gut. "I knew something was wrong," I said.

"What do you mean?"

"When she helped clean my apartment, we thought she had overdone it, or maybe that she was pregnant. It wasn't either, was it?"

Through closed eyes, I braved the swell of surging tears, but my heart split wide open.

"I'm coming back. This weekend," I said, once Karl finished giving details. "She'll fight it. I know she will." In truth, I didn't know at all, but I hoped I was right. I wondered if Eva had wanted to tell me when she called the other day. Maybe she was reluctant to add another burden after I shared news of Hal and his gun. Eva was always the more considerate one of us.

"Karl, I'm sorry. We'll get through it."

"We have to, Amber. We need her."

"Do Melody and Finn know?"

"Eva's not ready to say anything."

"Oh, Karl, I wish I could change this. And I wish I could help. I'm coming. This weekend. I promise."

As soon as we ended our call, I felt as though a bison had rolled on top of me. We all knew it was possible. Remission was not a cure. But even with it hanging over our shoulders, it was simpler to ignore it. To hope it had disappeared for good. But it hadn't.

Eva rose from her favorite living room chair, and we embraced as though our lives depended on it. Maybe hers did. She didn't look horrible, but I noticed a difference in the six short weeks since I had left. Together, we whispered, "Saddle burn."

For several hours, we sat quietly, her head on my shoulder. I didn't ask questions. She didn't volunteer an update. We simply sat, feeling each other's body rise and fall with our breaths, and feeling the warmth we had always felt. One day, long ago, we had been together in this way, with our mother's protective womb around us both and her heartbeat miraculously giving us life in a steady shared rhythm. I knew, in these moments sitting with Eva, as I had known many times before, she was part of me, as I was part of her. We would forever be one.

Next morning, Karl shared specifics. It was worse than the

first time. It was in her pancreas, and, he informed me with moist eyes, it had already spread to her liver. Maybe beyond. There was no clean way out of this. Surgery wasn't an option. Karl said it was common with this sort of cancer. I knew the odds of beating pancreatic cancer were slimmer than most. Eva would start chemo this week and face the odds, along with all the horrid side effects. I wanted to reach inside her and cut it all out. Every single despicable cell. I hated being so helpless. I hated having to wait. I hated the thought of losing Eva. I desperately wanted to cure her.

At lunch, I looked at Melody and Finn and saw beautiful reflections of Eva and Karl. Before I arrived, Karl and Eva had told them together. They were scared. As was I. My western magazine was insignificant. Who cared about a river, or anything else? None of that mattered compared to Eva and her family. My family. I was thankful Karl had help—his mom and dad, his two sisters and older brother. It would take a village. Eva, true to being Eva, felt nothing but guilt putting us through this. She shouldn't have, of course.

Maybe it was the defeat of knowing it had returned. Maybe it was that it had already spread. Eva was usually a strong but quiet warrior. The kind you overlooked on the soccer field until she drilled one past you. A quiet weapon. But she lacked the determination I was accustomed to seeing in her. She had fought so hard to get through it before. I prayed she could get the upper hand and free herself of it again, but an inner voice told me a different outcome was likely. It was a dreadful thought. And I was terrified.

At the end of the weekend, I felt helpless leaving my Eva. The entire flight back, I wanted to exit the plane and magically float into my sister's home to hold her in my arms and make her well. I wondered if I should have stayed and started over again in Philly. What would it have mattered to leave the magazine, but what would it have done to help? Either way, staying or coming back West, I was at the mercy of something I couldn't control.

I landed near day's end and saw Fletcher's truck at the church. It wasn't the first time I had seen it there late afternoon. He had been part of the church council for over ten years, and the conviction of his faith was strong. I noticed his eyes sparkle every time he talked of his church. But then, they lit up when he talked of many things. Fletcher was a down-to-earth, straight-shooting, crafty and wise realist with a warm heart, reliable intuition, and an enjoyable wit. Thinking of Fletcher's faith, I realized Eva's life was out of my hands. I took it as a sign that I'd seen his truck this day. A sign that, perhaps, I ought to join him at church services. The thought surprised me.

The beams, now giving strength to graceful arching ceilings instead of giant open canopies, were, no doubt, cut from local wood. The air inside the church smelled natural and fresh, as though I were still standing outside. And I felt light, and free, and safe, as though gently cradled by a pair of strong, protective arms.

As I sat, surrounded only by the quiet of the church, I recalled snippets of Eva's and my shared lives. At first, my heart pulled at my chest, as though on the verge of dissolving, but slowly, I gained hope, perhaps faith, and relinquished my pain to a sense of peace and acceptance. We had made it through once already. We had to do it again.

Outside the church, I saw one of Brody's barns as a speck in the distance. Another large wooden barn, less than fifty yards behind the church, struck me as an odd religious outbuilding. Beyond it, downslope, a beautiful river—not the widest or the wildest—flowed in a leisurely manner, navigating a route over and around clusters of rocks, before passing more rapidly through unimpeded space and seeming to relish its newfound release to flow freely. I edged around the far side of the church and discovered yet another surprise: a lake, bigger than I could have imagined, practically calling to me. It seemed a good omen. As I was wading deeper into my first issue and feeling the accompanying pressure of a deadline, I was also shifting through thoughts on the second issue, slated to cover TriState Art. If this wasn't a sign that nature, and our irrefutable desire to capture it, was at the heart of our relationship with this region, I didn't know what was. Reluctantly, I turned to head back to work. But on my way, I was determined to drop the souvenirs I had purchased in Philadelphia in Shelly's mailbox, even if Hal was standing right beside it. I was more than pleased with the replica Rocky Balboa statue that I intended to give Ted to keep his spirits up and his mind focused on his rehab, and I was certain Shelly would feel needed love and support when she saw the coffee mug I'd brought for her with the iconic red Philadelphia Love Park statue on it.

Even with my mind springing back and forth to Philly all week, I managed to send much of the edited version of our first magazine issue to Fletcher. It was my first creative journalism in years and would be my first full magazine ever. I was proud of how it was coming together. I hoped Fletcher felt the same. So far, doing the *TriState* had challenged me, excited me, and reaffirmed my capabilities.

Fletcher had said to tell it all: the enviable stuff, the ugly stuff, the murky stuff ... all of it. He wanted readers to see our authentic lives and for the message to be real. So, in went the sturgeon, the levees, the conflicts, and the factions. This magazine, under his eye, was going to tell the truth. The whole truth. I had made a career of digging into hard facts, so, from this standpoint, putting me at the magazine's helm made perfect sense.

As I awaited Fletcher's reaction to the first articles and the mock-up Simone and Jack Gordon had put together, I mulled over his instruction and wondered again why he wanted this sort of magazine, despite my having already asked. I recalled Brody's inquisitive words from the Eagle Feather roundtable, the words that had raised this same question. Why was there friction between Fletcher and Brody?

As soon as I found Fletcher, I asked if the good, the bad, and the ugly would bring criticism. Fletcher's answer was as direct as usual.

"Suppose it does? I want a respectable regional. It's a way to bring in different advertising and bring more visitors to help the economy, but it's more than that. I'm sick and tired of those fluffy glossies that sound alike, look alike, and don't do diddly except make me puke. They are as predictable as the sunrise. The *Western TriState* will be better than that. You are better than that, Phillips. It's why I hired you. By the way, what I've seen of your final is spot-on spectacular. Only a couple of hiccups. I'll let you know when I get through the rest. And I'd say you, Simone, and Jack make an irreplaceable team."

After another couple of weeks, all copy was edited and approved, photos were approved, and layout was completed. Fletcher was pleased with the final.

"We're going with it!" he said. "Come on down to my office!" He hung up his phone before I could answer.

Fletcher, ready to celebrate in grand fashion, popped open a can of local beer, handed it to me, and popped another for himself. We were each a few sips in when he pulled a small item from his desk and said, "For you."

I looked at a loosely wadded ball of blue tissue paper and smiled. It barely weighed a penny's worth. Just as I began unwrapping, Fletcher sprang from his chair and said, "Wait! I almost forgot." He rushed from the room, as though speed walking, and I heard him swiftly climb the stairs. Several minutes later, I heard his familiar gait, followed closely by a second set of shoes, landing step after step with a softer patter, descending from the second floor. Fletcher flashed back into the office with Diane right behind.

"What's a good beer without a homemade beer pretzel?" Diane beamed. She pushed forward a basket of warmed pretzels, offering first to me and next to Fletcher. Then, she took a seat, and Fletcher handed her a beer.

"Now," he said, settling back into his chair, "show me what I got you there, Phillips." He trained his eyes on the tissue-laden gift. After I carefully unfurled the paper, it revealed a softly colored stone, sandy yellow and smooth, barely an inch long and loosely shaped like an egg.

"It's from your river," said Fletcher. "The Yellowstone. Taken with permission from private property."

I wondered if he meant the church. I closed my hand around it and pulled it to my chest.

"It's perfect," I said. Even more perfect was seeing how pleased Fletcher was for having given it.

"Such a sweetheart," said Diane. "One of the best."

I couldn't have agreed more.

12

———

ART

"How's she doing?" Fletcher asked, referring to Eva.

"Not well." I took a seat beside his desk.

"I wish we could get a handle on this damned devil of a disease. It's touching way too many people," he said.

"She's on another round of chemo. It's hitting her hard. From that first IV, she's had nausea and diarrhea. As of this morning, fever reared up as well. The only sense of normalcy is she still has her hair."

Fletcher and I shared a pair of weak smiles. It was small consolation, but any sense of normalcy was welcome.

"She'll get another dose in a few weeks," I added.

Fletcher stood and said, "Sit here as long as you like." He gave a swift but solid touch to my shoulder and excused himself to look in on Diane.

A call from Simone, checking in on her newest colleague, boosted my morale. "I saw the proof of the first issue," she said. "Jack is a wizard. And so are you. It looks marvelous in print, and I read it cover to cover. Congratulations. I loved the part about the trout, and Fletcher was smart to rebuff the fluff and tell it like it is. Made it light-years more powerful and meaningful."

"We both did it," I replied. "So, back at you. I got my proof this morning, as well."

"I don't want to cut the celebration short, but you know I need your features for the next one. I want to be ready when you need me."

I described the art issue and heard her squeal.

"Spectacular. Go to Cody. You must."

"Cody?" My voice wavered.

"There's a place there—the Western Art Museum—where you can see firsthand the most exquisite work of Thomas Moran. It's on tour from the Smithsonian."

"Does it depict dead bison?"

"Oh, dear ..." Simone paused. "You've visited one of the other museums in Cody."

"Bull's-eye."

"An unfortunate time and very unfortunate events, but trust me, the Moran works—in the collection and on loan—are different. Spectacular and exquisite. They are well worth a look. And why were you at Cody anyway, if you didn't see the Morans and Remingtons?"

"Misguided curiosity," I admitted, not wanting to reveal the real reason for my first visit was to learn about the supposed glamour of Buffalo Bill and western history, something I had considered essential for understanding influences on where I lived and where I might take the *Western TriState*'s development.

Back in Cody, I stood mesmerized by how expertly Thomas Moran had captured the massive mountains, precarious ravines, and jewel-toned hot springs. *Genius*, I thought. Greta Mills was at the top of Fletcher's list of writers and now was at the top of mine. Though she'd been too busy to contribute to the first issue, I was determined to break into her schedule and assign her to the article on this important gem and other works of Thomas Moran.

As I unraveled the cryptic details of Moran's paintings, it struck me the world was ripe with defining moments. Some resulted from actions of earth or weather, completely beyond our control. Some resulted directly from human actions. Still others arose from the intertwined hands of people and earth, as was the case in Yellowstone, where the paintings of Thomas Moran brought an extraordinary landscape to others to imagine, and some of these people, in turn, imagined and created the first national park. Art was, indeed, an excellent choice for the second *Western TriState* issue. I was happy Simone had sent me back to Cody.

At the start of the weekend, I added several more Montana firsts to my growing list. The first of these was seeing someone I knew—Michael Bertram from Fisheries—at the next pump over at the gas station. It was an unexpected pleasure. The next was his response to my asking what was new: he was preparing to start up one of the park's plows.

"You what?"

"It's one of my spring jobs, helping clear the way. Other drivers are also gearing up," he said. "Even Mel is considering a shift. The truth is, we're short on drivers. Sam used to take shifts."

Apparently, plowing the park roads was a rite of spring. No one knew when it would happen until it was time to head out. Weather and funding rolled the dice. If I wasn't careful, Abby might recruit me to take a shift. I could only imagine. Since it was Abby, I would likely agree to it.

"We aim to open part of the park for overroad travel in April, and then bring passage from the East Entrance early May and South Entrance a week or so later. Some years, we have to push it back. This week, the roads were closed for oversnow travel. No more grooming for the oversnow vehicles, like snow coaches and smaller vehicles like snowmobiles. This means we're getting close."

I knew the weather had been milder this year, but a couple of big snowstorms before I arrived had an impact. This is what pushed the bison out of the park. When Michael said he could only plow about one mile or two a day, and some days much less, my jaw dropped. I felt it drop further when he revealed the plowing cost per mile was between $5,000 and $10,000. I asked if he was kidding. He assured me he was not.

As I snapped shut the lid to Justice's gas tank, with barely enough fuel to get me through another two days, I visually followed a glistening stretch of snow-covered mountains. The thought of plowing their roads sent chills. Ice, vehicles, and precipitous drops didn't mix well. I struck this thought from my mind with visions of how different everything would feel when it all opened up, the roads and the park. How different it would be to eventually see green grass and a summer landscape. Simone's photos had been tantalizing.

***

When Abby invited me on a shopping trip, she caught me off guard, but of course, I agreed to go. Midmorning, with the diner under control, I hopped into her truck. Seeing Abby behind the steering wheel of her oversize pickup made me smile. Thankfully, it also took my mind off Eva. I sensed I would soon enjoy a side of my friend I had not yet met.

As we neared Bozeman, a city of thirty-five thousand, I became increasingly excited by what popped into view: a real supermarket, box stores, and a real mall, not a tourist mall. It was anchored by several brand-name clothing stores and harbored a movie theater complex. Surprisingly, culture shock wedged its way next to my excitement.

I shook Abby's shoulder as she steered her truck past parallel-parked vehicles and shouted, "Holy cowabunga! Civilization!"

"No need to screech. You'll be sending us out of our lane."

I pulled back my arm.

"Shopping mall, here we come," said Abby. "I need new clothes! After that, we'll grab bulk supplies for my home and the diner. They're cheaper here. Then, we might have time for a movie."

Since Eva was the shopper in the family and I was simply the shopping companion, I was in familiar territory, and I was ready. Wide shopping aisles, polished tile instead of sawdust-covered wood, decorative planters bookending indoor benches, and fluorescent lighting to the moon and back put me right at home.

Abby was a smart shopper. She accessorized like a pro, to expand the basics inexpensively, which made me wonder what she did in her off-hours. This was not diner wear. In short order, Abby had gathered a well-rounded selection of clothes for spring, and I, surprisingly, had picked up two shirts, one pair of pants, and a new spring sweater. Success. Next, we purchased and loaded enough bulk toilet paper, paper towels, pasta, and sauce to fill the rear seats of her truck. Then, we window-shopped.

All buckled for the ride home, we sat a good while at a railroad crossing while more than a hundred freight cars eased past. Trains had a long and storied history here, and Abby knew all about them. Her ex-boyfriend, Cameron, had been a train buff, and Abby had seen a library's worth of train books during their time together.

"What don't you know, girlfriend?"

Abby said, "Lots. Trust me."

With the crossing bar rising, our conga line of vehicles rumbled over the steel rails. Barely on our way, I shared discouraging news of Eva. Abby was an excellent listener. She had lost a good friend to cancer growing up. She knew the challenges of the fight and the roller-coaster ups and downs of watching it unfold.

"Count on me with your sister," she said. "We're friends now."

I squeezed her shoulder, and then, in my typical manner, pulled back, saying, "You don't buy a truckload of TP with just anyone, now, do you?"

"Speaking of truckload," she said, "you must be about ready to take delivery of your new truck."

A broad smile raced up my face. "Tomorrow!"

"Yowwwwweeeee!"

"Yes, ma'am!"

Abby turned up the radio, and we sang along. At song's end, she lowered it again so we could catch our breath. For the next several miles, we listened only to the sound of tires circling over the pavement, in tune with our silent thoughts. Finally, Abby said, "What's the news of Brody?"

"News?"

"You toured his ranch. I only heard a few of the details."

"It was quite a tour. Informative. Interesting. Surprising. What's with him, anyway?" I asked. "Who is Brody Ross?"

"I told you my friend Cameron, who left town, used to hang out with him. For almost a year, they worked the ranch together. Cameron planned on staying long term, but he didn't like what he was seeing in Brody and didn't much enjoy the work either.

Brody was convinced he was the only one who could make a decision. He thought he knew everything and acted increasingly superior. Cocky and independent didn't sit well with Cameron, and he and I were distancing. So, he moved on. It was more than Brody, but part was due directly to Brody."

"So, what do you think about him?"

"I feel for him. He had some tough losses."

"What do you mean?"

"He lost his entire family in an accident when he was younger."

"Fire?"

"No. Car wreck."

"Ouch. That's rough."

"He tends to be a loner, though he doesn't need to be. People usually do better with a small group of friends, at least. Around here, especially, we need this: people we can count on. I think it all hit Brody too darn hard at a wrong time in life, not that there is ever a right time."

"I know what you mean," I said.

"He soldiers on and even boasts about his isolated life, as though he feels better on account of it, but I don't buy this as real happiness, and I feel sorry for him. I know some people keep their distance if they can."

"You and he seem like friends."

"Sure, but he's hard to get to know."

"I could tell he had been wounded."

We drove on in silence for a few minutes before I said, "Losing people doesn't have to make you bitter. Although at a young age it sure could have a lasting formative impact."

As soon as my words sounded, I questioned them. How would I feel if Eva lost her fight?

"I've lost people," said Abby. "You have to accept it. I think more's getting to Brody than this, including, these days, how he might go about getting to know you, when I doubt he's let down his guard enough to get to know anyone in his adult life."

It was not the thought I wanted lingering as Abby dropped me off, but it was the one that followed me into my apartment. And she was right about it. Brody had asked me to coffee twice in the past three weeks. Having set aside talk of bison, conversation had been pleasant. He was interested in my family, Philadelphia, and the East Coast. I was surprised. But, at times, conversation was awkward.

I patted Justice on the dashboard one last time and thanked him for time together and his steady hard work. It was funny how cars became more than machines. I credited it to our ability to love, which shaped so much of our individual worlds. Before I left the dealership, my new truck had a name. Sebastian.

Perched high above the road, I drove to the Lamar Valley, a part of the park that had long lured artists with its panoramic views and welcoming valley. I wanted to see what they saw and experience what they experienced, because it was this, as well as their resulting art, that I was determined to share with my *TriState* readers—the lure of the landscape. The artistic chase. Only by standing here did I believe I could give it proper consideration.

I recalled the Yellowstone photographs I had seen preparing to assign features, and my mind wandered from the present. I considered the artist and photographer of the earliest expeditions sleeping in tents for weeks in a row and lugging photographic equipment—three hundred pounds' worth—across the rugged landscape, with no benefit of roads or maps and only mules to assist. Could I have had their patience to develop images on site, or the mastery of chemicals and lighting to do so? Could I have overcome the disappointment of a mule sending a month's worth of work down a ravine?

As I thought of them working in an unknown wilderness, I imagined their sense of adventure, their sense of duty to their jobs, and the thrill of doing what they felt so inspired to do. This was surely an integral part of the TriState Art story.

13

FENCE

FLETCHER TURNED me on to a third-generation Yellowstone photographer named Jordan Jones. A single wall of color prints reeled me over with its display of barns, farms, ranches, ranchers, and cattle. It was the antithesis of the other walls at Jordan's, which displayed black-and-white nature scenes devoid of human intrusion. I slid slowly past the unframed color photos, alternately leaning down to better view lower rows of prints and rising on the balls of my feet to see two rows above my head. At the end of the wall, a single photograph pulled me to a stop. I zeroed in on details.

"May I help you?" Jordan's booming voice shocked me from my study.

Jordan was interested in my upcoming art issue. Truly and honestly interested. I was interested in Jordan. Interested to learn if we might license some of his photos for the *TriState* and interested to learn if three generations of family photographers could be an impactful addition to the TriState Art issue.

For nearly three hours, Jordan shared stories, photographs, slides, vintage equipment, and family and park lore. Jordan was an encyclopedia. A glorious, humble, quirky encyclopedia.

Subject matter, methods, and surprise wins in the field, as well as hidden disappointments or failures, spilled forth. Nothing was beyond his memory. His family had chronicled the park for more than a century, with the sole goal of sharing a reliable record with those present at the time and those to come. They had worked tirelessly, heeding the call of gut and intuition—that strange, unwavering personal voice that insists something must be done, and in a particular manner; listening to a heart that takes a number of defeats only to counter with continued, steady paces and even greater strength and stronger conviction; following a mind that doesn't take no for an answer, and forming a will that surely wavers but reignites and presses forward until goals—expected or not—are reached or revealed. Jordan's family had created an iconic log of the park's path. Then, as though sensing things might change, Jordan had ventured beyond park bounds to start capturing ranchers and cattle for the wall of images that had lassoed me when I entered his shop. Indeed, things did change. Now everyone carried their own camera. As if by some unspoken command, we left the park's journey and launched into the subject of his color prints.

"I'll get out there as long as I can," he said. "Not for the Park Service anymore, though I still create an annual catalog of park scenes to sell. But I'll do more of human life. And a bit of free-lance for Fletcher's *Gazette* and others."

"This explains why he sent me your way."

"Most people around here know the business. The residents, that is. In the past couple of years, I started doing some for the sheriff. It was rough taking photos of the Nelson accident. But, of course, they needed them."

I cocked my head and recalled Fletcher talking about them.

"Unbiased documentation," said Jordan. "I guess either to prove—or disprove—it was an accident."

I nearly jumped out of my skin waiting for Jordan to locate the prints. Until I saw them. In a nanosecond, I was back to

Philadelphia shootings, auto wrecks, fires, and other gruesome occurrences with unwanted consequences. He had arrived soon after emergency services. I thought of the beehive of activity in town on that same morning. I recalled the faint sounds of sirens in the night.

The details of the assault—hoof marks, skidding boot marks, patches of bloodied grass, and strewn bodies, all in color— ambushed me. I focused on Sam's overturned ATV, which had seemingly flipped after hitting a pile of fence posts. Ted's time-line became real. Jordan slipped a couple more images onto the counter.

"I went back in daylight and took these before more people messed up the ground."

I zeroed in on the fence. Then I turned to Jordan to ask about his display of ranch images again. I pointed at the lowest row, where earlier I had noticed a clear shot of Sam Nelson's ranch. Along with his horse corral.

"This Nelson Ranch photo. When did you take it?"

Jordan unpinned the print from the wall and flipped it over. "December tenth of last year. Between ten and ten fifteen a.m. I label all of them." I wasn't surprised.

Three months old. "Could I get a copy?"

He handed me the print. "No charge."

Jordan began perusing the other prints on the wall, slight smile on his face, perhaps reminiscing about the way things had been for all the years past. He suddenly turned to face me. "You aren't the one staying at Irv and Izzy's, are you?"

"How did you guess?"

"It's common knowledge they rented out. And I just put two and two together, what with you being new to the area. Come, take a look."

I followed Jordan to the edge of the wall, where he pointed to a print and said, "Here you are. Irv and Izzy's. Home sweet home."

I looked. Nothing seemed familiar.

"Taken from far out back, across the pastureland. Here's the home, up here near the horizon. The driveway's on the other side. You can't see much of it."

I was suddenly grounded. "It's bigger than I thought."

"Used to stretch right down to the church. In fact, that church land used to be part of it all."

"Really?"

"Look over here."

I followed him to a wall of black-and-white prints. "Here's the home—or what used to be the homesite before the new one went up—where you're at—and here's the view down the hills with no church. Just open land forever."

"When did the church go up?"

"Twenty years. No, might be twenty-five by now. You know how time flies. Ask Fletcher. He'll know. Or maybe better to not ask him. I'm sure there's a plaque somewhere at the church. In fact, I know there is." As if making a mental note, he said, "Surprised I don't have a photo of it. I'd best be getting out to that church with the camera."

Within minutes, I was out the door, clutching my bag with Sam and Shelly's ranch print tucked inside. As I drove home, minutes seemed to pass in seconds, and my mind raced even faster. I rounded the last curve, intending to take the turn into Irv and Izzy's at a no-nonsense pace, but instead had to hit the brakes hard. A sheriff's vehicle sat in my driveway. I eased off the road and slowed to a halt, feeling a heaping dose of apprehension. Where the hell had I missed the speed trap? Crap. Burt Holcomb emerged and stood waiting.

"How's your day going?" he asked.

I ignored his question and said, "Is everything all right?"

"I apologize for not giving notice, but I couldn't reach Fletcher for a number. May I come in?"

I ferried him into the apartment. Burt got straight to business. Had I known the visiting tourist? he wondered, having barely taken a seat. Before I had come to Montana?

I stared straight into Burt's eyes. "I didn't meet him until you let Fletcher and me talk with him in the hospital."

"You didn't hear of him in your work in Philadelphia?"

"No."

"Did you ever interview him for a story?"

"Not that I know of."

"Does this mean you might have spoken with him?"

"I don't believe I ever spoke with him, and I don't believe I ever met him, and certainly didn't know him. Burt, what are you …"

"I have reason to believe you lived near him. Or he lived near your office. I guess that's what he said."

"You spoke with him? Recently?"

Burt nodded. "Yesterday, at Shelly's"

This explained the interest in me. And told me Tourist might be a suspect in Burt's mind as well.

"Burt," I started. "Philadelphia is a city of strangers. You could live or work a block away from a number of people you never met. It's not like out here, where everyone knows everyone, despite large distances between homes."

Burt listened carefully.

"Does he claim to know me?" I asked, feeling an odd sense of self-doubt.

"He said he knew your name."

"He what?" I shook my head. "Maybe from the paper and my stories, but not me personally."

"I am not certain," said Burt.

I thought quietly a moment and regretted having given Shelly and Ted the Philadelphia souvenirs. "Does this mean you suspect him of harming Sam?"

"I can't talk about that. I just had to ask a few questions."

"Okay …"

"I believe you came into town the night of the accident."

I thought back to the sirens and the overflow of townspeople gathering the next morning. I relayed details to Burt. I thought of Jordan's crime scene photos in my bag and said nothing. After a few seconds, he said, "Don't think anything of this, Ms. Phillips. I am obliged to follow up on everything."

I watched Burt's SUV glide to the edge of the driveway and turn its way down the hill toward town with the stinging words *Ms. Phillips* echoing in my ears. What had just happened? And what did everyone else in this town think of me?

<hr>

"No more guns, I hope." Eva spoke matter-of-factly.

"None I know of. I did, however, have a visit from the sheriff yesterday."

In my former line of work, I had faced many situations others would never add to their autobiographies, but Eva thought I was joking. I could tell from the sound of her laugh that she was weak. It killed me.

"Oh, Eva ..."

"I'm doing okay," she said, knowing exactly what I was thinking.

I did my best to send positive energy and conceal my haunting thoughts. The ones that had scratched relentlessly of late, as though stuck in my skin like a painful burr.

"I have new photos of the fence," I said.

"You went back to that man with the gun?" Eva's voice sounded shrill. I hated to alarm her.

"No."

I shared news of my visit with Jordan and pulled out photos as I spoke. "Something is wrong, but I don't know what." I stared at Jordan's photo of the corral fence taken in the winter. As I did, I placed the photo beside the pictures I had taken at Sam's before Hal had come after me. I stared at the one of the single broken piece of fence post on the ground. Suddenly, it was as though the entire woodpile that had flipped Sam's ATV hit me in the face. I didn't see the difference very clearly on the photograph, but I remembered the difference well.

"Eva! I know what's wrong! I know. I know. I know!"

"Slow down, Amber. No need to go nuts."

I had had the answer all along, but hadn't realized it. "It's not the same wood," I said.

"What?"

"The fence wood and the piece on the ground are the exact same color."

"Okay. So?"

"But one is rough finished, and the other is smooth."

"So, they're different?"

"Yes."

"Which means what?"

"Which means Fletcher has been right all along about something not feeling right."

"It sounds like you have found yourself a good match out there," she said. "You and your instincts, and Fletcher and his *something-doesn't-feel-rights.*"

"You bet!"

As I headed upstairs after visiting Mitch, Mel popped through the *Gazette*'s front doorway, instead of Fletcher's secret side door on the sly.

"Is Fletcher in?" he asked.

"Somewhere, but he's been impossible to track down today."

"I have an appointment," he said.

I wanted to talk with Fletcher as well, but, instead, sprinted upstairs to my office to place a call. I hesitated before dialing the only number I had for Shelly Nelson—her home phone number.

With no answer, and no space for messages on her answering machine, I knew I would have to visit. Instinct told me it would be better to introduce myself in person anyway, but I didn't know if Hal was still on duty.

About ten minutes later, I decided to join Fletcher and Mel. I had to tell Fletcher about the fence, and I might as well tell Mel at the same time.

"Fletcher," I shouted through his closed door. "Incoming! It's Amber." If the door had been locked, I would have wrenched my arm from wrist to shoulder from the force with which I swung it open. I found Fletcher in his normal leaned-back posture and Mel across from him with feet up on an empty chair. They could have been watching a football game, as relaxed as they both appeared. In a third seat, also appearing relaxed, was a woman I had seen only once.

"Phillips," said Fletcher, "come on in." After a short pause, worthy of the best stand-up comedy, he added, "Oh, I see you have."

I huffed. Yes, I had. So, I had better have something good to warrant this turn of attention.

"Phillips," said Fletcher, "you remember Shelly Nelson?"

I looked at the woman, who now sat upright. My body stiffened.

"Shelly," he continued, "this is Amber Phillips. Maybe you saw the first issue of the magazine online. It's Amber's baby. Print copies are due out any day now. I'll drop off a copy."

Shelly and I exchanged a light handshake and quiet smiles. I tried to excuse myself, hoping to save my conversation for a later moment with only Fletcher and Mel, but Fletcher wouldn't hear anything of it.

I started cautiously. "It's about the fence photos." I flashed my eyes to Shelly's. Her expression remained unchanged.

"Go ahead," said Fletcher. "We're on the same side."

"I found something."

"You went back to Sam and Shelly's?"

"No," I said, giving a strong shake of my head as my eyes again met Shelly's.

Fletcher lowered his chin, to better see over reading glasses.

"I visited with Jordan Jones."

Before I pulled prints onto his desk, Fletcher confirmed Shelly wanted to look, knowing all too well Jordan was early to the scene. I thanked my lucky stars she deemed her business over and it best to leave. With Fletcher and Mel rising to escort her to the door, she came forward to look me eye to eye. "Thank you," she said, "for showing your respects to Sam. I didn't know you then, but it meant a lot—your attending the service."

With perfect honesty I replied, "I had to." Out of the corner of my eye, I saw Fletcher subtly smile.

"Thank you, also, for the souvenirs. They lifted our spirits."

Again, I said, "I had to." And I meant it.

"Well, Ms. Amber, I hope you will come visit. Diane has spoken of you."

"I'll coordinate with Diane."

"So," said Fletcher, with only three of us in the room, "what's up, Phillips? And how's your arm, after attacking my door?"

"The woodpile that Sam's ATV hit wasn't his wood."

"What do you mean?"

"Sam's corral fence, including posts, is made of smooth-finished wood. The pile on the ground was rough finished."

"From someplace else, you mean?" said Fletcher.

"Dumped?" asked Mel.

"That jibes with what Irv said about picking up the piles each night," said Fletcher.

"Last month, when I trespassed at Sam's, I leaned on one of Sam's posts and touched several others. They are all smooth-finished wood. And so are these in a photo Jordan took last winter."

"Smooth finished and decorative," said Mel.

"Yesterday, I saw Jordan's accident photos. The ones of the woodpile that flipped the ATV. I realized the splintered-off piece I shot while trespassing at Sam's was from a post, and likely from the pile. And it was definitely rough finished. You can see it here in my photo. I never put it together."

Mel and Fletcher leaned forward.

"But why would someone dump posts at Sam's?" asked Fletcher.

"No idea," I said, "but if the sheriff's office took the posts that Sam ran over as evidence, I'm sure they can check for fingerprints."

Fletcher laughed. "Maybe if they were in Philadelphia," he said, "but any rancher or resident west of the Mississippi would know not to handle a fence post without gloves. Besides, I suspect the sheriff and some friendly neighbors thought they were doing Shelly good by hauling the posts away. At the time, no one was considering this anything more than an unfortunate accident. Burt and all the rest assumed this was leftover mess from Sam and Irv's handiwork. They wanted any reminder of it out of Shelly's view. Irv told me they cleaned up the site every afternoon, so we were perplexed, but Burt didn't know any of this."

"So, what was the purpose of dumping posts at Sam's?" I asked.

"It's a question," said Fletcher.

"What if someone thought they were helping Sam out, giving him extras?" asked Mel.

Fletcher suddenly looked worried. "It would be just like Irv to help out. And it would be a hell of a lot of guilt to carry if he or someone else made this sort of donation and inadvertently caused Sam's death."

Mel and I remained silent.

Fletcher said, "I'll call Irv. Great work, Phillips. I see why you were so good at your old job." Then he gave a recap. "As it stands, we know the corral breaks had nothing to do with the bison. No bison should have been anywhere near Sam's unless he got help, which he did, with the outer fence breaks. We don't know if a rancher with cattle or a dude rancher fearful of Sam's art project was involved. But they are the prime suspects."

"Rules everyone in," said Mel.

"We may never know for certain," said Fletcher. "But you and I both know several ranchers who are more likely than others to do something like this. Some who, judging from how they're dressing and what they're driving, are doing mighty well with their own dude ranches and might not want anyone new in the game."

"Okay, Phillips," said Fletcher, after holding Mel in his gaze, "you're officially in the inner circle. Keep your mouth shut."

It wasn't as though I hadn't received plenty of inside tips before.

14

EVIDENCE

I shut off Sebastian's engine in front of the *Gazette* but made no move to unlock the door or step outside. Instead, I remained seated, feeling invisible and safe, protected from life's troubles. I watched Morris slowly awaken and sat so long, beads of sweat dribbled from my hairline. Heat, focused from the morning sun, had gathered in my cocoon, even on this early spring day.

When several tourists passed between Sebastian and the next truck over, they tugged me back to the tasks of life. I packed away my calm and pushed open the driver's side door. A modest breeze rushed me back into a familiar sensation of day-to-day business, as though a work switch had been lifted to the on position. I drew in a deep breath, climbed the steps to the porch, and tugged open the familiar front door.

Fletcher, leaning back in his rollaway chair, waved. He did this with such routine, I no longer feared for his safety.

"Brody came looking for you. He wanted to show you something."

I stopped.

"I think he's taking a liking to you."

"Is this an April Fools' joke?" I asked, seeing his smile inch higher and considering what day it was.

Fletcher shrugged. "Wouldn't consider it."

It was unnerving not knowing for certain. Before Fletcher could say anything more, I looked at the brilliant bronze cowboy seated half in and half out of the saddle atop the bookcase bucking horse.

"So, Fletch," I said, reverting to a nickname I had never used, "how'd you get the statue? The Wyoming bucking horse?"

Fletcher shone a vacant glare.

"It was my great-great-great-granddaddy's. From a long time ago." He set his gaze back to his computer.

I considered the incident throughout the day. Fletcher, usually happy to share, had shut down completely at the mere question. He hadn't pulled it forward, given me the story, or shown it off in the least. Someday, I was taking a closer look at the words on the nameplate.

After several productive hours of research, phone calls, and writing, my mental energy flagged me down for a break. I was exiting Abby's Diner with a cup of strong black coffee when Banker Frank prepared to enter. I hadn't seen him since Sam's service. He held the door and said, "Good day." It was perfectly uneventful until I was barely three feet from Sebastian and I heard Banker Frank calling, "I've been meaning to tell you, I like your new truck."

Before I uttered a word, he stood beside me. "I tried to get inside it the other day."

"You what?" I took a step backward.

"It looks exactly like my brother's. I was looking for paperwork, but when the door wouldn't open, I knew something was wrong; he never locks. Then I noticed there were no fuzzy dice."

"Dice?"

"I just wanted to tell you, in case you saw me and thought I was trying to break in."

"Didn't see a thing," I said.

"It looks new."

"I got it this week."

"That explains why I had never seen it. I'll be more careful next time Mo comes to town."

Instead of ending the conversation, I took a page out of Banker Frank's book and asked about his family. "Does your brother live here?"

"One of the next towns west. I got him into the insurance business. Sam had his policy with him, so Mo came to talk with Fletcher and me, to see if we heard anything new. I'm a silent partner because he's the sort of brother you have to look out for."

"Such a shame about Sam," I said.

"Mo doesn't believe it was self-inflicted, of course, and he'd like to help Shelly, but he needs all the facts before the company hands over a check. It's a big deal."

"Understandable. And no hard feelings on the truck."

On the verge of entering Fletcher's office, I heard his phone ring and stepped away. Less than five minutes later, Fletcher called me in.

"Your landlord, Irv, and I go back forty years, and I'd trust him with my life. Someone thought they saw Irv's truck near Sam's the night of the accident, and Burt's gotten wind of this report."

I listened carefully.

"Irv drove by Sam's a few times before leaving town to see if anything looked out of sorts. Brody's one-eyed bandit was the only vehicle that passed by."

"Brody's what?"

"His truck. Hasn't fixed the taillight in over six months. Don't know what's wrong with him.

"Irv also checked in with Sam that night and learned Sam was preparing to spend time out on the ranchland, gun in hand, looking for trespassers. Someone had been vandalizing. That's why they did such shoddy repair work. They figured a few more metal screws put in a post, beyond what was actually needed for post repairs, would increase the chance of breaking someone's saw if they returned to cut them again. Might slow someone down enough for Sam to catch him. Irv figured Sam had things under control, but leaving so late, he and Izzy spent that first night right up in Billings.

"Irv has some old posts of his own that happen to be rough finished. He thinks they might be similar to the ones Burt and friends hauled off—the ones that caused Sam's accident. Irv didn't leave any pile for Sam, although wishes he did, because Sam would have known to look for it and might not have flipped his ATV on some unexpected pile out back. Anyway, we need to make sure Irv's extras disappear. They're somewhere in his garage ... your garage."

"Where should I put them?" I asked.

"Any place out back where they can start rotting. There should only be a couple. Tell me if you need help. And wear gloves."

15
————————

GATHERING

"I'm visiting Shelly after work," said Diane, "and you're joining me."

Without a moment's thought, I said, "Indeed, I am."

It was to be a celebration of sorts, and a farewell dinner with Diane, Shelly, and Ted. The man formerly known as Tourist was preparing his return to Philadelphia. The four of us circled around a sturdy wooden table, glasses of wine joining us.

"Why art?" I asked when Shelly's dude-ranch plans joined our conversation.

"It was Sam's idea," she said. "He couldn't draw more than stick people, but it was his wild, beautiful dream to open this up to people who could, and who would enjoy the experience."

"It makes perfect sense," said Diane. "Especially since you were an art major in college."

"You what?" I said.

With a slight nod and a modest smile, Shelly confirmed Diane's comment. "He wanted to do it for me, but we also wanted to create a special space to gather, share, and let artists or would-be artists work alongside one another. A sort of retreat, with an increasingly far-reaching community growing from everyone who visited."

"We considered classes," added Ted, "because Shelly is certainly qualified to lead them, but in the end decided to first focus on artists working independently. To set up for a couple of days or weeks."

"Above all," said Shelly, "we wanted to share our gorgeous land. We have so much here, being on the edge of the park and forest and with our creeks and lakes. We have long felt we should share it, rather than keep it all to ourselves. A person can't ever really own this land."

"Lovely," I said. "And generous."

"And we're going to make it happen," said Diane.

"Yes, we are," said Shelly. "And I thank you, Ted, again and again, for helping." She turned to face me. "We met Ted through a search for small business consultants. We were pleasantly surprised to find someone who specialized in art-related start-ups. Galleries, art therapy nonprofits, and such. Sam and I felt it best to work with someone who wasn't from here so we hit the points nonlocals would react to. We wanted someone with art experience but also planning knowledge. Ted was perfect."

"Oh?" I said, seeking more information on Ted.

"I've helped many groups with exhibits and programming. I started in graphics, but each project gave me insight into other elements, so I shifted into conceptual design and development. I even do grant writing. I like the full-package approach."

"Do you do this all over?"

"Mostly in the East and California. Shelly's dude ranch was a first for me."

"It sounds rewarding. Congratulations."

"Yes," said Ted. "And Sam and I are still all in."

Shelly touched a hand to her heart. I wanted to hug them both.

"I bet we could get a women's group set up to help this off the ground, Shell Belle." Everyone looked at Diane.

Diane looked at Shelly. "Oops, couldn't help it." Then Diane looked at me. "I've called her that forever. We had better keep the name reserved for family, though. No offense intended."

"None taken," Ted and I said in unison.

"Are you far along with plans?" I asked.

"Shelly will start small this summer to gauge interest," said Ted. "We'll divide her second building into painting lofts— either individual or group space. She'll use the extra bedrooms in her home to put up as many as four at a time, some with private bath and some with shared. Right now, she's planning on setting up two round structures to give panoramic views of particularly scenic locations. They'll be roofed and enclosed, perfect no matter the weather, and safe to leave materials in at night. Of course, artists can work outside them as well and use them as a sort of base. And they'll be stocked with beverages and snacks."

"I'm keeping a couple of horses here," said Shelly, "to let guests ride if they like, but we expect we'll be ferrying everyone to painting locations with trucks or ATVs. They're faster and more convenient."

"And no one will have to deal with Dunston," said Diane.

"Dunston?" I said.

"He likes to lick your face. I love him to pieces, but ..."

We had a good laugh.

"With as strongly as this region is tied to art," I said. "a dude ranch for artists seems perfect."

"Without artists," said Shelly, "we might not have a park. Fur trappers told stories of geysers and hot springs, but people thought they were tall tales. When people in Washington set eyes on artwork and photography done out here, they finally believed the stories and set about protecting the land."

"Yes," I said. "And I just saw a magnificent painting done by one of our American impressionists, John Twachtman. It was his *Waterfall in Yellowstone* over in Cody. He set colors swirling around an incredible green river focal point that flowed forward and practically grabbed me."

"Sounds like I would want to surround it in a hug," said Diane.

"That, you would," said Shelly.

"Next time you are east," Ted said, looking at me, "we ought to plan a museum trip. New York City, perhaps. They have quite a few works of this time frame."

"It's a date. Well, you know what I mean." I was embarrassed by my overeager and poorly worded response. I caught Diane smiling.

"And you, Shelly, with plein air art out here, might just be starting a school of modern western art and impressionism," I said.

"The sky's the limit," she said.

"You know, I am doing my next magazine issue on TriState Art. I bet you could advise me on ideas."

Shelly cocked her head. "Why not?" Then, looking at Ted, she said, "A couple more go-rounds of the barn for you. You didn't think I'd forget your night's exercises, did you?"

Ted smiled. "I was certain you wouldn't."

"Amber, would you care to escort Mr. Steele? He knows the routine, and I believe he can use the company. I'm going to clean up with Diane."

Ted and I looked at one another. We rose for a few steady laps around Shelly's barn, both feeling set up.

"Do I need to hold an elbow or anything?" I asked. "We don't want a hospital visit to spoil our party."

"This walker keeps me steady," said Ted. "Tour time."

As we passed the kitchen windows, I saw Shelly and Diane together at the sink. I was grateful to see a big grin on both of their faces. Of all the cousins in the world for Shelly to have, Diane had to be the absolute best.

"It's good you're here," I said to Ted. "Keeping Shelly thinking forward, not back."

"It's good for me, too, you know."

"Of course. I didn't mean to minimize your trauma. How are you doing?"

"Getting by, but also trying to look forward, not back."

"Does it hurt to walk?"

"Some days, it's brutal. They say walking is good for my leg, breathing exercises are helping my lung, rest is good for the tail-bone, but this conflicts with the walking, and my liver is growing back. Honestly, I go hour by hour. Thank God I didn't land on my head, just jammed my shoulder. But enough about me. Come on in the barn."

"And skip the laps?"

"Only one." He smiled and turned on the lights. The barn was big, and crowded with barn junk.

"Not too much carpentry to do in here," he said. "A few partitions over on this side, and storage areas for each artist, but we want to keep it open. We'll be adding windows on this side for more natural light, but don't want to overdo it for the sake of keeping heat in if Shelly decides on winter guests. She insists we make everything beautiful inside and out."

"Artists are usually not used to much, given their modest budgets, but they, of all people, would welcome a beautiful interior," I said.

"Exactly."

I looked to the far end of the barn. "What's that?"

Before Ted could answer, I stood next to a woodpile.

"Those are the broken posts Sam and Irv pulled out. Sam said they were beyond repair. But he said he'd find a use for them."

"Recycling is good," I said, noticing they were all smooth

finished. It supported Irv's word that he and Sam had cleared the corral of debris each night and gave strength to the conclusion that the pile of rough-finished fence posts that had tipped Sam's ATV had been dumped from off site.

"My leg's not up to the climb for the upstairs tour," said Ted, "but I'll wait here if you want to look."

"Without a tour guide? Not a chance."

Ted and I did another two laps. It hurt knowing how hard it was for him, and how hard it likely would be for years to come, if not life. I comforted myself with seeing him alive and able to walk at all, based on what I had heard of his accident. He seemed a decent man, in the wrong place at the wrong time. He did not appear to be a liar, but Jake's voice had been stuck in my ear from the moment Ted and I left the kitchen: "Ask him."

"It might be a sore subject," I said, "given what you went through, but rumor has it you are not only a supporter of the arts but also wildlife."

"Ironic, isn't it?" said Ted, shaking his head. "That I'm on the board of the American Wildlife Protectors. It's been a long-time interest of mine. This accident doesn't change anything. Except, maybe, the way I walk and how I'm going to navigate airport security with all the metal in me now. Do you know, they had to give me a couple of fake ribs?"

I paused our walk.

"Sorry," said Ted. "That was definitely overshare."

"I'm just glad they had your size."

"Good one. Thanks."

Jake's voice nudged again, and I heeded it. "Before the accident, did you see anyone here who might not have belonged? Or who might not have liked Sam and Shelly?"

"I'm not exactly following. The only person I saw was Irv."

"My landlord."

It was Ted's turn to stop. "Really? Small world."

I held open the door to the kitchen, feeling better for having asked several lingering questions.

"Okay to drive?" asked Diane.

"Oh, sure. I have my new truck."

"That's right," said Diane. "Nobody messes with Sebastian."

"And you?" I asked.

"I'm lodging the night with Shell Belle. It'll do us both good. And it'll give my Gene more time with the guys. They're playing cards and watching baseball. Win, win, win. The rehab center is sending a ride for Ted."

16

CHURCH

I DROPPED off Sebastian for the installation of a specialty bumper, one I learned was good to have in case of wildlife crossing. It was an aftermarket part that hadn't yet come in when I took title to my truck. Life's timing often worked this way. The two-door loaner car I drove to work felt cramped, an odd revelation, as Justice had barely been bigger. Once in town, I found all parking spaces occupied, forcing me down the block. *Not again*, I thought. For all my years of Philadelphia reporting, I was used to bad news, but bad news here was different. Bad news here increasingly touched people I knew. As it turned out, Abby was simply selling hotcakes for a fundraiser, and Morris was supportive. Finally, good news.

At lunch, I ate hotcakes. After work, I followed Fletcher in my loaner coupe until he turned through the gates to the church. After a quick vehicle exchange, I came across the pastures near the church again and spotted through the long shadows of dusk a couple of men on horseback. Instinctively, I braked. Fletcher was easy to identify with the red-and-black flannel shirt he often wore over his work shirt. His posture was familiar, too, even on a horse. He casually trotted from church property to national forest land. The other man rode by his side. He didn't look familiar.

I urged Sebastian into a fast gait home and jogged up the stairs to my computer. Did the church own horses? It would explain the barn, but it would also mean *two* things not making sense: horses *and* a barn. Within seconds, Morris First Congregational Church popped up on the screen. Along with mention of its thousands of acres of grazing land and a reference to cattle operations. Was Fletcher ranching?

Late morning, when Fletcher stepped from his office for a walk down the hall, I stepped in. Within fifteen seconds, I had a photo of the bucking horse on his bookcase and was out the door. Back at my desk, I zoomed in on the inscription. Augustus Callahan, the recipient of the statue—Fletcher's self-described great-great-great-granddaddy—had put in twenty-plus years of service with the Wyoming Cattlemen's Association, and was a founding member to boot. While he was its president, the association's reach had grown from 36,000 head to 1.5 million head by the time he stepped down, right when the beef bubble popped. It was a lot of cattle and a lot of change, and his position carried clout. He was heralded as a friend of legislators, of cattlemen, and, in the second-to-last line, a "Friend of Presidents."

Holding the reins of such a powerful association undoubtedly put Fletcher's family on the map of Wyoming beef. This statue wasn't sitting in his office for nothing. But why was Fletcher hanging out at the *Gazette* instead of minding Wyoming cattle full time like generations before? My antennae of suspicion rose through the clouds.

The very next morning, I sat at the counter at Abby's, awaiting the crack-of-dawn breakfast group, and then lit the flame. "What do Montana ranchers think of the Wyoming bucking horse?"

Competing stories erupted like flaming fuel billowing from an oil truck. Mike Herbst believed many saw it as a symbol of like-minded ranchers. A man named Darnell vehemently disagreed. Patty Simon said no Wyoming rancher would ever credit a Montana rancher. "Might have some respect for us, since they know what ranching's all about, but isn't going to feel any kinship," she said.

"Even less so the other way around," her husband quickly added. "Those Wyoming ranchers are mighty close to their herds, but not nearly protective enough about the disease. We Montana folks have the cream of the crop, as far as I'm concerned, and don't want anyone or anything messing them up."

"What do you mean?" I pushed.

"We've had a step up on world-renowned cattle lines for decades."

"What do you mean?" I repeated, wanting more.

Before an answer came, Brody blurted, "All I know is my friends over there are dang tired of tourists lifting license plates off their vehicles. If they want a bucking horse, they ought to buy one. The Trading Post has plenty."

The roar of laughter put the conversation to bed until I said, "Art collectors nationwide take a fancy to the statues."

"The real deal is the only one that matters," said Mike.

My breakfast crowd had not given the clarity I sought when it came to state allegiance. I still didn't know why Fletcher had groused about the Wyoming statue taking up space on his Montana shelf, but with people stealing license plates for it, the bucking horse seemed as valuable a piece of art as any in this region. Unless Fletcher crushed the idea, the Wyoming bucking horse was going in the art issue, along with its history and lore.

What surprised me more than inconclusive talk of the

bucking horse was seeing Brody pulling a black-and-white plaid jacket over his shoulders as he prepared to leave. I had only seen it once before: a few nights ago, when clearly he was perusing church lands on horseback with Fletcher. It didn't make sense. Not with what Fletcher had said about Brody or Brody's tone of voice when he spoke of Fletch. Were they simply verifying boundaries? With as much land as the church had, it was conceivable they shared a boundary line.

"New jacket?" I asked.

"Sure is. You like it?"

"Of course."

Brody lit up a smile that could have warmed anyone's insides. It was equally surprising and disturbing. Abby noticed too.

"Any chance you'd meet me for lunch this week?" Brody asked.

"I don't have my calendar on me. I'll reach out."

"Still believe he's not interested?" Abby asked when we were alone.

My wagging finger ended the conversation.

Fueled by Abby's breakfast special—a true treat—I prepared to meet Shelly and Simone for a planning session for our TriState Art issue. Fletcher was thrilled I had pulled in Shelly, and nothing raised my energy and output like professional colleagues.

* * *

The next day, a productive afternoon dissolved into a difficult night when Karl phoned just as the sun was setting.

"Her current regimen isn't working," he said.

I shut my eyes, and a veil of hopelessness pressed me to the ground.

"We're trying something new. It's out of state. Specialized

treatments linked to genetics and her immune system. It's the best chance of beating it. I hate to say it, but this might be her only chance."

"Oh, Karl ..."

"We're going to Arizona."

"When?"

"Immediately."

"I'm meeting you there," I said. "Is she up to it?"

"She's in more pain, and her spirit is weakening. I wish I could give better news."

"What about Melody and Finn?"

"They're coming. My mom and dad too. Actually, they already left."

"What?"

"Eva and I fly tomorrow. The others started driving an RV a few days ago. Sorry, I've been so busy. I should have told you earlier, but it's been a moving target."

Hanging up with Karl, I knew I would ask Fletcher for time off. It was hard keeping up hope from how she sounded lately, and from the way Karl described her. But this was exactly what I was going to do. For her sake. I would stand by her side, hold her hand, and pray like the devil.

***

I drove into the parking lot of the Stiles Cancer Center and pulled my Arizona rental car into a space near the luxury RV. Karl had made it their home on the road. It eliminated back-and-forth trips from a hotel, and Karl's mother and father were doing well with sandwich-making and other care. Melody and Finn were keeping up with classwork. Best of all, the RV kept the family united. I wished they could have joined the Yellowstone crowd instead and had no reason for a clinic visit.

"Knock, knock," I said, gently rapping on the RV's side

door. I thought fondly of Diane as I repeated her familiar greeting. The door flung open, and Melody and Finn raced out, the excitement of a family road trip written across their faces. It was the blessing of innocence. Of course, they knew why they were here, but a certain playfulness couldn't be contained.

"Aunt Amber!" they shouted.

Thankfully, they were still young enough to appreciate my hugs.

"Who wants licorice?" I asked.

"Red or black?" asked Finn.

"Let's see, red for Finn."

"Oh, yuck," said Finn.

"And black for Melody."

I watched their eyes light up.

"Trade ya," they said in unison.

"Oh, come on. Do you really think I would forget who liked black and who liked red?"

I relinquished the sweets just as Karl's mother loomed atop the RV steps.

"Amber," she said. "Welcome to our cozy abode. Let me get you something to drink. Or perhaps a PBJ?"

"We could splurge," said Karl's father. "We have ham and cheese as well."

We went back inside, filling captain's chairs and fold-down beds.

"If you want to take my rental car for anything, feel free," I said.

"I call shotgun," said Finn.

"I get to drive," said Melody.

"Oh, right," said Karl's father, rolling his eyes. I stared at the two beautiful faces. It was exactly what Eva and I would have said. My throat constricted into a painful mold, pressed around an invisible painful lump. Life wasn't fair. They were far too young for this sort of reality. They had been through it once already. Perhaps the first outcome gave false hope.

"Oh, Mama Karl," I said, folding my arms around her. We both knew I needed a hug as much as she. I followed it with another long hug with Karl's father. It was difficult holding in tears, but for the sake of Melody and Finn, I did.

"Karl's gone for an afternoon check-in. We took turns seeing Eva this morning. Go to the front desk. They'll tell you where to go." Karl's mother knew exactly what I needed.

* * *

"Eva? It's Amber."

I saw my sister smile before she opened her eyes.

"Thank you," she said. "I needed you."

"I needed you more." We both laughed softly, knowing long ago, needing something more, loving something more, doing anything more had become a hotly debated element of many conversations.

"How are you doing? And what are they doing to you?"

"I don't ask anymore. They do what they know to do. All I do is take it all in. Not much more I can do. I'm letting Karl ask the questions."

"Oh, Eva."

"I know, Amber. I love you."

"Oh, Eva," I said, "you're so special. Please, please, please."

After a moment, she said, "We don't get to choose, do we?"

I couldn't speak. Couldn't even whisper "No." All I could do was wet her blanket with tears, despite trying my hardest to keep them contained.

We had shared as many tears as laughter and serious conversations in our lives. We had shared everything. At this moment, even in the face of a broken heart, I felt selfish for being so weak. I settled myself to offer a consoling hug. Eva relaxed as I stroked her temple with my fingers. She closed her eyes. I gazed at her and felt the overwhelming power of love. Along with a staggering sense of fragility. In another moment, all I wanted was to scream out my anger and make it all go back to normal. Instead, I sat silently and softly stroked her temple.

Facing reality, time and time again, required courage. One second of courage, followed by another, and another, until the darkness was behind. It always moved behind. But only after a first courageous step. I returned to the RV just in time for a game of Old Maid. We followed this with several rounds of Go Fish and finished with Crazy Eights. More than once, we collected cards from under seats as excitement swelled and cards were relinquished to others upon request with great animation. I thought back to all the games I had played with Eva and our friends. Then, cards were put away, and Melody and Finn settled into bed with me in between, on top of the covers. For a few minutes, I stroked each of their heads, as I had recently stroked Eva's. It didn't take long for them to fall asleep, but before they did, I was in my own world of thought, wondering how Karl would tell them and who would take care of them. It was so damned unfair. Cancer was stealing my family's innocence.

"I was afraid we'd lost you," said Abby several days later, when I returned from Eva's bedside. "That you had literally gotten lost or headed back to Philadelphia."

It was good to see her, and Brody, too, seated next to her at the Eagle Feather. We embraced. I told them about Eva and why I had stood up Brody on his lunch invitation. I hadn't meant to say much, but the news spilled out. Relief and vulnerability intermingled as I bravely gave the report. I rarely opened up like this with anyone except Eva. My journalistic persona—objective and unemotional—had carried over to my personal relationships. Winston, tending bar, assessed my pain and mustered up a pot of hot tea. When he gently set it on the table in front of me, along with honey, my favorite, I thanked his quiet kindness by sending several tears rolling down my face. I was a mess. But it was okay, because now I had friends.

I knew Abby had lost someone to cancer, and I was sorry to be poking at her old wound. She said she had long ago accepted it. Her words gave solace, but I doubted I could ever accept Eva's passing. Brody slid his chair closer and put his arm on my shoulder. It shouldn't have been comforting, but it was.

"We should have learned more by now," I said. "More about how to treat it, or erase it altogether."

"We have," said Abby. "Look at what your sister's doing. It's new. Because we have learned more."

"The problem," said Brody, "is we're creating more that causes it. Our world isn't as clean as it used to be. Our bodies can't be happy. But I'm sorry she's going through this."

A moment later, I recognized the same panic-laced fear that gripped me when I learned of Eva's first bout with it. But this time, I knew I could truly lose her.

The art of Mary Lockwood's Tribal nation was unlike other art I had explored. It wasn't leisure representation for aesthetic interests or personal expression. It was a fine interlacing of utility, symbolism, beauty, and celebration. It was the skillful creation and decoration of moccasins meant to be worn. Beadwork on clothing meant to cover and convey meaning. Feathered regalia, ornate but symbolic and powerful. Quillwork from the gift of the porcupine. Pottery and vessels used to sustain but marked with significant and meaningful color and color combinations. It was art, but it had purpose and significance. It had history, heritage, memories, and lessons handcrafted with intent. Art, too, was active, for it was dance and the hand creation of instruments using time-honored methods, and the creation of rhythms and song for both instrumental and vocal expression. It fit finely into day-to-day living. And it maintained the strongest of ties to nature, earth, and universe, for so much of what was created came from this earth and its offerings. It maintained bonds with generations who came before. And it represented an unyielding commitment to remain connected as humans to the earth and environment and to preserve the same.

Was it ironic, I wondered, that some of my last research for the art issue was taking me to the oldest realm, to the art of our land's Indigenous peoples? As Mary Lockwood opened a portal into her Indigenous way of art, I pulled together notes. She showed me stitching learned from others, knowledge passed down one person to another to another for generations, and finally to her. Her work had great meaning: the finished product and the source of all the materials. She was creating something that someone would depend on. It had to be strong.

Our conversation eventually shifted to contemporary Indigenous artists. Their art was never included in museums, aside from a few art exhibits. Mary referred to it as "walled-off" art. It, too, had meaning, as expressions of living artists. Of contemporary art through the eyes of ones so little represented and so fiercely impacted. Still connected to their surroundings. Connected to lives before theirs. And to lives yet to be born. Honoring the paths of those before, and their paths in this changing world. Mary recommended a future visit outside the region to a single museum dedicated to contemporary Indigenous art. I was more than interested to see what few were seeing.

By the time we ended our conversation, it hit me: Mary was only a few generations removed from significant loss and pain. How had she and so many others gotten through? It had been so much more than losing relatives. It had been the brutal stripping away of known ways of life and generations of life as well. A total disruption. Yet she sparkled with remarkable, steadfast resilience. A broader perspective quietly displaced thoughts of my personal situation with Eva. As Mary shared intricate details of this earth and its limitless gifts, I realized a single human's physical body was both critically important and influential and barely consequential, whether I considered my sister's life, my life, or any one single person's life. We had meaning as part of a bigger whole. It was with this understanding that I felt both singularly empowered and more lost than ever.

17

─────────

DANGER

TWENTY MINUTES after I settled at my desk, Brody's truck rolled across the gravel lot. He took a slow walk to Abby's. An hour later, his truck remained parked, and several more trucks sat beside it. Shouldn't these ranchers be tending cattle? When another ranch truck eased into another empty space, I made a beeline to the diner.

Abby had the news. It had happened last night at Brody's. Another bison break-in. Fences had been broken, and Brody had herded his cows to a remote pasture, hoping to maintain separation from an entire herd. The bison must have been females, being in a group as they were. Brody had sent shots into the air, attempting to scare off the intruders, but the shots had scared the big bodies into motion. Mixed up in the fray, Brody had caught his hand on a horn and fence. His wrist was wrapped; he had done the doctoring himself. Brody would have plenty more fence repairs, but he had already fixed key sections. Later today, the Park Service would check for bison, and Brody's cattle would be subject to special inspection, putting the town and ranching industry on high alert.

Every rancher would have done what Brody had done to safeguard his cattle, but everyone was saying he was lucky the horns didn't pierce anything else. Most were saying he should be thanking the good Lord he hadn't ended up like Sam or Tourist. A wild bison herd was unpredictable.

Late morning, I put bison news behind me to hike with a group headed to an overlook at the north end of the park—a partial climb of Electric Peak, below the snow line. I hoped to see where the bison entered dangerous lands. I also hoped to see church lands and Brody's further north. Maybe even glimpse my little garage apartment.

After an hour of strenuous climbing, our small group of tourists stood high atop the landscape, where we shuffled past one another for different vantage points. I took photos of others who had traveled as pairs, to help them memorialize their time in Yellowstone. Some planned to continue the climb with snow-shoes. I would be heading back down. I turned away and, cupping binoculars to my face, made several sweeps across the valley. I spotted Brody's cows and home, but saw no movement. I saw no one at the church either. Irv and Izzy's was hidden by a line of hills. I moved my binoculars between the two locations several times. On the third pass, a blur of light-blue color swished through my field of vision. In warmer days, it might have been spring flowers, but certainly not today. I tried to put eyes on it again but couldn't find it, despite moving back and forth and up and down and adjusting depth of focus. Finally, I caught a second glimpse, only to lose it again. I continued the hunt until, once again, I caught sight of the colorful vixen. It was small and too distant to see clearly, but the particular color of blue implied it was man-made, perhaps a bag or a garment. Fine-tuning the magnification once again, I made out something pink, but equally ill defined, underneath. I might have thought nothing of it, but the longer I stared, the more uneasy I felt. My inner voice and a tense body were screaming fear—my familiar, personal reaction to homicides. My eyes nearly pierced the lenses as I strained for better definition, but all I saw was a haunting possibility that a child had gone missing or someone was dead. A small someone. Call it a journalist's instinct.

I made my way to the Eagle Feather for a quick look around before starting my intended search for the blue-and-pink mystery item. Brody remained center stage, with plenty of others sitting close, thriving on details, lending support, and offering unsolicited opinions.

"Hey," I said, joining the group. "Are you okay?"

"Couldn't be better. Nice to see you." He held one beer in his hand and clearly had several more inside him.

I might have blushed with his words, given so warmly and freely in front of a crowd. "I thought you'd be fixing things up at your ranch," I said.

"Already did. Best I could with this hand."

His left wrist was well bandaged, but when someone noticed blood seeping through the gauze, Brody excused himself to apply a new dressing at home.

Of course, it was Abby who said, "If it's not closed up by morning, you need to check in with Doc for stitches."

When Brody departed, so did others. It left Abby and me sitting alone at a table for ten. Our chairs bumped as we scooted together.

"Half the ranchers in town stopped in the diner while we were open," she said. "Then, the search party moved over here. Brody's as sick as can be of repeating the news. I'm glad, for his sake, he started dripping and had to go home."

"Why would this happen?"

"As best I can tell, bison are returning. Maybe they know something, like we're getting an early spring after the last late storms."

"I could use that."

"I'm sure. After your sister and all."

I told Abby about my day's expedition and reported snow

had melted from the lower ridges. She raised a hand for a high five. Then, I eased into a troubling thought.

"What happens if someone gets lost out there? Is there a rescue squad you notify?"

"Let any park person know, and they are all over it. But I heard one person got lost and it wasn't until years later that they found his foot and nothing more. It was at a hot spring."

"Oh, jeez. We need to talk about something else." I thought a moment and said, "Actually, I saw something out there today. I had this weird feeling, like it was something bad, or maybe a person, either lost or not alive."

"What? Are you sure?"

"No, not factually. But instinctively, I'm having trouble letting it go."

"Like I said, you can tell any park person, but I haven't heard a word about a missing person, and usually this news is out in the wind like wildfire. I bet it was just trash."

"You're probably right. Let's talk about something better." I threw out a question. "If you could go anywhere on vacation, where would you go?"

"Hawaii," said Abby. "I'd read books, snorkel with the turtles, get some sun, and

take in the views."

"Ideal."

"And you?" she asked.

"After joining you in Hawaii, I'd go to Europe. Simone used to work in Paris, and I'd die for a visit."

"We're on a roll," she said. "Let's do this. Twenty questions."

"As long as it doesn't involve Brody," I said.

"You're on. Favorite color?"

"Blue. Yours?"

"Hot orange. Super bright, nearly blinding, like the fiery orange of some of the sunsets. Electric! You know what I mean?"

"But your truck is teal," I said.

"Orange would've cost more. I asked. So, Teal Turtle it is."

"Most embarrassing moment with a guy," I said.

"Oh, my God. I was about twenty years old, in college, and I got locked out of my sorority house. In the snow. In half my pj's. I had on a long-sleeve top, panties, and flip-flops, and I was picking up something that fell out the window. Of course, the cute guy I had hoped to meet for weeks comes by. I almost died. Never wanted to see him again."

"Yikes. Sorry. For me, it was high school prom. My date puked on my dress. In front of the world."

"Spiked punch?" she asked.

"Stomach bug. He was out for days. Then, I got it."

"Favorite things back in Philadelphia."

"Easy. Watch Eagles football, eat Philly cheesesteak, and watch either the Rocky Balboa movies or this movie about a walk-on Eagles player. Of course, I could watch those anywhere, but it feels more authentic watching in Philly."

"We must be clones. I was U of Missouri, so a Missouri football game, eating this special pizza they have there, and shouting it out to classic rock."

We went on to favorite song and favorite movie. Then, Abby said, "Favorite thing to do here."

"Easy. Hang out with you."

"Back at you," she said. "But we're going to get you meeting some of my other friends in no time."

We both took a swig and called it a day. Before I turned toward Sebastian and she toward the Teal Turtle, Abby said, "I heard Fletcher glowing your praises when he grabbed a sandwich yesterday."

"Thanks for letting me know. Say, you wouldn't want to take a hike with me right now, would you?"

"Right," said Abby. "Hope to see you tomorrow."

It was nearly dark when I began my search for the mysterious mound of colors. Dark from the departing sun, but darker still from black storm clouds racing my way. If it was trash, as Abby suggested, I would never in my lifetime live down a call to the parks department. But if it was a child, he or she would be in more trouble than ever with storms. I had to know.

Coming from the road on the north side of the peak, I followed my mental map to where I had seen it. I found nothing blue. Nothing pink. Nothing at all, except ... holy crap, holy crap ... more lightning than I had ever seen. It crackled the moment it struck and sent jagged bolts between sky and ground or ground and sky. Mystery be damned! I had to run! With bolts lighting my way, I followed the hilly terrain through pounding rain, feeling exposed to death and desperately praying I wouldn't slide over the steep edge on the other side. I thanked God I made it to Sebastian alive and slammed shut my truck door as another bolt crackled and lighted the sky. It was temporarily blinding. "Amber," I scolded, "you know better than this! What the hell were you thinking?" But I knew the answer. Someone might be in trouble.

Around one in the morning, I awakened in bed and saw the storm had ridden through. I had to try again. Under the light of a brilliant moon, I steered Sebastian back to the forest road nearest the mystery on the hill, hoping I wasn't too late for someone who might be lost or worse. A chill in the air followed me as I walked upward behind the beam of my flashlight. I had mentally measured the location, some seventy feet from a group of shrubs, but quickly realized I had miscalculated the true distance. Left to right, and back again, I illuminated the ground. Methodically, I pointed the beam increasingly higher up the hill. All the while, I felt I was being watched. By whom or by what I didn't know. Maybe only by my own spooked self. I stood very still and strained my ears, believing I heard an animal or, perhaps, another human. I called in a loud whisper "Is anyone here?" emboldened to ignore my fears. "Anyone here?" I quietly repeated as I made my way through grasses and patches of left-over snow. Ready to give up, I saw something move, and I froze. I couldn't make out anything more than movement. Another cool gust of wind raced past, and I saw it move again some fifteen yards away. "Hello? Anyone?" I held my bear spray tight, listened for another moment, and proceeded toward it. I stood ten feet from my target and saw a swatch of light-blue fabric caught in a shrub. I inched forward, and my left foot hit something straight on, nearly tripping me up. I lowered my lantern and jumped back as soon as I saw it. A pair of hooves. Lying still as could be. I swung the light further forward and gasped. It was more than one pair, and nothing moved. I inched closer and saw a mass of bloody bodies—a mixture of fur, animal faces, and hooves—with no life in them. I nearly dropped my flashlight. With brucellosis on my mind, I was certain I was staring at a pile of dead calves. Or were they dead bison?

I took photos, each time glancing around to see what else my camera's flash might reveal. I had seen plenty of gruesome scenes before. Call it journalistic instincts; I had walked into some sort of crime scene. If these were calves, I had to tell someone. But suppose a predator stopped in before I could bring someone back here? The photos wouldn't be enough. Forsaking normal protocols, I prepared to take essential evidence. It was the right thing to do. "Okay, Jake, here goes." Hoping to only find trash, I had balled up several large plastic bags in my coat pocket. I slid one over, under, and around one of the bodies. Next, I pointed my light at the fabric. It was a swatch of denim with stringy edges, as though hastily torn off, and likely cut with a knife. It hung limply, soaked from the storms and patiently awaiting another gust to bring it back to life. It was loosely tied around a broken branch, as though left as a marker.

I placed the denim in a separate loose bag and tied it to my belt so I could carry the bagged body with two hands. The little creature didn't weigh more than twenty pounds, and since it had been folded in the fetal position, it made for easy carrying. I would return for the others. Perhaps I would bring Fletcher.

Making my way down the hill, I heard a sound like hooves gently pounding the ground. I came to a dead stop. Were bison nearby? Did I sound like a predator to them? Would they run? I examined the surrounding space with my flashlight and saw nothing. But I felt my heart would jump from my throat with each slow step. Hopefully, anything out here with me was on the other side of Sebastian. I slid forward, feeling like a sitting duck. I touched the metal handle of Sebastian's tailgate and reveled in its cold embrace. I didn't know if it was the movement of bison, the closing of my truck door, or something altogether different that sent a couple of Brody's dogs barking in the distance, far down the valley. Floodlights flared into the sky, followed by a couple of gunshots. I cut off my flashlight but saw a faint and distant halo of light from headlights at Brody's place setting out close to his driveway. At two o'clock in the morning, he was checking for trouble. As best I could tell from the distant flickering of lights, he circled his front field, then climbed the mountain gravel way and looped by through his gulch. Clearly, he was armed, which was why I sat silently in my truck, waiting for Brody's lights to disappear. For the second time in less than twelve hours, I asked myself what the hell I had been thinking, going out alone. At least I had brought my bear spray! Schiste, Amber! How would *that* ever help if I encountered wolves? Or Brody's gun?

With the mystery items in my truck, I had a new problem: what to do with them. I slipped into the only twenty-four-hour convenience store for miles around and purchased five bags of ice—all they had—to pack around my haul. Once in the garage, I put ice in a bin and settled the little body inside. Hopefully, it would prevent it from reeking. Then, with my window shades drawn tight, I looked at the photos. I saw four bodies, each the size of a large Thanksgiving turkey, but seemingly all legs. They were pathetic, all lumped together. As though pushed by a calling to dwell on every ugly detail, I looked more closely. They appeared wet, but not only from the rain. They barely had a coating of hair. Facial features were not fully developed. I pulled back and tried to take a deep breath, but my constricted chest fought back. I considered the evidence. If my ice creature wasn't fully developed, a rancher had either dumped aborted cows or was ridding the ranch of aborted bison to save his cattle and hide a problem. I closed my eyes. Why had the denim beckoned like a flag?

A few hours later, I purchased a floor-model freezer and convinced the delivery department at Artie's Appliance, across the border in Wyoming, I needed it immediately. A year's worth of steaks sitting in my old, now broken freezer had prompted action. I hoped my lie didn't follow me back across state lines.

With the whole bloody mess, including the denim swatch, packed in my new freezer, I made a note to buy a lock. When I figured out what it meant, I would know better what to do with it. For now, I would simply save the evidence out of sight. It wasn't like I could run to a ranching association and ask them to look in my lost and found. Suddenly, I hated jeans. But I hated myself more because there was no easy way to make what I had in my freezer vanish. I should have left it alone. At least no one had gone missing.

I walked into the office, trying my damnedest to not look like I had a carcass in my spare freezer or that I had barely slept. I took a longer lunch than usual to walk around town and check every pant leg that passed. Everyone wore denim. I wanted to trust Abby with my secret, but I had a better option.

Midafternoon, I joined Fletcher in his office, where empty candy wrappers lay scattered on his desk. He stood, looking out his front window, chewing a piece of candy, and clearly not considering anything outside.

"Brody? Cattle? Bison?" I asked.

"Take your pick."

I closed the door and sat. Fletcher turned and instinctively offered up his candy bowl.

"What's not adding up in your mind?" I asked.

"Two break-ins? A month apart? Hasn't happened in all my years around this damned industry. And both at night? It feels wrong."

I glanced at the bucking horse on his shelf. If anyone would know, it was Fletcher.

"Did you check Brody's fence?" I asked, wondering if Fletcher's in-field snoop, Mel, had been on the prowl.

Fletcher smiled. "He—you know who—was trying to get out today for a look around. I haven't heard back. Brody wouldn't let Jordan on site for photos. The Park Service and Burt were interested, but Brody said repairs were done and didn't want to make it a news item."

"Surely he knew it was community news the second he pulled into the parking lot yesterday."

"Absolutely, and it made front page, but with no photos."

I looked at Fletcher's eyes.

"We'll find out, Phillips. We'll find out."

It was my clue to leave, but I remained seated.

"Yes?" said Fletcher. "I am detecting a journalistic glint in your eyes, Phillips. Out with it. What good idea do you have for the magazine?"

I placed a print of my night findings on his desk. I described my previous twenty-four hours. Fletcher gave a brutal stare that moved from the print to my face and back again. A few moments later, Fletcher and I slipped out his side door in search of the bodies. According to Fletcher, they were elk. And elk always gave birth alone.

We parked next to the road sand I had pushed into a small mound with my boots during the night. In daylight, it took barely ten minutes to climb the quarter mile. I saw many marks where I had walked in the darkness. I was surprised I had left such a noticeable trail. When I reached the shrubs, I had the strange feeling of being watched again. I glanced around but saw no one. The clearing was larger than I remembered. Equally surprising, I saw no babies. No bones. No skulls. No skeletons. No hooves.

"Well?" said Fletcher.

"It was here. I am certain."

The pile was gone. Every little body.

"It has definitely been disturbed, and it is far too neat to be the work of a predator," he said. "Whoever dumped them must have returned. Unless a tag team was working together, one to dump and the other to haul away."

"Is smuggling a possibility?" I asked.

"More likely an animal sacrifice. A ritual of some sort. It happens once in a while."

I took a slow look around. *Was* anyone watching? And had anyone bothered to count the bodies and suspect that I, standing here in the open with Fletcher, might have one in cold storage? I wished I had brought my binoculars to appear less suspicious.

"It's a good thing you took photos. Not to mention evidence."

I hardly felt like a saint.

"We have a decision to make," he said.

"Who do we tell?" I asked.

"More like, 'Do we tell?' A small town has many ears. As I said, a ritual isn't inconceivable. And hunters or ranchers are often faced with having to dispose of unborn bodies. It's the dilemma of late-season hunting, but this is even beyond that; it's out of season. A number of people wouldn't think anything of this find, except for where and when you found it. So, what's the gain? It's not like anyone's pulling a fingerprint off of something out here, or off of your freezer loot. Parks might want to know. State vet, too, perhaps. The cause of death could be of interest to them."

"Wouldn't Sheriff Burt want to know?"

"It's not necessarily a crime. As I said, ranchers and hunters face life and death all the time with animals."

"Would it be animal cruelty?"

"I doubt it. It's more like bad luck."

"So, do we or don't we?" I asked.

After a few moments' thought, Fletcher determined hunting out of season was punishable, but we were too late to identify a culprit. Poisoning—an alternative option—was certainly worth notification, but less likely than pure misfortune. We had made our decision.

Fletcher notified Montana Wildlife, and we relinquished the find so they could get input from the state veterinarian. I kept the denim and a small piece of the animal that had detached from the little baby. I felt like a mother abandoning her child as I handed it over to a stranger, but I didn't mind at all having someone take it off my hands.

18

HISTORY

I ENDED a call with Laura Lenci, expecting to soon receive information on art fairs scheduled for Yellowstone's summer and fall. Then, I practically bounded down the stairs to Fletcher's.

"If I'm not in Monday, send a search party."

"Planning a weekend hike?" he asked, barely glancing from his notepad.

"How did you know? Specimen Ridge or Artist Point, now that the road's open. I hear they are both big draws for artists."

Fletcher trained his eyes on mine. "Before you go up there by yourself, make sure to get some spray. They're out already."

I knew Fletcher meant bear spray. I declined to tell him about my full artillery—the ever-present cans in my bag, in Sebastian, and in three locations scattered around my apartment and Irv and Izzy's exterior doors. All I said was "Got it."

"And if you see anything," he added, "don't run, just shoot it!"

My eyes must have opened wider than I thought. He quickly clarified: "With the spray, Phillips. Not a gun."

I felt like an idiot for having already considered the firearm option. It was nothing short of top-grade Saddle Burn. I was pretty sure I heard a muffled laugh as I stepped into the hall, so I yelled back at his door, "Glad you care about me." A telltale creak assured me he was tilting back in his chair, no doubt looking to the ceiling and harboring a broad smile.

Not long after dawn, with fingers gripping my metal can of Bear-X-brand spray, I began my climb. As soon as I rounded the first bend, I felt as vulnerable as a field mouse under circling hawks. I stopped to feel the power of the wilderness as the singular speck of a human that I was. It was frightening. A nearby rustling of leaves halted my breathing. I was a city sissy. A couple of hikers passed me heading back to the trailhead, and I climbed further from my zone of safety. Others passed me, ascending at a faster rate, and I tried to keep up but couldn't. Nonetheless, they were another welcome distraction from the fear I carried. The fear of being alone and ill prepared for this natural world. I had a lot to learn.

At the top, I was greeted by a magnificent portal into an outstretched valley. It no longer mattered that my thighs burned and I was painfully out of shape. I stood at the precipice, as so many had over the past centuries, knowing wholeheartedly our earth was spectacular. This was Yellowstone. I inhaled deeply and forgot I was alone. Then, I saw prints. At the edge of a fir stand. I didn't know how, but I sensed they were bear. Alongside, I saw smaller prints—cub prints—preserved in the sticky mold of spring mud. I began my descent with fear so close to my skin, it could have burst into a blanket of goose bumps at any moment. I checked every turn for unwanted guests.

Centuries or decades ago, anyone would have known better what to do with bear prints or a live bear. Some sort of institutional knowledge would have been part of their makeup. We no longer had this. We were detached from this land, so many of us. From the comfort of Sebastian's front bucket seat, I happily morphed back into an urban tourist. Nature had many dangerous elements, and exploring it was a complicated dance. I was certain this revelation would make a future issue in some shape or form.

Mel's voice message alerted me to the secret hunt, as he called it. The Park Service was behind it. I couldn't believe it.

What I saw upon arrival looked like major police activity, with a low-flying helicopter and ATVs buzzing across the landscape. I realized this was exactly what it was. Only the criminals were bison. I parked beside Mel's SUV.

"I thought you should see this," he said. "Every year, this is how it goes. Usually, it's a bit later."

I watched the hive of activity and caught sight of someone I knew.

"What's Brody doing here?" I asked.

"Sharpshooter."

"What?" My voice sounded aggressive. "He told me he did contract work. He never said he was a sharpshooter."

"We let them into lower valleys," said Mel, "until we don't. And this is how we force bison back into the park. It's called hazing, and it's like a cattle drive with bison after hunting seasons have ended. If they are injured during hazing, Brody and these others bring them down."

Anger raged in my gut.

Mel's voice flared with anger as well as he said, "Migratory instincts be damned!"

"Mel, this is wrong."

He continued his monologue. "Sometimes, they're run for miles. Or they force them to cross high waters. Inevitably, some are injured on the way. A broken leg doesn't serve any wild animal well. What would a few thousand extra acres for wildlife mean, really? Raising a cow out here in Montana takes fifty times the acreage it takes to raise one in the Midwest. It's inefficient. As far as I'm concerned, we're wasting millions of dollars a year to haze and continue an inefficient system. I'd rather see my tax dollars buying extra land for the bison and letting them roam. Truth be told, elk mix more with cattle than bison, and they get off scot-free."

"I heard they carried it."

"We're still on the fence about bison quarantine. They used to just cull—sent the ones that had signs that it was in their blood to the slaughterhouse, and their meat and hides used. Now, they're trying to vaccinate and are hoping to send clean ones for release on Tribal lands. The idea has merit, but putting them in a feeding area for two years, with a diet of hay, is unnatural. They didn't used to do this to a wild bison. And being corralled and stuck in a pen can leave nasty gashes. On a bison, that is."

"Aren't we supposed to protect them?"

"We've been going round and round with management for decades, and we know we need to do something different. The problem is, we can't agree on what it is. We have interagency groups and an interagency plan. I don't know if we'll ever come together to everybody's liking. And I'm pretty certain it'll be a long time before we let the bison decide. Like they did for centuries. This year, they're aiming to cull six hundred to nine hundred from the Yellowstone herd. Seems a shame the bison don't get a vote."

"Six hundred?"

"Minimum." Mel pointed out Henry Mattson, representing one of Yellowstone's first associated Tribes. He was talking with the park people. I knew I had to hear from him, to learn his stories and hear from his heart. But I had seen more than enough.

"Mel," I said, "I have to leave."

Karl had plenty on his mind when he called. The prognosis for Eva remained lukewarm. He shared details for ten minutes before asking, "What's new?"

I ventured into my meeting with Mel. How Karl knew Pennsylvania also had bison at one time, he could not recall, but he was certain at least a thousand had been hidden away somewhere in southeastern Pennsylvania not long ago. I believed him. Karl's wealth of knowledge had surprised me innumerable times.

I phoned Herman Cox at the university the very next morning. Herman was a bison expert. One of several, as it turned out. I had to know: Were the Pennsylvania bison also culled?

According to Herman, true bison herds went out of Pennsylvania long ago.

"True bison herds?" I said.

"Last time I checked, there were roughly four hundred thousand bison grazing freely in this country. But most on private ranches or farms have cattle blood in them. Typically, we're talking a three-eighths-bison-and-five-eighths-cow combination. Not true bison. If you want to tame a wild buffalo, you cross it with a domestic cow and see if its personality becomes more domesticated. Tamer. If you want to experiment with different types of beef, you crossbreed a bison and a cow. Intentionally and unintentionally, a lot of bison with less than one hundred percent bison genes are walking around these days. Perhaps grazing freely so as to appear 'wild,' but nonetheless not pure bison."

"So, how many real bison are there?"

"Wild?" he asked. "Somewhere north of twenty thousand. About half in government herds. Some nineteen of them— herds, that is—on over four million acres. It's your Yellowstone bison that are moving this forward."

  E. B. LEE

"How's that?"

"Given the declared limit the Park Service and others have put on herd size, a relocation program is becoming integral to herd management, along with the hunts, culls, and slaughterhouse shipments. That quarantine program isn't perfect, but it's being done with the well-being of bison in mind. They're hoping to move clean stock and add to herds and numbers of wild head elsewhere. It's working. Slowly. Hopefully, some of the Tribal herds will soon be free to breed and transfer as well."

"It seems the least we can do," I said, "since we went from how many before the slaughter?"

"You mean the nationwide kill-off?"

"Yes."

"Guesstimate is thirty million minimum. Could be double that."

I found myself thinking of Cody, but from there springboarded to thirty million beautiful bison grazing the plains of a beautiful land.

"Then, straight down to about three hundred twenty-five," Herman continued. "Nearly extinct. The official number in Yellowstone was twenty-five, but truth be known, the herd was built, in part, with some brought up from Texas. They're as close to one hundred percent pure bison as any, and they are wild, not domesticated," he added.

The longer we talked, the more my blood boiled. Yellowstone bison were even more special due to their bloodlines and genes.

"Don't we care what goes forward?" I asked.

"Meaning?"

"It hardly looks like we're saving any particular gene pool. It looks more like catch as catch can and forget the rest. Sort of like 'Win some, lose some.' Zoos, I know, combine efforts to expand gene pools. Or save them."

"I hate to say 'You're right,' but there's truth in it."

"What's to say we haven't already killed the best of them—

the ones who knew better than others to migrate for the winter?"

Even over the phone, I could tell Herman shrugged. I was devastated. And livid that we weren't doing better for our public bison. My bison. Everyone's bison.

***

Mel and I sat in the easy chairs in his living room and shared a couple of lemonades.

"I saw the first one shot, or wounded, back in '88," said Mel. "I've been a Bison Guardian ever since."

Within minutes, he shared sufficient knowledge of bison and their plight to cause me to suspect he might have been their guardian since 1888, not 1988. What's more, he had built a contact list as long as the Yellowstone River. In a little under three hours, Mel presented the perspectives of seemingly every rancher, park person, BLM manager, senator, representative, state governor, Tribal leader, president (of the United States, that is), cattleman, cattlewoman, rifleman, rifleman's group, and more, known to have an opinion on bison. He could likely tell me where each and every resident for the nearest fifty towns stood on bison, cattle, hunting, grass, and grazing lands. Mel shared freely.

The biggest surprise emanated from a casual comment at what was to be the end of our meeting. It steered us into twenty more minutes of conversation. Fletcher had not always been in the newspaper business, as I had suspected. In fact, his saddle time at the church came as naturally as breathing and walking, given he was a sixth-generation rancher, part of the Circle C Callahan family.

"Details, Mel. Now."

"You journalists are all alike, always asking questions. It started over in eastern Wyoming when it was rustling, open grazing and a wilder West. Fletcher's great-great-great-grandfather Augustus—Old Augustus—started it all. Before the Wyoming Stock Growers Association formed. Before homesteading and before Wyoming was a state. Old Augustus is the one on that bucking horse in Fletcher's office. He was president of the Wyoming Stock Growers Association for twenty years. That was after it evolved from the Laramie County Stock Association.

"Old Augustus and his son, Marks Callahan, knew how to get land and water. They made out like bandits—though I'm not saying that's what they were—in the last quarter of the 1800s, known as the open-range beef bonanza years. Unlike others, they made it through the tough winter of 1886 to '87 in good stead. That winter is what prompted a lot of ranches to set fences and start leaving winter feed. It changed the face of ranching. By 1900, the grandson of Old Augustus was into the business too. His name was also Augustus. He hit his stride just right with an increase in beef demand from World War I. Then, it was his son, Fletcher's granddaddy Merwin, who started his own Circle C, over here in Montana. That was after he enlisted in the army and returned from duty. After the first war, the ranching industry hit tough times again with the Great Depression, the drought years of the 1930s, and an agricultural depression to World War II. Foreclosures were common, but he held it together. One of the smartest moves Merwin and his son— Fletcher's daddy, Mason Callahan—made was getting their grazing rights on government lands. That was back in the midthirties, when the Taylor Grazing Act came in.

"When Fletcher and I were teens, his grandfather passed, and about a year later, his daddy, Mason, had a stroke. It put him in his grave at age fifty-four, but before he passed, the Circle C had brucellosis run through its herd. My bet is it was the result of cattle and elk mixing near the watering hole, because I distinctly remember it had been a dry year. Mason never knew about it, so his passing was a blessing. But then, Fletcher and his sister had a decision—stay in or get out. Fletcher knew his family was onto something good. They knew the way to get what you wanted out of a calf was to breed what you wanted into the mother and father. Fletcher's family and a number of Montana ranches were breeding and selling favorable genetics. They sent what you wanted right to you and your cows, anywhere in the world."

As a confused frown sharpened my forehead, Mel said, "Artificial insemination. Anyone who knew Circle C said they were one of the best."

I considered Fletcher's former calling. Mel kept talking. "At about this time, Irv and Izzy took over the herd operations. They left the Callahans to their bulls, and Irv's cows became the breeders. Unfortunately, in the early eighties, brucellosis reared its ugly head back at the Circle C in Irv and Izzy's herd. This scared a number of others from working with Fletcher's stock. It almost cost the state its *Brucella*-free status. All that prized semen was suddenly in question, even though the brucellosis wasn't in the bulls. Fletcher had trouble bringing in new calves because no one wanted their good herd's name tied up with this black mark. The only rancher willing to take a chance was Brody Ross's father. But that herd went bad too. Brucellosis again. A lot of people said the Callahans should have known better than to have gotten mixed up with the Ross Ranch, but the damage was done. Someone even shot Fletcher's three dogs. Land that was once mortgage-free now had a mortgage. With no income, Fletcher sold his ranch and was suddenly outside looking in. He took on his middle name of Marks, moved back into Wyoming, and got a job at a paper called the *Tribune*. His daddy had known the publisher, who either felt sorry for him or felt like he owed Fletcher's deceased daddy a favor for having had the privilege of knowing him. Face it, if someone in your family had been president of the stockmen's association, no matter how far back, you carried a lot of clout, met a lot of people, and earned the right to ask for favors, even after you died.

"So, in the eighties, with his own bull business behind him, Fletcher decided to let part of the land go to the church and part of the land go to Irv and Izzy. That's how a church came into ranching. Not the most common activity for a church, but if it were going to happen, it would happen around here. And Fletcher moved the *Tribune* up into Montana and gave it a new name."

When I told Mel I'd seen Fletcher riding on church property, it came as no surprise.

"He'll be focusing on genetics again," he said. "Hoping to rebuild his family name and brand, but in a manageable operation. He already has two bulls out there somewhere. They're big," he said, "but the land is even bigger. Only one or two people know about them. That, in itself, is a miracle since just about everyone here knows each other's business."

According to Mel, Fletcher would do anything necessary to keep bison out of his life, since they had already taken his ranch and his pride once.

"Bison need to tread softly. But he'd hunt an elk, too, if it stopped in," added Mel.

Had sharing my find with Fletcher been a mistake? Had he known about the dead pile all along?

"If Fletcher's raising bulls," I said, "what would he do if he had a cow born with the breeding stock and not a future bull? You know … female instead of male?'

Mel shrugged. "Ship it out, I guess."

"Will he be having calves soon?"

"He hasn't started breeding anything yet that I know of. Just has the two bulls. And Fletcher's not looking to harvest meat. Calving's only a concern to perpetuate his stock program. I imagine it's a tad early for planned offspring."

Which meant it might be exactly the right timing for a dead

pile of unborn babes, but not from bulls, of course. Maybe I had found calves, and not elk, after all. I hoped my face didn't display my inner turmoil. I had to double-check my find.

"Take these," said Mel, as I stood to leave. "Light reading to bring you up to speed on the controversy and who stands where in this mess. As I said, it began with the State of Montana suing the national park to protect its cattle ranchers."

He handed me a sizable pile of reports and testimony from the Interagency Bison Management Plan and the group working to solve Montana's bison/cattle conflict. I started reading them as soon as I settled back at home. Input from the public, scientists, ranchers, wildlife proponents, and state leaders put theories, facts, emotions, threats, and fear all over the map. I began to see the alliances. I was hoping to discover suspects. It would take time to read the thousands of pages. After several hours, I set them aside and found myself considering Fletcher's story. There was something between the lines I couldn't pick up. He was a westerner. At one with the town. He ran a fairly conservative paper, but when it came to certain aspects of life, he was more liberal than most. Was it because he had been moved to the outside pastures when brucellosis struck his family ranch? Was it because he had lost something everyone prized? Then I shuddered. Perhaps he had been set up. Jealousy and competition had their ways of igniting evil thoughts, and even worse actions. I considered the details of Mel's story and was grateful I had not found a pile of dead dogs. It would have jolted me far more than a couple of dead elk or calves.

19

ADVERTISEMENT

IT WAS the talk of the town. A welcome change from bison breaks, but eerily unwelcome: a strangely threatening ad in today's *Gazette*. Someone was looking to buy up ranches and land in our county and immediate surroundings. That's what the ad advised in a quarter-page, lower-right-hand position. The most threatening part was no one in advertising knew anything about the out-of-state group that had placed it—SKRAM Lands. It became the new, all-consuming, and unwanted talk of the town. I suspected it could be related to my mystery fetus because nothing would get a person to sell out of ranching faster than tainted cattle. Or even the possibility of it.

"I placed it," said Fletcher. "Actually, Irv placed it for me through a contact he has in Georgia."

"You're SKRAM Lands?"

"Yes, but there is no real SKRAM Lands. Look at it in a mirror."

I mentally reversed the letters. "Marks? Why?"

"Call it a fishing expedition. I like to know what's going on around town that people aren't talking about."

I asked Fletcher what selling a ranch for development would mean. To the industry. To the town. To anything. I captured a wrapped chocolate as I spoke.

"It's always best to be first, to make money off of novelty, or last, to take advantage of a limited resource. Either way," he said, "it would be bad for the town. And could be bad for the bison if it sealed off their migration routes or sent them into greater conflict with more cars on the roads."

Fletcher's compassion for bison surprised me after Mel's description of Rancher Callahan.

"Adding homes," he said, "like what's happening in Jackson, Billings, and Bozeman is leaving a lot of people needing schools and other private and public resources. And the price of all this open land is not having tax money for schools and other public facilities. All you have is land. And things cost." I recalled the hefty price tag for plowing.

Fletcher admitted development wouldn't be ideal, either, for the region's open and rural character. It left him curious as to anyone who might call that number. "But," he added, "there's a whole lot more money to be made in professions other than ranching. And a whole lot of ranchers who wouldn't have to work for another dime in their lives if they sold out."

What Fletcher didn't say was this: it was likely only a matter of time before someone sold and we would seal the fate of the bison for good.

The news of the ad rolled off people's tongues for days, but I had plenty of magazine work to keep me occupied. Simone and I were coordinating photos for the art issue. I didn't realize how much of Eva's battle I had bottled inside me and how badly I needed to set it free until a single concerned inquiry from

Simone sent me talking for nearly half an hour. Finally, I said, "Photos?"

"Only if you're ready."

I shared a more refined list of story ideas and initial themes, approved by Fletcher. We tossed around numerous options and finalized remaining assignments. The collaboration reminded me of my competency as a journalist and professional, turning my spirits for the better.

Along my route to the airport, I passed tourists rolling in. Simone had been right. RVs were practically falling from the sky. I spotted at least ten from Quebec, a couple from California, and fewer from other regions. One displayed plates of my Keystone State—Pennsylvania. The lodges in the park must have been filling up since I had seen lengthening vehicle lines along the switchback roads. Yellowstone was likely the first stop on everyone's travel wish list. I was betting the bison had a lot to do with it, along with Old Faithful.

Eva was asleep when I walked in. I silently watched her for nearly a half hour. She didn't look well, but at least she looked peaceful.

"I thought you should see her ... well ... you know." Karl confirmed my worst fears. "Her pain is being managed," he said, "but this time she can't beat it. I'm afraid we'll have to let her go. She says she's ready."

"How long?"

"A few weeks."

"Weeks?" I froze; my breathing, my arms, my chest, my legs. My sister would be gone.

I had made the trip hoping to see the miracles of medicine. Instead, I saw Eva resigned to giving herself to life's end. Soon, I would say goodbye forever. This couldn't be happening.

Inside, the RV was alternately quiet—the influence of adults—and rambunctious—the beautiful innocence of childhood. I couldn't help but think of Eva and me as children as I drove Melody and Finn for ice cream. It was so unfair. The impact would leave a lasting scar. Their precious lives would be wounded forever. How would they do without their mother? I wanted to hide from life. Instead, I returned them to the RV, drove to a distant parking lot, and wailed my guts out where no one could hear. Then, I made a pact with myself. For all my days ahead, I would ensure their scars healed and they lived to enjoy the best in life and themselves. I wasn't giving in.

I returned to Yellowstone two days later, knowing Karl and Eva would start rolling home in another few hours. Eva wanted her final hugs in her own bed in Philly. Karl would let me know when to travel east. I wouldn't wait for his call.

***

"Phillips?" Fletcher had seen me coming up the *Gazette*'s steps.

"Not good," I said, shaking my head slowly. Fletcher nodded, and I quietly escaped to my office. For the first time, I shut the door.

For several days, the town passed outside my window in its quiet daily manner, except for drawn-out attempts of RV drivers trying to park in town. Morris hadn't been laid out with RVs in mind. It had grown in an age of coaches and small cars. To its credit, it had cleared and graveled an oversize opening beyond the Country Barbershop so visitors in oversize recreational vehi-cles, or trucks towing watercraft or snowmobiles, had an equal chance to park and visit. It was a nice gesture and a boost for the diner and others. It did, however, make for a steady stream of close calls by those uninitiated to coaxing jumbo rental vehi-cles into a single spot—the perfect distraction for my pain.

A week back from Arizona, I watched a familiar maroon-red truck speed into town so fast I thought it might ricochet off every other vehicle. Brody had barely parked when his driver's side door swung fully open and he slid awkwardly out to set boots on the ground. He slammed shut his door with a loose swing of his arm and walked a wavering line into Abby's. I had seen this walk before. Brody had been drinking. It was barely 10:00 a.m.

I pushed back my chair and dashed down the stairwell, crossing the gravel lot and making a beeline to Abby's. As soon as I stepped inside, my phone showed a message from Fletcher: "Tell me what you learn." Nothing got past Fletch, the Eagle.

Brody sat well inside the third booth down the wall, likely awaiting coffee he had ordered with a shout to Abby as he had staggered past. Abby was already on her way, emergency brew in hand. I settled at the counter. Upon her return, she casually leaned forward and whispered, "He lost some cattle."

"Lost?"

"Aborted."

I froze. Was the killer brucellosis in town? My hands shook as I relayed the news by text message to Fletch. He sent no reply.

Brody looked like he would occupy the booth all day. Or until the Eagle Feather opened. Within ten minutes, the first rancher entered Abby's, like a bear sniffing for honey. With three hundred head on the line, Ellis Strong walked straight to Brody and sat. They talked quietly for a moment. Then, loud enough to wake the dead, Brody shouted, "What do you think happened?" The handful of people at Abby's turned. "What do you think?" he added, again shouting. He slammed his fist on the table so hard the silverware popped in the air and landed with a cluster of clanks. Then, Brody leaned his face into his hands. Another minute later, Ellis had to scoot over for Banker Frank. In a quieter tone, I barely heard Brody say, "Three or four of them, at least." I steered my eyes to my mug of coffee. Was Brody telling them about something that had happened last month? Was this what I had had in my deep freeze? One of Brody's cows? Why had Fletcher said it was elk? Surely he would know the difference. This had to be something else.

I avoided two ranch trucks rolling in as I made my way back to Fletcher.

"At worst, brucellosis could cost us our 'free' status," said Fletcher. "At best, Brody's cattle are headed for early slaughter."

"They can't be saved?"

"Not a chance. He'll test them, of course, but it sounds like Brody found plenty of proof to send them all. No use risking it."

I thought of what Mel had told me about Fletcher's ranch loss to brucellosis. And I thought of what Fletcher had already told me about the impact selling a ranch would have on the town and to the bison. I inhaled deeply as though to compose a swirling tornado of thoughts and wondered if this would put Brody out of ranching. He seemed so proud of his operation.

***

My hands trembled and the draft pages of the art issue shook as I held them and thought of Eva. I had shared with her my vision for the issue in its most nascent state. I doubted she would see it published. It made reading Fletcher's comments difficult. Normally objective about editorial comments, today I felt like a failure with every blemish he noted or question he posed. How was I going to get through this? How would I live without Eva?

With Yellowstone reeling from an influx of RVs and a direct confrontation with brucellosis, Abby was still Abby. I loved her to death, a shocking admission to my usually shielded self. She wildly honked her truck's horn as I stepped from the *Gazette*. Then she pulled alongside and shouted "Hop in" from her open driver's side window.

We wound around the edge of town and headed toward the northern end of the park, where we stopped, overlooking open grassland.

"See them?" she asked. Her straightened arm and hand pointed toward the corner of the front windshield. "A bunch of the ladies are mamas now!"

I saw the mama bison and their calves. Some of the mothers carefully tended wobbly cinnamon-colored babies, new to their legs and new to this world. We counted eight little ones. Red dogs, they were called. My heart felt full.

"They'll keep this cinnamon-caramel color into midsummer. By then, they'll all have little horns—male and female alike." Abby had learned a lot in the years she had been here. "They say some of the mothering is instinct and some is learned. Some dams are better at it than others."

I watched little calves closely follow their mothers. The family bond was clear, as was the vulnerability of something so little and young in this open landscape.

"Will most of them make it?" I asked.

"I don't know." We looked at one another knowingly.

Lucky for Eva and me, we weren't born as bison. Twins were rare, according to Abby. When it happened, one or both came out weak or stillborn. If they both made it into this world alive, somewhere along the way, one would start being left behind, and it was downhill from there. Mama Bison was only meant for one. After Abby shared the details, I was relieved to see singles only dotting the grassland.

"Life is such a gift," I said, merely thinking out loud. "I wish Eva could see this. Her smile would light the entire grasslands and send warmth to every living creature around."

"How is she doing?"

"She's on morphine. They're back in Philadelphia, and we are preparing as best we can. I fly in the morning."

"I'll be thinking of you. And Eva."

She touched my shoulder.

20

PASSING

I MOVED QUIETLY into Eva's room, slid onto her bed, and lay by her side. I slowly, gently stroked her hair with my fingertips. She hadn't lost her golden strands. She was as beautiful as ever, though gaunt and weak, a shell of who she had been. She looked at peace. The morphine was working. It comforted both of us. In my heart and mind, I clutched my arms so tightly around her my body ached, but none of this desperate energy actually passed from my body to hers. Instead, I barely touched her, encircling her as gently as I could so as to not hurt her fragile body and to lovingly protect her and soften her passage. It was as though we were still in our bubble, sharing the first of life together. We had started out as one. Shared what few can share—the warmth of a mother's womb—with another. We would always remain one in some miraculous way. She would always be part of me. I gave one gentle kiss atop her head, touched my fingers to hers, and drifted toward the door with tears streaming and a pain in my chest both acute and numbing. Karl and I hugged one another for a long moment outside her bedroom doorway. Then, Karl took my place, slipping gently next to his wife on the bed to comfort her, and himself, as she breathed her last breaths. I shut the door. I knew when I next saw Karl, we would stare into one another's eyes and share a warm, consolatory embrace, and we would each move on in our own ways to face the finite, irreversible, unchangeable nature of a life and its end. And that was exactly what happened. I cried myself to sleep but breathed more easily, knowing Eva was at peace. It didn't mean I didn't desperately want to bring her back. Because I did. I couldn't believe she was gone. The pain was excruciating.

I helped with final funeral preparations, and we celebrated Eva's life in a short service, as she had requested. Melody and Finn planted peonies in a garden space dedicated to their mother. That night, after dark, I sneaked out to the corner of the property and I curled up on the ground, to be closer. I saw her beautiful, loving face and thought of her smile. I contemplated her natural, and sometimes meek, mannerisms, along with her quiet strength. In my mind, I once again ran my fingers across her radiant blond wavy hair. It was the most beautiful hair I had ever seen. She always glowed like sunshine. In fact, when sun caught her hair from behind, she seemed to wear a halo. Truly, she was angelic. I smiled and cried when I thought back to the time we got our first and only perms. Her fine blond strands of hair came out looking like crinkly potato chips, and there was nothing we could do about it except wait for it to loosen and grow, and marvel at how long it took to do so. How I loved her light-blond hair. It was thoroughly Eva.

In the garden, I touched the earth and rested my head on the grass. After a while, it didn't feel cold anymore. I spoke to her. "Eva, I don't like being one. Tell me you'll be with me forever. No matter what."

I landed in Montana but didn't remember walking to my truck. For several minutes, I sobbed for all the airport parking garage to hear, as though freeing everything I had held inside for the past months—the first news from Karl, the trips to Arizona, the pain of Eva succumbing to a lousy disease I hated with a vengeance, the sadness and pain for Melody and Finn, and the final, irreversible goodbye. Then I fell asleep, leaning into the passenger's seat, undeterred by the discomfort of the center console pressing against my midsection and strange contortion of my back. I must have slept several hours, because my body was stiff when the loud voices of several men and the opening of vehicle doors roused me awake. After clumsily juggling myself upright and blinking a number of times to dismiss cobwebs, I saw several men standing next to a maroon-red truck two parking spaces behind me. Why was Brody here?

Slinking down in my seat, I slowly reached up to adjust my rearview mirror just in time to see him shake hands with two gentlemen, strangers to me. I again lowered myself toward the passenger seat, made sure I didn't press my foot on the brake, which would have lighted like a flare, and listened while doors closed and engines started. Moments later, I eased out of the parking area following two strange men in a black four-door pickup truck with a Texas license plate. The back doors were the biggest truck doors I had ever seen, and the beast had an engine to match.

I pursued the Texans along Highway 90. Something I heard of their conversation sent me in pursuit of the duo. I wasn't bothering to think. I was reacting, as I had been trained to do.

Barely five miles from airport parking, the truck turned into the Somercrest Hotel, a slightly upscale three-story building with white-painted brick exterior. I followed the men inside, with my airline-tagged suitcase in tow. Mr. Schine and Mr. Schine, as they identified themselves, had reserved adjoining rooms.

"Here for business or pleasure?" asked the clerk. I crowded closer.

"Business," said one of the Schines.

"Hunting," said the other. "A little real estate hunting," he added with a sly laugh. After asking for directions, I practically flew home. Brody was selling out!

I raced through Fletcher's open doorway.

"I saw Brody. And two men from Texas. He's selling out. Did he call about the ad?"

Fletcher looked up. I relayed my scant details.

"Interesting" was all he said. Then, a moment later he added, "Take a seat. Forget about all this other stuff. Phillips, how are you holding up?"

I folded into one of his chairs as though I would never move out. "Any advice?" I asked.

"They say time heals all," he said, "but it's not always as simple as this."

I looked desperately at Fletcher.

"To my way of thinking," he said, "time softens, but we have to do the healing part."

"Meaning?"

"Our minds remold the experiences over time, removing the hurt and replacing it with memories we are capable of facing. If we don't do the healing part, we forever remain as wounded selves, unable to function, incapable of ever again sharing love. So, time can be a forever friend, but we must also be a friend to ourselves. Don't be hard on yourself, Phillips. Face it head on. Let yourself grieve. It'll help you heal. And leave this other stuff alone for a while."

I managed the slightest smile. The sincerity emanating from Fletcher's eyes was exactly what I needed.

"Before you leave today, stop back in my office," he said.

Almost certain Brody would show at the Eagle Feather dartboard, I stopped by after work. Luckily for me, he was interested in my absence, having heard it was for a funeral. I shared news of Eva. He already knew about it. In fact, he handed me a sympathy card from his jacket and took ahold of both my hands as he told me he was truly sorry. For several moments, it shocked me into silence. After thanking him, I assured him I would get through it and decided it was best to change topics. I asked a pointed question: Would he consider selling out? I wanted the lowdown on the Schine brothers. And it was a logical enough question, given the SKRAM Lands advertisement. Brody knew of the newspaper ad, of course. Everyone did. But he kept any plans under wraps. Fletcher had said selling out would be unpopular with every rancher around. Despite a second probe, Brody was more interested in talking about me than discussing land. Abby was right. He had taken an interest in me. I wasn't seeking a relationship, but it certainly felt nice to have him care.

"What do you like best about being here?" he asked.

I broke my stare. "In the Eagle Feather?"

"No, crazy. In Morris. In the West. Surely it's different from where you came from."

"Different doesn't scratch the surface," I said. "And I like lots of things here. It's beautiful in a way I had never seen. Open, vast, powerful. I guess it's intimidating too. I was scared to death to hike by myself."

"Ask me to come along next time."

This thought scared me too. I kept talking. "The town is appealing, with lots of caring neighbors, even though I don't know too many of them."

"You know me," Brody interrupted.

"To a point."

"I'm not exactly like others," he freely admitted. "I've had to do a lot on my own. It made me different. But I like the people here too. Most of them, that is."

When discussion topics dwindled, I was relieved Brody was called to a darts game. I watched carefully. He was, indeed, a loner, but not as creepy as I had first thought. He had family behind him in his mind, but not by his side. He had made the choice to remain independent. I watched as he gave another challenger pointers. Wrapped under a layer or two, he had a caring side to him. Then, I heard him laugh. Where did he hide this? And why?

In the midst of aimlessly watching and thinking, I heard Brody call, "Have you ever played before?"

I looked up to see him looking at me. He beckoned me with a gentle grasp of my hand. "You can't live in Morris and not learn to play."

Over the next minutes, Brody showed me how to hold the darts and how tightly to hold them and described how the dart should feel in my fingers. He told me how to stand and how to bend my arm and use my wrist, and he described the release. Next, he tackled what to see and what to think. I knew this was what made Brody the marksman he was, but his lesson quickly became too advanced. For my uninitiated brain, this part of the lesson was overwhelming.

"Pretend you are throwing your hand right into the center of the board. Keep your eye on your target until you see your dart land. Feel like you have a line between you and your bull's-eye. And feel like there is nothing around you."

"You mean, be the board!"

First, he grimaced. Then he laughed and said, "No, crazy. What are you talking about?" He stared straight at my eyes and finally said, "Be in charge of the board. Own the target. No one else has a right to it." His eyes were penetrating. I couldn't move. Fortunately, he did. In quick succession he spun five darts directly down an invisible line, each hitting centerline, splitting, or nearly splintering the one that had landed prior. I remained frozen, praying the intensity would thaw and drain away. A voice called out to him. I closed my grateful eyes. He had a game. I watched only the first release and quietly slipped away, hoping to free myself from the sensation of having narrowly escaped a dangerous quagmire. I couldn't be ready. Could I? A sense of guilt for having loosened my self-imposed relationship shackles rode home beside me.

I walked the perimeter of Irv and Izzy's house, then entered the garage and opened the freezer. After Eva's funeral, I had told one of Karl's Pennsylvania friends about my little animal find. Normally, this wasn't a topic I would have raised, but Max Chong was at a veterinary school. After discussing my foray into the land of cattle and brucellosis, I felt safe opening up. Perhaps it was because I was back in Philly, or maybe I was seeking a trustworthy shoulder to lean upon, with all my emotions tied up in Eva's passing. Either way, Max was fascinated. It was a purely intellectual fascination and had nothing to do with the gruesome, macabre, deathly or anything else I found my freezer stash to be. He offered to shed any light he could on my cache. Max took me by surprise when he recommended I be tested for brucellosis. I thought he was joking until he said, "You can't play around with this, Amber. You touched raw meat in Yellowstone, and it might be infected."

Testing in Montana sounded like a bad idea, so I had told the lab—in Philadelphia—I was concerned about my recent consumption of unpasteurized dairy products.

Staring through the clear plastic wrap I had put it in before shifting it to the new freezer, I contemplated how to best send a frozen body part cross-country. And wondered if I had the guts to do it.

After a weekend of giving the action more thought, I bought supplies and took Max Chong up on his offer. I wrapped the tangled, solid mess from my freezer in dry ice, double wrapped it in insulated bags, then secured the entire package in a small foam-lined cooler within a heavy box, using an abundance of duct tape. I sent it overnight express to the East Coast. I wouldn't know diddly without the science. I scratched my simple instructions on a note: "Tell me anything you learn."

For several hours, I poured over aerial photos of Yellowstone and the land beyond. Property lines from the government database, layered on top of natural features, afforded a better understanding of where I was and what stretched around me. It was part work and part investigative curiosity that pushed me forward. The influence of the federal government and railroad companies in the region's rise reflected clearly in the checkerboard of property lines emanating from both sides of the steel lines. For every mile of line planned, the government had granted the railroads land alongside in checkerboard fashion, assuming pieces kept by the federal government would more than double in price as development of the railroad sites in between took place. But land didn't sell as planned, and lagging sales, instead, prompted the Homestead Acts, with free land for willing takers.

I focused on Brody's ranch and Fletcher's church property. Both shared edges near the park and forest. I looked more closely as soon as I saw the names on a third adjoining parcel:

Irving M. and Isabel P. Wilson, my landlords. Their ranch sprawled forever down the valley from their home, even further than I had known. It hadn't registered when Jordan described the lay of the land.

I detected several fence lines from their shadows on both the church site and Brody's, and I noted a couple of buildings at the far end of Brody's. I didn't remember them from the tour on Gunsmoke, but I wasn't certain we had gone that far west. At Fletcher's church site everything looked as I remembered, but it stretched farther than expected as well. I saw what looked to be a faint outline of a trail passing from the park to the freedom of the northern valley. Bison often walked single file through snowpack and grass. This, I believed, was a mark of their travels. The biggest surprise was seeing the aerial view of the church's lake. What I had seen in person was but a small finger of a far larger expanse. I wasn't certain if it connected to the Yellowstone. Something about the shape looked unnatural, leading me to believe it had been artificially enlarged.

Back home, I checked my memory of this set of government aerials with internet maps taken more recently. The buildings at Brody's were missing, but all else looked the same. I found myself considering the landscape less and Brody's unanticipated ride in life more. How had he done it? Run a ranch of this immensity? It must have been devastating facing his losses. I knew all too well how it felt. We had both used hard work as a salve and a means to cover wounds to avoid thorough inspection. But Brody was additionally perplexing. It wasn't as though he didn't get along with people. He simply didn't care to do much with them, except defeat them at darts. Was he independent? Absolutely. Loathsome? Sometimes. Intriguing? Yes, if not for his bison hunting. Conversations with him were pleasant. And wasn't Brody an interesting one to set his cattle on a later birthing schedule and to plan for future fall birthing, an even greater risk? Having just seen other ranchers wearily pressing through spring birthing season, I understood why he smiled when he had shared his plans for fall calving. Many of the ranchers had looked dreadful. Even without fall calving, Brody had created a seemingly more manageable routine. It was testament to his independent mind, and it was admirable. Damn.

21

____

PEOPLE

We had a plan. The third *Western TriState* would highlight people—the many interesting individuals who had been lured by the land, whether they were ranchers looking to yield cattle from grazing land; artists assuming a natural, bohemian lifestyle and drawing inspiration from nature; individuals in search of small communities and impressive landscape in which to thrive on their own; jet-setters with a second or third home who enjoyed large parcels for entertaining or escape, as well as hopes of conserving the land for future generations; or service and resort workers seeking a lifestyle linked to open lands and the opportunity to share their love of it with others. They were here for the land. And most stayed for generations, making family a central tenet of their lives on this earth. It was as though nature quietly seeped in, became part of them, and then anchored them.

A noticeable common thread of all who were here was their willingness to work a long day. In a lot of ways, it seemed people were still working hard to survive. They had demanding jobs and faced a demanding climate and landscape, which could overpower but also nourish.

Being a newcomer was a blessing and a curse in putting this issue together. My uninitiated eyes saw much that others passed over. This was good. On the other hand, I was struggling to make contacts and select representatives of this western region, fearful of missing important people. I would have to dig into my Philadelphia grit to make it a success. One thing I knew: even Abby and Shelly would be included. Shelly as a future entrepreneurial female dude rancher, and Abby, who had put together a diner that perfectly suited the town, owing to its oversize breakfast specials for ranching appetites, free seconds on steak sides for your eggs, and a pair of toothpicks at meal's end, not to mention that it had become the town's impromptu community center.

Just as I was comfortable seeing more of Brody, I couldn't find him.

"Cows are birthing," said Abby. "Maybe he needs help."

"Abby, I am not reaching in anywhere for a calf."

"You could hold a bottle."

"Abby, I am not a rancher." Even as I spoke, I wondered what calving season was all about, wondered if I might swing by Brody's with a fresh cup of Abby's coffee to see for myself. Half of me—the reporter half—desperately wanted to do this. The other half knew full well I would regret it.

"Two black coffees, to go," I said. Abby handed them my way, surely expecting I was taking them to the *Gazette*.

I eased Sebastian down Brody's drive. I hadn't even called in advance. For all I knew, Brody could be sleeping. I prepared to turn around, but the next moment, I saw him walking toward me holding a calf and knew I had cornered myself into a visit. I smiled at the opportunity to ask questions.

I felt silly carrying coffee to a man covered in newborn calf junk, but Brody didn't mind. He smiled broadly, and he proudly declared, "I'm a mama now."

The little one clutched in his arms had been rejected by its mother. I was about to see mama and baby reunited in their personal maternity pen, with hopes they would better bond. In the meantime, Brody took a bottle to the tiny calf's mouth. I watched as it suckled, and I followed a tender expression moving across Brody's face, eclipsing his mask of exhaustion.

I gazed at his eyes, which were fully invested in watching the calf's singular intent to feed. This was humanity at its best. Unfortunately, as the calf greedily grabbed for the last drops, Brody spoke of the calf's survival in terms of financial implications and the impact of each loss. Even if they were cute miracles of life to him, they were also future profits. My spirit deflated, but I was happy to have made the visit. Brody was pleased by it too.

Max phoned while Fletcher and I tossed around ideas, so I disregarded the call. Ten minutes later, I phoned him back from Sebastian, with windows closed.

"What did you find out?" I asked.

"You sent me part of an elk. That's what all four of your little friends are."

"That's what Fletcher said."

"Who's Fletcher?"

"My boss. But he's also a rancher."

"Right. From your photo, they look to be roughly two months shy of full term. When did you say you found them?"

"Mid-April."

"I'm unsure of the birth cycle out there, but the timing seems about right, as most full-term births would likely occur late May to late June and weigh about thirty-five pounds. So, late-term abortion fits with when you found them."

"But why would there have been dead elk? Four of them?"

"Your guess is as good as mine. Mama elk certainly didn't pile them up. For starters, elk give birth alone, not in groups, not that this was giving birth. On top of this, elk cows, meaning mama elks, are fastidious about cleaning up after birth, removing all the birth materials, and what you sent me was part of the birth material. The placenta, to be exact. Their newborns have no scent, so good cleanup ensures safety. It can mean survival in a world of predators."

"How clean are they when they abort?" I asked.

"Just as clean. I'll run a few tests and look for a cause. I'm wondering if they were poisoned. Or if the mamas were shot and cleaned and the babies simply dumped."

I found myself sitting very still as Max gave his awful assessment of something so inhumane. It was what Fletcher had surmised. Then I said, "We talked of brucellosis."

Max was silent for long enough I wondered if we had been cut off. "I can check. It requires special handling and protocols … if I keep this on the up and up."

"So I have learned."

"I'm certified as a vet to handle it, but it's classified as a potential Category B bioterrorism agent. Why? Because it can undergo aerosolization. *Brucella abortus*, the bacterium, that is. Everything has to be reported."

"To a state vet, right?"

"To CDC if you contract it, and state vet. You got checked, right? Like I recommended?"

"Yes. In Philly. I lied about unprocessed dairy and precautionary testing."

"Test again," he said. "Since you handled it again to send it here. Don't mess around."

I found myself sitting still as a statue. "I will."

After the call, I remained in Sebastian, deciphering Max's information and considering the mystery. A hunter might have taken one mama and tried to hide an unborn babe, but odds were slim one or more hunters had taken four pregnant mamas and had hidden and reclaimed four lost babes. The only other one hiding an elk would be someone who couldn't afford an elk problem, or rather a brucellosis problem—a rancher who wanted the remains off site. Four elk babes were worse than one. I glanced at the windows of the *Gazette*. The most fastidious person I knew was standing through the glass, and he had plenty of reason to keep his lands clean. Even if Fletcher was only hiding a couple of bulls, he couldn't weather another brucellosis outbreak. But where were the mothers? And why would he leave the dead pile one night and move it the next? Surely he wouldn't want others to find anything on church property. Maybe he needed time to put them elsewhere. Time to dig a trench. But this would mean he'd hunted out of season. This was far fetched for Fletcher.

Any rancher or any hunter could have been responsible, as Fletcher had said. For a fleeting moment, I ran Mel through my microscope of question. Reading the lengthy reports he had loaned me led me to know a self-proclaimed bison guardian might happily share aborted elk with the public and officials to displace the blame from the bison. Only he hadn't shared it with anyone. I was back to square one—the only certainty was elk could get brucellosis, and I had to test again.

22

———

GEYSER

THE WAY I was going about my TriState People issue was frustrating, and it felt wrong. I was pressing too hard, trying to discover all the right people in one fell swoop. I would surely miss some important lives and would regret it. Fletcher and I agreed on a change. TriState People would be pushed back several months to a December publication, but it would remain available as an evergreen issue. We'd reprint it as an extra edition every six months, retaining profiles of certain individuals and adding new profiles to each new edition. Fletcher saw its value in making the great big tourist attraction called Yellowstone more recognizable as a community. It was an opportunity we wanted to get right. Pressure off, except I had lost a valuable week to pull together the next issue—TriState Water.

Perhaps it was the influence of this editorial change and my newly realized appreciation of several of the residents, or perhaps it had nothing to do with either, but I accepted Brody's invitation to visit Old Faithful. I was curious to learn about the geyser, but suspected I might also ask a question or two about elk. As well as looking forward to meeting the next day, I even felt a bit nervous, as though it might be a date. This was preposterous, wasn't it? I shrugged off Abby's influence. But I knew why he had asked.

I paid for hot coffees, despite his objections.

"I owe you something for the private tour," I said. "Besides, you've been busy with your cows. You deserve it."

"I have been. Yes, ma'am, but I'm in good shape. And the little ones are beauties."

Brody had a soft side, but he guarded it closely. I couldn't fault him for hiding behind hard edges, though. It was the only way he had survived a hard life.

"Are you still getting rid of them?" I asked.

"No choice."

"But did any abort?"

He looked at me as though I was crazy. "That already happened, remember? But no stillbirths, if that's what you mean. You usually have one or two of those each calving. I should be able to get something for them, but I can't keep them all season."

They were animal units after all.

I expected Brody would be an excellent guide. He enjoyed being certain of his knowledge. At times, he practically added footnotes and references for clarity, substantiative support, and proof of accuracy. I had, however, also witnessed many strong stances based solely on intuition. He rarely declined to voice an opinion. Certainty came easily.

Brody knew Old Faithful had been named by the Washburn Expedition, that it was once called "Eternity's Timepiece" even though it did not erupt hourly, and that there were more than five hundred geysers in the park. Of equal importance, he had judged the direction of the wind as we had walked, and he had steered me to the far side of the viewing area.

"All the people over there," he said, alluding to the side we had vacated, "won't get nearly as good a view as we will. In fact, maybe none at all."

I questioned him with my eyes.

"The geyser's steam is going to blow their way and block their view of the eruption. Being upwind, we'll see a magnificent attraction."

"Magnificent?" I asked, smiling.

"Exactly." Brody nodded. I looked at his face a moment longer than usual. I couldn't help it. He was smiling. I thought of Abby's words. Perhaps Brody was simply looking for a compass to help lead him. Perhaps his usually tough exterior could be exchanged for a softer persona after all, with the proper helping hand. I felt an unexpected impulse to protect him and free him from his painful past. Why? I had other things to do than be a savior. What it said, I immediately concluded, was that I was lost. Eva's passing continued to weigh heavily, and pain had an incipient way of forcing bad actions. But it also quietly suggested I might someday be able to move forward without Jake after all. As soon as I thought this, I immediately wished I could have saved Jake and Olive. And Eva.

I was grateful Old Faithful began its show. A small jet of water splashed upward from the earth, appearing to reach a mere couple of feet in height. It was unimpressive. Far more impressive was the excitement and anticipation of what would follow. I prepared my camera.

"You don't need that yet," said Brody. "This part is called the preplay, and it can last up to twenty minutes. Small splashes. Small jets of water shooting up. You have to be patient. It will grow."

I set my hand and camera back by my side and stared at another puny blast of water, smaller than what I had seen with Melody and Finn at a water park splash pad. While waiting and watching the occasional jet of water pulsing from a hole in the earth, I remained keenly aware of my proximity to Brody. He stared silently at Old Faithful, as did I, yet I could see him out of the corner of my eye. I continued to be intrigued by both the geyser and Brody's boy-like curiosity.

About ten minutes later, the splashing and jetting began to reach higher into the air. Another couple of minutes after that, a few pulses of water jumped skyward, well beyond the reach of previous spouts and well over our heads. It was, indeed, a spectacle. My thoughts jumped to Thomas Moran and his painting of Old Faithful, at very nearly this location, over a century ago.

"Camera time," said Brody, his eyes trained on the water. But then he turned his head to look at me and did it again—cast a self-assured smile toward me. I turned my gaze to my camera, afraid to look a moment longer. Within seconds, Old Faithful sent a water spout frenetically jumping into the air and then splashing downward. This time the geyser didn't recoil into the earth. With water already spouting upward, it sent another pulse higher, maybe fifteen feet above its last peak. As this jet of water fell toward the ground, Old Faithful sent another pulse upward, even higher, piggybacking on the previous emission. As this began to fall, yet another wave of steamy water pushed upward. For a lone minute, the earth gave us a powerful hint of the fire within.

"How strange," I found myself saying, "that we stand on ground frozen solid for months in the winter, and yet, deeper underneath our feet, a fire burns and water boils."

"Indeed," said Brody. "And with each eruption it thrusts thousands of gallons of water upward. Three thousand, five thousand, eight thousand in a matter of minutes. Best well around can't do a fraction of this."

As water continued to spray upward, powerful jets of steam exploded into the air and danced away from us, just as Brody had predicted. By now the magnificent geyser towered more than a hundred feet overhead.

"The water," said Brody, "has been measured at over two

hundred degrees, not quite boiling, and the steam has reached three hundred and fifty."

As Brody continued his lesson, I realized he likely could have been many things other than a rancher.

Within a minute, the eruption began to wane, and Brody said, "This is called the end play."

I looked at his face.

"I did not make this up. Promise. It might do these short spouts again for a couple of minutes, or it might end abruptly, just like that."

The geyser fell lower and lower to the ground, and its steamy water droplets, cooling and condensing, dissolved into the surrounding air, once again at peace. And just like that, it was over.

The crowd, which had circled Old Faithful several rows deep, scattered quickly, seeking the next items on their wish lists. Brody asked about plans for the rest of my day. I had none, and as long as I had Brody with me, I was going to get to the bottom of something.

"You asked once why Fletcher brought me on board," I said.

"That I did."

"It seemed you had some unspoken thoughts. Maybe I was wrong."

"Like I said, Fletcher has done a lot of good for this town. Still does. But something tells me he's hiding something."

"Like what? And why?"

"Beats me."

"Oh, come on. What's between you two? I've seen it. The cold shoulder. Barely a glance when passing. You two have some history."

Brody huffed ever so slightly. "It's not something to talk about."

"Let me guess. It has to do with cattle."

Again, Brody huffed softly. I felt him inching closer to a revelation.

"His family and my family just don't ..." Brody paused. "Just didn't get along much."

"Didn't? Sounds like you still don't."

Brody was silent, but something was boiling within, like the earth under Old Faithful. I remained silent, waiting for him to vent.

"We wanted the church land," he said. "My family didn't get it. He's off running a couple of bulls, and my family could have been using it for a lot more. It doesn't sit right. Never did. Never will."

"You're holding a grudge over grass?" I asked.

"Didn't you learn anything from my tour? Grass," Brody started slowly, "means everything."

"More than cattle?" I asked.

"Grass *is* cattle." Brody clenched his teeth, as though locking a door to additional thoughts. This time, it was my turn to blow.

"There are millions of acres of grass out here. I'm still missing something. Tell me what you mean. I need specifics!"

"What I mean," Brody said, turning very slowly to look eye to eye and suddenly towering over me, "is our lives depend on land. And all this free land and leases of public land came with a price. Sweat. Long days. Long nights. Sore bodies. Lost bodies. Lost to disease, tough times, broken souls. Free land cost a lot of people a lot of themselves."

"That was a hundred years ago."

"That was my family. And every other ranching family out here. And in a way, it still is. We're all working for those who put in the hard days to get us here today."

"Does it ever change? Does it ever change to working in the present and not living with family on your shoulder?"

"No. It doesn't. Family is always by our side unless you get out of it."

"Which no one here does."

Brody gave a strange look and then said, "Right. So, you keep on working. Keep on trying to make things better. We had a real nice plan for that church land. It would have given us hay and corn silage for our winters. Instead, Fletcher's on it with a church. Like I said, it never sat well with us, with my ma and pa. Land, plain and simple, is who we are. We depend on it for our way of life."

As I sifted through Brody's words, I felt myself slipping out of journalistic mode and back into a personable human with a heart. Guilt unexpectedly surfaced. Why had I been so cold-hearted? "Thanks for sharing," I managed. "I'm trying to fit in, but clearly I don't yet." This pulled a welcome smile to his face once again.

"Don't worry, you'll make it."

Brody bumped my arm, and we started walking. How I wished this elk mess and bison mess would disappear. And maybe even the cattle.

Even though geysers were certain to make a future issue, my tourist hours at Old Faithful quickly caught up with me.

"Who's fastest at turnaround?" I asked. "With the shift away from TriState People, we're behind."

"Peter Finch for the lead and Hoagie for another," said Fletcher.

As we huddled around our water supply notes, I was already feeling the deadline in my stomach.

"I'll do Nate's story myself," I said.

"You won't have time for it," he scolded. "Not on top of the editorial."

"Have you ever known me to back down?"

Fletcher sighed. My stomach squeezed even tighter. I had better deliver.

"We could pull out a sig if needed," he said, referring to a group of pages. "Might help budget-wise, and it wouldn't be the end of the world," he added.

While I agreed with Fletcher's budget thoughts, I was damned if I was going to drop pages.

23

REGRET

I AWAKENED SERIOUSLY HUNGOVER, my head throbbing with every slight move. I hadn't been skunk-drunk for at least a decade. Through the slits of barely opened eyes, I noticed the other side of my bed ruffled from footboard to pillow.

"Oh, no."

Like the ugly shimmering goo of a slug trail, the night slid back into my brain. I closed my eyes. I remembered being at the Eagle Feather with no food in my stomach and, by the time I left, far too many drinks. It was after another lousy day of trying to move past Eva. I only vaguely remembered Brody driving me home, but I definitely remembered inviting him in.

Holy Mother of God, I thought. Yes, I had been branded. As if to punctuate my misguided actions, I began to dry heave. I barely made it to the toilet in time to empty my guts and make peace with my body's fury. I grabbed for the handle and flushed, my chin resting on the bowl as water emptied and refilled. The noise of it was head cracking, but I couldn't make myself lift my chin.

Holy Mother, I thought again. The tile floor felt cold on my bare legs. I managed the return trip to bed, where I buried myself under covers.

After several hours, I awakened again and considered the damage. Brody's big belt buckle hadn't even hit the floor the first time he mounted me. Boots had stayed on too. It was edge of the bed, no holding back, fast and loud. I wanted to die. He had had the biggest pair of balls I had ever seen. Not that I'd seen a ton, but I'd seen my share. And they were commanding. Each time he pushed inside, they had pounded my flesh, and I had rocked with uninhibited pleasure. Even in my current pathetic state, the thought made my midsection tingle. The rest of me cringed. I was back in adolescence, with its horribly confusing combination of carefree and reckless behavior, embarrassment, heartbreak, and experimental learning. Schiste!

During the course of the night, we had gone several rounds.

Dear Mother of God, I silently repeated. What an idiot I had been.

With great effort, I moved to the kitchen to begin a cautious remedy of sips of water and crumbled crackers. Staring vaguely at homemade coffee sitting before me and cooling with every passing minute, I foggily brought back additional pieces from the night. I remembered the darts, Brody's gentle teaching style, and a couple of celebratory high-fives, which had turned into body bumps and, finally, hugs. We had danced to whatever background music was playing, and, well, he had brought me home. How could I have gotten in such awful shape? It had been years.

I closed my eyes and heard a truck—clearly diesel—powering up the hill and around the bend toward my home. I slit open my eyes just enough to watch it pass and thank the world it hadn't turned in the driveway. That's when I saw Sebastian, parked perfectly perpendicular to the road. I knew, at this moment, someone other than Brody knew he had come over last night. Someone had helped him bring Sebastian back to the barn.

Please, I thought, *let it have been Abby. And not another rancher*. I couldn't bear the humiliation.

I moved back into bed, intending to die, or at least hoping to. That's when I recalled a blurry conversation, an interesting conversation. It was well worth dredging from my murky brain. I thought as hard as I could. It seemed futile, but somehow, I recalled a few slivers, followed by a few more. Fletcher's and Brody's ill will hinged on more than the church land. I thought of Fletcher's family bucking horse statue. Details became clearer. Brody's ancestors, also from Wyoming, had been beaten out for the association's top spot. And it still mattered. The eldest Mr. Ross had wanted that presidency. He had wanted the clout, the spoils of the position, and the chance to run the show. He never got it. And he didn't think Fletcher's family deserved it. A generational grudge had slithered into a second generation and had continued to poison all the others down the line. This was why Brody and Fletcher would never mingle well. How, I wondered, had they both come back alive from their joint ride across the church land? And why were they even out there together? Maybe they were trying to politely untangle a boundary skirmish. I could only imagine the posturing that had accompanied the conversation.

None of this was particularly intriguing when I considered how Fletcher would look at me, and what he would think of me, if news of my night with Brody had hit the presses. It was all I could do to phone Abby, but I had to do it.

"No worries" were her first words. "Brody was kind enough to ask me to help him move Sebastian."

"Thank God. And thank you, Abby."

It wasn't that I wanted to give Brody another hug, but what he had done was, indeed, considerate. Perhaps he didn't want to share his actions with others either. I was reveling in this thought when Abby laid the bad news on me.

"He was kind," she said, "and looking as though he had won the lottery."

I flattened my head into my pillow and for the first time said aloud, "I am such an idiot. What have I done? This is so unlike me."

Then, I heard Abby's gentle voice. "You want me to bring coffee or anything?"

I assured her my home brew was being neglected to the point of no return so, no, she shouldn't waste a cup of her good stuff on me. I would unfortunately survive without it. Once I did, I would unfortunately have to face the world. After that, I was putting Abby on the cover of the TriState People issue on account of her kind heart.

It was the best timing ever for having to head to Philly. Furthermore, it shielded me from the tourist RVs that kept rolling into the area, reminding me of Eva, Karl, and the kids.

I peered out the window nearly the entire flight. Other than a few puffy clouds far to the north, the day and the skies from west to east were as crystal clear as stunning mountain creek water. I contemplated the immensity of the landscape and the passage of so many people traveling west over time, on the very land below, which now housed millions. I considered the European rushes for land, gold, and other riches. I imagined wagons, stagecoaches, horse trails, and walking shoes. I thought a moment of Brody's and Fletcher's ancestors moving west and sacrificing much for a new life. Then, I mused about the many peoples who occupied and crossed the prairies, rivers, and mountains long before others from foreign lands arrived. Finally, I focused on the bison that had moved freely and grazed the entire stretch below me, and beyond. It brought me spinning around to the numbers. Thirty million bison had once lived here. My plane was shooting across 1,853 miles in roughly six and a half hours of flight time. If the bodies had been below, I could have looked upon 1,200 bison per second. I pictured a blanket of bison covering the country below. Keeping the earth warm, while the earth protected them in return. Nourished them, fed them, and gave a place for newborns to lie folded in its soft embrace. My mind involuntarily flashed back to the mound of skulls, the killing, and the sickening hazing. Then, I closed my eyes, trying to block it out.

Together, we were moving forward. Beginning to accept. Continuing to honor Eva's loving spirit. Yes, she was still with us. And always would be. The thought was reassuring, just as being together with Melody, Finn, and Karl was reassuring. Brody had been right about family strength and forever bonds. Once again, I found myself giving thought to crossing lands leading west, when many had to continue without loved ones who didn't make it. Family was vital.

Karl's parents came for the afternoon to learn about my new life, but more to reminisce and hold Eva in our thoughts, now that the newness of her passing and the sharpest of the pain had dulled slightly. We sat in the garden, where hedges and fences kept us privately separated from neighbors—the Ferrence family on the left, Wexlers on the right, and Robertsons behind. How compact it felt now. A cozy half acre on one hand, but a crowded, active neighborhood on the other. It had been easier than expected to settle into the massive, untamed western landscape, despite its many surprises. I considered that the privacy of this one slightly oversize fenced-in yard would easily cost the same as over two hundred acres in my new western home. The sky was different here, too, even on a sunny summer day: grayer and not as clean. Humming traffic sounds filled the air, occasionally hurling a blast of frustration or warning into our gathering. Planes, too—many of them—passed over our heads with telltale whistling sounds gliding with them to their Philadelphia landings. Their cloudy streams of exhaust crossed the sky in an ever-changing but slow-moving display. I thought of Old Faithful's steamy clouds evaporating into the blue-tinted air, silently disappearing. Here, plane streamers increasingly widened before melting into the aerial expanse, to be joined anew by more freshly painted exhaust.

I proudly passed around copies of my first *Western TriStates*. As I did, I felt Eva watching. Simone's luscious photos made everyone swoon.

"This is Eva's art issue," I said.

"She would have loved it," said Karl, "and I can't wait to read it."

"What do you mean, Eva's art issue?" asked Finn.

"I dedicated it to her—your mom. Art was her calling. Along with being a mother."

Finn smiled wistfully.

"You know, you must visit me out there. You must see how big and beautiful it is, and how different. We have wild bison out there. You would like them."

Finn tilted his head.

"Buffalo," said Karl. "Aunt Amber calls them bison now."

Finn appreciated his father's clarification, and I imagined them visiting and seeing bison in the western landscape.

"Amber," said Karl, "if not this year, then next. Absolutely."

I couldn't wait. Then, as if Eva were speaking, I heard a familiar phrase pass through my brain: *Saddle burn. Yes,* I thought, *Saddle burn, sweet sister. I wish you could come, too, but we'll take good care of them.* I heard her say "Thank you."

That night, after conversation had gone quiet, I slipped into the guest bedroom. I saw Eva's garden spot outside and melted into a pot of memories. Everything was different now. Without her, I would be a guest in Karl's home, and no longer in my own space with my sister. I found myself considering the Brody entanglement and felt I was visiting with a college regret. What had I been thinking?

"Nothing," I lamented. I hadn't thought at all. I looked once more out at Eva's garden, glowing under the floodlights, as though lit by heaven. I didn't know how to do life alone. Eva had always been my other me. And Jake and Olive had made me invincible. Being in Philadelphia was tough. If I wanted to return, it would never be the same, and it no longer felt like home.

After long travels, a day shared with family, and a time zone change, I relied on my alarm to wake me in time to meet Max at the university. After an initial greeting, he said, "You got tested?"

"Yes. The first tests were negative. I get my second tests this afternoon."

"Keep checking, especially if you feel symptoms."

I knew by now, from my reading and from Dr. Hill, that lethargy, fever, and chills could be signs I was infected. I had been on the lookout for several weeks. I was glad I'd had the foresight to bring gloves to the dead pile, and I didn't recall any fluids marking my skin or my eyes or nose. In fact, I had done just about everything I could to remain as distant from the little body as possible and had been extremely careful about the disposal of the original plastic bags. At the time, I hadn't been considering brucellosis. At the time, I was only thinking "Important clue ... whatever it is ... handle with care." But as I realized later, I had done nothing in the way of special handling of my shoes, which had slammed straight into the bodies. I had to test.

With a bit of technology, Max gave me my first in-person look at *Brucella abortus*. He had found the cause of death. He carefully closed in on the microscope and projected the magnified slide onto a screen. I saw pink-stained life-forms that resembled tiny soft capsules.

"There was some degradation, since it was frozen, but what you sent me was covered with it. What I can't tell you is if this specimen was aborted."

"Meaning?"

"I can't say if the animal related to this was dead and aborted naturally, or if the mother was killed and the little one's death was an ugly by-product."

"Sounds gruesome either way."

"Well, having four dead in one location sounds gruesome too," said Max.

I noticed one of my photographs pinned to a corkboard. Together, we studied it.

"No signs of the mothers anywhere?" he asked.

"This was it. Then they were gone."

"I'm curious if I can pinpoint the strain. An academic exercise of sorts. Or perhaps not. A few people, I believe, are starting an informal database. Maybe it will give us a location of the herds the mamas came from."

"Strain?"

"You know—more specific markers. It can present in any number of genetic forms. Just like our flu."

When I took my leave, I headed to Dr. Hill's for a simple blood test, my second after handling the dead pile. Once again, I attributed it to precaution after ingesting unpasteurized dairy, and, once again, I remained resolute in doing tests in Philly. Anyone believing I was tied to brucellosis would shoot first and ask questions later. If at all.

As I embarked on my third errand of the day, I harbored a sense of excitement. I knew instinctively Ted Steele had answers or, at the very least, clues. Besides, I looked forward to seeing him again.

I rang the bell to Number 54 Walnut Street and waited until

footsteps stopped on the other side of the door, the latch was unlocked, and Ted stood in front of me. He looked remarkable. Far better than he had only weeks ago.

"Amber," he said. "Good to see you again."

"It looks as though Philadelphia is treating you well."

"Always."

He led me to his office space, starkly decorated in gray and white, with the exception of a bold orange modernistic painting crossing the wall behind his desk. It seemed out of place in an older home, with its dark mahogany door to the street. With the help of his cane, he walked well, albeit with a limp.

"Thanks again for meeting," I said. "As I told you in my message, I can often tell when things don't add up."

"I understand. How can I help?"

"I already know why you were there, how long you had been there, and what happened. What I don't know is if you remember anything … well, odd. What, for example, do you recall of Irv and Sam mending broken fencing?"

"Irv was there three or four of the days I was there. He was a nice guy. We talked a couple of times about the plans for the ranch and lamented the fact the fencing was in such bad shape. Sam was looking to keep a few horses, so the fence had to be reinforced. Plus, it couldn't look shabby for visitors.

"Sam and Irv and I all thought ATVs would be better for artists to get their supplies out to different locations, but having horses would look more authentic and add appeal. I asked a couple of times how the fencing came to be in such rough shape. Or I might have asked once but then commented on it again in a roundabout way, saying something like, 'You still here, Irv? Are you making two breaks for every one repair?' That sort of thing. Sam said it was old. Irv said it happened. Now that you mention it, though, at least once I saw Irv and Sam share a knowing look. It was like they knew more than they were saying."

I considered what Irv had told Fletcher about the extra screws used for repairs.

"Someone was vandalizing it." I studied Ted's face carefully as I relayed the information. If he had anything to do with it, I was hoping to see it.

Ted pursed his lips, considering my words. "This would explain the strange looks when I brought it up. It might also tie in to something else."

I cocked my head, prompting his words.

"Heading into the main house for dinner one night, before Sam and Shelly knew I was there, I heard them talking about a dude ranch that wasn't happy about the future competition. There were a lot of what-ifs coming out of Shelly, and a lot of reasoning from Sam. What if he doesn't think there's room for both of us? What if he says he was going to add painting this year? What if he starts saying bad things about us? It was this sort of thinking out loud. They agreed it was better to not make him angry. The conversation stopped when they saw me. I tried prying it out of them to address any concerns up front. I planned on talking with them again the next day, but that's when it all happened."

"Who were they talking about?"

"I never found out.

"You know," added Ted, "another night, early on, I overheard something different, which also concerned me. I was outside looking at the night sky. Sam and Shelly were in their home, but with a window opened just a tad for fresh air. They had a fire going in the fireplace, and it was smoking a bit, so they wanted to air things out. The same thing had happened the previous night: wet wood. Anyway, I overheard them talking, and I got spooked by it. Sam kept saying 'I won't do it,' and Shelly was agreeing with him, saying, 'They can fight their own fight.' And then Sam agreed again. He said that he wouldn't do it for any amount. Shelly said she wouldn't either. Honestly, I didn't want to know what they were talking about. I slid away as quietly as I could. I actually considered leaving and dropping my involvement, but I was excited about the project, and I really liked Sam and Shelly."

"You told people, and Fletcher and the sheriff and me, that Sam saved you."

"He did. I'm sure of it."

Ted recounted the noises he'd heard that caused him to walk toward Sam in the first place. Then he said, as he had in the hospital, that the bison had come charging at him, hooked him right through, and tossed him. From the ground, he'd seen Sam coming toward him, doing what the rodeo clowns do when they want to get a bull's focus off the rodeo rider. But Sam tripped or stumbled and took a fall, and the bison turned and trampled him.

"I learned later Sam died."

The story lined up exactly with Ted's previous account.

"Did Sam say anything about taking photos of a bison or having the future artists painting bison?" I asked.

"We talked at length about how artists might be able to capture the wildlife, since this is what a lot of them would want. Sam was adamant about ensuring anyone who stayed with him would be safe and wouldn't get too close. He was fully aware of the dangers. Not related to bison specifically, since they didn't normally travel there, but related to wolves and elk. We talked about using guides and how to incorporate them without ruining the experience. Being the tourist that I was, I was a trial guest of sorts. I told them I would feel better having a guide nearby. That landscape is wild and impressive but, let's face it, frightening. Besides, it would be best to not get lost anywhere."

"Did you tell Burt about these conversations?"

"No."

"Why not?"

"It wasn't my business to tell. If Shelly wanted it known, she could have told Burt directly. In retrospect, I should have said something, but I was in bad shape when the questioning began."

"I hear you're still sending ideas to Shelly."

"I'd be disappointed if the dude ranch doesn't come to fruition, even if I do still wonder what Shelly and Sam were discussing."

"It would be a fitting legacy for Sam," I said.

When Ted stood to walk me to the door, he lifted a hefty stack of papers to bring to his recycling bin. My eyes latched on to a familiar object that had been hidden—a bronze-colored statue of the Wyoming bucking horse, approximately four inches tall.

"Paperweight?" I asked.

"Paperweight?" He followed my gaze. "More like a new family member and happy reminder." He smiled. Ted had that rare positive life view that would carry him through anything. Maybe he was simply happy to be alive.

Before Ted and I hugged and I took my leave, I knew I had another meeting to set. The question was, How would Shelly take to my wanting to discuss Ted's clues? She would have every right to boot me out of her life forever. None of this was my business, but there was a reason I was making it my business. It was for her own good.

In between catnaps on my flight back home, I played mental roulette, with the circle of questions, suspicions, and doubt spinning. It was anyone's guess where the wheel would stop. I considered the options: Fletcher, Brody, the mysterious Schine brothers, Mel, and who knows who else.

I had already ruled out Fletcher. Though remotely linked to almost everything, he was too honest. Any congregant in his church might have rid church land of elk, a potential threat to the new bull business, but this, too, felt remote. My thoughts turned next to Brody, for whom elk would certainly be unwanted visitors, and infected elk even more so. But why dump a pile of dead elk? And then reclaim it? I had no logical answer.

I turned my spotlight on the Schine brothers. They didn't belong in the equation, didn't belong in this state, but they were here, with their middle-of-the-night rendezvous. I had a bad feeling about them. *Brucella*-infected elk, after all, might scare ranchers right off their land. Might accelerate development, the Schines' apparent forte. It was conceivable they knew of Fletcher's history with infected cattle. Word didn't stand still once it got out. Maybe Fletcher was next on their list. Mel, a man with myriad connections, which could readily translate into an equal number of reasons to do things and people to do them for, wasn't clear yet. Pinning a disease on elk would benefit the bison. What continued to nag was why Mel had voluntarily told me, a journalist of all people, about Fletcher's secret cattle operation. This reeked more than the dumped fetus that, thankfully, no longer sat in my freezer. There was definitely intent behind Mel's disclosure. It was time to put a closer eye on the self-proclaimed bison guardian.

I sighed loudly enough that the woman in the next seat raised her gaze from her book. With cordial smiles, we again retreated, she to her book and me into the wispy world outside. In the distance, a small congregation of clouds placed a gathering of shadows over an isolated landscape. As I peered at them, I wondered, Could the elk be the work of an Indigenous Tribal member? Taking elk off the land for personal use and consumption? I knew they could legally hunt bison beyond the Montana hunt seasons. I didn't know if they could do the same with elk. Perhaps leaving and retrieving dead elk had special meaning. Of all people, Mel would know. If he didn't, he had connections who would. As my thoughts returned to Mel, I recalled his mention of the Ranching Association, a strong-minded entity, as he had described it, with several even stronger minded members. I felt uneasy.

———

Midweek, Fletcher's truck was unmistakable, parked in front of my apartment. He had left the *Gazette*, purportedly to run errands. Had he expected me to stay longer at the office? Or was he intending to give me a pink slip in private, having learned of my night with Brody? I had eased into my driveway, ready to face the music, when I caught a glimpse of Fletcher out back, standing at least a football field away. If he had worn a darker shirt, I never would have seen him.

From inside, I watched him cross the grassland from one slight hilltop to the next a good five times before making his way toward my apartment. I greeted him as he closed in.

"Phillips," he called out. "Good evening."

"Fletcher?"

"Irv asked me to look at the land. To make sure there wasn't any problem. Have you seen any cattle here?" he asked.

"Cattle?"

Fletcher nodded, then asked, "Any bison?"

"Fletcher, what's going on?"

"Didn't answer my question."

"Bison? No. And no cows."

"Just wondering. No tracks out there."

"What the heck?"

"Someone told Irv he saw cattle grazing here. I'm Irv's eyes. A couple of ranchers might be trying to take over Irv's land. The whole world knows he and Izzy aren't here and aren't grazing anything. It's beginning to feel like the old days, when land grabs were a matter of fact. Let your cattle run wherever they want."

"Who talked to Irv?"

"Just keep an eye out for cattle. Let me know if you see any."

"Is anyone coming after them if they're grazing here?"

"They are, if I have anything to do with it," he said.

I watched Fletcher's truck ease onto the highway in typical Fletcher fashion—slow and steady—and then watched him gun it, clearly on a mission.

No more than a minute later, Mel's SUV sat in my driveway.

"Did I miss him?" he asked, as I walked out to greet him.

"If you mean Fletcher, he just left."

"Oh, hell. Sorry to bother."

"What's going on?"

"Sorry, Amber, I have to catch him."

"Good luck. He left in a gallop."

Mel buzzed off in hot pursuit. It gave me a chance to contemplate what a land grab would mean in this day and age. And if it was even possible. I was back on Mars.

24
____

WATER

"Pull up a seat. Let's talk water!" Nate Crowley's British accent amplified his energetic, down-to-business welcome. As Nate was manager at the water supply company on the Wyoming side, he was a fabulous first interview for my next *TriState*, a "ready-to-tell-all water issue." This article would have my byline. Nate had already, quite conscientiously, returned my emailed list of advance questions fully answered. Few people did this.

With my recorder, pad of paper, and pen at the ready, my mind felt like a detail-seeking missile. Reporter mode was always thrilling. Jordan Jones would join us to capture part of the interview and anything else Nate produced of interest to readers. Finally, we had an opportunity to use his photographic talent.

We looked over maps with rivers, lakes and watersheds, pipes, wells, intakes and outflow systems. Together, we peered at nearly twenty slides beamed from a microscope onto a screen to inspect what was in our drinking water before it was treated and what was not in it after. He gave a dizzying rundown of chemical tests and regulatory allowances. One of the big concerns was arsenic, a natural result of water moving through rocks and soils of Yellowstone. With constant testing and remediation, Nate and others brought unhealthy levels to acceptable EPA standards when water flowed from faucets. Organic materials also got a good look-over and reduction as needed. And any unwanted inorganic chemicals, radioactive materials, and something called microbes—little living critters like bacteria—were removed as well. Nate was a water wizard. I might even call him that in my headline.

"In a nutshell, we add specific chemicals here at the supply facility to glom onto other chemicals and certain bad stuff that is dissolved or suspended in the water. Once glommed together, they settle to the bottom of a tank, and we can remove them. We pass the water a couple of times through carbon filters— huge megafilters. They put the home faucet filter to shame. Then we pop in a bit of chlorine to kill off unwanted bacteria, viruses, and other microscopic unwanted, for lack of a better nontechnical term. Finally, we adjust the pH to meet standards. In the end, almost clean, potable water becomes potable in line with seventy-six specific chemicals, microbes, and water quality standards."

Following Nate's classroom discussion, we toured the facilities, with Nate carefully explaining the processes again. The machinery was impressive. Jordan was in his element. Then we tackled the other big part of Nate's water equation—water planning.

"Here, we have roughly one hundred and fifty year-round water-consuming residents," said Nate. "Big whoop. Easy to handle. A bunch are even on private wells. I could supply water to the year-rounders in an hour-a-week commitment, easy. Maybe even with my eyes closed."

"But?"

"Yes, exactly. Like it or not, we are called upon to produce fifty-three million gallons annually for an additional six thousand people a day."

I stared with eyebrows raised high.

"Last year's biggest draw was over three hundred and fifty-two thousand gallons one day in late July. Being as this was one of the dryer times of year, it was a double whammy," he said. "In late summer, water levels are lower due to lower precipitation and greater evaporation. So, any chemicals in the supply coming in to us are naturally more concentrated."

"So, more filtration, glomming, and the rest?"

"Exactly."

"How do you do it? Increase your supply by so much?"

"You mean by fortyfold?" he said. "You want to know all my secrets, do you?"

By now, I knew no one around here worked without maps. Nate fell right in line. On one large, rolled-up, yellowing page with blue ink lines and multicolored pencil lines, I saw a system of water infrastructure. Nate was eager to share details, but our meeting had been scheduled to carry over to tomorrow afternoon. Nate had a previous commitment.

"Save that thought," he said, checking his watch. "We will meet again."

As I drove onto the roadway, my first concern was what flavor ice cream I should buy for a burst of energy. Then, as soon as I arrived home, I made a peripheral search for roaming cattle. As expected, there were none.

The following day, Nate and I resumed our discussion by taking seats overlooking his map.

"The biggest draw for this region comes from the Firehole River." He pointed to a squiggly line bisecting the park. "It's spring-fed. Over here in West Yellowstone, in Montana," he said, pointing across the table, "water is drawn from the town's

Whiskey Springs collection area. It's also a natural spring and goes through the same types of processing to get a safe, clean product to taps and water bottles. Several wells are used also."

"This is all piped underground?"

"For the most part, so it doesn't freeze in the winters. What's under the surface is warmer than what's above. As for going from serving one hundred and fifty people to six thousand per day, there's a lot of planning and infrastructure. The challenge, of course, is it all must be maintained and healthy, to be used at a moment's notice."

In a region considered to be semiarid, it was impressive.

I knew of growing problems with backyard farm animals and bigger farms in eastern towns. Farm odors were villainized, and farm waste and water concerns had become intertwined. Nate assured me animal waste was a growing concern here as well. As a precaution, many were keeping an eye on it.

No sooner had we ended our supply conversation than I learned Nate had a side interest. Throughout our discussions, I had wondered about the multitude of photographic printouts covering his walls. It was as impressive as Jordan's wall of ranch photos. As soon as I asked, Nate's flood of excitement told me I had touched his soul. Nate led me to a corner cabinet and said, "These are like fingerprints. The bacterial fingerprints of the entire region."

"Hmm."

"Yes, exactly. What does Nate mean by this?" he said, assuming a third-person position. "The photographs you see are from these slides. On them, we show millions of water bacteria and other microbes. Each from a different location in the region and from almost a hundred different hot springs. I have collected water samples for quite some time now. Believe it or not, even in superheated acidic water, life is created and survives. And the interesting part? I am finding spring-specific critters. Bacteria that live in a particular spring but not else-where. Something called archaea are also location-, tempera-ture-, and pH-specific, and they can survive the hottest temperatures. It's like every spring has its own identity. Its own fingerprint. Even those with some of the same microbes show quirky differences because of specifics of their surroundings. So, a person who knew their stuff could tell where a specimen came from by the bacteria under view."

"You're kidding."

"I'm a bit eccentric about this, I admit. Looking to publish in a couple of years. The day job slows me down a bit."

I thought of my deadlines and wondered how a several-year deadline would feel. In another moment, Nate was talking about PCR, primers, and identification. He was also getting into the minutia of adapted survival mechanisms of things you couldn't see without magnification. At this point, my eyes didn't exactly glaze over, but my mind's inability to absorb the new factoids told me I had reached saturation point. I was glad Nate had a calling. I also knew my readers would find a simplified version sufficient, if I ever put it in an issue.

"One last look," he said. "Give me a moment."

Nate pulled two containers from another specialized cabinet, dropped liquid from each onto a separate glass slide, and set them up to project onto different screens.

"Show-and-tell time," he said with a glimmer. "Just got these today. Tell me what you think."

"Not to drink, right?" I was staring at orange-colored crea-tures, magnified.

"Of course not."

"These are from our water? Outside somewhere? It looks like they came from another universe."

"Yes. And right again. In a sense. They are from separate hot springs of medium-low temperature near the Norris Basin, but off trail. These would be cyanobacteria *Oscillatoria*, the more orange one on the left, and cyanobacteria *Calothrix*, the more brown-orange one, to the right. You can see there is iron mixed in with the feathery mat of bacteria. And they do form mats."

"And you collect the samples yourself?"

"Indeed. A bit tricky at times, but so far, I have managed to stay alive."

I knew it was a joke, but also knew it was a dangerous task traversing land that had many hidden hollows, high temperatures under and in the water, and acidic conditions unfavorable to humans. Not to mention, Nate might have to smile his way around landowners intent on keeping strangers off their property.

Despite all the big-picture stuff going on around me—mountains rising, grasslands stretching, and sky bending beyond view —Nate's catalog of microcosms was equally powerful. I was certain Nate was one who would make a difference.

***

Diane's familiar knock came rapping on my door. The comforting smell of homemade sweets followed.

"One for you and one for me," she said, taking a seat. "How are you doing? I know you are at the one-month mark without Eva. We tend to mark anniversaries big and small, so I assume this has crossed your mind. I don't know what we would do without calendars."

"You're a sweetheart. Yes, one month ago today. Time truly marches on. And we follow. But it's a good thing. Thank you for thinking of me."

***

Later, with lunch in hand, I headed toward Fletcher's church, knowing Fletcher was at the *Gazette*. I hoped to see his bulls, a long shot, even from a distance, but I was curious. I suspected they would look like any other cow, except spectacularly big, and I harbored a romantic thought they would in some way look gallant. While I drove down the hill, Brody, in his truck, came chugging through the pass. We each nodded but neither slowed. I owed him a straight conversation on The Night but was dreading it. Maybe he was too.

At the edge of Brody's ranchland, I saw a stop-worthy sight: the Schine brothers, standing near the open tailgate of their oversize set of wheels. Out-of-state plates stopped along the side of a road were commonplace here. It was Yellowstone. But I knew enough of who they were and what they wanted to take notice. With a neighborly wave, I steered Sebastian to a stop within a couple of yards of their makeshift worktable.

"Sure, Brody told me all about it," I lied. "Planning to do something real nice here," I lied again, hoping to pry them open. "What's going out there?" I continued. "Cabins? Hotel?"

The bigger, taller Schine shifted his eyes toward Shorter Shine, who shifted his eyes back to Big Tall. Neither wanted to talk, but I had given them no choice. They couldn't appear to be hiding something. One of them had to cave.

"Well, it seems you know something about this." It was Big Tall who finally broke. And he was damned pleased with their vision for Brody's property and their investment money. Moving closer to the plans for a better look, I saw buildings on points from north to south and east to west. From the valley to the flats to the slopes. Brody was selling out big time! Concrete pools and a lazy-river pool were positioned near the lone semicreek, seemingly making use of his land's only natural spring. Upscale cabins dotted the lowland. A hotel would perch near the creek as well, and chalets were planned for the gentle slopes. Residences on nearly one hundred acres surrounding Brody's current house site were planned, and an event center was envisioned on his middle hills. A separate dude-ranch setup, complete with camp outposts, down a new road through the middle of the property, was the last of Phase I. Brody's western acreage was marked off "for Phase II." I could only imagine what Schine and Schine would dream up for it. Selling out was an understatement. Progress meant development, of course, but what the plan didn't say was "breaking up this land will put a giant stop sign in the bison's migration route to the lowlands." As bad as the situation was now, worse yet would be fragmentation along their travel routes. I found myself lying once again as I commended Schine and Schine on an admirable plan and, yet again, when I said, "It's got my vote."

I had nearly tugged shut my truck's door when Shorter Schine shouted, "What'd you say your name was?" Through lying lips, I shouted back, "Meredith Clark." Shorter Schine combined a nod with a quarter wave. Big Tall followed suit. Someday, I would pay for these fibs. Maybe Brody would pay for all his too. What an a-hole!

As I continued my drive to the church, I recalled Fletcher's admonition: ranching kept the land whole, and what wasn't whole was broken.

Gliding into the church parking area was like burying myself under bedcovers, nestled away from a tough day in a tougher world. More troubling than the Schines' plan was how easily I had lied. I had never done it so brazenly. Instead of heading to the barn or poking around the edges of the fence to look for bulls, I needed a seat inside to reflect. Walking to the entrance, I passed another car, parked and empty. Its California license plates weighed strongly in favor of its being a rental for tourists making a visit of faith.

The moment I stepped into the church's warm wooden shelter, my body relaxed. I was ready to bare all my emotions to myself and my surroundings, when a man appeared from an office up the hall on my right. He took four quick steps into a room directly across the hall, not bothering to look at me as he crossed. At first, I startled. Then I did a double take.

"Irv?"

The mystery man poked his face back into the hall. It was, indeed, Irv. He quietly motioned for me to follow.

"What are you doing here?" I asked.

In a hushed voice he said, "It's nice to see you, but you didn't see me." I stared quizzically.

"Is Izzy here?"

"Florida."

"Are you coming to the house?"

"Can't," he said in a continued hushed tone.

I watched as he placed a large manila envelope into the top drawer of a desk. On its front side I saw the initials *F.M.*

What was Irv leaving for Fletcher?

After he slid shut the drawer, Irv said, "I'd best be getting out of here on the q.t. Otherwise, I could spend a lifetime explaining why I'm here in the first place."

"But why are ..."

Irv reached for a quick hug. As he released me, he held a finger to his lips and quietly uttered "Shh." Then Irv slipped out the door before I could ask about trespassing cattle, Fletcher's bulls, or the meaning of Irv's visit.

"Wait. Wait," I said, not so much talking to Irv as to myself. I jogged in pursuit and found Irv already sitting in the car with California plates. At a knock on his window, he lowered the glass partition roughly six inches. It was enough for me to ask in a hushed tone, "Why are you here?"

"Business," he said. "Had to get something to Fletcher without the postal staff looking at it. Or the local attorney. Or anyone at Abby's or ... you name it ... a million others."

"Irv, what's going on?"

"When it's time, you'll know." My mind jumped to the Schines. Was it coincidence they were in town at the same time?

Was Irv also selling out? I remained silent, but secret thoughts bounced within like corn kernels popping madly in a pot.

Irv's window slid up, and I stepped away from his car … having never seen him. I got into my truck to leave. Why did I care about Fletcher's bulls anyway?

25

———

RIGHTS

I took in a deep breath and exhaled slowly as I opened the door to a little Italian restaurant, newly opened, in an aging strip mall some thirty minutes toward Bozeman. A window sign flashed on and off, alerting everyone in bright-red lighting that Luigi's was *Open ... Open ... Open ...* even on Monday nights.

Brody and I met out of town to prevent the gossip tornado from swirling, and to prevent others from joining us as we sorted out The Night. Brody was seated in a booth, and stood when I approached. Nervous energy slid smoothly into more directed discussion.

"I'm sorry about the other night," I started.

"Yeah, me too. I didn't expect things to happen so fast."

"We both had things going on. I don't think either of us wants to pursue this." I spoke slowly, choosing my words carefully. Brody listened. "It just happened," I added. "Happy to put it behind us."

"Oh ... right," he said, clearing his throat.

I felt freed of a despicable weight. All I had to do now was forgive myself. When Brody said "I can't say I totally minded," I realized it wouldn't be that simple. I came face to face with both guilt and pain for having inadvertently hurt Brody or let him down. I made the cowardly decision to dance around the subject.

"I doubt there's a man on earth who doesn't mind a night of drunken sex."

This brought a smile, but his gentleman's pride and courage made me feel worse. I wasn't ready to turn away from Jake after all. I didn't know why, except I wasn't sure I knew how to. Maybe it was fear of being hurt again. Maybe it was guilt over even considering moving on. Or perhaps I was still grieving after all.

"I saw men at your ranch yesterday," I said. "Everything okay? It looked like they might be surveying."

Brody cocked his head. "State employees, maybe. They tend to do their work without notifying anyone."

"What would they be surveying?"

"How do you know it was surveyors? It could have been water people, electric utility workers, road engineers, anyone. About what time?"

I forced a vague response. Then, I practically spat out my anger at being lied to. "You know, Brody, I used to be a very good reporter. I learned all kinds of things that others didn't. Why don't you give me the truth about your friends, Schine and Schine, and their extensive plans to develop your land?"

Brody looked terrified.

"That's right. I've seen them."

Brody stared eye to eye. "I can't talk about it. You'll have to wait."

It was a fair response. Certainly straightforward, even if I didn't like it.

I launched another question. "You've been in ranching your whole life, haven't you?"

"Since day one," he said. "Parents, grandparents, great-grandparents were all ranchers. I didn't have a say in it."

"You like it?"

"My choice would have been special ops, but you don't always get a choice."

I thought of Brody sharpshooting bison and wished he had followed his dream. "Why didn't you do it?"

"Couldn't. Family needed me. Then … they didn't, but by then I missed my chance."

"Abby said your family's gone."

"That's right. Accident. I should've been with them, but I got sick and stayed home. Waited for hours after midnight to hear they were all killed. Rollover. Some think they swerved to avoid an animal. You know … bison."

I gasped and pictured a younger Brody: a boy learning the news. I imagined him sitting through family funerals. And in that same flash of a second, I focused on the considerable burden of guilt he must have carried for not having been with them. I reached forward to lay a hand on his forearm and found myself sputtering out a lame message of consolation. "I had no idea. I am so sorry. It must have been so hard. Brody …"

"It's long past. If it was going to happen, it was going to happen. Mom and Dad weren't too happy at that time, anyway. Had some ranch problems."

"Problems?"

"They were overextended. It wasn't like my dad. Or my mom. I don't know what got into them. Maybe competition. Maybe fear."

"Fear?"

"Afraid others might get bigger and they'd be one of the ones left behind."

"So, how'd you keep everything going? How old were you?"

"Life insurance. I was sixteen. Barely."

"You did it yourself? No other relatives?"

"Not that I know of." Brody smirked.

"But how …"

"When you have a job to do, you can't quit. Can't crawl into a hole. Can't run. You have to do it. I knew as much about ranching as any of them. And the association looked after me okay."

I sank into the booth and felt my nurturing instincts rising. I would always be the older sister. Even if I only had five minutes on Eva. What's more, she was the quieter of us two, despite having her own kind of strength, and I was often her voice. When Mom and Dad passed, she took it hardest. I was there for her. When boyfriends broke up with her, I was there for her. I was always a little older, a little taller, a little bigger, and I was never escaping birth order. My nurturing instincts always surfaced. Damn it!

Brody continued talking. "Abby's friend Cameron came along, and we thought we'd be a team. That fizzled. So, here I am."

All I said was "I didn't mean to upset you."

"No one's upset, except maybe you."

The guilt I felt would have exploded out of me if such a thing could happen. "I ask a lot of questions," I said, "to get information straight from the source."

"I'm fine talking. It was a long time ago."

"Yes, nearly half your lifetime, but that doesn't make it ancient history."

Brody and I trailed each other back toward our homes. He still hadn't fixed the taillight on his truck. I honked when he turned into his gravel drive and nodded slightly, but only to myself. I felt awful for not giving him more of a chance. He wasn't a bad person, only wounded. And of the two of us, I was clearly the more flawed.

As I lay in bed, thoughts of Eva, Brody, Olive, and life slid gently, one to another. In a different day and time, Eva's death in her thirties would have been the norm. How much more opportunity we were given today. How fortunate we were. Thirties were young. Barely at a point of embracing life. She would have had children younger, of course. They would have been well on their way to taking on adult responsibilities back then. These days, reaching your teens was just the start of independence. In good ways and bad, with so much adulthood left to learn, it only became more complicated. I wondered again if I should help Karl raise Melody and Finn. Karl claimed he was doing okay, and he had his parents and siblings near, but it had been hard enough losing Mom and Dad in our early twenties.

And then there was Brody. At age sixteen, he'd become an adult, with all the associated weight. It would be odd these days, but Brody, at age sixteen, had likely done the same things many his age had done when they came West in days gone by. They sacrificed. To survive.

Judging from the position of the moon outside my window, I guessed it was nearly two in the morning, and my mind was still churning faster than a waterwheel in floodwaters. I had not been sleeping well all week. My thoughts skipped to Irv's secret dash into town. I reaffirmed my belief that Irv's visit had nothing to do with Sam but clearly had to do with Fletcher. Maybe he was leaving cattle information for Fletcher. It hardly seemed to warrant the secrecy. Next on my nighttime mental travels were the Schine brothers' plans. Brody didn't have a lick of hot water pumping out of his God-given earth. Not a single boiling point. Only a warm spring. Yet hot springs were a focal point of his future resort. It didn't make sense. Clearly, I had an assignment, and with this, I settled my head more deeply into my pillow and steered my brain to slumber.

Driving to the *Gazette* was taking longer these days, thanks to tourist traffic. I joined the caravan of slow-moving cars, mini-vans, and a larger RV hauling a four-door coupe. As I pressed forward, I knew Nate had likely moved into high-production mode, even if not full tilt just yet. I considered the vacation dollars winding through the region. The Schines' plan made sense. I wondered if Brody was simply counting the dollar bills, or if he was finally answering his inner voice that said he had never wanted a cattleman's life. Just about everyone had noticed how cranky he had been lately. My guess was his double life as rancher and secret developer was creating pressure, along with the lies he was telling. Secrets took a toll. Plenty of people would want to have it out with him when they learned of the plans. But as Fletcher had said, it was best to be first. Brody was playing his cards right. It was another quality I hated to like: he was smart. But if his plans with the Schine brothers came to fruition, he would likely be leaving as fast as he could. Any personal relationship would end.

"Today," I said to Abby, "I need high-test and as large a cup as possible."

"Oh?"

"I'm stuck with the aftermath of a mind that wouldn't sleep."

"No kidding. Exact same thing happened to me. I wondered if it was the moon. Say, did you say something to Brody?"

"Why?"

"He was as grouchy as I've seen him in a long time."

"Great."

"What?"

"I said it was a mistake … our night together, and I didn't see a future in us. He took it like a gentleman, which made me feel even more coldhearted."

Diane held the door open for me as I entered the *Gazette*, then crossed the street to the bank.

"Phillips?"

"Hi, Fletcher."

"Any cattle?" he asked.

"Only the invisible type." What I wanted to add was "Just like Irv … Invisible Irv," but I didn't.

Fletcher got a good laugh out of invisible cattle and said, "Sometimes, that's the best kind. Touché."

My good mood vanished when I checked emails and found nothing from Peter Finch. I dialed his number, this time using my cell phone.

"Oh, Amber …"

"Hello, Peter. Any guesses why I'm calling?"

I listened patiently as I heard the excuses of the day.

"Peter, I am sorry your kid puked on you. Sorry for you. Sorry for your kid. I needed your story yesterday. You know it. I know it."

"I know."

"We gave you the lead for this issue. Fletcher and I are counting on you."

"I'll get it to you. Today."

"No later," I said. "We've been holding for you. All clear in the contract."

"I'll do it."

"Yes, you will. You've done the interviews. I called around. Get it on paper. Get it over here. I know you can do this, and I am excited to see it. You always produce outstanding pieces, but at this point, you are being both rude and unprofessional."

"That seems extreme."

"I don't think so."

I hung up the phone and shouted "Damn it!" at the top of my lungs.

"Problems?"

Diane stood in the doorway.

"This guy used to meet deadlines faster than any I knew. He used to write in Chicago. Now he doesn't think a deadline applies to him. I could scream. The lousy prima donna!"

"You just did. Should I call him later? You know, as Fletcher's ace?"

"Let's give him the afternoon. His kid's sick."

"So he says," quipped Diane. "Does he even have a kid?"

I worked the phones for the rest of the morning, lining up meetings, fleshing out thoughts on upcoming issues, but all the while unable to clear thoughts of the night from my brain. Then I popped back into Fletcher's office to inform him I was headed to Bennett Merchante's for a meeting on water rights, on recommendation from Nate.

"Any bites on the SKRAM Lands ad?" I asked.

Fletcher shook his head.

"What would it mean," I asked, "to have a new megahotel with hot tubs galore and all the amenities?"

"If I didn't know better, I'd say you know something."

"Nothing concrete. Just wondering about water. I heard western water was more than liquid. It was rights and claims and a whole lot more. This is where Bennett comes in."

***

I sat across a laminate-top desk from Bennett Merchante, the water permit man for the county. A beautifully detailed crossword maze of water supply, which was one and the same as outtake, included levees, swales and pipes, ponds, streams, collection points, and wells.

"The first premise of understanding how water works around here," stated Bennett, "is this: Wyoming owns all of its water. Montana owns all of its water. Idaho owns all of its water. Above ground and below. If it's wet, it's theirs."

I considered this premise, so strikingly different from anything I knew about water, and said, "If I want some of it, how do I get it?"

"Drinking water, irrigation water, cattle water, landscape

water—it makes no difference. If you want it, you have to get the rights to it. These rights are allocated by permit only, and people have fought over these rights for centuries. With population rising and a drought in the making, water rights are more important than ever, and I don't see this ending anytime soon."

I considered having to fight for water. In Philadelphia, I turned a handle, water flowed, and I paid my bill. No questions asked. Had I lived further from the city, I would have dug a well, like everyone else. A single well permit would do it. All the water that rose up would be mine for the asking and mine for the taking.

Here, according to Bennett, you had a right to water or you didn't. It was simple and complicated. Your rights were limited to a particular amount and purpose. They weren't ever-flowing. Some people's rights went back a hundred years, and the first one to apply was the one who got first dibs. If a dry spell hit and that source shrank, the next in line could be out of luck. First in was first right out.

"There's no such thing as group rationing for the benefit of all," he said. "Not really."

"So, how do you make room for more rights?" I was considering specifically how the Texas Schines might acquire spa water.

"It's more like, How do we make more water or make what we have go farther?" he said. "The more we channel floodplains and cover the landscape with asphalt and buildings, the less water stays put. Every roof, driveway, and roadway sends a bit more running through our fingertips instead of into our well source in the protected custody of the earth. Without a doubt, the fights are going to ferment and brew."

Bennett had been regulating water rights for thirty-seven years. He had seen and settled many conflicts, as a respected and levelheaded permit man and referee. He was forthright with three thoughts: we refuse to acknowledge the notion of finite, we refuse to accept moderation, and we aren't very good at foresight and planning for the greater good. He pursed his lips as though to say "That just about sums it up."

"So, here we sit," I mused, "on top of strictly permitted water, trying to corral human nature into sharing mode instead of our fallback fight-or-flight survival. Lots of luck."

"In a word, yes. So, if you're thinking of buying land out here, don't assume you can use that stream of water crossing your land. Someone else might already have rights ahead of you. With anything you buy, check with me to make sure your land comes with the water rights you need. Or get ready to just sit in a rocking chair and stare at the damned scenery!"

I told Bennett I was renting and not looking to buy yet but assured him I would remember his words. In the meantime, I gazed at what seemed to be a map of a million levees and channels. It was fascinating how everything was distributed.

"Renting? Where?" he asked.

"Morris. A garage apartment."

"It wouldn't be Irv and Izzy's place, would it?"

"How do you know them?"

"They have some of the oldest rights around here. A super setup. Maybe you already know this. They have a system of old levees, pumps, pipes, and wells that could get them just about anything and everything they could need for the entire acreage. With Irv and Izzy moving out of ranching, I'm concerned they might sacrifice these rights. Like I said, use them or lose them."

"When would this happen?"

"They'll get another two years max. Then, other rights will move up the line."

It seemed appropriate a storm came in as I inspected water maps with Bennett. Pounding rain drenched me through before I climbed into Sebastian, and heavy downpours for the next quarter hour put me upright in my seat.

Close to the park, I saw a rainbow in my rearview mirror.

The pavement remained wet, and levees I had seen on Bennett's maps were, no doubt, filling for anyone who had the rights. Across the valley, a few bison stood calmly, as they did every storm, content to wait it out, with water running off their coats and dripping from their nostrils. Their shaggy light-brown overcoats of winter had been shed, save a few raggedy patches clinging to shoulders. Had I really only been here four months? Where would they go once a handful of humans transformed a ranch into a major development? Brody and the Schines angered me. The land wasn't theirs to change. It was bison homeland.

Thinking of the plans moved the Schines up my list of dead-elk dumpers. I had to learn if their Texas license plates had parked at a local hotel on April 15. If the Texas Schines could create trouble for cattle ranchers, they could coax them into a new industry. Their industry. Maybe they were responsible for Sam's death. Was this what Sam and Shelly had said was not worth any amount of money? Was this the Schines' revenge for their not wanting to partner? Everyone agreed the Nelson land was remarkable.

I had to ask Shelly.

26
————

LIFE

I PLACED a wild daisy in a vase for Eva. For several days, I had been watching a group of them preparing to open out back of Irv and Izzy's. Setting the flower on the counter, I felt Eva close to my heart. The next instant I considered what I'd done to Brody and wondered if I had any heart. Except I felt sorrow, self-pity, and guilt, so I knew I did.

I stared past the single daisy, out the back windows of my apartment, and noticed something staring back. The rough mounds and parallel lines crossing parts of the fields jumped out at me. I was surely looking at dried-out gullies and levees, overgrown and, as Irv and Bennett had insinuated, abandoned. They had been there all along, ready to quench the thirst of animals and land, but I never knew to look for them. Irv had told me when he sold his last cattle, but I couldn't recall how long ago it had been. Bennett hadn't given an exact time frame. I looked through the small panes of glass at Irv and Izzy's sprawling hills, imagining the greenway once filled with cows. It must have been quite an operation.

I hopped into Nate's truck and said, "We'll be safe, right?"

"No worries, mate. Worst off, we'll lose a toe or two. But at least you'll have a better picture of everything I've been talking about." Nate's sense of humor put my fears to rest.

We arrived at an isolated spot along one of Yellowstone's most iconic hot springs, aptly named the Grand Prismatic Spring.

"Let's take a look," he said, "starting at the center, where the water rises from the earth and surfaces at close to one hundred and ninety degrees Fahrenheit. Not quite boiling. Tell me what you see."

"The most beautiful clear blue water I have ever seen outside of the Caribbean."

"Right. Why is that?"

"Because of beautiful blue bacteria."

"One hundred percent wrong, but nice guess."

Failing Nate's first quiz was embarrassing, but I overcame it quickly as he gave an explanation.

"This water, at the center, is too hot for most bacteria," he said. "It is lifeless water. Or nearly lifeless. The only thing we see is a clear deep-blue color as light bends through the water. Moving outward from the source," he said, "the water cools and certain bacteria can survive in it. We see a lovely yellow band of water from a type of bacteria called *Synechococcus*."

"It's beautiful."

"In order to survive the temperature—about one hundred and sixty-five degrees, which is actually higher than their most favored temperature—and also to survive the high sunlight up here in the mountains, these bacteria make a lot of yellow pigments called carotenoids, as well as their green chlorophyll. Believe it or not, this is like us creating pigments to tan and protect ourselves from sun. So, in midsummer, as we are today, when we couple more light with these higher-than-optimal water temperatures, these cyanobacteria produce more of their yellow pigments—carotenoids—and less of their chlorophyll, and we move straight away from the blue central zone of this thermal spring to the yellow ring around it."

I considered how remarkable it was that microscopic bacteria could adapt to sun.

"Moving further out," he said, "into even cooler water, a mere one hundred and forty-nine degrees Fahrenheit, these same bacteria make less yellow pigment, so they appear more orange. So, this is the color the water appears. At these cooler temperatures, different types of bacteria, called Chloroflexi bacteria, can survive together with the *Synechococcus* bacteria, and their combined colors appear carrot orange. Finally, at even cooler temperatures, we find additional types of bacteria added to the mix at about one hundred and thirty degrees, and the combined colors of everything living in these fringes create the deepest, darkest reddish-brown color."

"This happens in the winter, too, when air temperatures are so low?"

"Yes. Water coming to the surface remains the same. The biggest difference is the sun is less bright, so less tanning magic goes on, and the colors are slightly less vivid. A green layer encircles the blue section rather than going straight to yellow. Why? Because weaker sunlight causes the bacteria to create less of their yellow pigments."

I was struck by how closely interrelated everything on earth was. Even the microscopic world had it figured out. The only things out of sync were humans.

As I climbed out of Nate's truck and climbed into Sebastian, a gentleman swung the back doors of a van wide open, revealing a lineup of easels. The summer art schools and artists' camps were here! Surely, the Grand Prismatic Spring would welcome them.

"Phillips, come on in."

Fletcher caught me once again.

"I hear you had a tough call with Peter Finch."

"Peter Finch is the two-word definition of prima donna. It's ridiculous."

"Maybe so, but you need to come up with a three-word definition for apology."

I stared.

Fletcher spoke. "It's called 'Peter Finch apology.'"

"You can't be serious."

"I don't care if it's kid puke, dog vomit, or anything else. We can't treat Peter the way you treated him."

"The way I treated him was like the irresponsible writer he was being."

"Call him," said Fletcher. "Apologize. You'll see his article much sooner as a result. Somewhere along the way, I made this mistake myself and learned the hard way."

"Seriously? You want me to apologize?"

Fletcher nodded. I felt like a schoolchild being scolded.

"So, what's first?" asked Diane. "Sheets? Vacuum? And remember, I do windows if it comes with a piece of your home-made blueberry pie."

"Oh, Diane, what would I do without you?" said Shelly. "And you, too, Amber. Thank you for coming. I know you both put in long days at the *Gazette*. To tell the truth, I am completely set for the guests, and more than anything else, I could use a good visit. And a short walk around. It would do me a world of good to calm my nerves."

"Like we always used to," said Diane. "I'll have to borrow boots." She looked at my feet. "And so will Amber."

Shelly smiled. "Let's do it!"

We carried tumblers of refreshing iced tea as we set foot onto the grasslands, with no particular itinerary in mind. We simply started walking. Shelly's horses whinnied as we left the corral behind us.

"Beautiful land," said Diane.

"Hmm" was Shelly's response, a mix of a word and a content sigh. It was as though we had been put in a trance by the land around us and the slow, comfortable pace of our boots walking the soil.

We breathed in the air, which had a slight hint of summer-bloom perfume; watched a couple of hawks painting easy circles overhead; and felt no need to speak. We were here for the land and one another's quiet company. With no plan in mind, we made a wide walk around the first hills and found ourselves standing atop the next step of rising land. A breeze caught our hair, brushing it from each of our faces, and I knew I was not the only one to light a smile across mine.

Shelly turned and raised her tumbler, and Diane and I followed suit.

"Cheers," she said. "To a new adventure. To Sam, my love. And to us."

Our plastic tumblers met.

I heard a truck that sounded familiar and wondered why it was driving by at this late hour. It slowed, pulled to a stop just off the road, and idled. It was the one-eyed bandit. I turned off the light so Brody couldn't see inside, and I hid to the side of the window in my nightclothes. He surely knew I was home, but after a minute I watched him pull away and then predictably come circling back, headed toward his home. I was never going to admit I'd seen him here. But why was he here when most everyone was asleep?

When my phone rang close to midnight, I panicked, certain it was Brody, but Abby's name showed on the screen. She was too levelheaded to wake a friend at this hour unless she had an emergency. Adrenaline flowed and then dissipated as she explained her need for extra hands at a wedding the next evening. Her helper was in the emergency room with a broken ankle.

Assisting Abby at an outdoor ranch wedding sounded fun. We would meet as soon as she closed the diner, to arrive at the Anderson Ranch by half past three. They were expecting three hundred guests. Our job would be to serve and clear a spectacular dinner. Others would work the kitchen to create a rustic menu featuring outdoor barbecue.

27

WEDDING

Swags of sunflowers embraced wooden fence posts lining both sides of the long, straight drive. Signs directed guests to a parking pasture, the pathway to the ceremony location, reception tents, and restrooms. Abby parked behind a barn, in an area designated just for us. We wound our way around the back, past a lineup of roasting meats.

"Melissa, this is Amber."

A woman tending to rows of salad plates took a moment to gently touch my shoulder and say "Nice to meet you, Amber." Then she gently touched Abby and said "Thank you for coming through."

Melissa gathered us together with others. "You'll work as a pair. Two tables per pair. That's twenty guests. We start with shrimp. Salads are next. Main course: steaks. We need a rundown of meat doneness preferences. You'll collect those when you pick up the empty first courses. Leave a marker at each setting to make delivery easier when the main course is set out."

After completing prep work, we gathered near the ranch house to glimpse the wedding ceremony. Seven attendants each.

Western dress. Boots for the men and women, with the women in calf-length white dresses embellished with rich blue lace. At each of the outer ends of attendants stood a magnificent mare of good stature, also dressed in wedding attire: a decorative halter with silver-and-turquoise medallions across her muzzle and along the reins. Each mare had a handler dressed in fancy black-and-silver western wear. A familiar figure stood as the handler on the groom's side—Brody. A woman in dressy black western wear bookended the wedding party on the bride's side. They had walked the mares along either edge of the rows of guests attending the blessed ceremony. In synchrony, they had taken their places, facing family and friends. In synchrony again, the mares had stomped front hooves on the ground and nodded their heads when time came for the bride to slide effortlessly down the aisle on the arm of a man I presumed was her father. The ceremony under the arch of sunflowers was short. When the newlyweds walked back through the aisle, the last to follow were the mares, side by side. I hadn't noticed how wide the aisle was until I saw the two hoofed messengers of love being led together, like chaperones of Cupid. At the completion of the vows, Brody and the other handler had added blankets of blue lace, adorned with sunflowers and vibrant cornflowers, across the horses' backsides. Neither mare objected. It had been beautiful, but now, it was time to work.

The bars in the oversize tent bustled with thirsty excitement and boisterous neighborly greetings. Champagne made the rounds. I was part of the mingling hors d'oeuvres crew, passing through the tent in any manner I pleased, seeking takers.

"Nice to see you putting your weekend hours to good work, Phillips." I had been so intent on successful platter assignment, I had barely looked around. That hadn't stopped Fletcher from seeing me.

"Fletch, you said you'd be here. Nice to see you."

"Like I told you, I've known both families forever. It's like watching my own kids get married." Fletcher lifted the last two sausages and a napkin, and I turned to refill my platter.

"I bet that dress cost $100K," said one of the other servers. "I'm not sure those are rhinestones. I overheard someone say they're real diamonds."

"Who would do that?" I asked. "For a one-day wear?"

"Some down-to-earth people are also filthy rich. Knowing the little I know about Yvette, I'd say they're diamonds. She's always had high-end taste. And her family and new husband wouldn't object."

I made a mental note to take a closer look. At the moment, she was receiving guests rather than enjoying food and drink. In the course of the evening, however, I suspected I could wander over.

Melissa gave us a two-platter warning before guests were to be gently directed to dining tables under the tent. As I made my way through the conversations two more times, I noticed almost all men wore dress jeans. The same deep-blue, well-creased jeans that Fletcher favored. All shirts were button-down. Ties were skinny. Some ladies also wore high-end denim: vests, skirts, or shirts. Fancy buttons and embroidery on shoulders, backs, sleeves, and fronts, along with turquoise or rhinestones, were popular options. Lipstick seemed important. Most was deep and luscious. A few, though, selected summery pastel pink and glistening white to light their smiles. Perfume was every-where. If I had thought too long about it, I would have felt dumpy in my white blouse and black skirt, but I didn't. Instead, I felt invisible, which was fine.

"He doesn't look too bad, considering," I overheard one man say to others. They looked extremely comfortable sharing cocktails.

"No, but he said he's had fevers on and off for weeks now."

"They don't call it undulant fever for nothing. It comes and goes."

My offer of crab cakes was met with cheers, and they requested an immediate return trip. I wondered about the conversation as I wove my way to the cook tent.

When I passed my final platter, lined this time with meatballs and toothpicks, I found many takers. The conversation in the happy men's group had shifted to investments, but I overheard another group speaking of Brody. To the group's thinking, he had a heap of trouble.

Through the passing and clearing of three courses, including plenty of beef cooked rare, I heard snippets of conversations that included Brody's name. In fact, he seemed as much the talk of the night as the main event. What wasn't clear was exactly why. Brody sat at the wedding party table. He and the others sat in the same relative positions they had occupied during the ceremony, putting him at the far end. He looked bored. Had he been invited only to handle the mare—a necessary hire, not an inner-circle invitee? I assumed the mares had been returned to their stables or pastures but expected they might show again to carry the newlyweds away—unless, of course, they spun off the ranch via helicopter.

The cake—five tiers and glorious—had been assigned its own table near the wedding party. Sunflowers encircled the base, along with several vases of sunflowers in water. Additional golden blooms adorned the cake itself, spiraling around like a golden staircase. Deep-blue cornflowers spiraled alongside. At Melissa's signal, it was time to highlight its golden beauty, so with customary song, the bride and groom performed the cake ritual. Then, it was our turn to share the gift of dessert and coffee as quickly as possible.

Abby set a tray of servings on a stand and made a beeline back to the kitchen. I circled the table, presenting two plates on each pass. Eight servings for ten places proved awkward. As I awaited Abby's return, I assured the cake-less couple they would not be left out. Also, as I waited, I overheard one of my cake-less pair say, "He figures it was the bison. The night of the break-in."

Abby eased a second tray of eight desserts atop the empty first tray. I secured two servings to start our second table while she brought pieces to my couple's empty places. The conversation was suddenly behind me.

Fifteen minutes later, we cleared tables of all but water and wineglasses. Then, as the party began its next act, Abby and I piled into her Teal Turtle, ready to celebrate our good work and head home.

"Long night," I said.

"It would have been a whole lot longer without you. Thanks for helping."

We compared pain levels in our lower backs, laughed, and shared opinions of the event.

"I never did ask about the diamonds," I said.

"Maybe Brody knows," said Abby. "You heard about him and his brucellosis, though, right?"

"I got bits and pieces all night, but never the straight story. What does this mean?"

"He's got it," said Abby. "I guess he's on meds. But it takes a while to get rid of it."

"People said he didn't look well. I didn't see much difference."

"Seems he's having fevers and aches," said Abby. "I don't know what else."

"Well, good news," I said, "he's not going to abort."

I wondered if his repeat drive-bys of my home had anything to do with this news.

28

———————

SLAUGHTER

BRODY'S CATTLE were headed for slaughter. Even the little one he had carefully bottle-fed. I might have once been a hardened city crime reporter, but this news hit like a rocket crashing a foot away. It wasn't fair. He might not have tested for another week, but having undulant fever himself, Brody had decided to be safe. For the sake of the industry, he had told others. Several cows were positive for brucellosis.

Every year, Fletcher headed to his sister's to avoid the herds of humans who deemed Independence Day weekend their best time to visit Yellowstone. This year, he had left town as soon after the wedding as possible. Of all the times I needed his feedback most, this was it.

Monday, I parked at the Old Faithful Inn and felt I was walking the streets of Philly, nearly rubbing shoulders with others. Once inside, I headed straight to the guest book, interested to see who was here. A self-described eight-year-old named Tommy Merton had signed his family in with what appeared to be his best cursive—Mother, Father, Gertie, Tommy, and Shane from Madison, Wisconsin. Hilary and Wendy Moss from Oak Ridge, Tennessee, also penned their names. Along with J.P., Lucas, Mother, and Father from Oakland, California; the Witzers from Brooklyn, New York; the Wilsons from Dallas, Texas; and Tanaya, Phineus, Tiana, and Pherson from Atlanta. All of them here, this sunny summer holiday weekend, were likely capturing photos of a lifetime, with the backdrop of mighty bison. Iconic symbols of our history and our land's history. And a national emblem. Every visitor likely would leave Yellowstone feeling transformed. All I could think, after perusing the book, was how utterly deceptive our government was, in the land of Old Faithful. In a few short months, some of those grand bison captured in photos, which would branch out to every state, every old territory, and across our country's borders, would remain in photos only, never again to breathe warm puffs of air into the wind. Never again to leave their hoofprints in spring mud. Never again to nuzzle another's familiar muzzle. In a few short months, many would be hazed, corralled, contained, or slaughtered. Families would be broken apart. It wouldn't matter. It was luck of the draw. And so typically human. They had only months left of their six-month reprieve before it was back to the game of chance as winter weather and instinct collided with the ranching association.

Yes, my journalistic mask had once hardened me to death and tragedy. I wore it to do my job. I understood how ranchers built calluses on their hearts. The ones that let them accept life and death so easily. The ones that let them say "This is how it is. When one's time comes, it comes." They had to do it, just as I had to do it. Losing Jake and Olive, and then Eva, had stripped that mask away. It had taught me to value life more strongly than ever. Animal life as well as human. I doubted eight-year-old Tommy Merton's heart was hardened like this. I bet he believed his bison would be protected forever. If only he could stand in front of the Park Service, his senator, his representative, the head of Yellowstone, the head of BLM, and the Montana governor, and raise his voice.

Then again, nothing would change. For decades, my Park Service—our Park Service—had been a serial killer. Nearly five thousand slaughtered since 1985—twenty years. I wanted to scream so everyone could hear. I wanted others to join me. To send their voices echoing through Yellowstone, their screams rippling across the Nebraskan plains, their cries crossing the mighty Mississippi, lifting above the Ozarks, Smokys, Blue Ridge, and Appalachians, reverberating across the landscape, into the hallowed halls of the US Capitol and White House. If only. If only. Every visitor to Yellowstone, our iconic Yellowstone, our first national park, historic in its origin, was being deceived. Other states had included wildlife in the public domain. They had expanded the original definition beyond land. But here, bison were not public domain. In fact, through trickery, bison weren't even wildlife. In Montana, they called them livestock. And livestock were the same as deadstock. It was a strong association indeed.

I stepped aside so another family could sign in. With two packages of licorice—one black and one red—I sat at a wooden table and watched the chaotic movement of humans crossing outside. I tasted the sweet pleasure and healing medicine of anise. The Tommy Mertons of the world deserved better. I had to do something.

I pulled into Shelly's drive as excited as a glowing firefly to meet Shelly's first paying ranch visitors and celebrate the holiday. Little did I know, Ted Steele would be here. Shelly had never let on. It was a wonder we didn't scare off the other guests when Shelly, Ted, Diane, and I hollered out our greetings and hooted with excitement. Ted had wanted to be the very first paying guest. He looked well.

Three other guests—all women—had come as a pair and

solo. Two from the East Coast, and one from the West—Hannah, Betsy, and Gwen. For each, it was a dream come true to have found the Nelsons' dude ranch. I looked forward to learning more and seeing how their next days unfolded.

"You know," said Shelly, once we settled around a long dining table she had set up out back, "this—sitting with others—is a big part of what life out here in a small town is all about. It's land. It's people. It's time passing peacefully."

She had our attention.

"Of course, it's also a lot of work. The land does all right by itself to a point, but cows need people, and there's always things to be done. But at times, it's living a bit slower and enjoying what's around. It's accepting that this landscape, which you three have come to see and paint, has undeniable power over all of us who decide to live here. And not a single one of us can change this. So, I hope you'll let yourselves slow down a bit to really enjoy what we have here. And I hope your creativity will be sparked beyond all bounds."

"Hear, hear," said Diane. We added our voices.

"Tell me," said Ted, addressing the other guests, "what do you usually paint? And what brought you here?"

Landscapes were a big part of their portfolios. Gwen also did quite a few seascapes and harbor depictions, being from the coastal West. Florals raised a steady call for Hannah. Each of the women had answered an inner curiosity when they signed up for Shelly's. They had to see Yellowstone. They had to sit in a larger, possibly overpowering landscape, with nothing more than their canvas and their paints. They wanted to test themselves. To see what they would do. How they would react. How they would create. How they would feel. Each seemed to know that this strong but gentle western landscape would reach forward a hand and lead them into a sort of magical personal growth. I was spellbound by their passion and their words.

Shelly's ranch was giving back, as Shelly and Sam had hoped it would.

———

I found Fletcher leaning back in his chair, as usual, the first day after the long weekend. He nodded to his freshly filled bowl of candies as soon as I walked in and dropped the front wheels of his chair to the ground, in unison with his feet.

"Phillips?"

It was good to hear his familiar greeting. Good to see his familiar wise, knowing face. Good to see fresh chocolates. But mostly, good to see sanity in the flesh.

"Next year, I'm following you out of here."

Fletcher laughed. "What did I miss? Other than another bison accident due to a stupid tourist maneuver."

"The visitors were either smarter, luckier, or quicker this year. No incidents to report."

"Improvement."

"The question is, Did you hear about Brody's cattle?" I said.

Fletcher appeared solemn. "I heard." He nodded slightly and then put his hands behind his head as he tipped his chair back once again.

"What will this mean?" I asked. "For the state. And all the others? And ... and for you. Your bulls are so close and were set to breed cows soon, right?"

"Don't worry about the bulls. They're tucked away. The routine is this: a brucellosis-accredited vet must have looked at Brody's cattle and done tests. They'll create a plan to ship them out safely. They'll trace back the lineage to ensure herds of origin aren't infected. Cattle will be slaughtered. Brody can get new stock."

So, it was cut and dried. Zero guesswork. You got a test. You slaughtered your stock. You moved on. I was thankful it was

Fletcher sharing this information. I didn't know why it mattered, but it did.

I finally got ahold of Dr. Emily Kahn, veterinarian for the state and the one in charge of brucellosis. She described the steps of checking and controlling incidents of infection exactly as Fletcher had. When Brody described the testing, he hadn't looked me in the eyes once. I wondered if it was the result of guilt and sense of failure, or if he was hiding something. Instinct said I needed the tests. I wanted to know what he was hiding.

Diane, Shelly, and I nearly knocked each other over as we converged in a group hug to celebrate the first successful weekend of guests at the Nelson dude ranch.

"You did it!" said Diane.

"I did, and I can't believe it." Shelly beamed.

"Congratulations, lady. I'm proud of you," I said. "But I never had a doubt."

"Oh, Amber. I had doubt enough for the three of us. But Sam was talking to me from up above and in my heart. He got me through. Like always."

"No one this weekend, right?"

"No, but I have four each on the next two weekends after."

"When are the round houses going up? I plan on helping," I said.

"Next month, most likely."

"I'll make the food for the work parties," said Diane. "Best incentive ever."

"The structures will be up in no time. Tell me, Amber, what are you working on these days?" asked Shelly.

"A problem." It escaped from my mouth before I could stop it. I immediately weighed the risk of explaining my brucellosis dead end up front and telling Shelly exactly why I wanted samples from the *Brucella* blood draws on Brody's cattle, or coming at it from a slightly sneaky angle and tying my desire for blood tests into a future phantom *TriState* issue. Diane was here, which meant news could travel. But I was staring at two of my closest new friends. How could I lie to them?

"Assure me you'll keep a secret," I said. Shelly and Diane looked first at me, then at each other. "It is particularly important none of this gets to the *Gazette*," I added, looking straight at Diane.

"I'll pinkie swear," said Diane. "Then I'll be good till the day I die."

Shelly attested to Diane's surprising secret-keeping ability, when needed, then said, "Just like when we were kids. I want in."

I started slowly. "I want to see the tests from Brody's cows. You know, for *Brucella*. I guess it's a reporter thing—ever curious —or maybe a bit more. This is all new to me, and I want specifics. I hear not all *Brucella* is the same."

"All does the same thing," said Diane.

"What's the problem?" said Shelly.

"The veterinarian won't share a thing. I'm trying to figure a way around this. As a reporter, I gained all sorts of access, as long as I didn't disclose personal information or a source without permission. This time, I was shut down."

"You've come to the right place," said Diane.

"I know everyone over there," said Shelly. "We never had any brucellosis here, but Sam and I worked with them on vaccines. Maybe I can find a weak link. A way to get you what you need."

"Whatever you can do would be helpful."

"Other than work, how are you doing? I mean, without Eva."

"I'm still in the disbelief stage. It hasn't gotten much easier. And you?" I asked.

"I rock back and forth between pain, disbelief, and anger. I guess that's grieving. Diane has been my savior, and her shirts have soaked up many tears. Day by day, they say."

"Some days are better than others," said Diane. "But we always have smiles, talking of Sam. We'll get through it, Shell Belle. Love never fails."

Shelly reached for both of our hands, closed her eyes, and said, "I love you both. And I love you, too, Sam. I'll be all right. You'll see. I know you're watching over me." We tightened our grips, as though to seal the words into being.

Less than a day later, Shelly had news.

"The tests on Brody's cattle were card tests," she said. "They were the rapid tests, but not the most specific tests. They show if cattle have developed antibodies to *Brucella*, meaning they have been exposed. They don't show the actual bacterium. They still have some of Brody's cards, but they might not get you what you want."

"They wouldn't be the blood, exactly?"

"No, but here's a direct number for Elise. She works the lab."

I tucked the paper in my pocket, interested that the state veterinarian and Shelly's contact were both female.

"Are there many women in ranching?" I asked.

"Usually, it takes the whole family to run a ranch, so yes. As you've likely seen, it's as much a lifestyle as a profession. And it's a good one in an awful lot of ways. Every person has to be mighty independent, able to stand on their own but also work as part of a team. Women might not do all the same things as the men, although some do, but no matter what anyone does, it is equally valuable to the operation. All pieces must fit together. If there's one noticeable difference being a woman rancher, I'd say its women don't usually get the same representation or leadership opportunities in the associations, but that's the norm with most industries."

"I didn't anticipate the power of the ranching associations."

"They're powerful, all right. And mighty tight," said Shelly. "Strength in numbers, with a lot to gain from unification around political agendas and a lot to lose without it."

"Mel said I wouldn't find a rancher around who wouldn't want to keep the bison in the park or gone altogether. But he also said each was an ardent conservationist and believed it was his or her responsibility in the service of God or another power to leave these grazing lands better off than how they found them."

"Mel's absolutely right. Except ..."

"Except what?"

"Oh, there are a few bad apples. A few differing opinions. As with any association."

I recalled my conversation with Ted and decided to risk it. "I didn't intend to bring this up today, but we seem to have gotten to a particular conversation of its own accord."

Shelly frowned.

"Sam was a man of honor," I started. "I heard another rancher was intending to be far less honorable. Even willing to lie about a bison break. I heard you and Sam received some threats. Is this true?"

Shelly looked like she had seen a ghost. I should have kept quiet.

A few moments later, she surprised me. "I suppose it would be best for someone else to know. In case something happens to me." Fear flushed any regret from my body.

"Sam was approached by a trio of ranchers who offered

money. A lot of it. For Sam to let a bison on site so it could ruin a few things."

I listened intently.

"We couldn't tell a soul. It would have put us in danger. Like I said, that association is as strong and relentless as quicksand if you fight it." Shelly shifted in her seat. "Sam refused. Like you said, he was a man of honor, and I fully supported him. But our refusal put us on the outside of a mighty powerful group. One that had had our backs all along, then suddenly didn't. Like I said, there are always bad apples, and they can get mighty selfish about meeting their own needs. They can also be mighty persuasive. We let it slide, hoping the trouble would disappear. But we got a note in our mailbox. It had a photograph, and it said, 'This is what your ranch is going to look like if you don't help us.' It had a photo of a pile of sticks." Shelly inhaled deeply. "Sam tore it up." I put my hand on her shoulder. "When Ted arrived, people knew we were going through with Sam's idea of setting up a dude ranch. That's when we started getting different threats. And hearing strange noises outside on a few nights. Deep down, we knew it was someone in the business who didn't want us in it. We figured out who it was, most likely, but not for certain. Sam wanted to catch him red handed. So, he took that old ATV out, and that's the night I lost him. Honestly, Amber, I was afraid someone might have tried to shoot him. All these people can be nice as all get-out. But they can also be deathly nasty. Remember this."

"Who was it?"

"I can't say."

"You should tell someone. What if ..."

Shelly shook her head. I opened my arms, and Shelly, normally strong as a rock, folded into them like a soft sack of sugar. Sweet, sweet Shell Belle. I was glad I'd come for a visit, and glad I had given her the opening to finally let out her pain and fear. Somehow, we had to make things right.

29
____

MICROBES

UNWILLING TO ASSERT anything more than microwave power to squelch the hunger of having skipped lunch on my eleven-hour workday, I reached for a box of frozen mac and cheese. A second box slammed to the ground, whacking my big toe before sliding like a whirligig across the floor. Then, the hermetically sealed denim slithered down beside it, also hitting me on its descent. I had long ago considered the denim either too valuable or too vulnerable to be left in the garage freezer. I had felt safe commingling it with my frozen food options, in its double-bagged condition. But how many times, over one month alone, had I cursed this sealed denim as I had worked around it to fish out other items? At least five, I was certain. For a moment, I considered heating two boxes for a double-size dinner. Instead, I shoved the second box toward the back of the freezer, moved a package of frozen beans from the freezer door compartment, and set the bagged denim in its place, out of the way.

"This," I said, "is your new residence. Get in there, stay in there, and leave me alone." As I reasoned with the denim, something caught my eye.

Moisture had crystalized on the clear plastic in brownish feathery strands. Similar strands spread faintly across the denim, and smaller pieces of these same strands lay frozen and captured within ice crystals. The color wasn't just any sort of brown. It was a distinctly deep, dark orange brown. I knew this color. This shape. The feathery configuration of several strands. My memory for visual details never failed. "*Calothrix* and *Oscillatoria*," I whispered, recalling some of Nate's strange minutia. Bacteria! Thinking back to the day I picked up the jeans, I realized I had not yet been introduced to bacteria, or archaea, for that matter. I riffled through my mental notes of Nate's research. Each pond had a different population of microbes. Like a fingerprint. I was staring at a clue. While reluctant to share the story of my fetus retrieval, I had to trust Nate. He might lead me to a particular lake, hot spring, or creek having ties to the owner of torn jeans. I emailed him right after dinner.

The following morning, I awakened to disappointing news. Nate was out of town for the week. Luckily, Simone was back from a summer getaway!

"Darling!" she said in her self-assured voice. "It's good to see you survived the horrible, or perhaps I should say horribly long, July weekend. It was a rude awakening, I am sure."

"Simone! How was vacation?"

"Fabulous! My parents are well and feisty. They wore me out, like always. It's good to be back here."

We hugged.

"So, water," she said. "I read your notes and stopped in on Nate after you two met. I have Jordan's equipment shots, and some fabulous interview pics of Nate. They'll definitely work. I know Fletcher wants to put our water in context with the world: supply, population, climate impacts, local weather phenomena, et cetera. So, the two photographers we assigned have gotten some good things back to me. Oh, and I sent someone out with your irrigation guy. Looking to get the ranching and agricultural end of things covered. I'm sure those will be good. Basically, we're in great shape. As usual!"

This was what made Simone the awesome art director that she was. Her eye, creativity, organization, and understanding of how pieces fit together was uncommon. She had unusual zest for making each issue the best possible and most powerful display, recognizing that powerful could be subtle as well as bold. I was entrenched in photos and the joy of working with Simone, until mention of Nate caused the denim to leap into my thoughts. When Simone excused herself for a coffee refill, I began an essential research mission: Would bacteria remain viable on clothing if it was frozen? I knew Nate could give an accurate answer in a second, but Nate was out of town, and I was impatient. Much to my relief, the answer was a resounding yes.

"I'll give you my cover thoughts in a moment," said Simone. She set a fresh cup of coffee in front of me and coddled her own.

"But first, you're going to tell me if you are feeling quite at home out here. From all my moving, I believe six months is a magic marker, and you are almost there."

"As a matter of fact, yes. Work is better than expected, and I had high expectations. I'm meeting more people, calling more people friends. Oh, and I helped Shelly with her dude-ranch launch. We've shared some special time together—a sort of prolonged grieving party, or support group, what with her losing Sam and my losing Eva, and before that Jake and Olive. It's been oddly comforting. We thrive on human commonalities, don't we?"

"Yes, we do. I'm sorry but also happy for the shared support," she said.

"But we have a pin sticking into the heart of town these days."

"What on earth do you mean?"

"Brody and some of his cattle tested positive for brucellosis. It happened during your vacation."

"Oh, my. This is a big one."

"The facts are fuzzy. Both Fletcher and I have questions, but we might not be working the same story or untangling the same loose ends. I'll keep you posted."

"The mystery is enticing."

Nate was jet lagged but standing, having made the trip to see family outside of London. I gave him credit for swinging into work so soon off the plane.

"What have we here?" He gazed at the small cooler in my hand.

"You had best sit," I said. "The backstory is highly abnormal, and it will take a few minutes to share."

At his desk, I gave details of my near miss with lightning and showed him the photo of the denim hanging from the branch over the dead pile.

"Ghastly," he said. "What happened?"

"I don't know. But I suspect this denim carries a secret."

"You are telling me this for a reason, but I can't figure what it is."

I opened the cooler.

"Oh, I see," he said. "Is this ... the denim? Yes, of course it is. And these look suspiciously like ... well, matted bacteria, my goodness. What fun. All feathery. Albeit dried. Tell me more."

"You would know better than I, which is precisely why I am here."

"How long did you say you have been hiding this little goody in the freezer?"

"Three months."

"Viability should be intact."

"I was hoping you could match it to your database and direct me to a water source as a way of finding more information."

"Sounds most intriguing. You know, however, if I am the one responsible and this is from my blue jeans, I am not going to tell you the truth, right?" Nate laughed, and I shook my head.

I trusted Nate's assurances that our meeting, and any findings, would remain confidential. He wasn't tied into cattle ranchers or associations. To Nate, the only roundup in town was microscopic. I handed him the cooler and said, "You must wear gloves and a face mask. Just in case." I disclosed Max's brucellosis find. Nate understood.

"Give me a couple of days," he said. "We should have a winner by then."

Two days later, Nate's text came through: "Call me."

I dialed his number immediately.

"You aren't going to like my news," he said. "I don't have a match. I believe we have something new."

"New?"

"Not in my database. Maybe from a spot I have not sampled yet."

"Seriously?"

"Yes. I am not the killer hiding my identity. Promise."

My thoughts dashed to the Schine brothers, whom I had seen in light-colored, work-worn jeans and who might have been willing to hunt out of season while they were here.

"What is the possibility this is from Texas?" I asked.

"You mean washed onto the jeans in Texas and dropped in Montana intact? Most unlikely. I did see a couple of hairs on the denim, if it helps. Anyone you know have a dog or a cat? I don't think they look like elk hairs, but you're best asking a mammal expert for proper identification."

Nate's suggestion had me considering sending the swatch to Max in Philadelphia, but lots of people had dogs, cats, and guinea pigs even, and I knew fur didn't stay put. The thought was ridiculous.

Even more ridiculous was finding Fletcher, once again, scouring the hills of Irv and Izzy's pastures. He hadn't parked his truck near the house. This time, he was driving it out back. He stopped a few times to get out and look at something.

"What are you doing?" I shouted.

"Looking for cattle, like I told you."

"Don't drive into a levee."

Fletcher jerked his head around and pointed his gaze directly at me.

"Glad you are finally fitting in out here. It's proper you should know about these things."

His voice rang across the grasses as he slid back into the driver's seat.

30

DEVELOPMENT

News was bouncing off the mountain. The Schines' plan had gone public, finally filed for official review. Townspeople were talking and taking sides. Old-timers looking to keep the valley full of grass and sedge were bristling. To most, it was a major sell-out of land and old times to a brand-new world of hedonistic tourists who would like the views well enough but wouldn't appreciate what life here was all about. It would bring in jobs, but they would be new types of jobs, which few believed were needed. Oddly, ranchers were joining voices with bison lovers as land loss, despite thwarting bison movement, held the power to bond.

I scoured the plans and was taken aback by a concise note in small font on the edge of the last page. It said "Water share" and was positioned on the side of Brody's property abutting the church site and my home. Others must not have seen it, for surely, they would have talked of it. Fletcher and Irv would be the town's new worst enemies, being involved as they clearly seemed to be. My mind flipped through the aerial photos. And the water rights documents. It had to be related to Fletch's church pond. Quite a convenient day for Fletcher to be out of town, I thought. I called Bennett Merchante as I steered Sebastian toward his office. He had maps and permits waiting.

"What do you know of this?" I asked.

"What I know," he said, "is it is going to be a major change, but it is all legal, as proposed."

"Walk me through it," I said. "Every detail."

"These two property owners will be working together." Bennett pointed to Fletcher's church land and Brody's ranchland. The church's twenty-acre lake sparkled like a giant diamond on the satellite images. And Fletcher's church had first rights for a variety of uses, including irrigation, household, and domestic use. As Bennett reconfirmed, the clock was ticking for both the church and Irv and Izzy to put their rights into use or lose them altogether. I asked why it mattered if a western church kept an old water right.

Bennett answered with details of the plan: "They are expanding the church's reach to cover Brody's property through a water lease. All legal. Most of Brody's hot tubs are dependent upon this. In addition, the Schines will be digging wells, which have clearance in terms of acceptable impact on the underground water supply."

Fletcher was not only behind the development but one of its masterminds. I pushed aside the sting of betrayal as best I could to ask how the lease could help Fletcher and the church with their bulls. Hot tubs would be useless to them.

"True," said Bennett, "but Fletcher negotiated access to good hay land on Brody's ranch in exchange for the water lease."

The nail in the coffin, I thought, as Bennett pointed out the future hay land location smack in the middle of the valley. No bison would ever get through again. I was silently mulling over the disturbing thought when Bennett said, "As I told you, all this land has a major system of pumps, swales, and levees connected throughout, as well as a series of strong wells up the hills. In a sense, it's making the old Circle C whole again.

Putting water back to use on Irv and Izzy's and spreading the wealth to this new operation through a lease. Like I said, they are some of the oldest, most generous rights around."

"Wait. I'm on the old Circle C?"

"You didn't know? It used to include all the land from end to end on Irv and Izzy's, the church, and part of the Ross Ranch along the northeast side. I would have expected Fletcher to tell you."

"You know Fletcher. A rather good poker player." Fletcher, of course, hadn't been checking Irv and Izzy's for cattle. He had been checking the old water system. This opened a whole new can of worms.

"Any death threats, now that the plans are out?"

Brody smirked. "I considered staying shut in for a few months, but this is more interesting." He made room for me in his booth at Abby's.

"What made you do it? Decide to sell? And to those two goons?"

"Goons? What do you mean? Fletcher's part of it too." Didn't I know it. He was my next conversation. "It's been a long time coming," he said. "Bison. Brucellosis. Time to move on. I met the Schines a couple of years ago, and we went from there."

"You've known them that long?"

"Of course."

"Why did they choose Morris? And your land?"

"They said it was all about location, but you're the reporter here. I'm only the messenger of doom."

After staring Brody eye to eye, considering his remarks, I finally said, "How are your cattle?"

"What cattle?" He snickered. "They're as good as dead. I'm moving them next week."

"How's your ..." I wasn't sure how to phrase my next question.

"My what?"

"How are you feeling? Getting any better?"

"You mean the bison disease?"

I nodded.

"It comes and goes. Right now, I'm doing okay. Doc says it could keep on for a bit. Hopefully, I'll sell out, feel better, and move on."

I contemplated Morris without Brody. For as much as he kept to himself, he was an oddly noticeable part of our town, and not because he had suited me. Maybe everyone was. Maybe even I was now.

"What will you do?"

"Get as far from here as possible, what with everyone hating me for selling out."

"You will be missed. Might be some of them are jealous."

"True. Money does that to people, but what do you care about it all?"

What I had wanted to say was "Despite not wanting to pursue a relationship, I continue fighting my attraction to you." Instead, I said, "Me? I've been a naturally curious person for as long as I can remember."

Brody laughed.

"It used to drive my parents nuts, or so they said. Deep down, they saw I'd be able to stand on my own two feet."

"You certainly do that. And quite well. It's time for me to do the same. Make my own decisions and get out from the past. I'm giving myself a couple of months after the sale to do whatever I want. After that, I'll settle somewhere and get started on living again."

"Won't you miss it?"

Brody considered my question. "I missed not having family when I needed one most. I know I would have turned out different and seen life differently. I can't change the past. Ranching was in my blood, but without my family, it never felt right. Maybe, even with family, it wasn't what I was put on the earth to do. There's something else waiting for me. I'll find it once I'm free and clear of all this. I've carried an unearned burden long enough."

"I hope it goes well for you," I said.

Brody raised his coffee cup. I gave a gentle touch to his shoulder and left.

A single research report sent a light bulb flicking in my brain, like Kendra Sloane's feisty fluorescent. It quickly grew into a floodlight, and soon I felt like a deer frozen in its glaring luminescence. All I had wanted was clarity on Brody's condition—in particular, how much longer it might last. Instead, I learned brucellosis could occasionally be spread among humans ... by semen. A study noted two particular cases and reported the outward signs of infection in human males were noticeable enlargement and uneven or unusual shape of certain specifically male organs, i.e., enlarged scrotum, and testes often uneven in size. I recalled Brody's physique from The Night. The size, I knew now, was beyond the scope of simple genetics. I recalled seeing him pop a couple of pills into his mouth that fateful night before we left the Eagle Feather. Another moment came screaming back as well. It was the moment in my bed when he had seemed momentarily and inexplicably in pain. Not at all normal for what we were doing. These telltale symptoms dashed from my laptop and created fear that nearly stopped my breathing. Brody must have been infected before The Night. Most shocking was the realization that I could contract brucellosis as a result of The Night's activity.

Holy bastard, prepare to die! I thought, uncertain whether I was sending this message to Brody or to any *Brucella abortus* I might be harboring within my own body.

I phoned Dr. Hill in Philly to say I had felt tired lately. But brucellosis? I had to check.

Then, I phoned Dr. Emily Kahn, who was surely tired of hearing from me but was kind enough to answer my call. Despite my persistence, my request for a sample of Brody's cattle blood received the same answer: it was not available. With Brody's cattle being readied for shipment, I had only one other option. I huddled with Abby outside the diner, where we wouldn't be seen or heard.

***

"Remember," I said, "keep the mask over your mouth and nose, gloves on, and eye covering in place."

"Not to worry. I've done this before."

Even under her mask, I saw Shelly smile.

"You just keep all the tubes ready," she said. "I'll hand you one, and you give me the next. Clockwork."

Shelly and I slid among Brody's cows.

"We're getting about a dozen, right?" Before I answered, Shelly responded to her own question. "Might as well, since we're here."

As we prepared to collect the first sample of blood, my phone rang. Abby's voice sounded rushed. "Abort! I repeat, abort!"

"Very funny."

"I mean it. Brody's on his way home!"

"Schiste!"

Within minutes, Shelly and I folded up our traveling workspace, raced through the field, tossed our supplies in her truck, and departed. I ducked when we saw Brody coming up the road. Shelly sped past.

"We have to try again tomorrow. It's the last chance we'll have. I'm calling Diane," I said.

Next morning, with Abby presumably on lookout and Brody sitting across from Diane at a front booth at the diner, Shelly and I pulled into Brody's ranch.

"How does it look?" I asked, before we unloaded.

Abby's report came through my phone loud and clear. "Diane's a professional. She's talking to him like a mother, wanting to make sure he's thought it through and is making the best decision for himself, and not only for the Schines. I expect she'll bring up a few memories of his family, to keep him talking, and then go into some of her own family memories. She's got it covered for at least an hour. Of course, she's likely to want a couple of coffees. And might pull a friend or two over to refresh the conversation. I could join them too."

"We're good to go," I said to Shelly.

We once again blended into Brody's cows. Sure enough, Shelly knew exactly where to jab the needle and how to keep each lady calm.

***

"Okay, lady, let's do this. I'll start the conversation," said Shelly, "and you jump in when the time is right."

I followed Shelly, who was carrying our cooler, as we marched through antiseptic hallways to meet Elise in her lab. One way or another, we were getting Brody's cow blood tested. I needed results.

The next second, I nervously assessed what I was in the middle of doing. I had no right to be checking Brody's cows. We had illegally procured the samples. If word got out, I would be fired and likely sentenced to jail time. Worst of all, I had pulled Shelly into it. Brucellosis was a demon.

"Shelly ..." I tugged her arm, ready to turn around. A woman marched toward us.

"Elise," said Shelly, with her tone of voice deepening in a drawn-out second syllable, as though, at last, she was greeting a long-lost cousin.

"Shelly, you are a sight for sore eyes. And you must be Amber, the one doing the story."

I glanced at Shelly, certain we had not yet had enough chitchat to warm up Elise. As we casually waltzed into a sparsely furnished office, Shelly gave a rundown of all she had been going through since Sam's passing, including the early success of the ranch; continued conversations with Ted Steele, the unfortunate tourist caught up in the mess; and helping me with my TriState Art issue. It was through this last endeavor that Shelly had supposedly learned I was considering a feature on brucellosis and needed help. Here we were at Elise's doorstep, seeking information: Could she determine a particular strain of *Brucella*, and how many strains were there, by the way? "Amber is an excellent journalist," said Shelly. "Details are her specialty. She used to cover crimes."

Shelly had adeptly reeled Elise into our corner. Now, it was my turn. Since this was for research purposes rather than herd management, it appeared unnecessary to Elise to record all usual data on each specimen source. Though silent, I expected my internal sigh of relief might somehow sneak out and expose my intentions as fraudulent. Luckily, it didn't. Elise, as a certified immunologist, was willing to conduct the necessary tests and show me how testing and assessments of this sort were done. She did, of course, have to collect a fee. The tests were not routine and came with a hefty price tag. So far, we had escaped jail.

Shelly stuck around while Elise outlined the procedure, and then left us to begin the investigation. Standing side by side with Elise and wearing the protective gear required to handle

Brucella, I realized how vulnerable I must have been during my encounters with the dead pile and now Brody's cows. And I wasn't even the one handling the samples this time. Max's warnings of aerosolization flew to mind.

Elise's techniques looked as professional as the equipment looked qualified and specialized to perform the work. Through a process called PCR, we would learn more of the *Brucella*'s DNA and RNA, and, therefore, its strain. Elise would compare results with a genetic databank. I would await her call with results. As expected, my quest for information became so strong, I wished I was writing the article Shelly and I had said I was. Someday, ranching would, indeed, be a fabulous fit for the *TriState*.

31

ELK

I took a seat in Fletcher's office with a low level of tolerance sitting beside me.

"Have you ever killed a bison?" I asked. I fastened my eyes on his and lowered the candy dish back to his desk, declining a selection.

"I'm not proud of it."

"And now your church is going to hem them in."

"First things first," he said. "I was young when I shot it. Well, relatively young. We see things differently at different stages of life. Like I said, I'm not proud of it. And I'm embarrassed to admit, at the time, I was excited by my strike. But I wouldn't do it again."

"You said development and land fragmentation would be bad for the town and bad for the bison. Why are you and the church doing this? Cornering the bison for good? Likely forcing them to starve to death in winters with high snowpack. Don't you care?"

Instead of leaning his chair back, Fletcher sat straight up. "Phillips," he began, "life can throw you curveballs. It can have a lot of moving parts. I want you to be patient with your judgment. You know facts don't always surface at once."

"I've seen the plans. I've spoken with Bennett. It looks clear to me."

"Yes," he said. "Exactly."

I stared at him, wondering how someone I had trusted could be so deceitful. Brody had been right about Fletcher all along. And I had been wrong. I took my leave, hardly saying goodbye.

To my chagrin, the next issue of the *Western TriState* was slated for hunting and fishing. I had been dreading it for months, knowing it would put me face to face with my worst conflict: the voluntary killing of animals. The alternative was to resign. Later, I sat again with Fletcher.

"I could interview Brody, to discuss his trophy wall," I said snidely. Fletcher wasn't amused.

"Or you could get serious about this issue and start with Mel for all the contacts you need. Put someone on the state wildlife departments for regulations and management, hunting associations, and get someone else on some old-timers, who'll provide history of fishing and hunting here. Chin Zellers will be one of the best old-timers, I suspect."

"Taxidermists?" The word rolled off my tongue with little thought.

"Why not?" he said. "Make a user's-guide section. But the best way for you to get through this, Phillips, is to put aside your 'camera' bias, as you call it, and turn over the rocks for what really brings people here for these outdoor experiences. This is what we want to share. Quietude. Peace. Nature. The marvel of life. It's not all about death."

"Most people who hunt and fish," said Mel, "consider themselves stalwart conservationists. Safekeepers of our land and natural resources. I told you this once. Their hunting dollars go into the wildlife coffers, and most of them keenly appreciate this natural world of ours. Ranchers, too, are unheralded trustees and stewards. I feel a profound kinship with many of them, even if we don't agree on bison. It's why I am hell bent on resolving this damned dilemma, for the good of everyone and everything." Mel's words told me TriState Hunting would be more complex than I had expected.

"Look around you," said Mel. "Look at this wilderness. This expanse. This raw land. How can you beat this? You spend a day out here, and you become part of it. Totally entrenched in its beauty and the challenge of testing your skill. You follow the game, big and small. And you aren't going to get any bigger than what's here: bighorn sheep, antelope, bear, bison, and elk. Elk go shedding their antlers every year and grow 'em back bigger the next. Some of them reach four feet across. Put *that* over your mantel. But remember, the trophy is not just an animal head. It's the memory of the hunt, of time spent outdoors. Of a special bond with nature. And often a bond with friends and family. Now, that's special.

"There are two sides, minimum, to most stories. In this case, protecting cattle is one side. Protecting a lifestyle is another. Diversifying business is a third. And helping governments maintain all this open land is another. Out here, they're tied as tightly as a rope can be tied.

"You know about the Elk Refuge?" Mel asked.

"West side of the park? Near Jackson?"

"That's the one. Over ten thousand elk go there. Around here, we have even more. Down in Wyoming, outdoor feeding stations help them through the winter. And all these elk wander in and out of cattle grazing areas carte blanche. Not as large a percentage of elk is infected as bison, but when you gather them at feed stations, let them pass through cow country, where some will sneak into cattle feeding areas, you're asking for trouble. But elk equal money. Selling hunting trips is lucrative business for ranchers. Diversifying their business has helped some stay in business. And as much as ranchers fear bison, they see certain similar benefits to letting them onto their property, in grass-lands distant from their cattle, and with some even raising them for the purpose of selling lean, grass-fed bison meat, or offering a chance to hunt them. We're talking $6,000 a hunted bison and $2,500 a hunted elk. Not bad. I'll give you a list of hunting outfits. You can talk with them for yourself. Learn about tourism dollars. Return on investment in the land. Return on the high costs of labor to run a ranch.

"Did you know over fifty-five percent of land in Wyoming, thirty-eight percent in Montana, and seventy percent in Idaho is government owned in one way or another? Look around. You'll see national park land, national forest land, wildlife refuges, state parks, et cetera. Where's the revenue in that? And why do I raise the question?"

"You tell me," I said.

"It's that tight knot, tying it all together. Hunting packages help sustain ranchers. Ranchers help sustain the government when they pay for government land leases, and government keeps wide-open space nice and open. And around and around it goes. Everyone likes wide-open space. Ranchers depend on it. For the well-being of their herd, and I'd say for their mental well-being too. It all boils down to keeping these magnificent grasslands forever ranchlands. Maintaining tradition and life-style. Even though this tradition is less than two hundred years young."

Following this thorough exploration, I eased into the other reason for meeting Mel—why he was looking for Fletcher at Irv and Izzy's.

Mel studied my face. "At Irv's?"

"Yes. About a month ago."

"I heard Fletcher was headed over. Maybe to see you. I needed him for something.

Don't remember what anymore. Nothing much, I guess."

"Why was Fletcher there?" I asked.

"Who knows. He does all sorts of things I never understand. Maybe ask him again."

An opaque covering had slid between Mel's transparency and me.

As I drafted my notes into a piece to introduce the hunting and fishing issue, I paused. Could I change it? Could I change people's thinking? Not about hunting. About our national bison. I stared out my windows. It would require spreading information, disseminating facts. This was easy. Changing people's thinking was likely impossible.

Following Mel's leads, I assigned interviews with two hunting outfits, and I took on an interview with a third—Miranda Lake in Wyoming, which boasted the best ten-pointers in the areas. Bo Padillo removed his hat and shook my hand firmly to welcome me to Miranda Lake. He and his wife, Nell, were oddball newcomers, barely fifteen years into the ranching and hunting business, but now that they were in it, they wouldn't ever leave.

"Most people come in for a long weekend or a short week. Usually, they come as pairs or foursomes. Occasionally, we book a bigger group, extended family members and such. Likely, you get an elk but no promises. Whatever smaller game you want to bag we throw in for free. I mean, they don't cost us anything. So, gratis on the small ones."

"Sounds appealing," I said.

"People like freebies."

"Does everyone lodge here?" I asked.

"Yes. I'll show you our four cabins in a bit.

"If you come from out of state to hunt in Wyoming, by law you need a guide," said Bo. "To my thinking, this is the smartest law on the books. It works from a state employment and commerce standpoint, but more important than anything else, it is a testament to protecting human safety and lives. Out here, as you know, we are talking millions of unfamiliar acres, and people coming in might not be the savviest when it comes to using map and compass or noticing landmarks. GPS isn't always reliable. Neither is weather, except for the fact that it can sneak up on you in a big way and catch you in one swift swat like a grizzly. The last thing we want is to lose people to the elements, surroundings, or wildlife. Search and rescue isn't cheap, and it spooks other visitors. So, guides are required. In-staters don't need one. But out-of-staters, absolutely."

"Hunters need permits?" I asked.

"Permits and luck. You have to roll the dice in the elk lottery. If you don't get chosen this year, your odds of success increase next. So, keep rolling the dice. As a nonresident, your bag fee will cost you ten times as much as for residents. There's no guarantee you'll bag one, but you have permission to try. Next, you make sure your gun license is good back home. If it is, chances are it will be accepted here too. With these two permits in hand, you're ready to reach out to your preferred outfitter and plan your dates. Some outfitters offer access to their personal acreage only. Others know the Bureau of Land Management and national forest lands well and combine it with their own lands. Still others work the federal BLM lands only."

"Wait, you can guide people onto government lands to hunt?"

"Sure. Just like the song says, 'This land is made for you and me.' Unless an area specifically prohibits entry, or hunting, like the national park, these lands are available to everyone. You included. Didn't you know this?"

"Let's just say I didn't put it together quite like this." Bo's words prompted my thinking: If I could wander onto my land whenever I wanted, why couldn't I decide what happened to my buffalo?

"One of the nice things about our ranch is we sit next to public land and we're relatively close to a retrieval route. That's an area designated specifically for access to the animal, so we can get your elk cleaned, and the meat boxed and ready for you to take or ship, all within the required posthunt time limit. We know all the best retrieval routes, and trust me, it is easier to let someone else haul the weight of a big trophy."

From a comfortable four-wheeler, we were soon touring the seventy thousand private acres of Miranda Lake Ranch. He pointed out CRP land, which could be grazed if needed but not farmed, since he was paid to keep it natural. He described other acreage devoted to growing grasses for haying and winter feed. From atop a cedar ridge, we looked across an endless sprawl of lowlands. He pointed to a spot in the distance. I recognized the brown dots.

"We call them buffalo on our promotional materials, since most people know them by this name. We have about eighty that wander some thirty thousand acres. In the winter, our hunting parties cull a few."

My heart sank, even though I knew why I was here.

"There's no guarantee we'll find them, but usually we can track them down, and this makes everyone happy. Gives us a natural cull mechanism and fetches $6,000 per bag. More than an antelope, mule deer, white-tailed deer, coyote, and prairie dog combined can bring in. The elk is second most, at $2,500."

"How many weeks do you hunt?"

"We start in the fall and go through spring but take weeks off here and there, and we get all kinds: bow and arrow, rifle and muzzleloader. It's lucrative, and just like people love coming here for the experience, it's fun for all of us to get a glimpse into lives we'll never have. They're usually nice people too."

"What happens to the bison you don't hunt?" I asked.

"To market. When they're ready. We sell ours under our own brand—Miranda Lake. It's all online and direct ship to the buyers. Demand outstrips supply. Some customers commit to annual purchases for as far out as we are willing to go."

"I've never had it," I said. "Haven't even tried beefalo."

"Oh, man … seriously? You've been missing out. That is, if you're not vegan or anything."

"It's not that."

"Well, everything they say about buffalo being lean and tasty is true. Absolutely."

I walked inside the biggest of the four cabins. The heads were keeping it warm. The rest of the decor was equally natural.

"During hunting season, can you tell if an elk cow is pregnant?" I asked.

"It's noticeable, if you know what you're looking at."

"What would happen if someone shot a pregnant elk cow?"

"It would be a bad accident," he said. "The little one would be left. The cow would be harvested."

Maybe the dead pile was related to out-of-season hunters after all. Except someone had come back for them.

I knew, deep down, if I had to hunt for food, I would be willing. I didn't know how successful I would be, but I knew I would assume a different mindset. It was this mindset I hoped to unlock during my next meeting, when I would sit with Henry Mattson, one of the Tribal representatives of the bison management group.

Buffalo, or bison, needed to return, although to Henry Mattson, they would always be Bi'Shee. On the lands of his reservation, Bi'Shee lived as they should—free to move and free to help the earth and man recover from past human assaults. The bison not only could restore native grasses and wildlife habitat but could provide food, other goods, and emotional connection. A hunt was not a killing. A hunt was an honor. And it was done with gratitude. No part was wasted. Bison were protective brothers. Far more dishonorable than hunting bison was wasting what the bison had given. Slaughterhouses were not the answer.

32

———

CONFIDANT

I swung by Shelly's and was pleased to see Diane's car parked alongside the barn and Shelly waving from inside.

"Any word yet?" asked Shelly.

"On what?"

"The blood."

"Jeez, Shelly, can't you use a secret code name?" shouted Diane, as loud as possible.

Shelly smiled. "I mean, on the crimson paint samples? Or strawberry preserves?"

"Yes, but first we have to collect the presents waiting for you in my truck."

Shelly and Diane followed me to Sebastian. We reveled in matching "Kick-Ass Sister" T-shirts, and I was thrilled to give them matching gardenia plants in full bud.

"So?" said Diane.

"Yes," I said. "Elise showed me how she does the testing. Two of the samples showed *Brucella*. She determined the particular strain, and it was the same for both."

"Is this what you wanted?" asked Shelly.

"Honestly, I don't know."

Diane gave a cheer to not knowing. Then we set to work. Shelly and I tackled some corral posts. Diane tackled the menus for incoming guests. About an hour into our post duty, Diane joined us, wearing work gloves.

"What's with the new look?" I asked. "The ham getting harder to handle? Had to go to the heavy-duty work-glove oven mitts?"

"Oh, shush on you. For your information, I am here to lend a hand to your noisy operation. I can hear you swearing from the kitchen." I gave Diane a squinty eye. That's when she took the post from my hand, heaved it into the hole we had prepared, and said, "Mix?"

"Diane, what the …" I started.

"Can't help it," said Diane. "I wasn't raised to sit around and watch. It was all hands in when it was all hands in."

Shelly grabbed the concrete mix, and I directed the hose toward the hole. Then, we picked up the next post. The job was done in record time by three determined souls. After, thanks to Diane, we enjoyed fresh-baked cookies and beer. Life couldn't get any sweeter.

"I have a confession," I said, striding into Fletcher's office.

"You know I'm not a priest, right?"

"You'll do." Fletcher shrugged his acquiescence.

"I went back to Sam's. I had to see Shelly."

"After Hal nearly shot you and I warned you to stay away? What the …" He paused a moment. "Oh, Phillips, relax. I have feelers out everywhere. Do you think I wouldn't know about some girl talk?"

"Diane?"

"She can't help sharing every last thing she does outside of this office. It's as though the *Gazette* is family, bless her heart."

"Right," I said, desperately hoping Diane was keeping her pinkie-swear promise.

"Trust me, I don't need chitchat details. But thank you for sharing—I mean, confessing."

"It's more than that." Fletcher's face became attentive, and his smile rolled away.

"She confided in me. It's exactly like you said." I had his full attention. "Before Sam died, a couple of stockmen put him in a bind. They asked him to let a bunch of bison pass through. If he was leaving cattle ranching behind, they figured it wouldn't hurt anyone and they'd have more ammunition when it came to requiring better boundaries to keep them off grazing lands."

Fletcher frowned.

"Sam said no. Shelly and Sam would never do something fraudulent and taint the other good stockmen. After a couple of conversations, things started happening at Sam's. The fences were getting cut. Dead animals were showing up."

"Did she tell you who did this?"

"There were three of them. You know them all. Association members, but from across the state. She won't tell Burt for fear of retaliation if they feel cornered."

Fletcher nodded, carefully considering my words.

"She's hoping it's behind her, but she's practically sleeping with a gun under her pillow. She's worried about having fire extinguishers and hoses near every building on the ranch."

"So, what now?"

"I've convinced her to give you a note with their names. If anything unusual happens to Shelly or her dude ranch, you'll have a lead on helping Burt and written evidence of their past involvement. As long as no harm comes her way, she wants you to remain quiet. Not even give a gentle hint to those involved. She fears your letting on knowledge of the particular stockmen could prompt problems, either at her ranch or with your new bull operation. She was quite explicit."

Fletcher sat silently, thinking it over.

"So, the question is, Would you accept her letter?"

Fletcher didn't hesitate. "She has my vow of silence, unless circumstances warrant otherwise."

It was a weight off my shoulders.

"While you're here," said Fletcher, "some shop talk. How are the hunting-package interviews going? You had Peter Finch doing one of them. Is he on it this time?"

"He must have heard you thinking about him. His story came in an hour ago. I considered it a miracle."

"Kid must not be puking on him," said Fletcher. "Or"— Fletcher paused—"he appreciated your apology."

"I thought Diane traded him three of her cinnamon buns for his story. She offered to call on the water article when she heard my dissatisfaction shouted through the halls," I said.

Shelly slipped the letter into my hand, looked me straight in the eyes. "You're an angel." I nearly buckled to the floor, feeling the strength of the gratitude flowing from her heart and lighting her eyes.

"It's the least I can do. And Fletcher said the same."

I glanced at the envelope and saw no name on it, and no sender's name either.

"I dated the backside across the seal," she said.

I clutched her hand. "I'll take it to him immediately."

I was barely a half mile shy of the *Gazette* parking lot when Max phoned.

"Thanks for the callback," I said. "I have news of the research samples from Elise." I pulled over to retrieve paperwork. "She found evidence of *Brucella abortus* bacteria in two of the fifteen samples. One other sample had high enough values on the antigen test to suggest a possible former infection." I gave Max the strain isolated from Brody's cows. "All samples were the same. Does this tell you anything?"

"That's the exact strain I isolated from your elk," said Max.

"Which means?"

"We can't be certain a bison infected the cows. Not unless they also had the same strain as the elk."

"Is this possible?"

"Bison and elk could always intermix. Which means either one could be the source of the cattle infection. Unfortunately, we have learned both something and nothing. Sometimes, science is not as clear cut as we'd like. We do, however, have a valuable piece of information to add to our growing case file."

"Shall I send the results?" I asked.

"Let's keep it out of the email for now."

"Got it. I'm going to send along something else next week. It should be legal. Be on the lookout."

I had committed to sending Max the denim.

My heart leaped from my chest as I clicked the payment button. A confirmation number appeared. I took in a deep breath and leaned back into my chair, hoping to dispel my jitters. In a couple of days, I would head to Gary's Guns for my first lesson in gun safety and pistol use, as long as I didn't die of a panic attack first.

On an intellectual level, it made sense. I often traveled in isolated areas and almost always alone. Learning how to shoot in self-defense, or at least being able to come close enough to scare anyone or anything unwanted away, was smart. Also, I was a female living solo on a main road with easy access. It wasn't the same as living in a city. It was isolated. I probably should have signed up sooner, but every time I considered it, I had fought back. And the memory of Jake had fought with me.

Stepping into the *Gazette* pushed some of these terrifying thoughts from my head. Fletcher's voice, reeling me into his office, completed the transition back to my safety zone.

"How's it going, Phillips?"

"No complaints, except for this hunting issue I'm doing."

We both smirked.

"How are your bulls? You've been out of the office a bit lately."

"I was looking at possible additions. I also spent time with my sister."

"Everything okay?"

"It was shop talk. She'll be helping with the bulls."

"You mean your sister in our legislature?"

"She's had enough of the posturing and bickering and doesn't want to miss the fun of the new ranch."

"Mel told me you'd be keeping it familial. What, exactly, are you planning?"

"In a nutshell, we'll be one of the most highly selective sources of genes. We won't be big and won't be breeding them to death. My sister, her husband, and I are working to recapture some of the old bloodlines my family already selected. The industry has changed, of course, but we had some mighty important and special qualities selected out, and we have ample thoughts on how to make them even better." Fletcher's eyes gleamed. While I hadn't forgotten what this would mean to the bison, I wanted his family to succeed.

"Does this mean you'll change back to being a Callahan?"

Fletcher smiled. "Once a Callahan, always a Callahan, but the *Gazette*'s still my baby. Mr. Marks won't be going anywhere."

"Changing subjects, Shelly's getting ready to put up her first round house. She wants hands for a work party. Do you still have gloves?"

"Always. Tell me when. I'll get Joe and Mitch to help."

If I had to do a hunting issue, I was making it palatable to nonhunters as well. A friend of Mel's cousin Eleanor was a fellow historian who specialized in recent western history. His name was Lawrence Fields. I dialed his number.

"You want to learn how guns, or, more appropriately, mankind with access to guns, shaped our history?" said Lawrence.

"Exactly. Without guns, I doubt people could have hunted, eaten, and survived the same way. Without guns, I suspect people could not have created a country in the same way. It seems to me the hardware—and its power—was the enabler."

"Indeed. Humans do seek power, and we seek to amass resources and wealth, however those might be defined at any particular time or place. I have often wondered if this was a survival mechanism gone a bit awry. At any rate, we have done this century after century with guns, cannons, and gunpowder. Before this, we used other weapons.

"When we consider European imperialism on this continent, guns were critical. For starters, they enabled more efficient hunting, as you said. Without them, many more likely would have starved to death.

"Guns also proved powerful tools of trade and self-defense. They inched new people and a new country westward. And it's no secret they were critical to stalking millions of bison, to the intended detriment of the land's former nations. But it wasn't all might, mind you, that drew the lines of a new country. Much was ceded through treaties, sight unseen."

"What do you mean?"

"The land of the Louisiana Purchase became property of the United States only after it ping-ponged between ownership by France and Spain. Interestingly, what was purchased was 'the *preemptive* right to obtain Native American lands by treaty or by conquest, to the exclusion of other colonial powers.' Truth be known, despite all of the paper transfers of land, Europeans had not ventured to the western lands of the Louisiana Territory, in present day, Wyoming, Montana, and Colorado east of the Continental Divide. So, what made the purchase possible? Not might, as you would assume, but the threat of it. As you said, it was the power of guns and similar weapons that held sway. Imagine if France or Spain had retained control of this large expanse."

Lawrence's words gave hope that owning a gun might prove sufficient for self-protection and I would never have to fire one. But I still had to learn how.

All Billy Grey said was "Go ahead. Pick it up." I stared at the pistol. My teeth clamped together, my arms tensed, and the muscles in my midsection tightened against my insides, but I couldn't move. Anyone looking at me—which, realistically, could only have been Billy Grey or Cliff Shepherd, whom I had met as Pops when we sang together at Sam's funeral—could see I was petrified. Why did I ever think gun lessons were a good idea?

When Pops shared a wink from his chair near the cash register and Billy said, "Relax, Ms. Phillips," I shed a layer of fear. It returned as soon as Billy added, "Some of the best, smartest, and safest hunters I know started out a bit timid."

Great, I thought. *I don't want to become a safe hunter.* Why would I want to personally take the life of a man, moose, sheep, bison, horse, dog, cat, squirrel, or rabbit, or even a measly, harmless little mouse? The little thing would likely fly twenty feet into the air if I hit it and then splatter down in pieces. Why, oh God, did this seem like a good idea?

I continued my staredown with the handgun and my inner fight with intentional killing. Who in their right mind, I reasoned in spiraling thought, would want to send a missile through protective flesh, to send blood spilling out an unwanted and unfixable hole, or leave a ribbon of destruction in a lung, an explosion of brain matter in a skull, or a destructive bolt of fire to unsuspecting muscle, ligament, or tendon, to cause paralysis? I thought back to my first impromptu assignment at the *Gazette* and the horror of the bison's struggle to stand. The gun, idly staring back at me, was meant to kill. To take a life of something that ran, flew, slithered. It was meant to bring a heart to its final beat, stop lungs from drawing in air, send legs to the ground in stillness with single intent. *Why*, I questioned, again in utter silence, *would I want to shoot a gun?* Not once had I asked to hold Jake's service revolver. It was his. Not mine. With Billy cocking his head, as though straining to hear my inner conversation, I steadied myself with a stark reminder: Out here it was good common sense to know how to use one. Just in case.

I reached inside for courage as I lifted my hand forward. I rested three fingers on the pistol, as though trying to calm it with my touch. In return, it sent a cold, hard greeting. I slid my left hand alongside and took in a deep breath.

Calmly, Billy said, "Go ahead. It won't do anything you don't want it to do if you know how it works and treat it with respect. That's what I'm here to teach you."

His words nudged me forward. Once over the threshold, lingering alarm was joined by an unexpected thrill of holding a powerful piece of weaponry. My hands shook nonetheless.

After determining the gun was not loaded and making sure

to not point it toward anyone, I lifted it slowly and prepared to continue with the lesson.

The 9mm felt surprisingly light. With my hands wrapped around it as Billy instructed, my legs spaced apart, and my body balanced, I expected a sense of control to rush in but instead continued to feel an alarming sense of fear.

Just as I miscalculated the fear, I miscalculated the decibels associated with firing it, when it was finally time to pull my loaded gun's trigger. I noticed, too, even with protective headgear, movie effects were not accurate. I left the range feeling a strange combination of accomplishment, relief, and exhaustion, the afterglow of an adrenaline rush that had gotten me through my first gun encounter.

Amid a personal conversation between my common sense and my lingering fears, I decided to talk with Shelly about shooting. I headed to her ranch, where she met me at my truck.

"So, you want to know about guns?" asked Shelly. She slid her hand gently onto her holster to announce the gun sitting inside.

"I don't know if I can hug you with that thing on your hip, but I love seeing you, friend."

"Back at you, Amber, girl. Glad you stopped by. Let me take this thing off, and we can talk. I just wanted you to see there ain't no shame in having a gun. As long as you use it right. Lesson over."

"Thanks, Shell. I have Fletcher on board for round houses this weekend, and he's flagging a few extra helpers himself."

"Oh, baby! I'm taking you to dinner!"

The musical notes of my phone signaled an incoming call from Max Chong at 9:00 a.m. East Coast time. Though groggy, I answered. Max was not only happy to look at the denim but downright excited. The case had aroused his scientific brain. He was phoning to tell me it had arrived and had a question about its safekeeping since I'd found it. I hadn't bothered with a note.

33

———————

CONNECTION

INCREDIBLY, I now felt comfortable walking through the door of Gary's Guns, chatting with Pops at the desk, and getting my safety gear. I had forced myself to fit in two more sessions, following my pep talk with Shelly. Today, I beat the crowd for a third, and the range was empty. I hit within twelve inches of my chosen mark on seven of ten attempts, several times over. I aimed at head, heart, and shoulder. Aiming at a paper moose or bison never crossed my mind, though plenty of their silhouettes lined the wall. While I had come to enjoy the challenge of indoor target practice, I couldn't imagine taking it to the real world. Some of my ancestors must have owned guns, but for all intents and purposes, I was a first-generation gun holder. I was certain every resident for miles around was not.

I went through forty rounds and debated putting down money for another twenty. Instead, I started a conversation with Pops, the lone cashier and my singing partner at Sam's service.

"How long have you been holding up this counter?" I asked.

"Funny," he said, "I was just talking to my wife about this very same thing. I think she's looking for me to finally retire and cause more trouble around the home."

"They always say to be careful what you wish for."

"That they do, and to answer your question, this range and I go back nearly twenty years." He paused. "This was my second job. After I retired from my first, I needed something to do."

I was curious as to Pops's age but didn't ask. One thing I had learned along the way was once people hit eighty, they shared their magic number like some sort of badge, as though amazed they had made it. Ninety-four was Pops's magic number. His twinkling eyes told me he would likely be here longer than I.

"Have things changed much?" I asked.

"Yes and no. Like everything. We've automated a bit. We have new folks coming in, like you. And we've got the old-timers. I think they come to see if I'm still standing. When I say old-timers, I really mean youngsters—like your Fletcher."

I felt my gaze deepen. Fletch came to the range?

"He's not exactly an old-timer," continued Pops, "but he's old enough, and most of the real oldies—my generation—have died."

"Are you from here?" I asked.

"No. I came for my first job." Pops smiled as he looked off to the distance, which could physically only have brought him ten feet from where he sat but mentally could have taken him miles and years away. "My wife and I came out from Ohio so I could take a job at the Alston HVAC manufacturer north of here. Do you know we used to put together twenty thousand units a week, before all the automation? Three shifts a day. Fifty weeks a year."

"You didn't want to go someplace different once you stopped working?"

"By then, we were here for good, I'd say. Knew people, knew the ways of life. We knew we weren't Arizona or Florida types. You sometimes get to a point when you just accept things are going to stay the same. No rocking the boat, and it's fine."

I wondered if it would happen to me. It seemed such a long

way off and such a distant possibility. Pops said I should meet his wife someday. He thought we would get along.

The foundation, framing, and rough utilities for the first round house had been completed during the prior month by professional contractors when Shelly gathered her ragtag team of friends and neighbors around the plans and building materials. About twenty of us were eager to put our combined energy to work to finish it off.

Fletcher volunteered to lead a group of six in hoisting ladders and applying shingles to the roof. The rest of us formed three groups for siding and trim. The hammers started pounding. We moved like well-orchestrated ants.

Working in the same group as Diane, the day would be fun, despite a hot sun. Of course, she wore a floral print top and a matching floral bandanna around her head. We spoke of Ted as I handed pieces to my hammer man. His ribs were healing well, but his leg continued to nag, and sitting on his tailbone still required a certain amount of negotiation. Despite all, he was behind Shelly's ranch one hundred percent. He was prepared to field any questions our work crew might have. Diane had posted his phone number on an easy-to-find fluorescent-pink notecard.

At day's end, Shelly and Diane unfurled the goods for a superb cookout as we looked upon our accomplishments. With a few more hours' work, and final wiring and plumbing by the professionals, we could celebrate round house number one. Shelly already had smoky-green paint to cover it. What I found most astounding was everyone had the know-how and apparent experience to do all that we had done.

While a weekend of soccer used to wear me down, it felt oddly satisfying when exhaustion hit. After a weekend of round house detail, I felt tired, achy, and old.

As the new week began, Max phoned.

"Good morning, sunshine," he said. "How's the western vibe today?"

"Despite it being early morning, traffic is rather snarled in a national park sort of way, and the nights are turning colder."

"In August?"

"Frightening, I know. Up the mountains we've even had some hail."

"Well, this should warm you. I detected some *Brucella* on the denim. Along with elk tissue and elk blood. No surprise there. Oh, and cat fur. I don't know if this gives you anything new."

"The best I can say is some felonious feline in blue jeans lugged a couple of baby elk to a pile in the middle of nowhere. Alert the presses."

"And a very good day to you too."

"Sorry. But I had the thing in my freezer. My food freezer. I didn't consider it could have *Brucella* on it. I wish I had left the whole thing alone. Wish I could do this for once in my life."

"Don't be so hard on yourself. It'll likely turn out to be a good thing. Your knowing, that is."

"Max, do you ever feel you have totally failed?"

"From time to time, yes. Well, maybe not totally, because science is often trial and error, hypothesis and proof. Sometimes the proof doesn't prove what you expect it will. You can either view it as failure or added knowledge."

"Max, I am not feeling the slightest bit of value added. Only a lot of failure."

"Like they say, keep your chin up."

"Thanks, Max. I'll try."

"Tell me where this Lawrence Fields piece came from and what it's doing in this issue," said Fletcher.

I had made a bad decision to put it in the mock-up, and now I was paying for it. In front of Simone and Gary, I was about to debate the article with Fletcher.

"Not everyone hunts," I started slowly. "Some people find hunting and fishing offensive."

"And?" he said.

"And I provided something of interest, but on topic, to this sort of reader."

"Phillips," he said, looking over the rim of his glasses, "I don't condone this, but I don't bite. Next time, I want the heads-up. And for this one, please get a better quote from Lawrence so he sounds less academic and at least minimally approachable. I think we found the limit of the good, the bad, and the ugly in the one you included."

I was certain I wasn't the only one giving a sigh of relief. When Simone and Gary left, I didn't have to say a word to share a heartfelt thank-you with Fletcher. A look was all it took.

34

———————

COMMITMENT

Labor Day weekend whisked past, taking summer with it, and I learned I was clear of any *Brucella*. But Dr. Hill requested a callback upon his return from a conference. I put it on my schedule. Then, I nearly skipped into Simone's office, thrilled we would be tackling the loose ends of the hunting issue, the one we now only referred to as "The Dreaded."

After work, Shelly helped me into the saddle, and we took a slow walk to the pasture near the round house, she on Louisa and me on a tame old mare named Martha. Dunston had received a carrot for allowing us to leave the corral without him.

We intended to shoot at targets. Outside. Shelly had convinced me it would be fun. My nerves pulsed. My heart pounded. And when we came to a halt in the middle of a grassland where a section of fence allowed us to tie Louisa and Mary, I felt an ache in my thighs and calves. *Saddle burn*, I thought. A tear escaped, hand in hand with a memory of Eva.

"Amber?"

Sometimes, grief sneaked up on you. For several moments, I couldn't answer. Finally, I shared, with memories of saddle burn and all.

"Oh, I understand. One moment I'm fine, the next I'm crippled with heartache." Shelly gave a deeply felt hug, which I returned.

"You know," she said, "Sam and I had a special phrase too. It was *cow shit*. It doesn't sound so special when I say it now, but it was. Sam wasn't raised in ranching. When we were dating, he couldn't fathom calling something a cow pie. In fact, he vowed he'd never say cow pie, as he knew it would scar him forever when he ate dessert." Shelly chuckled softly. "No one refers to cow pies or cattle dung as cow shit. No one! So, he called it cow shit, and sure enough, *cow shit* became our special expression, just like your saddle burn. And he could say it angry, he could say it sarcastic, he could say it delicate, and he could utter it smooth as can be, with total pleasure. 'Well, cow she-it,' he'd say when he heard something fairly awesome."

Shelly's imitation of Sam had me laughing. "Oh, Amber, girl, I know how you feel. I truly do. Saddle burn and all."

I squeezed Shelly tight and said, "Cow shit sounds perfect."

After a few deep breaths, we set to business—shooting. Shelly had hauled out some big targets earlier in the day.

"Start with the old wheelbarrow," she said. "Don't think of it as an animal. Think of it as worthless trash. And help me get rid of it!"

Shelly was good. I was not. Louisa and Mary didn't flinch a hair as our shots fired. And fired again.

"Almost," said Shelly. "Just a bit lower. I told you it's different outside."

I followed her instruction. Several shots later, I hit my mark.

"Well. Saddle ... BOOM!" she shouted.

"Woo-hoo!" I was proud of myself.

"Boom!" Shelly repeated.

"Cow heist!" I responded. "No! Crow shit!"

"Saddle boom!"

"Crow shit!"

We both looked to the sky and let our shouts and laughter mingle to the clouds, our energy now positive. Thank God for Shelly. We stayed out for hours. Even spent some time simply letting the horses make their own paths across the land, grazing as they pleased, as we sat in the saddle.

"I did a full panel," said Dr. Hill. "With Eva's cancer, I wanted to be sure."

"Of what?"

"Your white blood cell count is slightly elevated, so if you continue to feel tired or have any pain, let me know. Sometimes the elevated counts result from viral infections, like common colds and such, and sometimes with UTIs, which can clear on their own but more often need antibiotics. Just keep an eye out. Otherwise, consider yourself as healthy as an ox."

I approached Henry Mattson with an odd but simple request: I wanted a small piece of bison meat from his freezer. Along with fifteen samples from other Indigenous freezers. Henry had told me during our previous discussion, the stored meat was from the spring culls, the ones NPS couldn't haze back into the park last April. I couldn't say why I wanted their precious commodity. Not yet. For some reason, he trusted me. Trusted my reason made greater sense than the request itself.

With proper introduction, all families allowed entry into their frozen goods. I sent them overnight express to Max. As far as frozen meat transport was concerned, I had, surprisingly, not broken any rules that I knew of. It was a miracle.

"Talk to me about faith," I said, sliding into Fletcher's office.

"At this time of day? What kind do you want to know about?"

I looked at him, blank stare firmly attached to my face.

"In my experience, I've come across three types of faith," he said. "The first is faith. The second is blind faith. The third ... dumb blind faith. It's the third one that gets a person in trouble. Dumb blind faith is no different than denial. It's putting faith in something because you don't like the other possible outcomes. It's not true faith. It's a cop-out. Next is blind faith. It's believing in something because you have trust in it. You're willing to go along with something because you have enough trust to accept that the outcome will be positive, supportive, or beneficial, as in everything will work out. In short, you believe. Finally, we have faith. True faith. A true belief that you are being watched over and will be led to good results, or the right results, for whatever it is you encounter. It is the deep and sincere belief that there is a plan for you and all will work according to this plan. This is the strongest faith. This is an unwavering faith. Or, if it wavers, it will return. For a number of people, this is faith in God's plan."

"How do you experience faith if you are not religious?"

"There are a number of defined gods in this world, but you don't need to be religious to live with faith. We're allowed differences in our beliefs. For true faith, you give yourself up. You have complete confidence in life's processes. You question your meaning, your values, your purpose in a bigger picture, but you fully trust. You let yourself go *to* trust. And you believe in your trust."

***

"Max?"

"I hope you don't mind a call at this hour."

"It must be midnight where you are. Is everything okay?"

"I have important news. I've looked at the bison samples and found some with *Brucella*. And it is different from the rest."

"What do you mean?"

"Your elk strain is the same as what's on the denim. Granted, the condition of what's on the denim wasn't perfect macroscopically, but genetically it is the same as your little one. This would make sense, of course, being found together, as they were. I would guess either hand, glove, or animal brushed against the denim before, or while, the denim was cut. This *Brucella* strain is also the same as the cow samples. The bison meat, however, has a different strain."

"Different?" I said. I was getting closer.

I racked my brain for clues as I inspected the region's aerial photos. In a strange, fleeting moment, with my eyes glazing over from staring at the images, I vaguely registered a faint spot with slightly different color than its surroundings. It was as though a message had been silently transmitted from my computer screen to my subconscious brain. I squinted to give it better definition, an odd but time-tested action. It was the warm spring Brody had alluded to when he showed me his ranch. The spot the bison sought out in winter. I had to find it. It was another hunch. And, just as Fletcher once said, he and I depended on our instincts and hunches. They rarely steered us wrong.

The grasses were changing seasons, preparing to rest. Straw-colored, crinkling underfoot, and eager to leave seeds. Winds brushed through their fine blades, sending them bowing in waves. I could feel the warmth of it just by looking. Autumn sagebrush streaked through the plain, like airy heather-gray tulle. The entirety of the plains was muted and watercolor soft. Even the mountains seemed muted. Pines, too, along the edges wore verdant needles coated by charcoal-gray shadows from overhead clouds. And there they stood. Hundreds of them. Accents. Having all assumed the deepest, darkest chocolate brown of their seasonal winter hides. As always, a few stood sentinel on the outskirts. I watched them basking. They were in no hurry, just like these gentle plains. Before they knew it, the warm winds would vanish, taking the last autumn warmth with them. Glorious. This was what their lives should be! This was how their ancestors grazed. These were the grasses they knew. Everything about them had been programmed by their past. They did as those before them had done for centuries. And now the colors of the plains were celebrating them. Creating an apt background and home, a nourishing landscape. Today, it was all about being where they were supposed to be, doing what they were supposed to do, about bison DNA so firmly implanted on the face of this western landscape. How dared we treat them as we had.

Refocusing on the grass, I closed my eyes and considered the reality of my own eventual end someday: thoughts of my mortality. I wanted to touch the grass in gentle strokes and continue to see sunrises and magnificent bison forever. I also wanted to go back to the good times in Philadelphia and never lose a soul I loved. My touches, like everyone's, were numbered. I had to make the most of my time here. Often, gaining something in life meant losing something else. As Brody had said, sacrifice wasn't free. I had to take a stand. I could be one person making a difference, even though it would cost me my new home, my new friends, my job, and my community. Eva's voice sounded: "Do it, sis!" She was with me, after all.

The thought prompted me to drive to Gary's Guns. Of all the things I wouldn't sacrifice, it was my TriState People issue. I had a good number of interviews completed for the upcoming issue, but I didn't have Pops. And Pops, and the issue, would be shared with others, come hell or high water. My personal evolution into self-recognized bison guardian would not steal this from me, no matter if I was run out of town for what I planned to do, and no matter the other consequences!

Pops and I talked for more than an hour. I couldn't wait to share his story.

I looked at a young man's photo posted on the wall behind him and said, "Who's that? A grandson?"

"That," he said thoughtfully, "is someone you know. Used to come in here all the time. He was like a grandson to me."

"Who?" I couldn't make a link.

"Brody."

I looked more carefully at the image. He was far younger and likely hadn't yet felt the loss of his family. He had a certain idealism etched in his eyes. It was a certain confidence we all have before we learn differently. Nothing would stop him.

"He acted like he owned the place," said Pops. "Being so sure of his shots. Challenging everyone to hit the marks. He was a hoot. He kept talking special ops. With his losing his family, he lost his dreams. I felt sorry for him. Tried to buoy him up. Then he got all tied down with that ranch. Didn't stop in much, except for a few times with a lot of anger. I had to tell him his anger and his gun weren't meant to mix."

I stared at the young rancher with his youthful confidence, pride, and hope, which had since changed form. I focused on his clothes—ranching work clothes, with broad hat, bandanna around his young neck, button-down shirt, and belt looped into his jeans. And I acknowledged, once again, the ranchers going to Abby's or cooking up their own meals weren't glamorized made-for-television characters, fulfilling our ideals. They were hardworking Americans doing their jobs.

I turned my gaze away from the photo. "What do you think about bison, Pops?"

"Now, they're something, aren't they? Everything we try to be out here. Mighty special." He was nodding his head and staring to the corner of the room, as I had seen him do before when drifting into thought. "You know, when you get older, I believe you do get wiser, though a bit slower. I'd like to see what they'd do if we let them wander. We like to control everything, but some things are left better off without this. Could be mighty powerful."

It seemed strange coming from a man whose life had relied on guns and HVAC units, both good at controlling our situation.

Pops smiled. "I like your new gun, by the way. No need to put that in your story."

35

DENIM

FOR OVER A WEEK, I struggled with how I might get the proof I needed. Then it came to me. I told Fletcher I would be including Nate in my people issue, shared information about Nate's research, and said, as an aside, that Nate was missing a particular hot spring. The one bordering Brody's property and the church's.

"What are we really checking, Phillips?"

"Instinct."

All he said was "Let's go."

Fletcher drove Nate and me in his truck partway, and we walked the rest.

"If Brody's out and about, he'll think I'm showing you pastures. Besides, I don't want to get the truck stuck down there."

"How often do you come out here?" I asked Fletcher.

"I hadn't been this far down for at least a year, until Brody and I came on horses."

It was the answer I wanted to hear.

While Nate nimbly collected samples, I took photos of the terrain, creek, and pastures: anything to get a better handle on the Schines' grand plan. It was gorgeous valley land. Bison would love it. The hot spring, or semihot spring, as Nate described it, would still offer winter warmth for their bodies and earlier spring vegetation. If only …

Fletcher stepped near me. "Do me a favor. Take a couple of shots down the valley over there. The chute where the bison travel."

"You mean your future hayfield?" I felt anger rising.

"Call it that if you like."

He had me fuming. Why wouldn't I call it this? It was on the plans!

With a big green marker, I zeroed in on October 3 on my wall calendar and boldly wrote *DONE* in all caps. Simone and I had finalized details of the dreaded TriState Hunting and Fishing issue. I would have all finals to Fletcher by day's end. I had told a complete story and was proud of it. The issue had stayed true to Fletcher's mandate of sharing the good, the bad, and the ugly. All I had to do was take a deep breath and look forward to his final comments, which had never been anything short of thoughtful and profoundly beneficial. Most shocking, I had survived.

Nate phoned days later, excited to share his findings: bacteria in the water sample from Fletcher's spring matched microbes on the stringy denim swatch. Finally, I had proof of a location. It didn't rule out everyone, but my gut narrowed the field, giving slim chance to its having been Fletcher, Mel, or anyone from the church, and shining a light on the Schines or Brody. I wasn't being scientific, and it didn't matter.

That night, when I saw Brody enter the Eagle Feather, I stared like a wolf with a singular focus. With the unforgettable look when it sees its prey. With ears fully pointed, upright and ready. Eyes wider and aimed directly at their target. Its entire body poised to strike. Brody walked through my line of unflinching vision, completely oblivious. He would have been easy prey had I been a wolf. I departed the Eagle Feather without a word between us. It was the way I wanted it. I wasn't looking for his reaction. I was gauging mine.

Back East, one lived, and when the time came, one died. Seasons passing, as it were. Out here, everything was bigger and more dangerous: blizzards sweeping across hundred-mile expanses, snowmelt rushing down dangerous gorges, rivers that ran for hundreds and thousands of miles. All the edges of Philadelphia had long ago been tamed, and the city paved. A few parks and community gardens safely joined front and back yards. A stray cat crossed. Dogs remained on leash or contained by invisible fences. An occasional black bear wandered the landscape to make headlines. Out here, people didn't have first dibs on the land or control of the elements. Out here, it was live *or* die. My near encounters with death yesterday set me to thinking about disclosure.

A snowstorm developing earlier than expected had caught me at higher elevations as I returned from a meeting. Blizzard winds whipped snow across the two rural lanes like a forceful breath scattering dandelion seeds. Visibility shifted from moderate to whiteout in an instant. I was certain the road would close as soon as I exited. Five times at least, I was forced to make delicate but lightning-quick corrections to avoid whipping back end to front end into spinning circles off the roadbed. And that's when I realized I could die, with my truck sliding off the road, quickly hidden by snow, invisible to passing vehicles. It was up to me, my ingenuity, and dumb luck to stay alive. No different from a rabbit dodging an owl, sheep avoiding wolves, a deer escaping man's hunt for venison. It was live or die.

The mountain snowplow had rattled toward me from the west and made the turn up the hill right before I made mine coming from the east. It gave as clear a path as I'd ever get, winding upward with craggy gneiss on one side of my truck and thin air on the other. It was a damned good thing I lived at Irv and Izzy's, the first home up the next hill. As I followed the plow, I set my mind to sharing my findings as soon as possible!

"You know, it's a biohazard," Fletcher said, looking at me across my kitchen table.

"I've broken a lot of rules lately, which is why I didn't include you. That, and I didn't know where it would lead, if anywhere.

"Once I learned of the Schines, I had second thoughts about dismissing it. I considered they might have deposited the elk fetuses on Brody's as a means of buying insurance. Scaring him out of ranching. Preventing him from backing out of their development. I thought he might have removed them from his property and tossed them where I found them until he had time to bury them somewhere else. He certainly would not have wanted the Park Service or anyone else catching sight of them. It could explain why they disappeared; he had a way to dispose of them when people were no longer inspecting his ranchlands after his break-in."

"Plausible," said Fletcher. "But here's my piece of the puzzle: I found a tire mark and a small piece of a small body on church land right after you and I took a hike to the drop zone you discovered. It shocked the daylights out of me, until I saw a boot print close by. It told me it likely was a hunter. Anyone else would have covered their tracks. And from what I've seen, the Schines don't wear boots with treads."

I considered Fletcher's remarks and began my confession.

"The water sampling with Nate had as much to do with the dead pile as the *TriState*." I revealed Nate's findings and the correlation between the water bacteria and the bacteria on the denim.

"My bet," I began slowly, "is on Brody now. The way I figure it, he circled along the boundary between his land and the church's, caught a foot in the edge of the warm spring, and picked up the two types of water bacteria—cyanobacteria *Calothrix* and cyanobacteria *Oscillatoria*, that orangey-brown stringy stuff—on the bottom of his pant leg. Then, he left a piece on the snag as a marker. What I don't know is why Brody would have walked around the warm spring with or without the young elk, other than, perhaps, he *was* removing a Schine brothers present."

"To hide his tracks?" said Fletcher. "Or to rinse his jeans. Maybe he knew he had elk on them." We shrugged.

I revealed Max's findings: the baby elk and Brody's cows both had *Brucella*, and it was the same strain. Bison meat from animals slaughtered last spring also had *Brucella*, but the strain was different.

"What?" Fletcher's stare plunged deep into my eyes and he held it for so long, I nearly stopped breathing. Instead of sharing details of my investigation, I backed off and said, "Can't you stop the land sale and swap of water rights? Just pull out? What's in it for you, anyway?"

"Patience, Phillips. Don't assume bad things about me. Not yet. I didn't know Brody and the Schines were going to create this monstrosity. Use the water rights in this way and close off the lands. They weren't up front with details."

He couldn't stop it.

"Thanks to you, Phillips, I worked in a deal to keep those three hundred acres of lower land for hay. Brody never said a word about a hotel, but you did, inadvertently," said Fletcher.

"You said development would be the start of the town's ruin."

"I have faith it might work out differently," said Fletcher.

"Faith?"

"Like I said, patience, Phillips. I have it covered. We'll have a big enough passageway for all of them."

"Them?"

Fletcher nodded. Was he talking about the bison?

"Give me another week and I'll fill you in."

I slid into a chair next to Brody and Abby at the Eagle Feather. After several minutes of casual conversation, Brody said, "Darts?"

Abby and I looked at one another. I volunteered.

"You want to play?" he said.

"Absolutely. I've been practicing."

"Oh, right," said Brody.

Oh, right, I silently thought, but stood to lead the way.

I managed to take a number of points. I *had* improved. Maybe it had something to do with my gun training. Brody, of course, drilled every toss like a professional. We had collected our darts for a fourth game when I turned, and he turned, and my darts scraped across his bare skin, where he had carefully rolled up his sleeve.

"Oh, God," I said.

"Oh, shit! Amber! What the ..."

A bright-red line of blood surfaced. Not because the wounds were so deep but because I had scratched nearly the length of his forearm. Without thinking, I took ahold of his arm and pressed my shirtsleeve against him. It was faster than finding napkins. Blood continued to spill out. The wounds were deeper than I had thought. What had I done? I watched as blood seeped from his body to mine. I pulled one arm out of my shirtsleeve to more easily apply pressure with the fabric and stop the rush of blood from his arm, warm from the games and sharing freely.

"I'd better get bandaged," he said. I helped him to a first aid kit, all the while pressing firmly with my sleeve. Winston, tending bar, took over as soon as he saw us.

"I'll be fine," said Brody. "You go. Get cleaned up."

I had never stabbed anyone. Or semistabbed them. The worst I had done was inflict accidental soccer injuries. After lifting my shirt over my head and pulling my other arm out of the sleeve, I steered Sebastian away from the Eagle Feather. About halfway home, I slowed to a stop. I had what I needed. Through dumb luck, I had Brody's blood. Nearly in shock at my realization, I continued driving.

The next afternoon, following a committee review of their plans, the Schine brothers held an impromptu press conference for the many interested reporters. Fletcher and I listened in. Then, Fletcher deftly caught them alone before they drove away. I clearly overheard mention of poaching out of season. Fletcher was gauging their reaction. Checking if they knew anything about the dead pile. If anyone could see a slight wince, it was Fletch. And I knew the Schines weren't as slick as they thought they were.

36

———

CULL

In barely a few weeks, Montana's first hunting season would begin. Permits had been allocated months ago. Meteorologists were predicting a snowy winter, which would push bodies beyond park bounds at the height of winter. Managers were excited to see this happen. They needed a lower number. I had walked into the park office with trepidation, wanting to learn the anticipated cull number, and walked out nauseous but nonetheless determined. They were looking to cull another six hundred bison by spring, and I was going to let the world know —everyone from Los Angeles to Philadelphia, Boston, and New York City. A bison burger from a raised animal wasn't the same as a protected natural resource. Trust was at stake, as well as lives. Along with a connection to our land and history. We were trusting our government to protect this magnificent connection. But our government was secretly and underhandedly letting us down.

"What is the most drastic thing anyone has done to try to stop the killing?" I asked Mel.

"Human chain. Blaring horns. In the end, it failed to make a difference."

"Can't we do anything to stop it?"

"Nothing short of a miracle," he said. "They are not allowed to cross a number of thresholds, the biggest being human tolerance."

I argued on their behalf. Told him they were mine and his and they needed protection. All he said was "Good luck."

This made me angry. I stopped ranting and asked, "What do you think of the development plans?"

Mel wished Brody would sell to Fletcher, or at least another local, and leave town on good terms. Many others thought the same. But Brody wasn't interested. He saw more dollar signs in the sale to the Schines.

"Brody's biggest problem," continued Mel, "is he never got over losing his family. He's carried a grudge all these years."

I knew it was more than that. I knew, from Brody's and my talks, he carried deep-seated anger and distrust of his own association, several generations after Fletcher's family beat out the Ross family for the top position. Additional anger had melted into the pot when the church got old Circle C land and Brody's family did not. He was fighting for a family he no longer had, with survivor's guilt to boot.

"The truth of it," said Mel, "is he has a lot more of people's respect than he realizes. Heading up a ranch at such a young age, making the decision to overwinter stock and birth later, and succeeding at it, he's shown a lot of people a whole lot of good. Hell, he showed me we have another plausible way to reduce the conflict, by pushing calving back. But Brody has never come to peace with himself, and I'm not sure he ever will. Though maybe, once he gets out, it will be different. I hope so. For his sake."

The next time I visited Gary's Guns, I made a point of stopping in with Pops to hand over a couple of Abby's special cookies— the ones she'd purchased from a home bakery some forty miles into Montana. "One for you and one for your Mrs.," I said. "What's your wife's name, anyway?"

"Lena."

"German?"

Pops smiled. "Both of us."

"Sweet."

"Well," said Pops, "that Irv and Izzy are mighty nice people, and I'm glad they found such a nice tenant."

"You know them?" I asked.

"Of course I do."

"They're talking about moving," I said.

Pops cocked his head and looked toward the ceiling a moment. "Things go around and around, don't they? I remember when they first moved to that old Circle C land."

"When they bought from Fletcher's family?"

"Yes, ma'am." He nodded, as though recalling the very day he and Irv and Izzy had met.

"They knew what it meant to Fletcher to sell. They worked with him to parcel off part for the church. I went by a few times before Fletcher sold. Helped him keep the old pumps running and all. He knew I had a knack for that kind of work. He said he trusted me, and said the old pump man had died. Heart attack, I think he said. It was a while ago."

"Pumps?"

"The old well pumps. Irrigation pumps too. There were quite a number of them. Three wells. A couple of water pumps. Big ones. Fletcher had quite a system set up at the Circle C. You know, for the channels and all. Connected that big lake down the hills there and the thumb of the river with a whole mess of acreage. Some of it's church land now. Irv and Izzy used to grow so much hay and forage, they had enough left over to sell. It was real nice stuff."

"Pops, you're a miracle!"

Pops looked like he had peeked under the Christmas tree on Christmas morning. His smile glowed across his face. I am certain mine did too.

"Fletch, I need you."

"Emergency?"

"Yes!"

Twenty minutes later, we stood outside Irv and Izzy's, and I demanded an explanation. Calmly, Fletcher said, "Come. I'll show you something."

Already in my boots, I was ready for a walk. Fletcher guided me into his truck instead, and we rode slowly over bumpy grassland, up and down gentle hills, around areas wet from collected rainwater, toward the far end of Irv and Izzy's land. Fletcher pointed out several well locations as he drove. I should have known the mysterious mounds covered something important—well houses visible from the back.

"You were never looking for phantom cattle, were you?"

Fletcher smiled.

"It's all about your water rights and the old Circle C. Has nothing to do with hot tubs, cattle grazing, bulls, or hay, does it?"

"In part," he said as he again smiled.

"What are you up to?"

At the top of a rise, far from the house, we stepped from his truck. Fletcher said, "Look ahead, Phillips. Tell me what you see."

"Grassland. Miles of it, stretching forever through the valley. All the way to the church lake," I said.

"Think about it, Phillips. We're setting up a small family venture. Bulls don't need this much land. Or this much water. They don't even need all the hay I'm supposedly preparing to grow and harvest. From here over to there," he said, pointing out an enormous chute of valley land coursing between rolling hills to the left and rolling hills to the right and crossing the land designated for hay, "is their future trail to freedom."

I jerked my head around to see his face covered by a content smile. He wasn't hemming the bison in. He was trading for their perpetual freedom. I couldn't believe it.

"Mel and I have worked something out."

"Why didn't you tell me?"

"I told you to trust me. And I told you about some of it. I didn't know you were this invested in the bison, and such a die-hard ... what do you call them ... *camera*. Don't worry, Phillips, we've got this. We're looking at setting aside way more than three hundred acres, but we needed that acreage to make it work."

"What do you mean?"

"When you asked about a hotel some time back, I knew Brody and the Schines were up to something different than what they led me to believe. That's when I demanded this lower land for haying, in exchange for the water lease."

"And now you're not really growing hay there. You're pumping water back up to Irv and Izzy's part of the old Circle C to irrigate here instead and are leasing the rest."

Fletcher smiled. "You found out about the wells, pumps, and levees."

It was my turn to smile.

"Bennett?" he asked.

"Your friend Pops was the key. It was beautiful."

"Well, thank you, Phillips, for keeping it on the down low.

Long live the Circle C. Yes, that's the plan, along with the freedom."

My heart danced, for the bison and for seeing Fletcher so alive.

"But not a word to anyone. Not yet."

———

So many people had visited Yellowstone this year that the the Old Faithful Inn's sign-in book had spilled into a second edition. With the *Gazette*'s credentials to back up my request, I borrowed the first book to begin my planned campaign. For hours, night after night, I recorded anyone who had given a home state when they signed in. By the end of the week, every state, except Alaska, had a separate list of its state residents who had visited Yellowstone this year. My total count was over three thousand people. Soon, our bison would be recognized. I was certain. With any luck, I would return the book within the next week, and my lists would be more than doubled. Taking a break from my lists, I gathered my thoughts and started typing.

Dear _____,

My name is Amber Phillips, resident of Morris, Montana, and journalist with the Western TriState, *a sister magazine of the* Gazette, *a daily published in Morris. I write, not as a journalist but as a citizen, to inform you that at least ## of your constituents visited Yellowstone National Park this year and signed in to the guest book at the spectacular Old Faithful Inn. As you likely know, many people visit Yellowstone to catch a glimpse of our magnificent bison, or buffalo, as many call them. Your constituents likely do not know that these majestic animals, which grace their family photographs and for so many hundreds of years graced the land of our plains, have a good chance of being slaughtered every year. Some are hunted, others are penned, and others are injured during human quests to round up or move the animals to places we wish for them to be, rather than where the buffalo would naturally like to eat and wallow from season to season. Every year, our country spends millions of dollars for these activities when we could, instead, spend on more appropriate land use and allocation, which would support bison management for the betterment of larger, more free-roaming bison populations. Although I do not write on behalf of your constituents, I do believe I voice the opinion of many visitors who are trusting in their government and your governance to safekeep our national mammal, a symbol of our United States, our land, and our wild past and a brother of our Indigenous peoples, when I respectfully request you stand up as a voice for our bison. They deserve greater respect. I am certain your constituents would be shocked and devastated to learn of plans to slaughter, in the next few months, up to six hundred of the very bison they came to see and admire.*

Please see below a list of your constituents who visited this year, as recorded in the sign-in book at the Old Faithful Inn, and please address Mr. Mel Headman, of the Bison Guardians, with remarks supporting the protection of the bison in lands of the Greater Yellowstone region in a more natural manner.

Sincerely ...

I would begin sending emails, one state after another, as soon as I had each visitor list as complete as possible.

"Are you okay?" Abby asked.

I felt wobbly on my legs but lied. Then, when the diner had emptied out near closing time, I said, "Join me."

We slid into the booth.

"Something doesn't feel right. I've had a slight pain in my abdomen. My Philadelphia doctor just checked me, and in his words, I'm as healthy as an ox. But he said I had something going on with my white blood cells."

"Uh-oh," said Abby. "Could be nothing. Or ..."

We both knew it could be big.

I said, "No, he checked. Because of Eva. I am all clear. But

I'm still afraid to go to a doctor. Afraid they might find something."

"I know exactly what you are thinking, but if something feels wrong, you have to go. In the meantime, let me get you a coffee or tea. It might help."

"Any cookies left?" I asked.

Later that evening, I considered the depth of Abby's concern. In less than a year, in this strange new home, I had fallen into a community. I was no longer an outsider. The next moment, I realized I had to shift the TriState People issue yet again. Restricting it to a series of individual profiles was not good enough. I had to focus on community. I had to illuminate the ties that bound a group of individuals together and the added value of intertwining the lifestyles, livelihoods, and opinions of each member and each person's particular gift and contributions. As independent as so many here were, it was the interlacing of them all that made Morris special. It was Winston presenting a hot pot of tea when I faced my sister's cancer; Abby's warm hug and boisterous greeting when anyone came to her diner; Mel's fight for the bison, but moreover his quest to bring sides together for lasting peace; Brody's willingness to freely tour Old Faithful and his ranch; Shelly's wish to share her land with strangers; and on and on. It was a group of individuals who supported each other and knew they had the support of others in turn. It was the community that had taken me in. And in such a short period of time. It was open hearts and guiding hands. This issue had to share this gift of Morris, a population-eight-hundred town in southern Montana, the epitome of small towns everywhere. In one issue, I wanted to include all of them and what they meant to one another and the town. In another year, a follow-up people issue could highlight a different community. I would hire a freelancer to write that one, but I was claiming Morris for myself.

I organized my assignment, knowing I already had write-ups

for Pops, Shelly, Abby, Fletcher, Nate, Mel, Henry Mattson, and even Brody. But my incomplete column was rather long: Michael Bertram, Irv and Izzy, Simone, Mitch and Joe, and even Sheriff Burt. And others, including Stella and Art at the grocery store, Herman Swan at the gas station, and Fred Hanover at the feed-store. I would include them all, so as not to neglect any of the nuances of my special hometown. It couldn't be any other way.

———

I drove to an outdoor shooting range half an hour into Wyoming. It was my first practice without Pops sitting nearby or Shelly cheering me on. It was strange being on my own. I felt exposed. Bolstering my mood, my shots were good. But I continued to feel queasy—just a bit off.

After a fitful sleep, I inched myself into an upright position and swung my legs over the edge of my bed until my toes touched the floorboards. The simple task required significant effort. After work, at Shelly's, I must have looked about the same as I felt. The first thing she said was "You all right there, Amber?"

Shelly touched my shoulder and tilted her head.

I said "We're shooting, right?" to assure her I was fine.

"If you say so," she said. "This time, I'm getting the win. I don't care how much you've been practicing."

She was beautiful. Coming along so well after all she had faced. We shot for an hour and called it a tie. Afterward, I told her of my letter campaign and immediately felt horrible for raising the subject.

"If you're pro-bison, then that's what you are. You can't change how you feel about something."

"I'm sorry, Shelly. It was thoughtless of me. I was so consumed ..."

"Amber, girl, don't you worry. I'm more of a ... what'd you

call it ..."

"A camera?" I said.

"One of those. I know bison threaten the industry, but they're mighty beautiful. Sam thought so too. I mostly agree with you and Mel, and Sam and Mel talked a lot about land. We need to improve our sharing skills. If you want help, call me."

"Shelly, are you certain you don't want to press charges?"

"How could I? Sam tore up their note. It would be my word against theirs. Sure, I get angry thinking about it. I get bitter. But in the end, I don't want to live with hate and anger. It'll wear me down. I'd rather live with love. Like Sam did. Those three know they made a big mistake. And that's what it was. A mistake. And an accident. And they have to face it every day they wake up. I feel sorry for them for that. And the other one, who we think was sawing our corral posts, is likely shutting down his dude ranch at the end of the year. I suspect he's feeling too much guilt to stick around. I feel sorry for him, too. So, no, I don't want to press charges. Not for vandalism that I can't prove. Not for a threat. Not for greed. In the end, Sam's death was an accident. And I know Sam will always be with me."

"Everyone told me you were tough."

———

"Phillips," said Fletcher, "it's time for thoughts on next year."

"Oh?"

"The *TriState* is being very well received, as you know. We're on the good side of the balance sheet, and ad sales are looking strong. You're doing a spectacular job. Congratulations. My biggest concern is getting you more inside help, if you'd like it. Let me know a good time next week when we can dig into this deeper, after you've had time for your own evaluation."

All I said was "Absolutely," but my mind had spun around many times over with very different thoughts.

37

———————

PREPARATION

THE FIRST SEASON opened to bow and arrow. A gentle snowfall shed flurries, as though trying to hide the wounds. Tourist dollars were pouring in for guided hunts, and meat was being put in freezers and packed for transport to homes well beyond. Unfortunately, some of the bodies were also traveling the roads tied to vehicles, in clear view. I assumed Bo and Nell were enjoying visitors to their ranch. No sooner had I considered their ranch than my thoughts skipped to Shelly's visitors and to Ted Steele. Why hadn't I thought of this sooner? Ted had ties to a wildlife group. I shot off an email. I'd take any help he could offer from his wildlife network. I kicked myself again for not thinking of it sooner, and I hoped I wasn't too late.

———

Fletcher was hunched forward, eyes trained on his computer, when I entered his office.

"Just a minute," he said. I waited until he straightened up, clicking out of his computer screen as he did.

"What's up, Phillips?"

"I have a dilemma. A conflict of interest." I took a seat and started talking, based roughly on my prerehearsed presentation.

"You aim to send letters to every US senator and congressman?" he said after I revealed my plan. Fletcher folded his arms.

"I must do what I feel is right."

"And you believe you must resign to do this?"

I nodded.

Fletcher adjusted his glasses and inhaled deeply.

We sat silently a few moments. I was about to offer justification when he lifted a single finger in the air.

"Let me consider this a bit," he said. "Do yourself and me a favor, and don't send anything yet."

Despite Fletcher's suggestion to hold off on sending letters, I continued sorting names and consolidating lists. While making progress, I needed help. Ted had been a miracle in supplying contacts, which added to my workload.

"What's the password, again?" asked Diane. She and Shelly agreed to help me sort the visitor lists.

"Jake of all trades," I said. "All one word, all lowercase, and *all* is spelled with an *O*, not an *A*."

"Sweet," said Diane. "For Jake and Olive."

I smiled.

"We're getting this done tonight, Amber, girl, so you can get some rest," said Shelly. "You have been burning the oil at both ends, I can tell …"

Diane interrupted Shelly. "We can all tell."

"Right," said Shelly. "So, we are plowing through these names and tucking you in. Don't drink too much coffee."

"Got it. Thanks," I said.

Sure enough, after three hours of steady clicking on our

computers, flipping pages of names in the guest sign-in book, and sorting names by state, we heaved a joint sigh of relief.

"Done!" said Diane.

"Done," I said.

"And done," said Shelly.

"You're my girls," I said. "Best of the best. Drive home safe. I love you both. And please, take the rest of these donuts."

"Call Mel," said Fletcher, catching me on my way to work. "We'll do better piggybacking our efforts. I'm meeting the governor as soon as I can get there. I'm driving now."

I called Mel and was soon directing Sebastian in the opposite direction from the *Gazette*.

"Fletcher told me about your campaign," said Mel. "It's a good idea, and I give you a lot of credit for dreaming it up. I intend to steal it."

"What?"

"We want to keep you off the hot seat and send the letters from the Bison Guardians. Fletcher doesn't want to lose you. And he doesn't believe you want to resign. We want to time it right with the review of the Schines' and Brody's plan and Fletcher's hayfield proposal. If we get all the parts working together, the pressure is going to mount."

"I have additional contacts," I said. "Wildlife proponents from Ted. Organizations. We want them to spread word of the proposed culls to local news outlets. Nothing hits home with voters, representatives, and senators like news from their districts."

"Yes, indeed. A few screaming constituents, and an issue becomes an instant priority."

"Exactly," I said.

"And national attention is going to make the development

plans harder to turn down. If all goes well," he said, "this could become a case model: sound, cohesive development with well-thought-out environmental considerations. Fletcher's talking to the governor now about funding to buy out a few of the other ranchers. A couple of them are getting older, anyway, but one of them is going to be tough as nails. There's a nonprofit that might bridge the financial gap, given the lengthy government timing associated with this sort of thing."

I agreed to relinquish my files, giving Mel leeway to push forward when the time was right. He and Fletcher were right. It wasn't a bad idea to step out of the hot seat, particularly in a ranching town I enjoyed calling home.

I intended to do a final organization of my list of names but fell asleep soon after dinner. When I awakened in the middle of the night, fever, weakness, and a strong pain in my abdomen had me considering a walk-in clinic visit. I had shrugged off my previous day's stomach pain as nerves related to the campaign, but nerves would not cause a fever. Brucellosis, however, could. Even with this unwanted thought, I lost my fight to stay awake.

38

BISON HUNTER

BRODY STOOD FORTY YARDS OFF, his long gun steadied in his hands. Three bison stood further away. I took a photo. A fourth lay on the ground, an arrow plunged in its backside. I was thankful Brody had given it a humane ending. No doubt it had been hit, but not killed, when the group had wandered too far, and had refused to let human convenience interfere with ages of instinct.

I recalled Mel's words when I had asked the most drastic thing anyone had ever done to try to stop a hunt. Then, I inhaled deeply and slowly pulled my pistol from my pocket. I had worn baggy pants to make this part easy. I turned my back to Brody, inserted the magazine, and raised it slowly to firing height.

I would knock his gun askance and perhaps even cause him to drop it from his hands. He would abandon his shot. I had practiced this. I was certain it was the proper drastic measure. It would make the news.

I closed my eyes and silently prayed. Then, I turned back around and pointed straight at Brody's left hand steadying his rifle. I didn't feel excitement. Or dread. Or fear. Not adrenaline either. I felt nothing except certainty. I rechecked my target and pulled the trigger.

Brody's sixth sense startled. He swiveled around, intending to point his gun directly at my heart. And with that maneuver, he opened his own heart to my bullet. He dropped to the ground. I stared, too stunned to move. This wasn't the plan. I dropped my gun and ran to him.

I knelt by his side and watched a red stream seep outward into his shirt. As I stared at the widening stain, a heartless thought emerged from deep in my hollow depths. I would rot in jail for it, but this, surely, was going to happen anyway. It was a moment of reckoning. A moment when the only thing that mattered to me was Brody's blood. Call me callous. Some sort of primordial instinct zeroed in on the vibrant red liquid gushing generously into his shirt. I looked at his eyes, open to the sky, and placed the sleeve of my shirt atop his open front. I stared as it sopped up Brody's blood as quickly as it exited his chest cavity. Then, I ran to Sebastian and sped away, vaguely mulling over the fact that I had killed a man. The bison had barely moved. The sound of my single gunshot, mingled with Brody's, meant nothing to them.

I raced faster than I ever had on the two-lane highways, skidding slightly around several turns. I phoned EMS to report a mishap. When I passed emergency vehicles speeding toward Brody, I didn't slow. I arrived home and put my blood-soaked shirt in a clear plastic bag, found a box, added ice. Bag upon bag. And sealed it shut. At the overnight air express depot in Bozeman, I handed off my medical freight, making their flight deadline by minutes. Brody's blood taxied down the runway for an unexpected flight to Philadelphia and Dr. Maxwell Chong. I sat in Sebastian until I saw the plane in the sky. If my hunch was wrong, so be it.

I saw the flashers on Sheriff Burt's SUV actively making their way around bends in the road. He sailed into the driveway and shut off the engine. Instinctively, I raised my hands over my head.

"Amber, that you? Stay where you are."

Burt approached, with gun drawn.

I turned around when instructed. He joined my hands at the wrists. Then Burt said, "What in God's name did you do, Amber? And why?"

"It was an accident."

"But why, Amber? Why did you do it?"

Burt wasn't asking for a confession. He was voicing disbelief. I answered him anyway: "To awaken the world to injustice. He was set on killing my bison. And they are mine, you know. Yours too. I wanted to stop the hunt. For people to take notice. I was defending my property."

"Amber, have you gone nuts?" Burt shook his head, disbelieving. Oddly, Fletcher appeared next to him.

"I don't know. Perhaps I have."

"Amber, is that you? Amber ..."

Why was Fletcher asking this?

"Amber! Are you okay? Wake up. Stay with me!"

It sounded like Abby's voice. I wasn't certain. Along with the wail of a siren. I opened my eyes momentarily. Why was I sitting in Sebastian? Where was Sheriff Burt? I heard his voice but couldn't see him. I had to vomit. A sandwich I had packed for lunch slid out of its paper wrap to the floor. I felt woozy, and the world around me blackened.

"There you are. Welcome back."

It was a woman's voice I didn't recognize. I flickered my eyes open to see bright fluorescent lighting, white walls, white bedsheets, and IV tubing taped to my arm. As my lids fluttered shut, I vaguely registered a beeping sound coming from a machine near my bed but nothing more from the woman. I didn't have the energy for a second peek.

A different woman's voice, also unknown, was next to float through my thoughts. I opened my eyes for another scant moment, but again, they forced themselves shut before I could see who had spoken.

When I awakened again, it was a man's voice I heard. The sun was no longer bright through the window. I must have slept for hours. Or was it more?

"Next time you want your appendix out, just ask, instead of scaring us all to death."

"Fletch?"

"Yes. I wondered why I hadn't seen you at the candy bowl lately."

"Did I kill Brody? What happened?"

"Brody? We heard Sebastian's horn blaring outside the *Gazette*. Diane and I found you slumped into the steering wheel. Thank God you had already opened your door. And you had already parked. We rushed you here. They found a ruptured appendix, and you have been in and out of surgery."

"But what about Brody?" I asked.

"What about him?"

"Did I shoot him?"

"Of course not."

I stared at Fletcher through dazed eyes and with a mind still hazy, postsurgery.

"For you," he said. "It arrived yesterday, but you hardly looked up to reading."

"You were here? I don't remember seeing you."

Fletcher handed me an express mailing packet. I saw Max's name on the return address and, in nearly one action, grabbed the envelope from his hand, pulled out its contents, and let the envelope drop to the bed, eager to read his words, but then felt too weak to do so.

"He phoned," said Fletcher. "Dr. Chong wanted to confirm this arrived since he hadn't heard from you."

I acknowledged Fletcher's words with a slight nod, but my focus, though fuzzy, returned to the letter. As I read, my heart slid into an uneasy acceptance.

"Read it," I said, holding the note forward.

Silently, Fletcher absorbed the information. Then he looked straight into my eyes but fell deep into thought.

I let him mull over the meaning of Max's letter a bit longer before breaking the silence. "It was Brody," I said. After a deep breath, cut short by a touch of unwanted pain, I continued. "Last week, I sent Brody's blood to Max. I got it from a dart wound. It was accidental, but in the rush of the moment, I realized it was exactly what I needed. I told Max to look for *Brucella*. I gave him fair warning to handle it carefully. I wanted the strain. But I didn't tell him the source."

"Strain?"

"I told you last week, the bison meat from last spring's cull harbored a strain that differed from Brody's infected cows, the dead-pile elk, and the denim. According to this letter, Brody's own strain matched the cattle and the elk but not the bison. He was never injured by bison."

"That son of a ..." Fletcher as much as growled. "That lousy son of ..." His eyes widened. He looked beyond my shoulder, as though glaring through my hospital room wall to Brody's ranch.

"I knew it," he uttered. "Mel and I saw no hoof marks. Or not enough to match his story. We were investigating him for insurance fraud. Frank Bishop and his brother went along with us."

I was surprised Fletcher had it in him—to trespass.

"Mel and I found marks on a gate that weren't from bison,

even though we found bison fur on it," he said. "Now I'm certain he broke through that fence with his ATV."

I stared in disbelief as I considered Fletcher's conclusions, identical to mine: there had been no bison break. Brody had made it up.

"So, he set up his cows for the insurance money," he said. "Or set up his property for failure with a fake break-in so development would look like the best logical alternative," said Fletcher. "But a few things don't make sense. And how did you get your samples?"

"First things first," I said. "Henry Mattson helped me secure last spring's bison meat from a number of freezers. He didn't ask why. Another person, who shall remain nameless ... until I tell you it was Shelly ... helped me collect samples from Brody's herd. Elise thought she was helping with a future article when she showed me how to test the samples and then sent me the results." I let the words sink in. "I guess we're doing a ranch issue.

"I finagled a few tissue samples from Brody's cattle at the slaughterhouse. It cost me a week's salary, and I had to go there myself with an unknowing accomplice. I've gotten better at being bad, but it was absolutely horrid."

Fletcher nodded, sifting through the news.

I took in a deep breath, then said, "When Shelly and I raided Brody's cows, she found evidence of carcasses. Babies. Calves. I trusted her to know and took note when she said how peculiar it was. Collecting water with Nate and you, I saw the same thing, slightly submerged, while you were inspecting the chute. I'd say Brody was trying to rid his ranch of calf bodies for some time. Everyone dumps things in water."

"You mean, aborted calves. No rancher's trying to dissolve a viable baby beef cow."

I swallowed.

"Which means," I said, "he had a brucellosis problem before his supposed bison break-in."

Fletcher silently connected his thoughts.

"Years ago, we placed a couple of large stones in that waterway," he said, "to make crossing easier. This explains why I saw more stones there than I remembered."

"It made it easier for him to place bodies in the middle of it," I said. "To spread them around."

Fletcher considered my words.

"I am ninety-nine percent certain Brody's jeans were flagging the dead pile so he could find it again and use the elk to infect more of his cattle."

Fletcher's attention pierced through me, front to back. "Intentional infections?"

"According to Max, bison couldn't have been the cause, even without a break-in. It had to be from elk."

"Years ago," said Fletcher, "when the Circle C had its last brucellosis, we all suspected Brody's family somehow gave us bad cattle on purpose, and there were plenty of whispers that it was on account of my family was named head of the association. I was too naive to believe the Ross family would hold a grudge down generations. And also too naive to believe his family would risk an industry to get even. But this could be how they did it, since all their cattle were clean."

Fletcher's eyes darted to mine.

"We wager a lonely war between selfish desires and helping the greater good all the time," said Fletcher.

"I bet he just wanted out," I said. "He didn't want to admit a problem or failure and didn't know how else to do it. Surely, some of his cows were going to test positive for it anyway at slaughter. He was trying to beat the bad news to the punch. And perhaps," I added, "he wanted revenge. Wanted to ensure bison stayed in the hot seat. Weren't they the cause of his family's tragic deaths?"

Fletcher solemnly considered my words.

"On top of that," I said, "my guess is he needed people to feel sorry for him."

"Love," said Fletcher. "And family. What he missed out on all along."

———

I couldn't believe what a difference a day made. My mind was at least twice as alert, and I was only half as tired. My morale soared higher when Shelly, Abby, and Diane hip-checked one another racing into my hospital room.

"Me first."

"No, me."

"Let me in there."

If I hadn't had bed rails, they likely would have piled on top of me. It was the greatest gift ever.

"Look at you!" I said.

"Read these," said Diane.

"In between recovery naps," said Abby.

Shelly handed me a folder. I opened it to a pile of printed news articles.

"Your letters—or the Guardians' letters—are making the news," she said.

"Oh, no! My letters! I never sent Mel the names."

"No," said Diane, "but we did."

"You what?"

"We couldn't let a sister down," said Abby. "And we knew your password, after all."

"Even hiding in this hospital bed, you're making quite an impact," said Shelly. "People in town are talking. Newspapers are covering it. I even saw something on the TV news."

The country was awake. Demanding justice. But local ranchers were having a say as well. Tension was mounting.

"Good to see you up," said Fletcher, joining the group. "You get out tomorrow. You'll need a driver. I hired Brody for you."

"Very funny," I said.

"I'm serious."

"What? He could kill me for what I did."

"Ah, but Phillips, he doesn't know any of what you did. I told him my own investigative skills had found discrepancies in his bison-break story. Helping you out, and continuing with a slimmed-down plan with the Schine brothers, was part of his get-out-of-jail-free card. That, and his turning down every cent of insurance money, which he had already done. He was appreciative, particularly since public knowledge of what he did would infuriate the association, and, God knows, rightly so. He was reckless. But small towns have a tendency to turn a blind eye and protect their weakest. He lied, of course, and acted wrongly, but he did, after all, test his cows and send them to slaughter, without sickening any others. The only problem, is the state has one mark against its *Brucella*-free status. It would have received that one way or another, though, since he had some infected cows."

"You did right by him, Fletcher. And by Morris," said Diane.

"You know," he said, "it was difficult watching a young boy grow as he did and wanting it all to be different for him."

"He's not a bad person," I said.

"No," said Fletcher. "Just wants to move on. And we're doing everything we can to finally help him do that."

"Promise me you'll get your land back," I said.

"It will happen. The development is being scaled back, but will be economically lucrative for all. I know for a fact planners will approve it. My sister will run our operations at Irv and Izzy's. It looks like Mel's and my plan for a large bison swath will get the go-ahead. And you, Phillips, made this happen. The governor is on board. The outside pressure is helping. The Jensens are even considering selling. We have several others to approach. As you said, they might believe they have been on their sites forever, but it's only been a lone century. We'll make sure they have good places with extra dollars in their pockets. In the end, they'll likely feel they've done a good deed for humanity when, in fact, they will have served both the bison and people. Most of us, it turns out, have the ability and desire to do good things."

39

JUSTICE

BRODY WALKED beside me as the nurse pushed my wheelchair into the sparkling daylight sun.

"You're not permitted to drive for three weeks," he said. "My job is to get you to the *Gazette* any day you feel ready. If you need to cut your day short, Diane is on call. Once the diner closes, Abby takes over for a couple of hours. And any evening emergencies have been delegated to Fletcher or Shelly. Oh, and tomorrow afternoon, we're coming over to Irv and Izzy's for a welcome home party. We're holding it in the main house, not your apartment. So, no need to tidy up for company."

"As if," I said.

The debate was flaring in Morris. Fletcher had been wise to let the Bison Guardians take the lead. Letters with news of the bison culls had elicited lightning strikes of rage. People across the country were demanding justice. But longtime residents of Morris, whose families lived and died by ranching, were demanding justice as well. They sounded increasingly like thunder that darts from the clouds, causes you to jump, vibrates through your body, and rattles your teeth.

Had I made a selfish mistake? People I knew were being judged by Americans across the country. I was the spark that had started the storm.

Fletcher, of all people, called a spade a spade. Seeing me stand up for what I believed was right meant a lot to him. And he and Mel were taking a big risk in righting this uncomfortable and unsustainable dilemma in their own ways. It didn't matter to him if some of the ranchers would have to change habits, shift lands, shift to other grazers or bulls. He had lived through a lot. He knew our system could change, and he was willing to fight for it. This brought some comfort, at least.

But as I rested, I considered my actions, Brody's actions, the quest of ranchers to protect their herds and livelihoods, the campaign of outsiders and others to protect a different ideology. Every story had sides and facets. Idly, I stared at shadows of leaves that had invited themselves through my window. They danced on the ceiling with sun reflections from my bed stand's nearly empty water glass. Together, they shimmered and wiggled and blithely overlapped, twisting into one another's defined spaces and blurring their individual lines and outlines. I froze my gaze, inexplicably questioning the meaning of justice. Wondering if there was no single justice. Wondering if justice could, indeed, be explained and carried out in many different ways. Wondering if justice was in the eye of the beholder, after all.

40

———

HOME

I LOOKED around the room at faces of people I now called friends. They had taken me in to their community, shared themselves, and allowed me to share myself with them. I knew I could become better at it and knew, over time, I would. Abby nodded when she saw me looking her way. It was her way of saying "We've got you." Shelly and Mel were sharing a good laugh. I laughed, too, seeing it. Diane, of course, had just come from the kitchen, carrying a platter of cinnamon buns. She, too, smiled when she noticed me watching her. Brody was noticeably absent.

"How are you holding up there, Phillips?" asked Fletcher.

"To be honest, so many people have come to visit I am exhausted."

I looked at Fletcher's warm expression just as he began to speak again.

"I specifically recall your telling me, the first time we met, you wanted to live in a small town."

"I remember."

"I'd say you are home."

I was, indeed.

Despite the jovial conversation, my energy seeped softly away, my chin slid low into my chest, and my eyes became heavy. I fought in a most feeble manner, straining to scan the room, for barely a flicker of a second longer, until I felt my surroundings trailing away and I floated into a dream. Somewhere, vast and alone, I flew through a cloudless sky, with my arms stretched wide as my wings. In a moment, I detected a soft rumble a distance behind me. I turned to look. Bison magically appeared, barely detectable. Only a few. My path opened before me as though completely boundless. I floated on an invisible, silent wind, while at my back the sound grew. I saw hundreds now, or perhaps a thousand, increasingly clear and closer than before. Their steady rumble, like approaching thunder, came gently drumming across the gap. Gaining quickly. Moving closer. Sounding louder. Until their clamoring but harmonious hoofbeats and racing bodies were upon me. A thick cloud of dust rose from their dancing hooves and covered me with its grit, clods of grass were flung overhead, and a near-deafening noise overwhelmed, like disparate cymbals crashing, the brass instruments taking turns blasting, strings plucking and tuning, wind ensemble whistling … right through me: the orchestra warming up with its usual chaotic frenzy. Preparing. And then, as though the performance was about to begin, all fell silent. I became one of them. I sensed excitement from racing bodies and felt warm air pulsing urgently from flaring nostrils, every breath vital to our motion. Yet all was silent. I looked into their knowing eyes as we traversed the plains and ran together. The silence remained. I was ready to watch them roam forever. To no one in particular, I spoke.

"Join me," I said. "Come. Watch me hunt bison in the sky. Hunt them running free again. Hunt them with my eyes. And my arms. And my open heart. I am the Bison Hunter. Living to see them run again."

EPILOGUE

MORRIS, Montana, does not exist, but the heart of its story, as presented in the pages above, does. It is a place where cattle, ranchers, and bison make their homes. It is a place of peace and conflict. It is a place where justice must be defined. It is a community, like and unlike many others.

AFTERWORD

Some things stay the same.

In the late 1990s, before this story begins, the State of Montana sued the federal government for allowing bison to migrate out of the park, an action deemed a significant threat to Montana cattle, due to a stated risk of brucellosis transmission to cattle. There is not a single known case of direct transmission of brucellosis between bison and cattle.

In 2000 the Interagency Bison Management Plan was signed into effect to maintain a wild, free-ranging population of bison; to address the risk of brucellosis transmission; and to protect the economic interest and viability of the Montana livestock industry. The goal of maintaining a population of 3,000 to 3,500 park bison was established.

Since 2005, the year in which the story is set, Yellowstone bison have continued to travel beyond invisible human lines. From 1985 to 2023, some 13,958 Yellowstone bison were recorded as culled. In the particularly tough winter season of 2022 to 2023, 1,272 bison gave their lives to humans. The majority taken in 2022–23 were by members of Indigenous Tribal nations. Treaties bestow rights to certain Tribal nations to take buffalo in accordance with historic taking. Pushback from nonhunters became more apparent during this year of heavy cull.

Some things change.

Montana's governor proposed a law to enable Yellowstone bison to move outside the western side of the park, year round, onto 330,000 acres of public land beginning summer 2016. It was the first time bison had been allowed outside the park into Montana in 130 years. This action garnered support from some landowners and discontent from others.

Bison management is showing a shift toward reduced slaughterhouse culls and increased conservation and transfer of Yellowstone bison, free of brucellosis, to Tribal nation lands across the country. These new herds are bringing bison back into the lives of many for whom ties to bison have been historical, cultural, traditional, and spiritual. The first transfer occurred in 2019, when the park moved fifty-five bison to the Fort Peck Indian Reservation in northeastern Montana. The Intertribal Bison Cooperative, formed in 1992 by a handful of Tribes, has expanded to over eighty member Tribes and works closely with federal government agencies to increase the conservation and transfer of bison. In 2009 this cooperative changed its name to the InterTribal Buffalo Council.

In 2022 Yellowstone increased the capacity of the Bison Conservation Transfer Program facility in the park from eighty to two hundred animals, with help from several nonprofits.

As development and visitation in the Yellowstone region has expanded, so, too, have wildlife/traffic concerns.

To increase understanding of brucellosis in elk herds and the possible threat to cattle, Montana Fish, Wildlife & Parks initiated a targeted elk brucellosis surveillance project in 2011, and it tests elk herds in different locations each year.

In the spring of 2023, the US Department of the Interior established the national Bison Working Group to restore bison and prairie grassland ecosystems, strengthen long-term bison conservation partnerships, and engage Tribes in a meaningful way through future actions and inclusion of Indigenous knowledge and the best available science.

Dive into another great read from E. B. Lee now.

Carli Morris was looking forward to retirement. Instead, she would find a purpose. Join her on the streets of Manhattan.

See Clean Sweep A Novel

Leave a review

I hope you enjoyed *Thunder in Yellowstone*.
Is there something in particular you liked about this novel?
Please share it with other potential readers in a short review on my Amazon book sales page or Goodreads page.

Reviews help others and they help me, as an author.

ACKNOWLEDGMENTS

I wish to acknowledge with sincere gratitude the exceptionally thoughtful and astute comments, questions, and suggestions of my editor, Stephen Parolini, www.noveldoctor.com. You are, indeed, one of the best. As you envision a sound big picture and the necessary supporting arcs and details, you nudge me to do the same. My writing and this story are better for it. It was an equal privilege to work with you on *Thunder In Yellowstone*, as it was to collaborate on my debut novel *Clean Sweep*. Thank you.

Thank you, also, to Elyse Lyon, for topnotch proofreading, an essential element of every novel. By sharing your extensive grasp of grammar and rules of writing and publishing, you not only improved the manuscript, but offered invaluable lessons from which I will learn.

To Lynn Adreozzi, I offer sincere thanks for creating a gorgeous cover design to seamlessly bind the visual heart of the novel with the story within.

To family, friends, and readers – your constant support has carried me through page after page, edit upon edit, decision upon decision. Thank you, with love always.

ABOUT THE AUTHOR

E. B. Lee began writing contemporary fiction following life chapters working in the environmental field, raising children, and flower farming. She received her B.A. from Yale University and Masters of Environmental Studies, also from Yale. She currently writes in North Carolina and Connecticut. This is her second novel.

For more books and updates:
www.eblee.me
Be sure to sign up for my newsletter to learn the latest.

www.instagram.com/eblee.author
www.facebook.com/EBLeeauthor

Also by E. B. Lee
Clean Sweep A Novel

ALSO BY E. B. LEE

Clean Sweep A Novel

Carli Morris was looking forward to retirement. Instead, she would find a purpose.

Selling her Madison Avenue ad agency for billions, Carli Morris, the self-assured career woman, pursues her love of art and spends her spare hours volunteering. But her comfortable confidence turns to horror when a routine food delivery to a homeless encampment leads her to discover one of its residents dead and her two dogs orphaned.

Peeling back the grimy curtain concealing our own ghosts, Clean Sweep reveals the deep human need for connection and love.

If you like strong women, elegant writing, and journeys of self-discovery, you'll adore E.B. Lee's unforgettable story.

<u>Buy *Clean Sweep* to see with new eyes today!</u>

Praise for Clean Sweep

"Lee's story is ... absorbing and convincing ... intriguing mysteries quietly lurk in the background ..." – *Kirkus Reviews*

"... a beautiful story of human connectedness, separation, and loss, hope, and love ... E.B. Lee is masterful in her development of characters." – *San Francisco Book Review*

"... The plot twist ... will catch you off guard in the best way possible." - *Manhattan Book Review*

"Among the novel's many strengths are the smart, relatable main characters." – *BlueInk Starred Review*